FALLEN FROM GRACE

Fallen from Grace

Laura Leone

Five Star • Waterville, Maine

This novel is a work of fiction. Names, characters, places and incidents are either the product of the author's imagination, or, if real, used fictitiously.

Set in 11 pt. Plantin by Ramona A. Watson.

Printed in the United States on permanent paper.

Library of Congress Cataloging-in-Publication Data

Leone, Laura, 1962–
Fallen from grace / Laura Leone.
p. cm.—(Five Star expressions)
ISBN 0-7862-4708-8 (hc : alk. paper)
ISBN 1-4104-0181-2 (sc : alk. paper)
1. Women authors—Fiction. 2. Runaway teenagers—Fiction. 3. Sex-oriented businesses—Fiction. I. Title. II. Series.
PS3568.E689 F35 2003
813′.6—dc21 2002035943

This book is dedicated to my editor, Russell Davis, who is smart enough to believe that romance readers want a good story more than they want a safe one.

ACKNOWLEDGEMENTS

Special thanks to Valerie Taylor for walking through the story ideas with me. I'm also grateful to Mary Jo Putney for her support and encouragement. Many thanks to Theresa Medeiros, Susan Wiggs, Kathleen Eagle, Anne Stuart, and Barbara Samuel—with friends like these, who needs fairy godmothers? To the understanding folks of the Space Coast Writers Guild, I offer my apologies for spending the whole weekend locked in my hotel room trying to finish this book. As for Karen, Julie, and Lee Ann . . . I *told* you that those books I brought on our trip were legitimate research.

Praise for *Fallen from Grace*

"*Fallen from Grace* is an amazingly powerful, emotional and thought-provoking book . . . Leone's gift for storytelling shines in a truly provocative, gritty, tender and unforgettable story."—*Romantic Times*

"In this realistically gritty, sometimes violent, and gripping tale, Leone reveals the seamier side of society's maneuvering while she spins an unconventional romance between two unhappy people who find that love, like respect, can grow out of friendship and shared experiences and that new beginnings are indeed possible for those with the determination and courage to pursue them."—*Booklist*

". . . a fast-moving, compelling read . . . *Fallen from Grace* is recommended for its unusual pairing, its audacity to examine the seamier side and its ultimate message of hope and redemption."—*The Romance Reader*

"Laura Leone writes every woman's fantasy—real men and hot heroes to warm a cold winter's night."—Patricia Rice, *New York Times* bestselling author of *McCloud's Woman*

"Laura Leone will keep readers up all night with this fascinating, passionate and emotional novel. This unusual love story, told with freshness and authenticity, gives new meaning to the term 'tortured hero' and illuminates the healing power of love."—Award-winning author, Susan Wiggs

"Laura Leone . . . crafts an interesting and emotionally compelling love story that resonates on many levels."—AllAboutRomance.com

"Innovative and thoroughly engaging, Laura Leone has done it again! She's one of the few on my Must Read list, and *Fallen from Grace* is her best yet."—Kathleen Eagle, bestselling author of *Once Upon a Wedding*

". . . a powerful, soul-searching story . . . this book is a keeper. . . ."—LoveRomances.Com

PROLOGUE

Afternoon sunlight streamed through the windows as the woman in his arms gasped with startled passion and arched her back off the bed. Her hands moved uncertainly over his naked shoulders as she sought something more from him.

He obliged by lowering his head to kiss both her nipples, then he took one in his mouth and sucked—gently at first, then harder when she started stroking his hair.

"Mmmm . . ." He moaned in his throat, wordlessly praising her, then caressed her torso with slow, admiring hands . . . and turned his head to take a discreet glance at the clock on the nightstand.

They had about twenty minutes left.

She had wanted more foreplay than he'd expected, given that she'd only set aside an hour for this. Since this was their first time together, he wasn't sure how long it would take her to climax, let alone how long she'd want him to stick around afterwards. And since he was supposed to be out of here by four o'clock . . . he now set about rushing her without seeming to rush her.

He nibbled on her breast, urgent without being rough. As she shifted restlessly, he slid his hand between her legs and started stroking her.

Damn.

She wasn't as ready as he'd hoped.

Nerves, undoubtedly. Women were often like this the first time, unless they'd done this before with someone else and felt confident about what they were getting into.

He was experienced enough to have sized her up quickly, so he knew that his best bet was to do too little rather than too much. He let his hand go still on her barely-damp mound and just pressed the heel of his palm there, exerting a subtle, steady pressure as he lifted his head and gazed into her eyes.

Oh, yeah, he thought, studying what he saw there. *Nerves.*

He brushed his mouth against hers, letting his lips caress hers with intimate laziness.

Give her the control. Give her the power . . . And hope that she can get off fast once she relaxes.

"Do you want me inside you?" he whispered, nibbling all around her mouth as he spoke.

"Uh . . ."

"I don't have to," he murmured, pressing the heel of his palm against her. "Not this time. Not if you're not sure."

"Um, but you're, um . . ." She sighed and tilted her head back, eyes closed. He was kissing her throat and under her chin as she said, "You know. *Hard.*"

He nudged her hip with his erection, letting her know that it was okay to talk about it, that it was nothing to fear. "It doesn't matter."

He started circling his hand against her. Just a little. Barely moving at all.

She swallowed. "But . . . don't you want—"

"Yes, but I can wait until next time. Or the time after." He kissed her with exquisite gentleness. "It's only going to happen when you want it. When you're sure."

She met his gaze again.

Ah . . .

There it was: a little relief in her expression, a little relaxation of her facial muscles.

"Then maybe . . ." She licked her lips.

"You want to wait?" He nodded as he asked this, so that she'd know she could say it.

"Yes." Now she nodded, too. "I, uh, I want to wait."

He could tell it surprised her. Not just that she had a choice about it, but also that this was the choice she now made, after having come here.

"Then we'll wait," he agreed.

A slight quiver of a smile. "Okay." Now she let her breath out on a sudden puff of stifled laughter. More of the tension leaving. "I thought I . . ."

"This is for you." He kissed her shoulder. "This is whatever you want. *Whatever* you want."

Well, within reason. If she wanted him to stay late, she'd have to live with the disappointment.

"I guess . . ." She nodded again and started to look a little more comfortable. "Yes, I guess so. Whatever *I* want."

He lowered his head to let his breath flow into her ear as he whispered, "But you do want to come, don't you?"

Her breath escaped her in a rush. She gave a silent grunt of assent as he circled his palm more firmly against the juncture of her thighs.

Experience—as well as a good mentor—had taught him that the brain was a woman's most important sex organ, and since he was starting to feel pressed for time, he turned his full attention to *this* one's mind to keep things moving along.

"You want to come all over my hand, don't you?" he whispered, his lips brushing her ear.

"Um . . ."

"Because *I* want that," he assured her, pushing her with words and images. "I want your legs spread wide . . ." He nudged them farther apart. "And I want you wet . . ."

"Mmmm . . ."

"And rubbing against me." He explored her with his fingers now, feeling her whole body quiver as he did so. "And slick . . . and sweet . . . and hot . . ."

"Yes," she whimpered, starting to go there now, getting all tight and loose at once.

"How does that feel?"

"That feels . . . *good.*"

"And that?"

"Oh!" She gave a convulsive buck.

Okay, getting closer.

"Is this what you want?" he murmured.

Her head tossed on the pillow.

"More?" he asked.

"More, yes, *more.*"

She started moving her hips in response to his caresses, and her grip on his left shoulder was carelessly rough. Her other hand clutched the sheet, and her face was turned away from him as she started moaning freely, beginning to lose herself in sensation.

He kept whispering to her, but he asked no more questions. Not now. He didn't want to distract her, make her lose momentum by interacting with him, because they had—he took a quick glance at the clock—barely ten minutes left. So now he just murmured erotic nothings to her, keeping her mind stimulated along with her body, praising her femininity, her beauty, her responsiveness.

She came with pleasing clarity, ensuring that no guesswork need be involved. She cried out, arched off the bed, pumped rhythmically against his stroking hand . . . and finally collapsed, flushed, limp, and breathing hard.

He held her for a few minutes, waited for her to open her eyes and look at him, and then commenced the postgame wrap-up. No multiple orgasms today. Not with three minutes left on the clock.

"How do you feel?" he murmured, brushing her tousled hair away from her face.

She looked simultaneously satisfied and wary. "I feel like . . . like we've just made love."

Score.

"We did." He kissed her gently and brushed his fingertips across her belly.

"I didn't expect . . . I mean, I didn't think . . . I thought—"

"Shhh." He kissed the corner of her eye, where fine lines showed. "This is whatever you want."

She nodded. "Whatever I want."

She hadn't had any plastic surgery as far as he could tell. Nature showed on her—unless she was coloring her hair. He nuzzled her neck, guessing she was about fifteen years older than he was.

"Are you all right?" he asked.

"Yes." She suddenly smiled. It made her look pretty. "I mean . . . Yes! I feel . . ." She laughed and said no more.

"I have to go," he whispered.

"Oh?" But she looked more relieved than sorry.

He wasn't surprised that she wanted to be alone with this now. Maybe she'd call a friend and tell her the details, or maybe she'd take a long bath and pamper herself in solitude. Maybe she'd just lie in the sex-scented sheets for another hour and replay everything in her mind. Whatever she would do, she welcomed the privacy his departure would give her now.

He rose from the bed, went to wash up in the impersonal but elegant bathroom, then came back into the bedroom and started dressing. He put his clothes on slowly, garment by garment, letting her study the body she'd been too nervous to stare at earlier, despite her obvious curiosity. She watched him zip his trousers over the bulge in his briefs.

"Are you . . . Will that be all right?" she asked.

"Don't worry about it." He smiled reassuringly at her.

When he was ready to go, he returned to the bed and gave her a brief kiss.

"I hope I'll see you again." He stroked her arm in tender farewell, then turned and headed for the door.

When his hand was on the knob, she said, "Kevin, wait."

He turned around. She rose awkwardly from the bed, dragging the sheet with her, unprepared to let him look at her the way she was entitled to look at him.

She clutched the sheet to her breasts. "I don't think I realized just how anxious I was until you said . . . you know . . . that we didn't have to . . ."

"I know."

"And I appreciate . . ." She laughed nervously, then said in a more normal voice, "You're really very kind, aren't you?"

He shook his head. "You don't have to—"

"I don't mean that. Well, not specifically. I mean . . . overall. You made this . . ." She shrugged. "I . . . I enjoyed this very much. In a way that I didn't expect to."

"I'm glad." He touched her cheek.

"So I, uh . . . Well, of course, I already . . . And maybe you don't . . ."

"What?" he asked.

She suddenly crossed to the dresser, dug into her purse, and pulled out her wallet. She avoided his eyes as she said, "I don't want to insult . . . but, uh . . ." She removed a few green bills from her wallet, folded them around her fingers, and extended the offering to him. "Is this all right?"

He grinned. "Always."

He had taught himself to accept tips in a graceful, easy-going way so that anyone who did it the first time would feel comfortable about doing it again. Preferably, *every* time. It was money he never had to share with Catherine. And now that he knew this woman was a tipper, he'd be more willing to put in a little overtime with her if he had to; Catherine wouldn't pay him for it, but as long as the client covered his time, he'd cooperate with good grace.

He kissed her hand as he took the money, smiled at her as he slipped the cash into his pocket, and said, "Have a good weekend, Alice."

"You, too, Kevin," she replied.

Once the hotel room door was closed solidly behind him, he reached into his pocket and pulled the money back out to count it. Eighty. Not bad.

He reached inside his jacket and found his cell phone. He hit the autodial and waited for an answer.

"Hello?" Catherine said.

"This is Kevin," he said, walking down the hall towards the elevator. "I just finished the Van Offelen appointment."

"Did everything go all right?" Her voice was, as always, smooth, courteous, cultured.

"Yeah, fine. You might want to suggest two hours to her next time."

"There'll be a next time, then?"

"I'm pretty sure." He stepped into the elevator when it arrived, already full of people heading for the ground floor.

"Good. Just a minute." He heard someone else's muffled voice, then Catherine replying to it. After a moment, she returned to their conversation. "And you think she'd like a longer appointment?"

"Yes."

"Hmmm. Newly divorced women," she mused. "It's always hard to tell if they'll become regulars or are just looking for something to cleanse their palate."

He shrugged, feeling the elevator's descent starting to slow. "I don't think *she* knows yet."

"Is she going to ask for you next time?"

"She liked me," he said non-committally as the elevator doors swished open and he stepped out onto the marble floor of the lobby.

"That's not what I asked."

Mindful that he was in a public place, although no one was paying attention to him, he lowered his voice as he crossed the vast lobby and headed towards the front exit. "Probably. I think she'll want the same guy every time. At least for a while."

"Any singularities?"

"No," he replied. "She's just shy and nervous. Being with a total stranger bothered her." Which wasn't unusual.

"All right." Done with that business, Catherine changed the subject. "I've got the details now for this evening. You're expected at six-thirty."

He checked his watch. "Where?"

She gave him an address on Russian Hill. He memorized it and started mentally rearranging his afternoon plans to accommodate the appointment being earlier than he'd expected. As he left the hotel, a sudden gust of wind off the bay nearly blew him back inside.

"Jesus!"

"Kevin?"

"Yeah, I'm here." Rush hour traffic was getting under way in San Francisco, raising the decibel level on the street. He couldn't make out her next comment. "What? Speak up."

"I said it's formal."

"A tux?"

"Yes."

He sighed in unguarded frustration as he handed his ticket to the valet waiting outside the lobby doors.

Catherine asked, "Is that a problem?"

"No. No problem." His tux was at the dry cleaners. He'd have to stop off there, go home, shower, dress, then double back most of the way to Russian Hill. So much for the rest of the day. "What am I doing?"

"Escorting the client to a political fund-raiser. In her own words: bad food, worse entertainment, astronomical prices." Catherine made a sound of amusement. "I'll never understand why people get involved in politics."

"Disgraceful, isn't it?" he said. "At least I give good value for *your* astronomical prices."

She ignored that. She almost always ignored comments like that. "The client will decide this evening, after meeting you, whether or not she wants you to go home with her. If she does, she'll say so. Otherwise, she wants no overtures from you."

"Understood." Some clients wanted the fantasy of an ardent lover; other women wanted a presentable escort who wouldn't pressure them for so much as a goodnight kiss.

"Call me tomorrow to let me know how it turns out," Catherine said, "and I'll bill her accordingly."

Catherine didn't charge for sex, of course; that would be crude—and so blatantly illegal that it would lead to busts on the basis of sheer stupidity. No, Catherine would charge the client for Kevin's time. And since he wanted to get paid for every minute he was working, he'd certainly tell her whether he and the client parted company after dinner, after a little sex, or after dawn.

"Fine, I'll talk to you tomorrow." He hung up without saying goodbye, then pulled a couple of bucks out of his wallet to tip the valet when he saw his Infiniti pulling up.

Great, he thought. He'd get into his monkey suit, look politely interested all evening at some excruciatingly dull event, and wait for the client to decide whether or not she wanted to fuck him before he could go home. Yes, indeed, so much for the rest of the day.

Oh, well. That's what whores do. Get over it.

CHAPTER ONE

"Are you out of your *mind?*" Sara's sister demanded.

"It's this sort of moral support that I really value in our relationship," Sara told her.

"You've gone crazy! I'm not giving moral support to insanity!" Miriam insisted.

Sara looked around at her new apartment. "You don't like it?"

"I can't believe you gave up a condo in Richmond for *this.*"

"You know why I gave up the condo. And let's *not,*" she added hastily, "argue about it again. The condo is sold. End of story."

She'd made a sizeable down payment on the place seven years earlier, and then she'd paid for significant improvements to it a couple of years later, using the money from her first book sale. The condo's location in a desirable neighborhood north of Golden Gate Park also helped to ensure that, upon selling it last month, Sara had made a tidy profit.

Miriam shook her head. "It happened too fast. You put that place on the market on the basis of a desperate, impractical impulse, and two days later you had a buyer. You never had a chance to come to your senses." Miriam tried to shove some moving boxes aside, discovered she couldn't, and wound up squeezing awkwardly past them as she entered the kitchen. A moment later she called out, "*This* is your kitchen?"

Sara sighed and remained in the living room. "There's nothing wrong with the kitchen."

Miriam squeezed past the boxes to re-enter the living room. "It looks like it hasn't been renovated since Eisenhower was president."

"I like it," Sara opined. "It's homey."

"Sara, you had that gorgeous modern kitchen—"

"This one's bigger."

"This one has appliances that poor people brought over from the old country before we were born."

"It's not the apartment that bothers you, it's the choices I've made."

"That's true." Miriam put her hands on her hips and looked around. "But the apartment makes it clear just how bad your choices are."

"Mir, this is how I lived before I got the condo."

"But now you're thirty-five and unemployed, instead of twenty-seven with a good job."

"I hated that job. And I really appreciate the positive way you've expressed my circumstances."

"Of course, I probably don't have to worry about you becoming destitute in a year, because it's very likely you'll soon die of a heart attack climbing those stairs."

Sara grimaced. "The stairs are a little daunting," she admitted. "The movers looked like they were going to throw up by the time they finished, and they charged me two hundred dollars more than the estimate."

Glen Park was a hilly neighborhood with curvy streets. It was safe, charming, and more affordable than the more famous San Francisco neighborhoods north of here. Sara thought it had a real community feeling, almost like a mountain village. But there were undeniably certain steepness issues here—particularly *within* the building.

"It's pretty obvious why this place was vacant despite the reasonable rent," Miriam said. "Not one person in a hundred could face climbing those stairs every day."

"They'll keep me in shape."

"Don't try to look on the bright side. There is no bright side."

"I'll get used to them," Sara lied.

This eccentric old Victorian building was near the summit of a big hill, and Sara's second-floor apartment was at the top of two long flights of steep, uneven stairs which leaned precariously to one side—with nothing but a flimsy railing to prevent a dizzy climber from the sort of fall usually favored by bungee jumpers and suicides.

Miriam looked at Sara's enormous, cushiony couch and wondered, "How on earth did the movers get that up here?"

"I had to shame them into it."

"And what," Miriam said, turning to look at the long wall which separated this one from the apartment next door, "is *that?*"

"It's a mural. The guy downstairs—he owns the building—is a mural painter."

An elaborate abstract mural covered the entire wall, floor to ceiling.

Miriam asked, "Has your landlord ever been imprisoned for his crimes against art?"

"You don't like it," Sara gathered.

"I'm sure that, like the stairs, it'll grow on me."

Sara studied the mural. "I think it's kind of . . . stimulating."

"Stimulating? I can't decide if it's obscene, or violent, or pastoral, or—"

"That's what stimulating about it. I haven't a clue what it is. I figure I can sit at my desk and stare at it, seeing new things in it every single day."

"Yes, I know. Writers spend a lot of time staring into space." Miriam shook her head. "But wouldn't staring at thin air be preferable to this?"

"I also have a nice view to stare at," Sara said, heading toward the French doors on the far wall. "See?" She opened them and led the way out onto the balcony.

"Wow." Miriam's eyes widened as she came out into the breezy late afternoon air. "Okay, this is nice. I admit it."

The balcony, which overlooked Glen Canyon Park and part of the neighborhood, was enormous, a large wooden terrace jutting out from the building, bordered by big, sturdy railings which came up to Sara's midriff. The late afternoon sun beamed down upon a dozen potted plants positioned around the balcony.

Miriam noticed these. "You don't grow plants."

"They belong to the guy next door. We share the balcony."

Miriam squinted at her. "What's he like?"

"I haven't met him." She reminded her sister, "I just moved in three hours ago."

"So you're sharing your balcony with a strange man."

"He may not be *that* strange."

"A man who can look through these windows into your home whenever he wants to. A man who will have access to these flimsy French doors at all hours of day and night." She paused in her critical examination of said flimsy doors. "Good God! The lock doesn't work!"

"I'm going to ask the landlord to fix that," Sara said.

"You *have* gone crazy."

"Look, there's only the one neighbor—"

"Oh, good, he can rape and murder you in perfect privacy."

"And Lance—the landlord—says he's a nice, quiet guy."

"And the LSD-crazed manic-depressive who painted that mural in your living room is undoubtedly a shrewd judge of character whose definitions of 'nice' and 'quiet' are above suspicion."

"It's quite possible," Sara said, "that my neighbor is not a drooling rapist or slavering serial killer."

"It's equally possible that he *is*."

"*Equally* possible? No, I don't think so. There are only so many of those in the city, after all. The odds—"

"You are so naive."

"Excuse me, *I* am the eldest here. Besides, Mir, I am the mystery writer, not you. I know more about—"

"*Were* the mystery writer," Miriam reminded her.

"*Ow*. That hurt."

"And writing whodunits about medieval Jews does not mean you know anything about survival in the modern world. Far from it!" Miriam sighed. "Reality has never been your strong suit."

Sara flinched as something shrieked behind her.

"What's that?" Miriam cried.

"His bird."

"Whose what?"

"My neighbor's bird." Sara pointed to the tall bird cage standing in the shadowy corner of the balcony beyond her neighbor's own set of French doors. It was on wheels, presumably so the owner could roll it outside on sunny midsummer days like this and easily take it back inside at night.

Miriam crossed the balcony to look at it. "This cage is so big. And so ornate."

Sara came to her side and stared into the cage with her. A little orange-and-teal bird stared back at them.

"It's a small bird for such a big cage," Miriam said.

"Look at all those toys," Sara murmured.

"He spoils it," Miriam concluded.

"See? He's probably a nice, quiet guy, just like Lance said."

"I'm sure the Birdman of Alcatraz was nice and quiet, too, despite being a depraved killer."

The bird suddenly pounced on a toy that looked like a miniature bird and started pecking it with vicious intensity.

"Well," Sara said. "I think we've covered everything. I'm making a terrible mistake with my life and my finances. I've chosen a dreadful apartment. And my neighbor will murder me in my sleep, but only after he rapes and mutilates me."

"If I've forgotten anything, I'll send you an e-mail." Miriam kept her eyes on the violent bird for a few moments before finally saying, in a different tone of voice, "I just worry about you."

"I know. That's why I put up with your shit." Sara sighed. "But I hope you're done now, because Dad will be here any minute, and I can't deal with the two of you ganging up on me. Moving day is bad enough without that."

"Okay, I'll stop," Miriam promised. "I won't stand up for you, but I'll stay out of it when he starts in on you."

"Fair enough."

Sara supposed she could understand why her family was appalled by the gamble she was taking now. It probably did look crazy to any sensible person. Still, she had to do it. Her heart wouldn't let her do anything else.

The French doors swung open, nearly hitting them. Miriam grabbed her arm, pulling her away from the flying door. Sara whirled around, startled into momentary alarm—and found herself face to face with a man.

He looked even more surprised than she felt. He glanced

from her to Miriam, then relaxed a little. "You're the new tenant?"

"Oh!" Sara smiled. "I'm sorry. Yes. I'm Sara Diamond. I moved in today. This is my sister, Miriam. You must be my neighbor?"

He smiled, too. Soft and slight, but a nice smile. Friendly. His blue eyes were bright, warm. She liked his eyes.

He was *not* a serial killer.

"Ryan Kinsmore." He looked down at the load he carried: an armful of bird supplies. "I'd shake with you, but my hands are a little full."

"We were gawking at your bird," Miriam confessed.

"She has emotional problems, doesn't she?" Sara said.

He sighed. "Is she beating up on that toy bird again?"

"Ah," Sara replied, "so it wasn't something I said?"

He smiled at her again, then peered into the birdcage and shook his head. "I don't know why she does it. Does she think it's a guy bird, and she hates men? Does it smell like some enemy species she thinks she has to destroy? Does it look like her ex?"

"Actually," Miriam said, "I think it looks a little like *my* ex."

"No wonder he's an ex," Ryan murmured.

Sara reached for the bag of birdseed Ryan was holding and said, "Here, let me help you out."

"Thanks."

Miriam eyed his supplies. "Those look like welder's gloves."

"They are," Ryan replied.

Sara said, "You were planning on doing a little welding before dinner?"

"They're for cleaning Mrs. Thatcher's boudoir."

"Excuse me?"

He nodded towards the birdcage.

Sara snorted. "Mrs. Thatcher?"

"Her previous owner named her. An English guy who used to live in your apartment."

"He left her behind?"

Ryan nodded. "He moved back home after I moved in here. Said it was too hard to bring animals back to England. None of his friends here would adopt Mrs. Thatcher—"

"Go figure."

"—and I was afraid she'd die if he just turned her loose."

"So you took her in."

"I can tell what you're thinking." He grinned at Sara. *"Sucker."*

"I didn't actually *say* that."

"I have to feed her and clean the cage." Ryan flexed his hands inside the elbow-length padded gloves. "Believe me, this is something only a brave man would attempt. You ladies might not want to watch. It could get ugly."

"No," Sara said, "we'll stay. There should be eyewitnesses."

"Well, don't say I didn't warn you."

He waited for the bird to turn her back to him, then opened the cage door and shot his gloved arm inside. Mrs. Thatcher shrieked and attacked him.

After watching in astonished amusement for a moment, Sara glanced at her sister. Very quietly, Miriam whispered, "Hubba hubba."

Sara nodded in agreement. About six feet tall, maybe a shade less, Ryan had a long-limbed body with straight, square shoulders, a flat stomach, and a tight butt. His pants and shirt, both good quality, were cut well enough to show off everything without being vulgar. His thick, medium-short hair was a little ruffled by the wind; it was a sun-seeking brown color, looking almost as if it wanted to turn blond in a few places. He had a light tan, long-lashed blue eyes, a nice nose, and a mouth that . . . Well, a guy with a mouth like that had better be a great kisser or it was a criminal waste of lips.

He was obviously younger than Sara. And she didn't think he was from San Francisco. There was a slight drawl in his vowels, a softness around some of his consonants. It added to the melting-butter quality of his voice.

Drooling rapist? Hah! He'd probably been defending himself from worshipful women since puberty.

He was talking to Mrs. Thatcher now, trying to soothe her as he restocked her food and water and cleaned her cage, all the while wearing those bulky welder's gloves. Immune to the seduction of his gentle murmuring, the bird was clutching one of the gloves with both feet and biting it like a mad dog.

"That is not a well animal, Ryan," Sara said.

"She's got some issues," he admitted, "but she just needs a patient touch. *Ouch!*"

"You're working wonders with her, I can see that."

"Come on, sweetheart," he crooned. "Let go now. Let go of the glove."

Man, if this guy crooned to me, *I'd do whatever he wanted.*

Mrs. Thatcher, however, was made of sterner stuff than Sara. She shrieked and redoubled her efforts to amputate one of Ryan's fingers.

"Shall we call 911?" Miriam asked.

Sara said, "It's too late for help."

"No, no," Ryan assured them through gritted teeth. "Everything's under control."

"He did say it could get ugly," Miriam reminded Sara.

"Try shaking your arm," Sara advised Ryan. "Dislodge her."

"She's just a little bird. I could hurt her."

"I had no idea a four-ounce bird could be this menacing."

"Ow! Damn it, bird, give me back my hand!"

"So much for the sweet talk," Sara said.

"Try distracting her," Ryan instructed Sara.

"Distracting her?"

"Yes. And since I think I'm bleeding now, could you move a little faster?"

"Oh! Okay."

Sara approached the cage and put her hand on one of the bars. Mrs. Thatcher immediately lost interest in maiming Ryan and leaped towards Sara—who flinched and jumped back. Mrs. Thatcher shrieked at her. Ryan removed his arm from the cage and slammed the door shut a split second before Mrs. Thatcher could escape to kill them all. Then the bird returned to shrieking at Sara.

She asked Ryan, "Why did you *care* that Mrs. Thatcher might die if you didn't adopt her?"

"It just didn't sit well with me."

"What do you do when I'm not here to rescue you?"

"She's not usually this bad." He eyed Sara. "Your presence seems to upset her. I don't think she likes you."

"Sure, blame me."

"Maybe she resents sharing the balcony with a prettier female."

Caught off guard by the flirtatious comment, Sara looked into the cage. With no human victims to attack, Mrs. Thatcher returned to beating up her toy bird.

"That isn't healthy," she said. "You should take that toy away from her."

"I gave it to her, I can't take it back. Anyhow, it makes her happy." He winced as he flexed the hand Mrs. Thatcher had bitten.

"So you make her happy, and she makes you bleed."

"The universal story of men and women," he said.

"Not from where I'm standing."

He smiled. "Probably not from where she's standing, either."

Sara smiled back, and their eyes held—until a sudden pounding on Ryan's front door surprised them both. Then Sara heard a gruff, half-hearted bark.

"You have a dog?" she asked.

"Yeah. Macy. He hardly ever barks, though. Excuse me." He brushed past her and went through the French doors.

"Okay," Miriam said, "maybe this apartment wasn't such a terrible idea, after all."

"So you've given up your theory that he's going to kill me in my sleep?"

"Maybe he'll be busy doing other things in your bed."

"Miriam!"

"What?"

"Don't be stupid."

"Stupid about what? Come on, you can't tell me you're not interested. I know you, and you're *interested*."

"I'm also older than him."

"What, five years?" Miriam said.

"Maybe ten."

"Oh, so what? He's well above the age of consent, and he obviously likes you, too."

"The point is—"

"Sara! *Sara!*" a man's voice shouted.

The sisters looked at each other.

"That's Dad."

"What's he doing bothering Ryan?"

They stuck their heads inside the living room just as Ryan was opening his front door to their father.

"You're not my daughter," said Abel Diamond, applying the razor-sharp perception that had made him a renowned scholar.

"That's true," Ryan agreed while the large, hairy, black dog at his side—Macy, presumably—wagged its tail. "But Sara's right here."

"Dad!" Sara said, coming inside.

"There you are." Abel was breathing hard and looked flushed. "My God . . . is that a dog . . . or a bear?"

"I'll get you a glass of water, sir," Ryan offered and headed for the kitchen.

"Thank you, young man." Abel collapsed into a burnished leather easy chair and pulled a handkerchief out of his pocket. "Sara," he panted, "I don't want you . . . to take this personally . . . but I am never . . . visiting you again."

The dog greeted Sara and Miriam, then investigated Abel for a moment. Evidently deciding the old man wasn't that interesting upon closer inspection, Macy lay down and gave an exhausted sigh.

"I'm sorry about the stairs, Dad."

"So am I," Abel wheezed, "because we've always been very close."

"But I have a big balcony and a good view."

"And I'm sixty-four years old . . . with arthritic knees."

"You probably came up the stairs too fast. You should pause to rest on the landing halfway up."

Ryan returned. "Here's some water, Mr. Diamond."

"Thank you." Abel gulped down half the contents of the glass, then closed his eyes and rested his head against the back of the chair. "I'm not even going to ask . . . why a handsome young man . . . whom I've never met . . . knows his way around my daughter's kitchen."

"Uh, Dad—"

"No, no," Abel insisted. "I'm not asking. No need to explain. A father . . . with two unmarried daughters . . . who aren't getting any younger . . ."

"Dad."

". . . is only too happy . . . to find a polite young man in their company."

"You're probably hoping," Sara said to Ryan, "to meet *all* of my relatives now."

Abel reminded her, "We *haven't* met. Introduce your father to your friend."

"Dad, this is Ryan Kinsmore."

"Kinsmore? That's not a Jewish name."

Sara said, "I admire the way *nothing* slips by you."

"Pleased to meet you." Ryan shook Abel's hand. "More water?"

"No, thank you, son."

"Dad, Ryan is my next door neighbor. This is his apartment."

"Oh! I *thought* you had unpacked awfully fast. And none of this looks like your stuff."

"And the amazing thing," Miriam told Ryan, "is that Dad's a tenured professor in the physics department at Berkeley."

Ryan wisely said nothing.

"I gave you the right apartment number," Sara said to her father.

"Across the hall." He nodded. "I knocked and knocked. The doorbell doesn't seem to work."

"Gosh, what a surprise," Miriam said.

Sara gave her sister a quelling look. "I'll get it fixed."

"And no one answered," Abel said. "So I tried this door. Then I heard a strange noise in here."

"Macy barked at you," Ryan explained.

"I'm sorry, Dad. We were out on the balcony. I didn't hear you."

"Thank God your neighbor isn't so cavalier. I thought I was going to faint in the hall after climbing those stairs."

"But y—"

"I am not bringing Aunt Minnie to your housewarming party."

"Aunt Minnie walks two miles a day and is in much better shape than you, old man."

"It's terrible," Abel said to Ryan, "how my children speak to me."

Sara started trying to haul him out of the chair.

"What are you doing?" he protested. "I like this chair!"

"Let's stop bothering Ryan and go into my apartment, Dad."

"We're not bothering Ryan. Are we bothering you, son?"

"Dad, he's got much better manners than you do, so it's not fair to ask him a question like that."

"Do you hear how they speak to their father?"

"Let's go, Dad," Miriam chimed in. "Don't you want to see Sara's apartment?"

"Oh. Yes. All right," he conceded.

"So get up."

"Well, help me, then, help me!"

"I'm trying." Sara held his arm and heaved, then staggered backward as he popped out of the chair like a cork.

"So, Ryan," Abel said, "after I see the apartment, we're going out to dinner to celebrate Sara's descent in the world."

"Gee, thanks, Dad."

"Would you like to join us?" Abel invited.

"Thank you for asking, sir, but I've already got plans."

Sara noticed formal eveningwear lying over the arm of the couch, still wrapped in plastic from the dry cleaners. "Come on, Dad, let's motor. We're probably making Ryan late for something."

"I like that chair," Abel confirmed. "It's a good chair."

Ryan said, "You're welcome to come sit in it any time, sir."

"You're a nice boy." Abel added to his daughters, "He's a nice boy."

Propelling her father to the door, Sara said, "Thank you, Ryan. Sorry about this."

"No problem," he said. "It was nice to meet you all."

He even sounded sincere. A nice boy, indeed, Sara reflected.

CHAPTER TWO

Sara sat alone in the dark and wept.

Oh, this is pathetic.

She blew her nose, stuffed the crumpled tissue into the pocket of her bathrobe, and tried to pull herself together. Needing some air, some space, something besides this dark living room full of boxes, she rose to her feet, went to the French doors, and opened them. She stepped out onto the balcony, then looked cautiously in the direction of Mrs. Thatcher's cage. It was gone. Evidently Ryan had rolled the cage inside for the night. The balcony was empty and quiet.

Sara gazed out over the neighborhood. A couple of lights shone like beacons in the dark expanse of Glen Canyon Park. The streets were faintly illuminated, but most of the homes and businesses were dark. Which made sense. It was three o'clock in the morning.

Insomnia was a common curse among writers. Especially out-of-work ones.

The cool night breeze ruffled Sara's shoulder-length hair, tangling the dark, curly strands. She rested her folded arms on the balcony railing, turned her tear-streaked face up to the night sky, and tried to count her blessings.

I'm alone in a strange place. I'm unemployed at thirty-five. I'll be penniless in a year.

And the career she had built was now all ashes.

So much for trying to find the silver lining.

She started crying again.

Stress, she assured herself, it was just stress.

Moving was supposed to be one of the most stress-inducing things a normal person did. The first night in a new home was always disorienting. Given that she was also depressed about her career . . . Well, a few tears were natural, perhaps even healthy.

Yeah, yeah, just give into it. Get really *depressed. WALLOW. Go on. You know you're dying to.*

Sara caved in, lowered her head, and started crying in earnest, letting herself sob as if someone had just died. If she was going to feel sorry for herself, then, damn it, she was going to be thorough about it.

"Sara."

She shrieked and nearly leaped over the balcony rail.

"It's just me," Ryan said. "Easy, easy."

"Ryan!" She stared stupidly at him, sniveling and sobbing.

He came closer, but not too close, and he didn't try to touch her. "What's wrong? Are you okay?"

"I'm fine," she choked out as tears streamed down her cheeks.

"Did something happen?" In the faint glow from the city lights, he looked genuinely concerned.

"No!" She realized that sounded too vehement to be convincing. "No, nothing happened."

My whole life fell apart, that's all.

Sara sobbed harder and turned away. Something poked her thigh. She gasped and looked down to see Macy, big and black and hairy, panting anxiously. He burped at her.

"Macy can't stand to see someone he likes crying," Ryan said.

"So I'll go inside."

"Sara . . ."

"I'm really embarrassed," she blubbered. "It's nothing."

"No," he said, "I'm pretty sure it's not nothing."

"I'm sorry. I'm bothering you," she whimpered. "I'll go inside now."

"Shhh." Now he touched her shoulder. "Maybe you shouldn't be alone."

She just stood there crying. Macy whined.

Shit.

"Come on," Ryan said after a moment, gently trying to tug her away from the balcony railing.

She sputtered with mingled amusement and tears. "I wasn't going to jump."

"I know." He smiled slightly. "I mean, why don't you sit down?"

"Oh."

Sara let him lead her over to the two wooden chairs set up between their respective balcony doors. She sat down and mumbled, "It's so late. What are you doing up? Oh, no! Did I wake you?"

"Yeah, I always sleep dressed like this, Sara."

She heard the dryness in his tone and looked up at him. That was when she noticed he was wearing a tuxedo. "You just got in?" she guessed.

"Uh-huh."

"Oh, your thing."

"My thing?"

"Your . . ." She eyed the tux, which fit him beautifully. "Concert appearance? Gala embassy reception? Magic act?"

He snorted. "Nah, just a thing. Bland food, warm drinks, boring speeches."

She nodded and sniffed. "Been there, done that. Bought the T-shirt, read the book . . . *Wrote* the book." She started crying harder again.

He put his hand over hers for a moment. "Stay here. I'll be right back. Okay?"

She nodded, because as embarrassed as she felt, a little undemanding company seemed more appealing than the strange bedroom full of boxes that awaited her when she went inside. She hadn't even been able to find the box with her linens, so she'd have to sleep rolled up in an old army blanket tonight. That seemed so sad she quivered with another hard sob. Macy approached her and panted on her knees.

"Macy," Ryan said, returning to the balcony, "move. Come on."

There was a slight scuffle of shoes and paws, then a box of tissues appeared in front of Sara.

"Thanks," she sobbed, yanking on several tissues in a row and then holding them up to her wet, puffy, grimacing face.

"I'm putting the box right next to you," Ryan said. "On the table here."

She nodded, eyes closed, and sat with the tissues pressed to her face. Then the chair creaked under Ryan's weight as he rested his butt on its arm. Sara suddenly felt his body next to her, warm and solid. She shifted nervously when he put his hand on her back.

"It's okay," he said, his voice like melting butter. "Sometimes a good cry is what it takes." That slight drawl in his voice made him sound so soothing.

So Sara wept. Just cried like a kid whose favorite toy had been broken. The hand on her back stroked her, sure and gentle, an undemanding human contact silently telling her that her tears were all right. Needy and shameless, she shifted and leaned against him. He slid his arm around her and squeezed, settling his weight comfortably against her, then continued those slow, sympathetic caresses along her back and shoulder.

She didn't know how long she cried like that. She was tired when she was done, and light-headed. She sighed and, realizing she'd have to do it eventually, she pulled herself away from Ryan's comforting embrace. Avoiding his eyes, she turned and reached for more tissues, keeping her face averted as she blew her nose. Noisily. Several times.

He rose from the chair. Who could blame him?

Then he picked up something else on the side table and handed it to her. "Here. Drink this."

She accepted a glass from him. The strong smell made her shudder. "What is it?"

"Scotch."

"Oh, good. I'm not nearly maudlin enough yet." She took a bold swig—and suddenly felt as if her esophagus was melting.

"Sara?"

"Ohmigod!" Gasping and choking, she handed the rest of the scotch back to him. "That was diabolical!"

"Maybe a smaller sip—"

"What did I ever do to you to deserve a dirty trick like that? Besides collapse on your balcony in tears at three in the morning, I mean?"

"It's your balcony, too." He sat down in the other chair. "I guess you don't like scotch?"

"I guess not."

"Can I get you something else?"

"No, I think I'll throw up if I add anything to the scotch."

Ryan took a sip from what had been her glass, then leaned all the way back in his chair and sighed. Macy yawned and lay down between them, giving an exhausted moan as he settled in.

With her sob-muzzied head starting to clear—okay, so the scotch hadn't really been such a bad idea—Sara finally noticed that Ryan had removed his jacket, undone his tie, pulled his shirt out of his waistband, and opened the buttons at his throat. It suddenly seemed very intimate to be sitting here in her robe with this stranger who was in a state of dishabille while he drank from her glass—after holding her while she cried her heart out.

"Thank you, Ryan," she said.

He lifted his head. She couldn't see his eyes, but she could tell he was looking right at her. "I won't pry," he began.

"It's okay," she said. "It's not a big secret. It's not even very interesting."

He shifted in his chair. "So do you want to bore me a little?"

"You know," she pointed out, "I could be some neurotic who does this every night, and you're inviting a world of tension headaches by being this nice to me."

"You could be. And I could be preying on your moment of weakness to get you into bed, or maybe just to get into your wallet."

"So *you're* the reason the rent is so reasonable here."

Sara had heard the words "get you into bed" loud and clear, and her rich imagination immediately conjured up . . .

No, don't go there.

He gave a soft puff of laughter. "No, our landlord is the reason. Not many people can live with Lance's murals."

Ryan clearly wasn't going there, after all. He'd expressed it as a joke. And that was okay, Sara decided. Gorgeous young men were not notoriously easy for aging women to monopolize, and she would make herself crazy if she tried. Mirrors didn't crack when Sara looked in them, but neither did heads turn when she walked down the street. She was an ordinary-looking woman with curly dark hair, brown eyes, and acceptable features. Her figure was that of a thirty-five year old who spent most of her time sitting in a chair staring at a computer screen. And she'd only get hurt if she fell for her gorgeous, younger, undoubtedly much sought-after neighbor. Besides, she had more important things to do now than lose her head over some guy.

Here in this dark light, with his shirt unbuttoned to bare his throat and his posture weary, Ryan looked even younger than he had this afternoon. All the same, he looked like someone who understood disappointment and fear, and she'd already discovered that he was definitely someone who understood sorrow.

"I suppose I've been keeping things bottled up for too long," Sara said at last. "I might not have gone to pieces tonight if I hadn't been so rigid about holding myself together until now. There was just so much to do, so many things to accomplish in a short space of time. So many decisions . . . It all kept me busy. Focused. Determined. Sure of my choices." She sighed. "But now that's all done, and tonight . . . all that's left is me."

"And you couldn't keep out the rain anymore," he guessed, watching her.

"Yeah."

"What made you move here?"

"A fork in the road," she said. "A new beginning."

"A fresh start?"

"Exactly."

"A fresh start." Butter melted with honey in his wistful voice. "A second chance."

"Are you making a fresh start, too?" she asked, looking at him curiously.

"Me?" There was a pause before he said, "No." He finished the last of the scotch. "Well, maybe I did. I made some changes a couple of years ago. When I moved into this apartment."

He didn't give the impression of wanting to talk about it, but Sara wanted to know more. She tried a question that wasn't too personal: "Did you move here from out of state?"

He nodded. "Originally. But that was a long time ago." He stared into his empty glass and added, "Another lifetime."

"You don't look old enough to have run through one life already."

"Oh, I've run through a few."

"Then you must have made a deal with the devil."

"What?"

"I mean, your past doesn't show on your face."

He gave another soft puff of laughter, but he didn't seem amused this time. "A deal with the devil," he repeated.

"Where are you from?" she asked, sensing his withdrawal.

"Ah. I've still got some of that accent, don't I?"

"It's slight." After a pause, she added, "I like it. It makes you sound . . . I don't know. Soothing. Friendly." *Sexy.*

After a moment of silence, he evidently realized it was his turn to speak. "I was raised in Oklahoma."

"Do you ever go back there?"

He shook his head. "Nothing to go back to."

"So you were already living in California—in San Francisco—when you moved to this building?"

"Yeah."

"And made your fresh start."

"It wasn't really a . . . Maybe I wanted it to be," he

said, "but it's not that easy, is it?"

"No, it's not easy." When he didn't say anything, she risked asking, "Has it not worked out for you?"

"Well . . . the apartment has worked out for me." He added much less moodily, "I like it here. You will, too, once you're unpacked." His tone indicated he was ready to change the subject. Perhaps even regretted having said as much as he had.

"I'm sure I will." Sara sighed. "But I'm not really worried about that."

"Then do you feel like telling me what *is* worrying you?" he invited.

She knew he didn't want to talk about himself anymore. And since her self-absorption was running high tonight, she was quite willing to let him shift the conversation back to her. "My career went on the skids recently. I'm trying to start over. Go in a whole new direction. Wrest success from failure."

"What do you do?"

"I'm a writer."

"What do you write?"

"You mean, what did I *used* to write?"

"You've stopped?"

"I've been terminated."

"Fired?"

"Dumped."

"I don't understand."

"For five years, I've been writing a mystery series set in the Jewish community of Moorish Spain. It was a time and place of high culture and relative intellectual freedom for Jews." She paused. "You did get that my family's Jewish, right?"

"Yeah, somehow I clued into that," he assured her.

"But, Sara—you're a novelist?"

"Yes."

He leaned forward. "That's so cool! I'm not sure I've ever met a novelist before. I've definitely never sat around talking to one, anyhow."

"It follows, therefore, that you've also never watched one bawling her eyes out and blowing her nose?"

"So I could go to the bookstore and find some of your books?"

"Yes. Well . . . Maybe not the first bookstore you tried. Not anymore." Since that sounded morose to her, she added, "But they're definitely at the library."

"That's—Wow!" He grinned. "A real live novelist living right next door."

"A real live one," she agreed. "It's amazing how many people think you have to be dead—like Thomas Hardy or Agatha Christie—to be a writer. Trust me, being dead makes it *so* much harder to write."

Ryan seemed much more animated now than he had been when they were talking about him. "How many books have you written?"

"They've published six. I turned in my seventh a few months ago. It'll be released in the fall. But you'll probably need to hire a team of detectives to find it, since I doubt they'll print more than eight copies or even mention to head buyers and distributors that they're publishing it."

"Why?"

"I didn't make them enough money, so they've cancelled my series and ended our relationship."

"Oh." He thought that over. "I'm sorry."

"I'm much sorrier," she assured him.

"Can you sell your next one somewhere else?"

"Not in that series. No one wants it. The way publishing

works, the writer has to show a certain growth in sales figures as her career progresses or she's no longer an interesting investment to her publisher—and often not to any other publishers, either."

He leaned back again and said thoughtfully, "I guess it's that way in a lot of lines of work, isn't it? The boss picks up newcomers cheap, tries them out for a while, eventually figures out who's bringing in the most money—and just gets rid of the rest. Cuts the losses and moves on."

"What do you do for a living?" she asked.

"Me? Oh. I'm a model."

"Really?" Well, that made sense. Just look at the guy.

"Nothing glamorous," he assured her. "Mostly I do clothing catalogues."

"That's so cool!" She grinned. "So I could open a catalogue tomorrow and see your face?"

"Well, no, not my face."

"Huh?"

"My face doesn't photograph so well."

"You're kidding me." Since that sounded bald, she added, "I mean, you have a beautiful face, Ryan."

"Thanks. But the camera doesn't really like it."

That was hard to believe, but she assumed professional modeling had a whole set of criteria about which she knew nothing. "So they chop off your head when they take your picture?"

"Pretty much. I mostly model below-the-neck stuff. Boxers, briefs, trousers, shoes."

"Do you like the work?"

"It's a living," he said. "Do you like writing?"

She felt him again turning the conversation back to her. She let him. "I *love* it. I'm obsessed with it. When I first started writing, I knew I'd found my true work, the thing I was meant to spend the rest of my life doing."

"Did you know your sales weren't going so well?" he asked.

"No. In fact, I thought things were going fine. I won an Agatha, and I got nominated for an Edgar Award. I got good reviews and nice letters from readers. My editor loved my writing." She sighed. "But I made mistakes. I didn't pay enough attention to the business end of things or prepare in advance for something like this happening."

"But if you didn't know—"

"I should have known it was *possible*. It's not uncommon, Ryan. Writing is an incredibly competitive profession, and publishing has narrow profit margins. I know other writers to whom this has happened. I should have prepared better." She shook her head. "But, as Miriam always says, reality isn't my strong suit. So when my agent called to tell me the publisher wasn't going to buy my next book because they had decided to cancel the series, I was caught off guard. I was shocked. Devastated. And financially vulnerable." Sara shrugged. "For a few days, I was a total mess."

"And then you made plans?"

"Yes. Stupid, impractical, risky plans which everyone—particularly my father and my sister—condemns."

"Oh. I see." After a moment, he asked, "Were they kind of hard on you at dinner tonight?"

"Oh, no, not at all." She waved her hand dismissively. "My sister did her lecturing well before dinner. And my dad just repeated all of his earlier objections, in case I'd failed to take notes the first ten times he told me not to do this."

"Do what?"

"I sold my condo—which had turned out to be a really

good investment—and have come here to write a new novel on spec."

"Spec?"

"Speculation. It means I don't have a contract. No one's paying me. There's no guarantee whatsoever that a publisher will buy it. I'm starting my career all over from scratch, in effect."

"What are you writing?"

"It's sort of a historical thriller. I've been thinking about it for a few years and have done a lot of research for it, but I've never had time to write it because . . . well, until now, I was always under contract and busy writing my mystery series."

He tilted his head. "So, on the bright side, now you have time to write your blockbuster."

She grinned at the word. "And when I'm done, I hope it'll be a book some publisher will want to buy for lots of money. If not . . ."

"So you're really taking a big risk." He nodded. "A life gamble."

"Yes."

"And if it doesn't work, you'll lose everything, even the money you made on your condo?"

She shivered. "Yes."

"That's a brave gamble, Sara."

"I hope so. After just panicking for the first couple of days when I got the bad news, I came up with this plan. I contacted a real estate agent right away, before I had time to talk myself out of it. The condo sold just a few days later to a buyer who wanted to take possession as soon as possible." She ran her fingers through her wind-tangled hair. "Suddenly I was apartment-hunting, and packing, and swamped with doing all the stuff you have to do when you move. And since my family thought I was crazy and weren't at all shy about telling me so, I took a very strong, confident stance about what I was doing . . . Until one night, I found myself sitting all alone in a strange room full of cardboard boxes, with nothing left to do now but write this fabulous novel that's going to resurrect my career and keep me from starving when the condo money runs out."

"Oh, well, if *that's* all that's left to do . . ."

She smiled. "Yeah, what am I whining about?"

After a pause, he said, "You've got guts."

"You're too polite to say I'm crazy and impractical."

He ignored that. "I admire guts. I respect determination."

"You should hang up a shingle," she said.

"Huh?"

"You're good at making people feel better about themselves."

"That's not what I'm . . ." He shrugged. "I just mean, I think it's a good plan. It's what you should do. And I'm glad you're doing it here."

"I guess I picked the right next door neighbor."

"I guess you did."

"It's very nice of you to be so supportive. Granted, it's probably because you have no idea what a big mistake I'm making—"

"But I gather your father will explain it to me the next time he comes here to bond with my leather chair."

"Oh, God." She put her hand over her eyes. "I'm so sorry about that."

He chuckled. "It's okay. I liked him."

"He shouldn't be let out of the house without supervision."

"No, I did like him. Honest." After a pause, he added,

"You have a nice family."

"I do," she agreed. "They're like all families—a lot of times I want to kill them. But mostly they're good to have around."

"They're not like all families," he assured her quietly.

"Is your family—"

"Where's your mom?" he asked.

Okay, his family was evidently something else he'd rather not talk about. "She died," Sara replied. "Three years ago. Cancer."

"I'm sorry."

"I think it's still pretty hard on my dad. He misses her." A long silence followed this. Finally Sara said, "I'm keeping you up."

"No." But he glanced at his watch. "Christ, I didn't realize how late it is."

She pulled her robe across her throat as a breeze swept across the balcony. She hadn't noticed until now that she was chilly. Even in July, nights were cool in San Francisco. "I should try to get some sleep. Lots of unpacking to do tomorrow."

He stood up and held out his hand, quite the gentleman, to help her rise from her chair. "Do you feel a little better?"

"Oh, yeah." She nodded. "All the crying and babbling and blatant self-pity was very cathartic."

"Well, you certainly *sound* better."

She paused before entering her apartment. "Thank you, Ryan. You're a good listener."

He shrugged. "I like listening to you."

"The old man was right," she said. "You're a nice boy."

"Good night, Sara."

"Good night."

CHAPTER THREE

"What are you *doing?*" Sara exclaimed.

"He doesn't like the stairs."

Ryan was carrying Macy up the steep, sloping flights of stairs leading to their two apartments. Sara thought the dog must weight at least seventy pounds.

"So this is how you keep in shape," she said, standing at the top of the stairs and watching Ryan ascending towards her with measured, trudging steps.

"No, I keep in shape so I can do this," he corrected.

"And here I thought you kept in shape so you could be photographed in your skivvies."

"Well, that, too."

He put the dog down when he reached the top step. Macy poked Sara in the leg by way of greeting, and then stood at the door and waited to be let into Ryan's apartment. Ryan remained standing on the top step, his hand on the fragile railing, and tried to catch his breath.

"I've got to work out more," he said, glaring at Macy. "That dog is gaining weight."

"Maybe *he* should work out more."

"I think he's got a thyroid problem. I should ask the vet." He shifted his gaze from Macy to Sara. "I didn't think you'd be up so early."

It was the following morning, barely six hours after they'd said goodnight.

"I didn't sleep well. Lots of new noises here that I'm not used to yet," she explained.

"Oh, of course." He nodded at Macy and said, "He woke me when nature called."

"I can't find my damn coffee maker," Sara said. "You might want to get out of my way now, because I'll kill you and trample your bloody corpse if you keep standing between me and caffeine."

He laughed. "Okay, before it comes to that, maybe you should just come inside with me. I started a fresh pot before I took Macy out."

Now Sara was embarrassed. "I wasn't angling for—"

"I know."

"And I've already intruded on you enou—"

"It's okay." He brushed past her and opened his door, gesturing to invite her into his apartment. "I'd feel guilty about letting you loose on the neighborhood in your current state of mind."

"Well, you have a point," she admitted, accepting the invitation.

"How's it going?" Miriam asked over the phone a few days later.

"Good," Sara replied, unpacking books with one hand while she held the receiver in the other. "I found my toothbrush this morning. Why didn't I pack it where I could find it right away?"

"Because you're disorganized and you plan badly."

"Oh, yes. That would be the reason."

"Are you almost done unpacking?"

"What do you think?"

"Oh, I'd bet a week's pay that you're now realizing I was right and you should have culled your possessions before moving from a two-bedroom condo with storage into a one-bedroom apartment without."

"I think I'll have to get rid of some stuff."

"Color me *so* surprised."

"But *maybe,* if I arrange it all very cleverly—"

"No, you'll have to get rid of some stuff," Miriam said.

"God, to think I paid the movers to carry it all up here, and now . . . No, maybe I'll just try to squeeze it all in."

"I won't even bother suggesting you get rid of some of your books."

"Good."

"I am curious, though, about the structural integrity of the building. Does your landlord think the second floor can hold the weight of all those tomes?"

"We haven't really discussed that."

"Figures. How's the neighborhood?"

"Fine."

"And the neighbor?"

Sara started shelving some of her reference books. "I hit the neighbor jackpot."

"So he's still a nice, quiet guy?"

"Yeah. No Mr. Hyde side, no split personality. In fact, he's been really thoughtful. Above and beyond the call."

"Oh?"

"He's helped me move some furniture. Gave me breakfast two mornings in a row. He's been showing me around the neighborhood a little." She heaved another heavy pile of books into her arms and crossed to the bookcase. "He's made me feel at home here."

"So you've been spending some time together?"

"Uh-huh." She started alphabetizing, wishing she had thought to do that when packing all this stuff.

"And?"

"And what?"

"And is he showing interest? Are *you* showing interest?"

"Aw, drop it, will you, Miriam?"

"Why? I saw the click between you two the day I was there. You can't tell me there was no click."

"Shit!" Sara looked down at her filthy hands and arms, then sneezed twice. "Why didn't I dust these books before I packed them?"

"If you'll recall, I told you—"

"Yeah, yeah. I didn't have time then. I'll do it now."

"Do you know where your cleaning supplies are packed?"

"Oh." She looked around at the chaotic living room. "I probably should have been more methodical about this."

"You're changing the subject."

"What was the subject?"

"Ryan."

"Mir, he's twenty-six, okay?" She'd weaseled this information out of him yesterday over a shared pizza on her living room floor.

"Nine years younger than you. Hmmm. Well, that's perfect for a fling, and it's not an impediment to a serious relationship."

"Right, because gorgeous young men are always on the prowl for middle-aged women."

"You're not middle-aged. If you're middle-aged, then I'm *approaching* middle-age, and I don't accept that."

"Hah! Do you remember how *old* we thought Mom was when she was my age?"

"You were nine and I was six then. One could reasonably suppose Ryan has a slightly more sophisticated view of these things."

"One can also reasonably suppose that Ryan has his pick of beautiful, long-legged, sloe-eyed, accommodating women who are ten years younger than I am."

"And one can just as reasonably suppose that he's not that shallow, and that he—"

"Look, whether he just wants casual sex or is seriously looking for a lifelong partner to become the mother of his children, a twenty-something guy who's that good-looking and charming, and who makes good money—"

"If he makes such good money, why does he live there?"

"*Now* who's being shallow?"

"I meant—"

"He likes it here. So do I. Anyhow, I don't know what he makes, but he drives an Infiniti, he's got great clothes, an expensive wristwatch, nice furniture. He's obviously making better money than you or I were making at twenty-six."

"I was in grad school then," Miriam reminded her.

"My point is, he's a good catch. Hell, he's a *great* catch. And even a lot of men *my* age aren't interested in women my age, so a man his age—"

"Might not be that shallow, I repeat."

Sara sighed. "He and I are becoming friends, okay? I like him, and I live right next door to him. We're in each other's pockets on that balcony. So I'm not going to make things awkward by throwing myself at him."

"You don't have to throw yourself at him. But you could let him know the door is open if he wants to walk through it."

"Why should I?"

"Because you're interested. Don't tell me you're not interested. I saw the click between you."

"Will you stop with the clicking, already?"

"Just listen to yourself, would you? He's gorgeous, he's charming, he's thoughtful, you like him."

"Why are you harping on this?" Sara demanded. "Why are you suddenly desperate for me to date?"

"Because you've been by yourself for too long. You haven't even *had* a date in over a year, am I right?"

"Yes. And I so appreciate the reminder."

"And you haven't been *involved* with anyone since Nathan. That was four years ago."

"Eeek. Nathan. A synonym for self-absorbed."

"Agreed. I'm not saying you should have kept him around."

"I didn't think so. Because then I might be forced to say you should have kept David around."

"No, you wouldn't. There is no provocation in the universe that could make you say that."

"True. Your ex-husband was a schmuck."

"Ever since you started writing full-time," Miriam persisted, "you've hardly dated."

Sara went back to alphabetizing the books on the shelves. "Well, it's hard to meet men if you're always home alone all day with imaginary medieval people."

"Which is why I think your yuppie next-door neighbor—"

"He's not a yuppie. He's a model."

"Yeah? Well, that figures. Just look at the guy."

"Sometimes when you talk," Sara said, "it's like I'm hearing an echo."

"You like him, he's nice, he likes you—"

"For God's sake, Mir, do I have to be afraid you're going to send a marriage broker to speak to the poor guy about me?"

A pause. "I'm being pushy, aren't I?"

"Well, I didn't want to be the one to say it."

"Sorry, I know, I know. I'm being pushy. I'm being—oy!—like *Mom*."

"Just a little. What gives, anyhow?"

Miriam laughed. "I don't know. I guess . . . Hey, love is

wonderful—I mean *wonderful*—and you deserve it, too."

"What about you?"

Now Miriam's laugh was nervous. "I'm working on it."

Sara paused in her task. "No!" She felt her jaw drop. "You're seeing someone?"

There was a pause, and then Miriam admitted, in an undeniably happy voice, "Okay, yeah, I'm seeing someone."

"Since when?"

"Well, um . . . a while, actually."

"What?"

"We met in April."

"So you've been seeing each other for three months?"

"Uh-huh."

"And you haven't said a word to me!"

Miriam laughed nervously again. "Well, at first I wasn't sure it was worth saying something."

"What do you mean *worth* saying something?"

"And then you had all that bad news about your career, and you've been dealing with that, and I didn't—"

"God, Mir, am I really *that* self-absorbed? You thought I wouldn't—"

"No, no," Miriam said. "I don't mean that. That's not what I meant at all."

Sara frowned. "So what do you mean?"

"Well, just . . . the timing didn't seem right."

"Miriam, so I'm having some ups and downs. Big deal. You think I don't want to know what's going on with you?"

"No, that's not what I—"

"You think I'm so selfish that I'd be upset that your life's going well when mine's a little bumpy?"

"No."

"Then what's the deal here?"

"I guess . . . Oh, maybe the deal is that I just want to

keep this to myself a while longer. Dad doesn't know, either. And don't tell him!"

"Okay. But are *you* going to?"

"Eventually."

"So can you at least tell me something about this guy?"

Miriam made a sound. "Maybe not right now, Sara."

This was unbelievable. They'd always been close. Maybe they didn't tell each other *everything,* but for Miriam to keep quiet, even now, about someone she'd been seeing for nearly three months . . .

"You don't think we'll like him," Sara guessed. "That's it, isn't it?"

"Something like that," Miriam conceded.

"It's because I was so nasty about David after you and he split up, isn't it?"

"No."

"Because I told you that I'd always wondered, from the very start, what the hell you saw in him, and so now you're afraid—"

"This is not about David," Miriam said. "Not in any way. Okay?"

"Miriam, *whoever* you choose—whether he's around for just three months, or for the next fifty years—is okay with me. With Dad, too."

"Now you're bullshitting me."

"Well, yes, I really mean it's okay with Dad as long as he's a Jewish Democrat."

"Yes, that's closer to the reality we all know and live in, Sara."

"But I'm not like Dad, and I want you to know that whoever you love—or date—is fine with me."

"Good." Miriam paused. "Thanks." After a moment she added, "I hope that's true."

"Oh, my God," Sara said suddenly. "I know what it is."

"You do?"

"He's a book reviewer, isn't he?"

Miriam sputtered with laughter.

"That's it, isn't it?" Sara demanded. "My God! How can you date someone like that? What could you possibly be thinking?"

"No! Not a reviewer, okay? But thanks for bringing up yet another type of date I can never introduce you to."

"Another type?" Sara repeated. "You really are afraid I won't like this one."

"Look, we've only recently started talking about meeting each other's families. And given how frightening my family is—"

"What's so frightening about *me?*"

"I'm just not ready. So you're going to drop the subject."

"The way you dropped the subject of Ryan the moment I asked you to?"

"That's different."

"What the hell is so different about that?"

"Because I'm right," Miriam said. "I saw the way you two clicked."

"I don't get it," Ryan said. "You work on this thing almost every day, right?"

"Yes," Sara agreed, watching him set up her computer at her desk the following week.

"It's your primary professional tool, right?"

"Wrong." She pointed to her head and said, "*This* is my primary professional tool."

"Okay," he conceded. "Point taken." He paused in his work for a moment and studied her with a contemplative expression.

"What?" she prodded.

"I was going to wait until I was done before I told you."

"Done doing what?"

"I'm reading *The Seven Deadly Blessings.* I bought it a couple of days ago."

"Wow, you mean to say you found a bookstore that carries my books?"

"It wasn't hard, Sara," he chided. "The first store I tried had three of them. I bought them all."

"You didn't have to do that. I have spare copies I can give you."

"Oh, *now* you tell me."

She grinned. "Few things are more pathetic than a writer forcing her books on her friends. But if you actually want to read them—"

"I don't mind buying them," he assured her.

"I don't mind giving them to you," she countered. "And it's not as if your purchasing the remaining titles is going to save my career. So if you ever want to read the rest—"

"I do if they're all as good as this one," he said.

"Ooh! I knew there was a reason I liked you. You're a man of superior taste and rare perception."

"I kind of want to ask you if I'm right about who the killer is. But I don't want the ending spoiled, so I'm not going to ask."

"I wouldn't tell you, anyhow."

He grinned. "That's other reason I won't ask." He returned to hooking up the computer. "It's kind of scary, though, living right next to a woman who could think up some of the stuff in that book." He cast her a sly glance as he added, "Especially because it's so *you* in some parts."

"So me?" she asked cautiously.

"It makes me laugh. Usually when I least expect it."

She smiled, pleased.

"And some of it," he continued, "is so grim. And all of the history and culture—it's really interesting."

"I'm glad you think so."

"I can't believe the publisher dumped you. You're so good! I'm staying up too late reading you."

"I wish you were running a publishing house."

"Straight up, Sara. I'm glad you're not quitting. I'm really glad you're writing another book now." He added, "And I'm glad I'm here to set up your computer, since it's obvious you'd never manage by yourself."

"Now that thing," she said, "is a *real* mystery."

"But it's important. You deal with it every day. All your work is stored in here."

"Uh-huh."

"So how can you know so little about it?"

"These things are designed by men." She nodded. "That says it all."

He rolled his eyes. "Hand me that power cord. On your left. No, your other left. Yeah, that's it."

Sara watched as he continued connecting her computer. "I really do appreciate this, Ryan."

"Consider it an act of self-preservation. The squeals of frustration coming from here were making Macy agitated, and he was drooling all over me."

"I'm not good with technology," Sara confessed.

"I'm no expert," Ryan said, hitting the power button on the computer, "but this thing seems pretty straightforward. Ah-hah! And it's working. Now let's see . . ."

She sighed. "You're like all men. Give you an expensive electronic toy with many parts and indecipherable instructions, and you come to life as never before."

"That's sexist," Ryan said, "but probably true."

He sat down at her desk to fiddle with the computer. Sara moved to stand behind him and look over his shoulder. She was about to suggest he stay for dinner again—maybe Thai or Chinese this time—when the computer screen popped into life, its colored patterns looking like one of their landlord's murals.

"The monitor's not supposed to do that," Sara said with some concern.

"Give it a minute," Ryan advised.

She wasn't completely settled in yet—there simply wasn't room here for everything to come out of the boxes—but she had, by now, unpacked and put away the essentials. Once the computer was set up, she could commence work and establish a real life again.

Her vast desk was in the living room, with an easy view of the balcony. All of the walls that weren't covered in Lance's mural were now dominated by overflowing bookcases. The place was starting to feel like home.

"Maybe we should reboot," Ryan murmured. He looked down at the ergonomic keyboard. "Where's your Alt button?"

Sara leaned over his shoulder and showed him.

"Oh, okay."

Ryan's shoulder brushed into brief contact with her midriff as he shifted in his seat. His hands moved gracefully across the keys.

Everything inside of Sara went on tilt. She looked down at his thick, sun-burnished brown hair. The nape of his neck, smooth and touchable. His shoulder, sturdy and warm, just scant inches away from her body.

There was a sudden, hungry quiver inside her. For affection. It had been such a long time. And for this particular man. Because she couldn't find anything about him that she didn't like. A whole lot. Inside and out.

Sara closed her eyes. *Down, girl.* She wasn't going to embarrass them both.

"There it goes," Ryan said.

She could hardly hear him through the tumult of her thoughts.

His hand brushed her breast. Sara gasped and flinched, feeling guilty. Only when her eyes flew open did she realize she hadn't caused that scintillating moment of contact; Ryan had started to fold his hands behind his head while simultaneously leaning back, not realizing how close she was standing.

With my eyes closed. While I fantasized about touching him.

"Sorry," he said, frozen with his hands by his head as he looked at her, perhaps surprised at her overreaction. "I didn't mean—"

"I know. It's okay."

He turned back to the computer, mercifully saying nothing and letting the moment slip into the past. Sara sat down on the side desk, at a saner distance from Ryan, and watched as the computer rebooted.

"Good," she said in a normal voice. "*That's* what it's supposed to look like."

"Let's make sure the modem works."

A phone started ringing.

"That was fast," Sara said, puzzled.

Ryan smiled at her. "No." He reached into the pocket of his cambric shirt—she'd noticed by now that he dressed very differently at home than he did when he left for work—and pulled out his cell phone. He stood up and moved away from the desk. "I'll be right back," he assured her.

Sara nodded and took his place at the desk, sitting in the

chair left warm by his body heat. She resisted the urge to squirm or to think about the butt that had been there only moments ago.

She stared resolutely at the monitor as she heard him exit the apartment via the balcony, forbidding herself to watch him. Lately, she'd been giving in to the urge to ogle him when she thought he wouldn't see, and that had to stop.

She heard him answer the phone on the balcony, but then his voice faded away as he went into his apartment. He always had that cell phone with him, and he always sought privacy when he answered it. Another example of his exquisite manners, she supposed, and she appreciated it. Sara thought cell phones were a social abomination which should be illegal everywhere except New York, where editors and agents should be required by law to carry them at all times.

Since the monitor screen looked normal and she knew Ryan had connected the phone line to the computer, she decided to go ahead and try to get online.

"Eureka!" she cried when she accessed her e-mail.

"It works?" Ryan appeared at the balcony door, putting his cell phone back into his pocket.

"Yes," she said, then frowned. "What's wrong?"

He looked distracted. "I've got to leave town, and the vet's office just told me they can't take the animals. Too short notice. They're full for the weekend. And the pet sitting service I usually use isn't answering."

"When are you leaving?"

He glanced at his watch. "I've got to be out of here in about forty minutes."

"What?"

"That call that just came," he said. "Sudden assignment. I'm sorry, Sara, I've got to find a place that can take the animals if the pet sitter doesn't get back to me in the next half hour. But you're pretty much all set up now, and if the modem is working—"

"Ryan, come on. What are you saying? I'll take care of them."

"No, I don't want to put you out. They can be a lot of trouble."

"So can I," she pointed out.

He smiled. That soft, seductive smile. God, she liked looking at him.

Down, girl.

"You're no trouble," he assured her.

She could melt in the warmth of his voice.

"You've been so nice to me ever since I moved in," she said. "If you've been this nice to everyone else who lived here, they were idiots to move out."

"I steered clear of the woman who lived here before you did." He shrugged. "We never hit it off."

That gave her a little glow. So it wasn't just that he had nothing better to do with his time than pal around with whoever lived next door.

"So the least I can do," Sara said, "is help you out now that you're in a jam. I'll look after them."

"It's a lot," he warned her. "The dog, the bird, the fish, and the cat."

"Yeah, I know." She had learned by now that Ryan had a veritable menagerie in his apartment. He also had tidy habits and a Colombian cleaning lady who worshipped him, which was how the place stayed cleaner than Sara's apartment. "I'll manage. How long will you be gone?"

"Just for the weekend."

"Okay. Don't worry about a thing."

He gave in. "I'll write everything down," he promised.

"And I'll show you where everything is."

She stood up, grabbed a pen and a pad of paper, and headed for his apartment. "You don't have much time. You talk while you pack, *I'll* write everything down."

"Oh, yeah, that's makes sense." He smiled again. "And to think people say you're not good at organization."

"*You* said that after you saw my kitchen," she reminded him.

"Macy! Come *on*. Come on, boy!" Sara lost all patience. *"MACY! COME!"*

The dog had lost heart halfway up the stairs and now lay on the landing in an exhausted heap.

"Thyroid problem?" Sara muttered. "You're borderline catatonic!"

She tugged on the leash. Macy groaned.

"I can't carry you. We've been over this before. You're too heavy."

He was always sprightly going down the stairs. By the time they had walked once around the block, he was usually flagging. And he invariably balked right about now.

Thank God Ryan had told her she only had to walk the dog twice a day. Thank God Ryan was due back late tonight.

Maybe she should just leave Macy *here* until Ryan got home.

At that moment, she heard the door opening downstairs. Macy gave a faint woof without lifting his head. Sara doubted it was Lance, since Ryan had told her Lance never came upstairs unless repeatedly begged to do so. So unless it was a very energetic thief . . .

"Ryan?" she called.

"I'm home," he called back.

"You're early."

"Change of plans."

There seemed to be a lot of last-minute change of plans in the modeling business. Sara shrugged and sat down on the stairs, relief flooding her. "Thank God, you're back."

She heard him race up the stairs, and a moment later he appeared on the landing. He saw her dejected posture and the prone dog and—unforgivably—he laughed.

"So happy to amuse you," she said.

"You can't say I didn't warn you."

"Yes! Yes, I can say that! Because you did not tell me he would do *this* twice a day."

Ryan was trying not to laugh as he sat down next to her. "I'm sorry. I didn't think before I left. I was in such a hurry."

"No wonder your neighbors keep moving out, one after another."

"No, no, you're the only neighbor I've ever inflicted my pets upon," he assured her.

"Oooh. I'm *special*."

"You are." He put his arm around her. "Was it that bad?"

"Your bird is psychotic."

"We already knew that."

"Your cat is missing. She disappeared the moment you left, and I haven't see her since."

"She's really shy. She doesn't trust anyone but me. It's hard on her when I go away."

"She was a homeless stray. Mrs. Thatcher was abandoned. Macy was wandering the streets with no collar when you found him. And you *claim* he was skinny at the time."

"I think he has a thyroid problem."

"So talk to the vet already, would you?"

"Soon," he promised.

"And the fish were in some algae-infested bowl in a carry-out joint and had to be rescued."

"I'm a soft touch," he admitted.

Was that why he was so nice to her, too? Because he was a soft touch?

"I'm glad you're back," Sara said, still a bit grumpy.

"I'm glad to be back." He squeezed her shoulder.

"How was your trip?"

He shrugged. "Okay. How was your weekend?"

"I hauled your dog up and down the stairs. I battled with your bird. I searched for your cat. I fed your fish." His thigh was pressed against hers. Hard and warm.

"I'm sorry," he said. When he kissed her cheek, she wanted more.

"You can't ever make it right," she told him.

He grinned. "Come on. I'll take Macy upstairs, and then I'll take you out to dinner."

"Hmph."

"And," he added, "I'll tell you how much I liked the end of *The Seven Deadly Blessings*. I finished it on my trip."

"Yeah?"

"I was wrong about the killer."

"Well, of course you were. It's my *job* to make sure you're wrong about the killer," she informed him.

"And you do it so well." He rose and held out his hand to her. "Come on. We'll eat. I'll pay. We'll talk. I'll tell you how talented you are. What could be better, Sara?"

She had a sudden flash of wisdom and knew she should say no. She was going to get hurt. It was foolish to hope he might want the same thing she wanted.

Yeah, she should definitely say no. Put the skids on. Be sensible. Protect herself.

"Okay," she said. "Dinner. It's the least you can do."

CHAPTER FOUR

"Alice Van Offelen has asked to see you again, Kevin." Catherine's cool smile was pleased. "At her home next week."

He knew it was significant. The client had satisfied her curiosity. Now, instead of closing this book for good, she was making their dates part of her life. Alice was becoming a regular.

His regular, at least for the time being. She had specifically asked for him yet again; and she had changed her own schedule to accommodate his availability last week. She might continue to book him exclusively for quite some time, enjoying the illusion of a relationship with him; many clients preferred that arrangement. Or she might choose to indulge her curiosity and try other companions. It was, of course, up to her—not him.

He asked, "Same as last time?"

"Yes. Two hours."

Sex only, no dinner, no public events, relatively little conversation required. Easy enough.

"Okay." Kevin was sitting across Catherine's desk from her in her elegant and discreetly luxurious office. He'd come to the agency today with the results of his monthly blood test. A copy of it was provided, upon request, to every client he serviced. Now Catherine was briefing him about some upcoming jobs.

"And," she added, "don't stay late—even if Alice tips you nicely, Kevin." When he didn't react, she continued,

"Because you'll be leaving for the island right afterwards."

He paused. "That afternoon?"

"Yes."

"For how long?"

"Two nights. Until Friday."

He looked up.

She saw his expression. "Yes?" she asked coolly.

He shouldn't say anything. But he did, despite knowing it was a mistake. "I've gone out of town three times in four weeks. Three days last week, an overnighter the week before. And before that, I did that weekend job at the last minute when that new guy, Trevor, got sick and couldn't go."

"And you'll be going away again. Next week."

"Can't someone else go?"

"I've interviewed the client and determined that you're the one who's right for the job. She's seen your photos and agrees." She arched her brows. "Is there a problem?"

He didn't want to go away again so soon. "No problem."

"Good," she said.

He didn't let himself think about it. Feel it. Want what he wanted. Hell, he didn't even know what he wanted.

All the same, he heard himself asking, "I'm definitely coming back on Friday?"

"Yes. Be sure to check in. I may book you for the following day."

"No," he said.

"What?" Her tone was exquisitely calm and courteous. It almost always was. But he knew how much she hated the word *no*.

"I have plans."

She looked at him. He looked back without saying anything. Almost anyone who worked for her would feel compelled to start babbling explanations in the face of that cool, impersonal gaze. But not him. Not anymore. He had learned.

"What kind of plans?" she asked at last.

"I only need Saturday," he said, deliberately not answering her.

Her lips curved, and he realized she hadn't expected him to answer. Not anymore. She was just testing him to see if the door was still locked. It was her way.

"All right," she said. "No work on that Saturday."

"So what's the job on the island?"

She picked up one of the file folders on her desk and handed it to him. He knew he'd be expected to study it here. Client files never left Catherine's office.

"Movie producer," he murmured, perusing the file.

"She's bringing her new lover to the island," Catherine explained. "They want you to watch them together, and the client wants to watch you with her lover."

He glanced at her sharply, ready to throw down with her if he had to.

"The lover's another woman," she clarified. Businesslike, calm. She hadn't even been toying with him. It was just a lapse in communication.

He went back to studying the file. "Any singularities?" he asked, using Catherine's tidy word for dysfunctions, vices, and fetishes.

"Some drug use."

"Right," he acknowledged without looking up.

Catherine insisted that none of her employees use drugs. Ever. But some employees were a little weak-willed, whereas she knew that Kevin wouldn't touch the stuff. He'd never done drugs, not even when he was living on the streets. She also knew he could handle whatever emotional confrontations arose on this job—working a couple was often fraught with their relationship problems—because he never crossed the line, got involved, lost his head, or said the wrong thing to a client.

Catherine's agency leased a fully-staffed luxury villa on a small island in the Golfo de California, off of Baja. Kevin's job would include meeting these two clients at the private airport there and ensuring that their entire visit went smoothly. He usually went there with a solo woman or else as part of a large group that included other agency employees. This particular job might be a little stressful; but at least these clients had only booked two days.

When he finished reading the file, having memorized everything relevant, he gave it back to Catherine. "Anything else?"

"Yes." She picked up another file folder. "I've got your schedule for the rest of this week."

"All right." He took the folder from her.

"Gayle Thompson," Catherine said.

He nodded. "I remember her from last year." An Australian businesswoman in her late thirties, slightly uncomfortable about having a hired escort, but even more uncomfortable about eating alone in a strange city in another country. And wealthy enough to pay for a costly dinner companion.

"She liked you, she's asked for you again."

"How many evenings?"

"Three, starting tomorrow night. Pick her up at the hotel at seven o'clock every evening. Dinner, possible sightseeing, nothing else."

"Same as last year." No sex, no physical contact, no overtures or hints. Gayle Thompson wanted a dinner date without the unwanted pressure a real date might put on her for something more.

She would also want, as he recalled, to talk his ear off each evening about her business—before moving on to pumping him about his life. He tried to remember what lies he had told her last year, but couldn't recall now. Oh, well, maybe she'd enjoy all-new lies this year. One thing he did remember: she was eye-crossingly boring. However, at least she was sober and amiable.

And he could be home before ten o'clock each night.

He tried not to think about it. Feel it. Tried not to want what he wanted. He didn't even know what the hell he wanted.

Oh, Jesus, I'm playing with fire. I know I'm playing with fire.

He should stop. But he couldn't. Didn't want to. *Couldn't.*

He knew it was wrong. Knew that with all his heart. He had passed the point of pretending to himself that no harm would come of it. *God,* it was wrong.

Yet he still couldn't stop it.

"There's one dinner that's pre-arranged," Catherine said, "a banquet on the third night. I've booked you into restaurants on the first two nights."

"Huh?"

She looked at him. "Am I boring you?"

"Oh," he said. "Dinner. Gayle. Right."

She folded her hands. "What's going on, Kevin?"

Instead of answering, he asked, "Is there anything else, Catherine?"

She held his gaze for a long moment. He didn't squirm, back down, or try to rush her.

"Yes," she said. "One more thing. You're taking over a

weekly appointment of Derrick's. Effective as of tomorrow morning."

"A regular of Derrick's?" That surprised him. Derrick was an exceptionally good-looking man who loved money, expensive things, and sex. Derrick liked being an escort and was not prone to canceling his appointments—unlike that new guy, Trevor, for whom Kevin had already filled in twice in two months.

"Yes," Catherine replied, "a regular of Derrick's."

He accepted the client file from Catherine but didn't open it. "What happened to Derrick?"

"He got drunk on the job the other night. Embarrassed a client."

"Ah." On the other hand, Derrick wasn't exactly bright. "He's being punished."

"He knew the rules. He broke them."

The rules were very specific: only one drink on the job, and only if you could handle it. If Catherine found out you'd had a second drink, you didn't get paid for the job. As for getting drunk . . . Oh, yes. This would cost Derrick some income. And knowing Derrick, he'd be angry about it.

"What does Derrick's regular get?" he asked, opening the file.

"A massage and whatever else she wants," Catherine replied.

"What if she wants Derrick?" Regulars didn't like sudden switches like this.

"I've already dealt with it. And you're not to discuss him with her."

"Of course."

"It's a two-hour appointment," Catherine continued, "and she always pays the full fee, even if you're done sooner."

An easy gig, then. Derrick would indeed be angry about losing it. Especially if the client tipped, too.

He studied the file while Catherine rose and came around the desk. He felt her gaze on him, but he ignored it until he was done reading. Then he put the file folder back on the desk and looked up at her.

She was in her mid-forties now, and still a very beautiful woman. Dark-haired, sloe-eyed, with a feminine build, graceful gestures, and exquisite taste. Everything about her presence spoke of money, culture, and discretion. In truth, he suspected her origins were no grander than his own, but he had once, long ago, believed she might be royalty in exile—and even now, he didn't wonder at the memory.

She was leaning against the desk, her arms folded across her breasts, her legs crossed. She wore a pale suit of wild silk, and he had no doubt that her stockings were silk, too. Her long-lashed gaze softened as she studied him, letting a little fondness creep into her cool expression.

It made him wary.

"We . . ." She smiled at her own hesitation. "We haven't really talked in a long time."

"*Really* talked?" he repeated.

"Yes."

He considered this. "No, we haven't. Not since you so generously helped me stay out of prison."

"Things don't have to be this way between us," she said gently, overlooking his sarcasm.

He rose from his chair. "I believe that's been my point all along."

"You're angry."

"Your perception is as sharp as ever."

"I feel . . . things might have been different if I hadn't let so much distance come between us."

"We've *never* had enough distance between us."

She put her hand on his jacket and used it to pull him closer. "But things could be different now," she offered in a seductive whisper.

Their gazes locked and held. A new tension filled the room.

He was surprised. There hadn't been anything like this between them in years. He couldn't even remember the last time she had touched him. And his infatuation with her had ended several lifetimes ago, as had his sexual obsession.

"What are you doing?" he asked.

"I've missed you." Her voice caressed him.

"When have you had time to miss me?"

"I've always missed you."

"What next? You'll tell me you'd like it to be the way it once was?"

She smiled, pulling him still closer. He let her. "No," she said. "We can't go back. No one can. And you wouldn't want to."

That much was true.

"But we can go forward," she continued, her voice so soft he wouldn't have heard her if they weren't standing toe to toe with their breath brushing each other's faces.

Her breasts rose and fell in a slow, steady rhythm beneath the pale silk of her bodice. He smelled good perfume and expensive soap. Catherine nudged his knee with hers and let him see a thousand promises in her wide, dark eyes.

He had forgotten how good she was at this.

She murmured, "We can give each other things we couldn't before."

He looked at her mouth, so lush and ripe. "I gave you everything I had."

"Everything you had *then*."

"It's still all I've got, Catherine."

"No," she assured him, "you're growing into all your potential now. As a man." She leaned forward to brush a damp butterfly kiss on his lips. "As a lover." Another kiss, deeper this time. "As a partner." Her tongue touching his was so full of erotic promise, so rich with forbidden nuance. Once upon a time, he'd have felt like an eager stallion. "And now," she murmured, her voice dark with heat, "you're finally ready for all *I've* got."

Good shot. Full marks for effort.

He snorted, pushed her away, and stepped back. Her expression blazed with momentary fury before she masked it.

"Nice try," he said. "What are you after?"

Her eyes narrowed. "There's something you're not telling me."

It caught him off guard. She was good. Oh, yes. Looking back now, he knew he'd never had a chance. Not from the very start.

Still, he didn't play her games. Not anymore. "There's a lot I don't tell you."

"But this is something special."

He felt violated. He didn't even wonder how she guessed. Didn't let himself wonder *what* she guessed. "Are we done now?"

"If I find out you're free-lancing again—"

"I'm not. You keep me too busy, and I'm not as young as I used to be." Who was?

"If you're lying to me . . ."

Their eyes met. Hers were intense, but he wasn't sure what he saw there. He prayed she couldn't see anything in his.

"I'm keeping my promises to you," he replied.

She continued to hold his gaze for a long moment, evidently trying to decide if she believed him.

Finally she said, "Good."

He turned to go, not caring whether she was done with him now or not. Even so, he paused in the doorway when she said his name.

"What?" he snapped over his shoulder.

"I'd hate to think," she said in a gentler, warmer voice, "that you've forgotten you're lucky to even be alive."

That got him, as she knew it would. He didn't look at her, but his banished memories came flooding back, and he knew she was telling the truth. "I haven't forgotten," he said.

"Good," she repeated.

"Maybe he's gay," Miriam said.

"Gay?" Sara bleated.

Miriam looked at her. "Would it bother you so much?"

Sara sat back in her chair and stared at her Mu Shu Chicken, suddenly losing her appetite. They were eating in Chinatown. Miriam, who lived and worked in Palo Alto, was in the city for a seminar and had an hour free for lunch, so she'd offered to treat Sara.

And they were talking about Ryan. Again.

"Ryan. Gay." Sara tried out the idea. Then rejected it. Forcibly. "No. I can't believe it."

"Why not?"

"No way."

"Let's review," Miriam suggested. "A gorgeous, charming, employed man of twenty-six. He has never mentioned a girlfriend, past or present. He's never brought a woman home, not even for a cup of coffee, never mind for, shall we say, a romantic interlude."

"Discreetly phrased," Sara said.

"He dresses wonderfully. He's—hello!—a *model.* He nurtures stray animals and is good with plants. He has good taste in furniture. He smells nice, is well-groomed, and, as far as you know, has no revolting habits." Miriam sighed. "Sara, Sara, how could this man be anything *but* gay?"

"Oh, now if that isn't just catering to every stereotype imaginable," Sara chided. "That's like saying if a strong, independent woman reaches her mid-thirties without having married or lived with a guy, then she's obviously a lesbian."

"Oh. Good point," Miriam muttered.

"I mean, that describes *me.* And I'm completely straight! I don't even like going to an all-women's gym."

"You don't like going to *any* gym."

"Ryan goes to the gym," Sara said, unable to get her mind off the guy. "Religiously. I mean, like, almost every day. If he's home, that is. He travels a lot for his work—photo shoots on location." She sighed wistfully. "I've seen him without his shirt a couple of times . . . Oh, my *God,* he has a great body." She clutched her head in her hands and moaned, "Of *course,* he's gay! He'd have to be! Because that's the way the world works. A man like that is either taken or gay. Always! Without exception!"

"I admire the way you're facing up to reality," Miriam said. "Does it bother you that he's gay?"

"Of course it bothers me!" Seeing how taken aback Miriam looked, she lowered her voice. "I am not keeping my perspective about this man. I swore I would. I've tried . . . Well, okay, maybe not hard enough."

"Maybe if you asked him about this, and got it all out in the open?"

"I don't know. I don't think so. He's like that damn cat of his."

"His cat?"

"She was a starving stray. She's shy and wary. You have to be patient and let her come to you. Ryan's the same way."

Miriam frowned. "He's been coming to you since the day you moved in, Sara. I was there. I saw the—"

"*Don't* say click."

"And when I visited you last week and he popped in to say goodbye to you on his way out of town, if I hadn't known better, I'd have thought you two were a couple. You have private shared jokes, you finish each other's sentences, you seek eye contact with each other about every three seconds . . . And you can't say goodbye to each other in under a half-hour. So I don't see why you can't ask him about his love life."

"Because he doesn't like to talk about himself. I mean, yes, he talks to me all the time, and there's nothing he ever actually *refuses* to discuss. But there's a lot he doesn't want to talk about. He's good at changing the subject or evading the question. And I . . . I feel like it would be a violation of our friendship to push. I feel like I've got to wait for him to come to me."

"If he is gay, why do you think he wouldn't tell you?" Miriam probed.

Sara shrugged. "Maybe he's not ready to come out. He said he was raised in Oklahoma. Maybe he's from such a traditional background that being gay is unthinkable, so he hasn't even admitted it to himself yet."

"I don't think so," Miriam said. "His whole unconscious manner is too comfortable—and too sexual—for that."

"You're right." Sara sighed. Whatever Ryan's sexual proclivities were, he wasn't in denial about them, even if he was maddeningly discreet. "Maybe he just assumes I know."

"Maybe, but if he's never said anything to you to indicate that he is—"

"Maybe he wouldn't. Or maybe he did and I missed it. Ryan is very delicate about any kind of sexual comment or innuendo."

"He does have awfully good manners," Miriam conceded.

"He might think it's in bad taste to talk to me about his sex life."

"Or maybe he's afraid if he just came out and said he was gay, you wouldn't accept him the way you do now." When Sara didn't reply, she asked, "Would you?"

"I've lived in the Bay area all my life," Sara reminded her. "It's not like this would be something new."

"But you've never been this close to somebody gay, have you?"

"I've had gay friends."

"No lesbian friends, I notice."

"Well, you know." Sara rolled her eyes. "Lesbians."

"What does that mean?"

"It doesn't matter."

"It does!"

Sara eyed her. "Why does it matter?"

Miriam poked grumpily at her food and shrugged. "Because maybe this is what Ryan senses in you."

"That I don't like lesbians?"

"Ah-hah! You see?"

"Why would he care?"

"It's all one and the same prejudice, Sara."

She paused and thought about that. "Maybe."

"Why *don't* you like lesbians?"

She shrugged. "Two women together . . ." She shuddered. "I'm just uncomfortable with the image. And there's this whole socio-feminist political *thing* about lesbianism that doesn't seem to have anything to do with sexual passion. It's as if a woman chooses to be lovers with another woman because, in some bizarre leftist way, she thinks it's the socially responsible thing to do."

"*Jeez,* Sara! You are so full of polluted misconceptions!"

"So you think I'm scaring Ryan?"

Miriam blinked. "What?"

"Ryan," Sara repeated, "*Ryan.* The object of my obsession. You're saying you think I have some innate anti-gay pheromone that he can smell?"

"Oh, don't flatter yourself that it's a pheromone. It's a prejudice."

"But I like gay men."

Miriam sighed. "Lots of women like gay men. It doesn't mean that you're truly comfortable, deep under your skin, with homosexuality."

"Well, I don't need to get that comfortable with it."

"You might, if you're close to someone gay." Miriam added with a certain relish, "If, for example, you're falling for a gay man."

"Oh, God." Sara threw down her napkin and quit all pretense of eating. "I feel sick."

"Sara . . ."

"I don't *want* to be in love with a gay man. What could be more frustrating?"

"In love?" Miriam studied her. "*Are* you?" When Sara didn't reply, she prodded, "Are you in love with him?"

"I don't know." She shrugged irritably. "We don't . . . He's never . . . And it's too soon to know."

"Not necessarily. Mom and Pop were engaged by the time they'd known each other as long as you've known Ryan."

"But I don't want to be in love with someone whose nature means he can never feel that way about me," Sara said unhappily.

"Oh, well . . . I wouldn't worry about it," Miriam said after long moment, digging into her Ma Po Tofu. "He's not gay."

"What?" Sara frowned at her sister. "But only a few minutes ago, you said—"

"No, whatever else is going on, Ryan's straight. That much is obvious."

"Then why have you been saying—"

"Oh, I was only playing devil's advocate. What I actually think is that Ryan's a miracle of nature: a straight man with the best attributes of a gay one."

"If that's what you think, then why are we wasting all this energy talking about gays and lesbians?"

"Wasting . . ." Miriam sighed and shook her head. "I was just curious, that's all."

"About *what?*"

"Never mind. Look, I've got an idea."

"I don't think I want to hear any more of your ideas today."

"Invite Ryan to bring a date to your housewarming party."

"What?"

"The party's a week from Saturday, right? Plenty of time for him to ask someone."

Ryan. Date. *No.* Sara felt queasy at the very thought. "I don't want—"

"It would casually open the door to discussing his sex life. And your lack of one."

"I don't want to open the door," Sara decided, retreating from territory which suddenly felt dangerous.

"Okay? Let's just stop. I wouldn't be happy to learn he sleeps with men. Or sleeps with women who aren't me. Or took a vow of celibacy. Or was wounded in the war." And she couldn't stand the thought of him bringing a date to her party. Couldn't stand the thought of seeing him with someone else.

"Then you know your only other choice," Miriam said. "Tell him how you feel, and see what happens."

Sara rubbed her forehead. "He's never made a move. He's never shown—"

"Maybe he doesn't know you want him to."

"Lately I've sort of tried to . . . you know." She made a vague gesture. "To let him know the door is open, so to speak, if he wants to walk through it—"

"If you'll recall, that's what I told you—"

"Yeah, yeah. The point is, I have to be careful how I behave, since I don't want to do something that would make me pathetic and him embarrassed."

"Oh, such as *what?*" Miriam said impatiently. "Would it be so bad if—"

"Yes! It would."

"So what are you going to do? Just keep tying yourself up in knots over this guy?"

Sara rubbed her temples, feeling a headache coming on. "I think," she said at last, "I'll just return to my regularly scheduled theory, which is that he's just not sexually interested in a woman ten years older—"

"Nine."

"Nine years older who was never, even at her peak, in his class, physically speaking."

"That's insecurity talking."

"And it speaks loudly and carries a big stick."

"He cares about you," Miriam insisted. "Anyone who's

seen him with you for two minutes can tell that he cares about you."

Sara shrugged irritably. "He cares about his dog, too."

"Yeah, yeah, I've met the dog. But when Ryan looks at you . . ." Miriam shook her head. "Well, it's no wonder you're obsessed. It's incredibly seductive when one person looks at another that way. It's not fair for him to do that to you if he's not interested."

"Yeah?" Feeling vindicated in her obsession, Sara prodded, "How does he look at me?"

"Like there's no one else in the world, and that's just fine with him."

CHAPTER FIVE

He sat in the holding cell and prayed the goddamn lawyer would get here. He was going to lose it if he couldn't get out of this place. Get out *soon*. Right now, thanks. This very minute would be good, folks.

Fucking hell.

The urine-rich, chemical smell of places like this made him want to cry with despair. The other inmates brought a wealth of horrifying memories rushing back to him. The sense of helplessness was overwhelming. Bars imprisoning him. Walls closing in on him. He'd been arrested twice before, and it made him sick with fear every time.

Now some burly tattooed guy was staring at him with speculative interest.

Kevin had only survived on the streets because he'd learned to be tough. You had to show them it would take nothing to make you throw down, while no power in this world could make you *back* down. You had to show them every single time.

"What are *you* looking at, asshole?" Kevin snarled.

The burly guy grinned. "You're pretty fucking pretty."

"Go fuck yourself."

"Ooh! You got a pair, huh?"

Kevin kept his stare hard and mean.

The guy shrugged dismissively. "Relax, pretty boy."

Kevin was overreacting. He knew it. And, hell, there was good reason for others to stare at him here: The lock-up wasn't exactly swimming with clean-cut guys in Armani casuals.

No, indeed. I seem to be the only one, go figure.

He felt ready to gnaw off his own paw by the time they called his name. He rose to his feet, weak-kneed with relief, and shot out of the cell like a bullet the moment the guard opened the door for him. The vaguely familiar lawyer who greeted him was dignified and impressive-looking.

Well, sure, I get a first-class lawyer. After all, I'm a first-class whore.

"Kevin," the lawyer said, "I'm Edmund Dryden."

Kevin blinked at him. Everything seemed unreal. "Yeah, I remember you," he said after a moment. It had been two years since they'd last seen each other.

"Are you all right?" Dryden asked. "Have they treated you appropriately?"

"Yeah, very appropriately," he muttered, "except for the part where they arrested me and locked me up."

"Well, it's over now. You're free." Dryden said.

"Free?" he repeated, afraid he misunderstood.

"Yes. I've come to take you home."

His heart thudded. "You're not taking me to be arraigned?"

"No. They've dropped the charges. You're free to go."

"Dropped the charges?" he felt dizzy as the news sank in. *Free to go.*

"Yes. Come on. We can talk in the car."

He wanted to cry with relief. "She sent you?" He didn't use Catherine's name. Not here. She was the one who had taught him, long ago, the value of discretion. She had also taught him to invoke his right to remain silent whenever he was arrested. Catherine guaranteed her clients that her employees would never embarrass them, and Kevin had nothing to gain by breaking that rule. Today, as always, he'd kept his mouth shut.

He was confused, still not sure why he'd been busted this morning. He'd been wondering for hours if Catherine had set him up, as punishment for his behavior in her office yesterday. She of all people knew how much this would scare him. So he hadn't been sure she'd get him out of this mess. Nonetheless, he had used his phone call to ask her for help. Who else could he call, after all?

"Yes, she called me as soon as she heard from you," Dryden assured him jovially. "She's very concerned, eager to make sure you're all right." Dryden was cautious about using names here, too. "My instructions were to get you out as quickly as possible. No, this way, Kevin."

Disoriented, he let the lawyer guide him through the correct door. "My stuff," Kevin said.

"Yes, we're going to get your belongings on our way out. Right here, in fact. Officer? Thank you." He pushed some paperwork towards Kevin. "You just have to sign here."

Kevin nodded, resisting his body's urge to start shaking with reaction now that he was free. He signed his legal name and then, a few moments later, received a plastic bag with his personal possessions in it. He started pulling himself together, willing his hands to remain steady as he checked his wallet, put it in his pocket, then sorted through his other belongings.

Dryden kept a casual hand on his elbow as they navigated through the hallways. Once they were outside in the sunshine, the lawyer signaled to a waiting limousine. When it pulled up, Dryden held open the door. "We'll take you home now."

"No, I . . ." He ran a hand through his hair, trying to pull his thoughts together. God, he'd been scared. Shit scared. Witless and desperate. He wanted to throw up now. He cleared his throat and said with all the dignity he could muster under the circumstances, "I want to get my car."

"Of course." Dryden followed him into the spacious backseat of the limo and said, "It's still at the scene?"

The scene. How tactful.

"I guess. Parked outside."

Dryden nodded, picked up an intercom phone, and told the driver where to go. Very well prepared, the lawyer was, knowing off the top off his head where Kevin had been arrested a few hours ago.

As the vehicle got under way, gliding down the street like a ship on calm seas, Dryden offered Kevin a drink. He accepted. Just one. He always stopped at one, even when he wasn't on the job. But he really, really wanted this one right now.

"There will be no further trouble over this incident," Dryden assured him. "It was a bad bust—"

"A bad bust?" He let his agitation take over now that they were in private. "But when vice grabbed me in the hotel, they said they had a video of me fucking this woman and then accepting fifty bucks from her—which they found when they searched me."

"Oh, rendering the tape inadmissible would have been no problem at all, as I told the police," Dryden said dismissively. "As for the money, you didn't ask for it, did you?"

"No, of course not." If Catherine ever heard of one of her boys asking a client for money, she'd fry his balls for breakfast. "But I—"

"And the client didn't say, 'This is payment for the sex acts,' did she?"

He rubbed his throbbing temples. "No, she didn't."

"Legally," said Dryden, "you merely showed up for a romantic interlude and then borrowed some money before leaving. And the police illegally intruded on your private life."

"Okay, now I really *do* want to throw up."

"Vice was almost certainly hoping for a lot more," Dryden mused, "one way or another."

"Oh, really? What the hell did they think I was going to do in that room?" he demanded.

"I mean," Dryden said patiently, "they expected something much more incriminating today, given the trouble they went to."

He frowned. "But why would they think . . ."

Holy shit.

He already knew. Which meant that Catherine already knew. And knowing Catherine, she was already doing something about it.

He picked up the phone and buzzed the driver. "Change of plans. Turn right at the next light."

"What are you doing?" Dryden asked.

Kevin gave the driver a new destination.

Dryden looked at him. "Why are we going there?"

"Because I'm really pissed off."

He ignored further attempts at conversation as the car cruised towards Cow Hollow, an expensive and crowded district of businesses and residences which sat between Pacific Heights and the Marina. He opened the car door before the limo had even come to a full stop, and he was at the door of Catherine's elegant townhouse before the lawyer had left the car. After Kevin was buzzed in, he let the security door shut and lock behind him.

"Where are they?" he demanded of Jolie, the impeccably groomed employee who was now buzzing in Dryden behind him.

"Who?"

"Catherine! Derrick! *Where?*" he shouted.

Jolie flinched. "Upstairs! They're upstairs, Kevin."

He hadn't been upstairs in years. That was where Catherine lived. That was where she got personal with people.

And that was just fine, because he was feeling pretty fucking *personal* about having been arrested.

He raced up the stairs, taking them three at a time, and kicked in the brass-handled double doors he found on the second floor. The security alarm immediately went off. Its shrill, deafening clamor would have made his teeth rattle if he weren't grinding them with barely-controlled rage.

Dressed in a dark, superbly-cut pants suit, Catherine whirled to face him as he burst into her living room. Her flushed face and agitated posture, both of which he noticed instantly because they were so unusual, were an answer to the question which had plagued him in his holding cell.

He asked it anyhow: "Did you set me up?"

"No."

He stood there panting with agitation, anger, and rampant emotion. The shrill alarm made his head spin and his ears ring.

He and Catherine both turned their gazes on Derrick, whom Kevin had suspected would have been summoned here by now. He was an exceptionally handsome, well-built, bi-racial man, two years older than Kevin and about three inches taller. Derrick's green eyes flashed with open resentment, and his café-au-lait complexion was vivid with hot emotion.

"Did *you* set me up?" Kevin snarled at him. "Did you?"

"That was *my* trick!" Derrick raged at Catherine. "I worked that trick for almost a year. She never asked for anyone else! Never! You had no right to give it to *him!*"

Catherine shouted, “You screwed up! You lose! Those are the rules, Derrick!”

“Oh, yeah?” Derrick pointed to Kevin and demanded, “What did *he* pay for screwing up? He fucked with you until you were foaming at the mouth, and he’s *still* your number one boy!”

“It *was* you!” Kevin was livid. “You set me up!”

“You deserved it, man! That was *my* regular!”

“You sonofabitch!”

“You want a piece of me now? Is that why you’re here?” Derrick shouted at him. “Is that what you want?”

“You bet your candy ass I do!” Kevin shouted back. “I’ve been in the goddamn lock-up because of you! I’ve got another *arrest* on my record because of you!”

“Well, come *on,* then!” the other man taunted him. “You wanna do this? Do you? Huh?”

“Yes!”

“Then DO IT, you prick!”

“No!” Catherine screamed at them both.

Consumed with fury, Kevin ignored her. He dodged when Derrick leaped, then he knocked him down, followed him to the floor, and hit him in the gut, the face, and the gut again. Derrick fought back wildly. A blow to Kevin’s eye made the lights waver and the room spin, but he didn’t back down. He never backed down. *Ever.* He knew that once you backed down, you died; he’d seen it too often to doubt it. He slugged Derrick in the face, then grabbed his head and banged it against the floor. Derrick was bigger, but he’d never lived on the streets, and Kevin had. Derrick had never had to become tough; Kevin had never had any other choice.

Catherine was screaming. So were a few other people who’d evidently been attracted by the commotion. Kevin ignored them. He sat on Derrick's chest, pinning the man's arms to the floor with his knees, then grabbed his lower lip and twisted. *Hard.*

Derrick howled.

"Stop!" Catherine screeched. "Stop it this instant! And, *God,* will someone shut that alarm off?"

Now that he had Derrick's undivided attention, Kevin said, "If you have a beef with *her,* you take it up with *her.*" He twisted harder and the lip started bleeding. Tears of pain gathered in Derrick's eyes. "If you ever involve me in your problems again, I will cut off your dick and feed it to your former regular with hot sauce. Do you understand me?"

Derrick whimpered.

Kevin yanked on his lip, making Derrick scream again.

"Sorry, I didn't quite catch your reply?" Kevin said. "That alarm is so damn loud, you know."

Derrick started babbling while tears streamed out of the corners of his eyes. He was a little hard to understand, since he didn't have use of his lip, but the gist of it seemed to be that he was terribly, dreadfully, sincerely sorry he'd squealed to vice, set Kevin up, and got him busted.

"I'm glad to hear that, Derrick. So this was all just a bad choice and an unfortunate misunderstanding, wasn't it?"

Derrick grunted affirmatively.

The alarm abruptly stopped. Kevin's ears buzzed in the sudden quiet. He heard a number of people breathing hard and muttering.

"Well, misunderstandings and bad choices happen sometimes, Derrick." He didn't slacken his vicious hold on Derrick's lip. Not one bit. "But if you and I ever have another misunderstanding, life as you know it will be over. I hope that's very clear now."

Derrick grunted again, glaring in mingled fury and pain.

Kevin let go of Derrick's lip—then slugged him once more across the face for good measure, because he could never emphasize enough just how much he hated going to jail. He rose from Derrick's prone body. Trying not to tremble in the aftermath of the sort of violence he hadn't exercised in years, he walked over to the window and stared down at the normal, ordinary, weekday street scene below.

"Get up," Catherine said to Derrick.

Kevin watched a woman who was pushing a baby stroller go into a building down the street.

"I said get *up*."

"Goddamn," Derrick muttered. Kevin heard him lurch to his feet. "God*damn!*"

A delivery truck pulled away from the curb. A street musician was playing the violin. Two men in business suits walked past him. One of them paused to toss a dollar into his case.

"Last week, you embarrassed a client," Catherine said coldly. "Today you exposed a client to the police."

"It wasn't fair to give my regular to him." Derrick's injured lower lip made the sentence a trifle hard to understand.

"Shut up!" Catherine snapped.

There was a small crowd gathered outside, staring at this building.

The alarm, Kevin realized. Of course. People in the street would have heard it. People in *Canada* had probably heard it.

In a neighborhood like this, and with the brass sign on the front door indicating that this was a consulting firm, it would never occur to anyone out there that a couple of very expensive prostitutes in here had just lost their heads and thrown down with each other like street boys.

Even that street boy out there surely didn't guess the truth.

That street boy who . . .

Kevin blinked and looked harder, then snorted.

That street boy who's trying to pick pockets.

"Now what happens?" Derrick asked, his speech barely comprehensible. That injured lip would soon swell up like a balloon.

Gosh, that's gonna hurt in the morning, Derrick.

"I'll have to give it some thought," Catherine said.

She was in an awkward position, Kevin knew. Derrick had worked for her for four years. He knew too much to be cut loose in this frame of mind. Even Catherine couldn't entirely protect her clients from an angry ex-employee who knew as much as Derrick did.

Luckily for her, though, Derrick was too stupid to realize the leverage he had. Right now, he was mostly afraid of losing his job. All that money, more than guys like he and Kevin could make any other way, and all they had to do was make the clients happy. Derrick was one of the ones who thought he was swimming in honey and couldn't understand why Kevin had tried so hard to get out.

Staring down at the crowd gathered outside, where that street kid was still prowling, Kevin waited for Catherine to take control again. She wouldn't let a loose cannon like Derrick roll free of her supervision. Instead, she'd punish him enough to bring him in line and to make the others wary of crossing her as he had—but much more subtly than Kevin had just made them wary of crossing *him*. In the end, Derrick would remain on the payroll, albeit at reduced pay and under the yoke of discipline. Much like Kevin. Only Derrick would be grateful.

"I was doing you a favor," Derrick insisted to Catherine, lisping a little now. "He's trouble. He's *always* been trouble. You should have let him take the fall. And you should have let him take it two years ago."

Kevin didn't give any sign that he was listening, but his heart pounded a little harder. Even *he* sometimes thought he was crazy to push her as he had.

"You want to talk about Kevin?" Catherine asked.

"I'm just saying . . . You shouldn't have given him my reg—"

Kevin turned to see what had suddenly made Derrick utter a high-pitched choking gasp.

Oh, that's what.

Catherine had Derrick by the balls. Literally.

Now that's got to hurt.

"You want to know why Kevin's worth trouble to me?" Catherine prodded, her voice even and friendly.

Kevin saw half a dozen people watching her with riveted fascination. Except for the lawyer, who glanced at his watch.

"Do you know what a woman really wants in a man, Derrick?" Catherine asked. "No, of course you don't. Let me give you a hint. It isn't washboard abs, broad shoulders, perfect skin, or a big dick. A woman wants a man who's *intelligent,* Derrick. Who can use his head. Who can figure out what she needs."

She must have squeezed harder, because Derrick flinched a little and made a pretty awful noise.

"Kevin is my number one boy, Derrick, because he's smarter than you. In fact, if there were *five* of you, he'd still be smarter than you. Do you think you understand now?"

Derrick nodded, his face contorted with pain. When she released him, he slumped and sank slowly to the floor again.

Kevin whistled. "And here I was thinking you were going to be more subtle than I was."

She gave him a bland look. "It just seemed like too much trouble."

Kevin shrugged and went back to gazing out the window while Catherine told someone to help Derrick into one of the bedrooms, then suggested the rest of the gathered group return to their business. Not everyone did, though. A couple of them dawdled, hoping there'd be an epilogue to the melodrama.

Meanwhile, that kid in the street, Kevin noted, was smart enough to have chosen a perfect time and place—a dense crowd of people with their attention fixed on this building—but he wasn't much good at the actual mechanics of picking pockets. Kevin, who'd been a pickpocket himself in the bad old days, watched his technique with a critical eye.

He saw the kid miss several easy opportunities, then nearly get caught by someone else, thereby drawing enough attention to himself that he'd have no more chances with this crowd—which now started to disperse.

Ah, youth. Kevin shook his head.

"You should put something on that eye," Catherine suggested, coming close to him now.

He pulled away from the hand she raised to his face. "Later."

"You can't meet Gayle Thompson in . . ." She checked her watch. ". . . less than three hours. Not like this. I'll have Jolie call Trevor."

"Gayle Thompson? Oh, right." The client from Australia. Dinner and conversation, maybe a little sightseeing.

Catherine added, "I'm sure Trevor will be happy to help. You've filled in twice for him, after all."

He shrugged. "Fine. Whatever."

"I'm very sorry this happened, Kevin." Her voice was soft and warm. "The arrest, I mean. I know how you must have felt in—"

"I really don't want sympathy or commiseration from *you.* My sense of humor is strained enough as it is, right now."

"I won't let this mess get any bigger," she assured him.

"Good," he said. "I'm leaving now. It's been fun, but let's not do this again any time soon."

"Is there anything you need?"

He glared at her, shook his head, then headed for the door.

"Kevin," Dryden said, "I've got a meeting in thirty minutes, so I don't have time to take you to your car now. If you'll give me your keys and your address, you can just take a cab straight home, and I'll have someone deliver your car tomorrow morning."

"No," he said. "I'll get it myself."

"But you look like you need—"

"He doesn't want us to know where he lives," Catherine explained dispassionately. "He thinks he can keep his work and his life separate from each other. You see, he's not *always* smart."

Okay, he was in a bad mood, he felt like hitting back.

So he paused in the doorway and said to Catherine, in front of her expensive lawyer and several of her employees, "I just noticed. You've had this place redecorated since the last time I was up here to fuck your brains out." He nodded. "It looks good. Love the drapes."

Only when he was outside in the sunshine did he really start to feel the pain. He'd been too keyed up to notice it before. Now it made up for lost time.

Jesus, Derrick hit hard. He was bigger, heavier, and stronger than Kevin, and he must spend four hours a day working out. (Well, he certainly didn't spend any of the day improving his *mind,* anyhow.) So if he'd had either a little skill or else the element of surprise, Kevin would probably be dog food now.

Gosh, what a rewarding day. He'd given a fifty-minute massage and a forty-minute fuck to a woman who'd treated him like furniture. Next, he'd been busted, frisked, cuffed, verbally humiliated, and locked up. His eye was throbbing like his head might fall off his shoulders, and he had assorted aches and pains. And now he got to compete for a taxi in rush-hour traffic so that he could go collect his car from the scene of his arrest.

If things kept going this well, he'd be the victim of a drive-by shooting before sundown.

Someone suddenly careened into him. Kevin staggered, clutching the smaller person as they both tried not to fall down.

"Oops! Sorry, mister."

"No problem kid," he said absently. "Just calm down, okay? Where's the fire, what's the hurry? All that stuff."

"Yeah, right, *whatever.*" The teenager brushed past him.

Insolent, smart aleck brat.

Kevin shrugged his jacket back into place and kept looking for a taxi. As if he had a hope in hell . . .

Shit.

He reached in his pocket.

Goddamn it!

His wallet was gone.

That was the same kid he'd seen working the crowd earlier.

He looked up at the sky. "I don't *believe* the day I'm having."

CHAPTER SIX

Sara was lost in her work when the storm commenced. The first clap of thunder made her jump out of her skin. The second killed all the electricity in the building and shut down her computer in mid-sentence.

"Damn!" She rose and looked through the French doors. Thunder, lightning, and torrential rain. "Oh, *great.*"

It was a sign of how much Ryan had conditioned her to his passions that, after Sara gnashed her teeth furiously over her lost work, her next thought was for his bird. He'd left Mrs. Thatcher on the balcony this morning.

Sara ran out into the rain, crossed the balcony, opened Ryan's French doors—his had a lock, but he'd stopped using it ever since Sara had become his pets' secondary caregiver—and then grabbed the bird cage with both hands to wheel it inside.

Mrs. Thatcher bit her.

"Ow!" She moved her hands, finished rolling the cage inside, then ran back to her apartment to look for a flashlight.

Had she unpacked a flashlight? She was pretty sure she owned one. She just couldn't remember having seen it lately. What about candles?

Sara suddenly recalled the lengthy list of household supplies she'd been meaning to go purchase this week. And heading the list? Candles, of course. Ryan had warned her that the electricity sometimes went out in this building.

Exasperated, Sara opened her front door, stepped out

into the hall, felt for the banister, and began making her way downstairs. As hazardous as these stairs were under normal conditions, descending them in the dark was positively suicidal. However, since turning around and going *higher* again didn't hold much appeal, she kept going down.

When she reached the bottom step, she let herself out into the pouring rain—naturally, she had not thought to bring an umbrella—and circled the building to climb the front porch and knock on Lance's door. Hard. Several times. His doorbell didn't work (of course), so she tried shouting. Nothing.

Lance was not home, damn him.

Lance was never home! Sara had seen her landlord *once* since moving here back in July.

Cold and wet and discouraged, she circled the building again to commence the precarious climb to her apartment—and nearly screamed when she bumped into Ryan coming home from the other direction.

"Ryan?" she blurted.

"Shit." He flinched as if he felt an impulse to run and hide.

"What *happened* to you?" she cried, stopping him as he tried to turn away from her.

His jaw was slightly puffy, there was blood at the corner of his mouth, and the whole area around his left eye looked *awful*—swelling and darkening.

"Nothing happened to me." Perhaps realizing that sounded less than convincing, he amended, "I was mugged."

"My God! And you're soaking wet!"

"So are you," he pointed out, dabbing at his lip.

"I'm just damp. You're drenched." Not that the difference really mattered. "Did you come home on foot?"

He shook his head, then winced. She suspected he had a killer headache, given that eye. The mugger had landed a hell of a blow.

"I caught a bus," he said. "I had some pocket change left. The sky opened up just as I got out. Naturally."

"Where's your car?"

"It's a long story."

"Why didn't you call me?"

"Can we go inside?"

"Oh! Yes. I'm sorry."

Bludgeoned and soaking, he still didn't forget his manners; he opened the door and gestured for her to precede him.

"The electricity's out," she warned him.

"Of course it is," he said wearily. "It's been that kind of a day."

When she started leading the way upstairs in the dark, he reached for her, pulled her close to him to stop her from ascending, and said, "Wait. Where's your flashlight?"

"I came down without one."

"Candle?"

"No."

"You came down these stairs in the dark? Jesus, Sara, are you trying to die young?"

"Just hug the wall," she advised.

"Wait. I've got . . ." She heard him searching his pockets. A moment later, a lighter flared in the flickering darkness.

"Better than nothing," she admitted.

"I'll go first." He took her hand. "What's wrong?" he asked when she hissed in momentary surprise.

"Your damn bird bit me." It still stung.

"Oh." He gentled his grip but didn't let go. "I'm sorry."

His fingers caressed her palm, then he lightly rubbed her knuckles with his thumb. "Come on." His voice was soft as he pulled her near and led the way. She followed, staying close to him . . . and felt painfully aware of being close to him.

Ryan . . .

After a dozen steps, he drew in a sharp breath and the lighter went out. She supposed he'd burned himself.

"Ryan?"

"It's okay."

She touched the hand holding the lighter, meaning to offer to carry it—but he flinched away. She'd felt the roughness there. "What's wrong with your hand?"

"Nothing."

She realized what must have happened. "You fought back?"

"Let's get upstairs."

The lighter illuminated the staircase again, and they made it the rest of the way up. She followed him into his apartment without thinking. He let her follow, without protest or acknowledgement, as if he expected it.

Macy was whining and panting, distressed by the storm. Ryan spoke to him soothingly while Sara went to put the night cover over Mrs. Thatcher's cage, since the bird was making a racket. When Ryan lit two candles on the stereo cabinet, she took one.

"I'll be right back," she told him.

By the time she returned from her apartment a few minutes later, he had lit half a dozen candles, and his living room was bathed in a warm golden glow while steadily falling rain drummed on the roof. No more thunder and lightning; the worst of the storm had passed.

Ryan had removed his wet clothes and put on a pair of

gray sweat pants. A towel hung round his neck, and he rubbed at his damp hair with one end of it. He wore no shirt.

Sara briefly closed her eyes and called on her composure.

He was putting down the telephone with his other hand. "No answer," he said. "Lance isn't home."

"You have his *number?*"

"Oh, that's what you were doing downstairs in the rain." He looked at her armful of first aid supplies. "All right, before I let you near me with that stuff, I'm entitled to know: Do you have the slightest idea what you're doing?"

"Please. I'm a mystery writer. I've watched autopsies."

His brows arched. "Not the reassuring answer I was looking for."

"I'm not splinting a bone, Ryan, just patching up some cuts and bruises. Sit down."

He sat in the leather easy chair. She sat on the arm and held a candle up to his face.

"Will I live?" he asked.

"It's too early for a prognosis."

"Ow."

"Sorry." She dabbed around his injured eye with damp cotton, to make sure the area was clean. Then she gave him a cold pack. "Hold this over your eye." As he did so, she asked, "Have you talked to the cops?"

He flinched. "The cops?"

"Yeah." When he just stared at her, looking dumbstruck, she prodded, "You know. About, oh, being *mugged,* for example?"

"Oh!" He looked strangely relieved. "No."

"No?"

"No."

"Ryan." It was so self-evident, she didn't quite know what to say to him. "We have to call the cops."

"No!" He stopped her when she tried to rise from the arm of his chair.

"What do you mean, no?" When he didn't respond, she asked, "Is it because you fought back?"

"Um . . ."

"Did you hurt the other guy?"

He sighed. "Okay. Straight up. I wasn't mugged. I got into a fight."

"You got into a fight?"

"Yeah."

"You don't . . ." To cover her confusion, she started washing the blood off his face. Tending him. Caring for him. "You don't seem like a violent person."

"I'm not. These were special circumstances."

"Do you know the other guy?"

"Yeah." He sounded depressed.

She reached for his hand and studied it in the candlelight. The knuckles were bruised and bloody, some of the skin torn. As she gently cleansed it, she asked, "So what does he look like now?"

Ryan gave a soft puff of amusement, which she gathered meant the other guy looked worse; but he didn't answer her.

"Well, you're not badly hurt, thank God. There'll be bruises for a while, but swelling will be your main problem." She broke out two more cold packs, resting one on his right hand, then holding the other against his jaw. "Thoughtful of you to provide me with a chance to use all this stuff Miriam gave me."

"And to think some people," he said, "are doing boring things like dinner and the movies this evening."

"Each to his own."

She was way too close to him. To that hard expanse of ever-so-lightly furred chest, those bare shoulders, that smoothly muscled stomach. Too close to the beautiful, bruised face in need of healing. Too close to the troubled eyes which avoided hers right now.

"Are you going to tell me why this happened?" she asked.

He was silent for a long time. She saw that he was trying to figure out how to tell her, and he evidently couldn't find a way.

"Whatever it is," she said quietly, "I'd rather you tell me nothing than tell me lies."

"I know."

She barely heard him, his voice was so soft.

He still looked conflicted, undecided about whether or not to answer her question.

She tried to be more specific. "Is it something to do with your car? Is that why you didn't drive home?"

He seemed briefly amused. "No, I just couldn't get the car because it's parked so far from where I lost my wallet."

"You lost your wallet?" she exclaimed.

He sighed. "It's been a bitch of a day."

"I don't suppose you've reported your lost wallet to the cops?"

"No."

"Ryan—"

"I can probably find who took it."

"Someone *took* your wallet? You're saying someone stole it?"

"Um. Yeah. Someone stole it."

"Okay, I give up." She took away the cold pack from his jaw. He moved his mouth experimentally, testing for pain while she spoke. "You're in a brawl, and you try to tell me you were mugged. Your wallet's been lifted, and you won't call the cops."

He looked away.

She stared at him. "Are you in some kind of trouble?"

"Most of my life." He sounded uncharacteristically bitter. "But the fight's over and doesn't matter now. I'll get the car tomorrow. And I think I can get my wallet back."

"Your credit cards won't still be in it," she warned.

"I never carry more than one. I've cancelled it. Made the call on my cell phone while I was on the bus." He scowled. "But I want my stuff back. And my money. Well, whatever he doesn't spend before I find him."

"But why don't you call the cops about—" She stopped herself. "Wait. You know who took it?"

"In a way."

"Still, why won't you—"

"The cops are not the right people to call in a situation like this. Believe me, Sara."

"No, Ryan, the cops are exactly the people you call when someone steals your wallet."

"I'd rather handle it myself," he muttered.

Needing something to do, because she had no idea what to say, she took her dirty cotton pads into the kitchen and threw them away. He was still sacked out in the chair when she returned to the room. Still half-naked and painfully gorgeous in the golden glow of the candles. And still avoiding her eyes.

"What kind of trouble are you in?" she asked at last.

"Nothing I'm not used to." His dismissive tone closed the subject.

But Sara wouldn't let him close it. Not this time. "You don't want me to know about it, do you?"

He met her eyes now. What she saw in his face made her

want to shake him, because his whole expression was telling her he didn't mean to shut her out.

It would be a lot easier if he'd tell her to mind her own business and ask her to leave him alone now. That was the answer she was braced for—not this look of longing she got instead. Miriam was right; it wasn't fair of Ryan to look at her this way.

Unable to walk away from that expression, Sara sat down on the arm of his chair again. She sifted her thoughts carefully before she spoke. Ryan was like his damn cat. She had to let him come to her.

"You've had trouble with the cops yourself, haven't you?"

He nodded, his gaze turning wary.

She took his injured hand, checked to see how it looked, then held it in on her thigh as she reapplied the cold pack. "Is that why you don't want to speak to them about whatever happened to you today?"

"It's not their business." Seeing her speculative gaze, he amended, "Yes, that's why. Well, partly why. I mean . . ." He looked down at his injured hand as she held it in both of hers. "Cops never did me any good, Sara. Not when I needed help, not when I needed to be left alone. I don't want them in my business, and I don't put them onto anyone else's business."

"So, instead, you're going to try to get your wallet back yourself."

"Yes."

"And if you can't?"

"I'm pretty sure I can," he said.

She could tell it didn't worry him that much, either way. But she certainly didn't understand this, and she wasn't sure how to proceed.

They were quiet for a long moment, the air between them thick with unspoken words. Heavy with unacknowledged longings. All that smooth, bare skin bathed in candlelight . . . All the warmth in the hand she tended . . . All the dark sorrow in that beautiful, bruised face . . . All the weariness in Ryan's posture as he closed his eyes, lowered his head, and rested his cheek on her leg.

She couldn't breathe for a moment. Couldn't think. Could only feel. A hot river of tenderness gushed through her, making her hand tremble as she stroked his hair. So soft and thick, clinging damply to her fingers.

He sighed shakily, keeping his eyes closed. A moment later, his other arm came around her leg in a slow embrace, his hand moving along her denim-clad thigh until it found a place to rest, gripping her lightly. Then he nudged the cold pack away from his injured hand with a flick of his wrist and laced his fingers with hers.

They stayed like that for long, silent minutes, hands linked, Ryan clinging to her, his eyes closed, while she stroked his hair. Rain danced on the roof, and the wind blew it against the darkening windows. Sara's mind spiraled around their conversation, trying to understand his words, wondering what had happened to him today and why he felt he couldn't tell her what his trouble was. Meanwhile, her heart filled and overflowed, moved that he turned to her for comfort and rejoicing that she could give it to him. And slowly, her body filled with tension as instinct urged her to comfort him much more intimately.

Maybe he felt her tension. Or maybe he knew he couldn't stay like this forever. He'd have to move sooner or later. Say something sooner or later. Break the truce of their warm silence. He took a breath, opened his eyes, and turned his face towards her stroking hand. She went still, watching him. He didn't look at her. His mouth was against her wrist now. Not kissing her, not moving. Just there, his breath brushing the sensitive skin. Warm. Soft. Ryan's breath on her skin . . .

"Sara, I'm not who you think I am." His whisper sounded weary and bitter.

She was surprised, but after she absorbed this obscure statement, she told the truth: "I don't care."

That almost seemed to amuse him. "You have no idea what you're saying."

"I do."

"No. You couldn't possibly."

She made an impatient sound. "Look, Ryan, I'm a lot older than you—"

"Oh, no, you're not." He sat upright with sudden restlessness, abandoning his embrace and letting go of her hand. Withdrawing from her.

She said, "I'm nine years older—"

"Eight."

"Nine."

"I have a birthday coming up."

"You do?" Her bright tone won her a sardonic look. She sighed. "I have a birthday coming up, too, Ryan. Anyhow, my point is, I'm not some dense bimbo—"

"Jesus, you think I don't know that?"

"—or naive schoolgirl. I'm an adult. An adult who's *older* than you are—"

"Oh, Sara, for God's sa—"

"So whatever it is that you think you can't tell me, you're wrong."

"What if I killed someone?"

Okay, that gave her pause.

He saw.

"*Have* you . . ." She choked on the words. "Are you telling me—"

"No." He shook his head. "But there are things that make a difference, Sara. A big difference."

She tried a different approach. "Don't you trust me?"

His eyes flew up to her face, his blue gaze stricken. "Of course, I do." When she didn't reply, he insisted, "I *do*."

She pressed her advantage. "No. You think I'm just some needy, self-involved airhead who intrudes on your life whenev—"

"I don't!" He looked appalled. "Sara, I l—" He stopped himself. "I—" Frustration swept across his battered face. "God, that's not how I think of you at all! How could you even think that? How could you not know how much I . . . *Sara*."

Her heart was pounding. She leaned closer and put her hands on his cheeks, careful to be gentle with his bruised face. "Then tell me what's going on. Tell me this thing about yourself that you're so sure makes such a difference, Ryan." She could feel the barely perceptible shake of his head. "It won't matter to me," she insisted. "It won't change things between us."

"It will."

It hurt her to see how sad he looked, but she knew they had to go forward now—because they certainly couldn't go back. "Tell me," she whispered.

"I *can't*," he gritted out.

"Why not?"

"Because . . ." He covered one of her hands with his. His other hand slid up her leg, and then it was at her waist, seeping warmth through the damp fabric of her blouse.

"Ryan," she murmured, melting under his touch, going hotly mindless under the desperate intensity of his gaze.

Her blood caught fire as his eyes grew misty. "Because," he said slowly, starting to pull her into his arms, "if I tell you, you'll never look at me this way again."

She made a sound of desire and relief, of mingled joy and pent-up frustration as their lips met. He was so gentle for a moment, his full mouth soft and tender against hers . . . but the hand at her waist clutched her too tightly, the fingers digging into her skin. Sara reveled in this sign of explosive emotion trapped inside him, and she kissed him harder, reckless in her need for his heat and hunger. He grunted as he fell back against the chair, dragging her with him, and then they were a wild, clumsy tangle of arms and legs, taking rough, biting kisses from each other as they struggled to get closer, closer, as close as possible with all these clothes still on.

His mouth was all over her neck, her face, her hair. She heard him murmuring her name, his voice hot and breathless. She couldn't touch him enough, couldn't feel enough of him beneath her eager hands. His hard shoulders, his luxuriant hair, the smooth length of his back, his firm chest with the faint shimmer of hair, his nipples puckering boldly under her palms.

She drank his kisses, welcoming the agile invasion of his tongue, wanting more, much more . . . She couldn't breathe, and she didn't care. His arm, more powerful than she'd ever realized, banded around her, holding her captive as he plundered her mouth with kisses so hard they hurt, and all she could think was, *Yes, yes, more, give me more . . .* His other hand was in her hair, holding her head as they devoured each other, ravenous and awkward and unashamed of their mutual greed. She pulled against his grip on her hair, ignoring the pain as he tried to make her kiss him again, because now her mouth was hungry for the curve of his shoulder, the hollow of his neck . . . And then he was massaging her hair instead of pulling it. Holding her head against him as she sought the subtle curve of his breast, the hard pebble of his nipple which she bit because she couldn't help herself . . .

His head fell back on a startled moan, and his hips rose convulsively into hers as she straddled him. She felt the hard thrust of his erection moving blindly against her, muffled by his sweatpants, and she wanted to touch it, wanted it so much she whimpered as she fumbled with his waistband.

He kissed her again, groaning into her mouth when her hand found him, smooth and hard and twitching with frantic impatience. Then Ryan slid his hand up under her damp blouse and impatiently ripped the delicate fabric of her bra where it shielded a breast from his eager touch.

"Yes . . ."

Clamoring need pooled heavily in Sara's loins, and she knew he felt it, too. His body trembled and his hips moved with a will of their own. He pressed his forehead against hers, panting incoherent words of delight as she caressed the restless wild thing between his legs. She wanted it, she had to have it, she told him so, whispering her desires to him before she kissed him again. Their tongues moved as their bodies wanted to, melding, mating.

Until Ryan's pleasure-rich groan turned to a choked gasp, and he tore his mouth from hers.

Sara felt his grip on her wrist. Hard. Hurting her. Rejecting her. Flinging her hand away from his body. Then there was a wild heave, like the world turning upside down, and she fell, sliding down to the floor, where she landed with a jarring thud while he leapt out of the chair as if it were on fire.

Winded and stunned, she lay there for a moment, her clothes disheveled and her tumbled hair covering her face. Then she heard an emphatic pounding sound which was even louder than her own frantic heartbeat. She shoved her hair out of her eyes with a shaking hand and looked in his direction. With his naked back turned to her, his ribcage pumping in and out like a bellows, he leaned against the wall with one hand and hit it repeatedly with the palm of the other.

"Goddamn it!" he raged. "*God* . . . Goddamn fucking hell!"

"Ryan?"

He didn't hear her over the racket he was making. Even the dog, apparently comatose until now, awoke and rose, whining in agitation.

Real alarm seeped into the hot whirlwind of Sara's passion. Concern for Ryan made her pull herself together. She used the sturdy bulwark of the chair to haul herself to her feet and then, trembling with reaction, went to him. She touched his shoulder to get his attention—and he nearly jumped through the ceiling.

He backed away, shaking his head, his eyes wild. "*Don't* touch me," he panted.

"Ryan—"

"I mean it!"

She stared at him, wounded beyond coherent thought. Humiliated beyond anything she'd ever known. Hurt beyond anything she'd ever imagined.

She put her hands over her mouth, trying to stifle the sob that rose in her throat, the sudden pain which madly sought to escape because her body wasn't big enough to hold it.

The sound came out anyhow, and it was just awful.

Tears were hot on her cheek. She staggered away from him and tripped over Macy, who pursued her in whining confusion.

"Oh, God," Ryan said, this time in a completely different tone of voice.

Sara pushed past the dog and sought the balcony doors, fleeing blindly towards the dark safety of the rain and the wind.

Ryan got in her way. "Sara."

She was choking on her humiliation. "Get away from me!"

Macy barked at them both.

Ryan's hands stopped her, his body blocking her. "Sara, my God, I'm so sorry, *Sara,* no, wait—"

"Let go of me! Let go!" She shoved at his shoulders. Macy panted nervously and tried to get between them. "Let me go!"

"Shhh, sweetheart, no, don't . . ."

"Get away!"

She tore herself out of Ryan's arms and hunched away from him, covering her face so he couldn't see her shame and mortification. Her raging hurt.

His hand touched her shoulder. "Sara—"

"Don't touch me!"

He backed away. Macy cowered near him.

Sara strangled on her tears, trying to stop them. Trying to stifle her sobs until she could get away from Ryan and curl up in private to howl with unchained misery.

"Are you listening to me?" His voice was firm, soothing.

"No! Leave me alone!"

"We have to talk."

She looked at him. "What could we possibly say that won't make it worse?"

His eyes were tormented, his face flushed. "I'm sorry."

Her breath gusted in and out as she stared open-mouthed at him. Some feeble flicker of intelligence kicked in, some shred of pride, and she used it to bring her hysterics under control.

"Okay," she said at last, still breathing hard, still hot with rampant humiliation. "Saying you're sorry may not make it worse, but it sure as hell doesn't make it better. Can I go now?"

"Not like this." His voice was hoarse. "Sara. Come on. *Please.*"

They'd been friends. She had to try to remember they'd been friends. She needed to end this nightmare remembering that they'd cared about each other.

"All right," she said. The unconcealed relief that washed across his face made her want to slug him, because she couldn't be his goddamn friend anymore. Not after this.

"I'm really sorry," he began.

"So am I."

"You don't have anything—"

"Oh, stop it, Ryan," she snapped.

"This is my fault," he said, soothing the dog absently with his hands and encouraging him to sit down.

"No. Yes." Sara sighed. "I don't know."

"I'm the one—"

"Look, I've had . . . feelings for you . . ." She turned away, too embarrassed to look at him. "That I didn't act on . . . because I knew you weren't interested . . . and I didn't—"

"Not interested?" he repeated loudly. "Not *interested?*" When Macy whined, he added, "Shh, shh, it's okay now. Shh."

Sara looked at the floor. "I know you could have anybody. And I'm not . . . I'm just . . ." She folded her arms across her chest, trying to hold herself together. "I know this isn't what you want from me."

"Not what I . . ." His voice grew edgy as he said, "When did you decide this isn't what I want from you? When I had my hands all over you? When my tongue was halfway down your throat? When I nearly came all over myself just because you reached inside my pants?"

"Well, guys are like that, aren't they?"

"*I'm* not." He sounded irritated now.

She glanced at him. His exasperated expression was almost comical. She didn't feel inclined to be amused, though.

Then he sighed and eased himself down onto the arm of the chair. He winced and touched the darkening bruise around his eye, then touched his lip. Her frantic kisses must have hurt his battered face, she realized dimly. She edged further away from him.

"I'm such an idiot," he said. "I think I know so much about women, and then the one I . . ." He gave a disgusted puff of laughter and shook his head. "I had no idea. I thought you kept your distance because I'm not smart enough for you . . ."

That got her full attention.

He went on, "Not educated enough." He shrugged. "Not Jewish."

"I don't care about that." She made a sound. "Not being Jewish, I mean. You're smart enough. For me. For anyone. And I don't care how educated you are."

"I know you think I'm too young for you—"

"Or I'm too old for you."

"Sara." He sounded exasperated again. "You really have no idea what you're talking about."

She waited for him to say more. Because she was still so hurt, and she didn't want to be.

"And I let you *keep* your distance," he continued, "because it was better that way. I knew from the start this was wrong. But I couldn't stop. Couldn't stay away. Even knowing . . . Oh, well. But it never occurred to me," he said, shaking his head at his own lack of perception, "that you didn't know what I wanted. Sure, I thought you wondered why I didn't try to touch you—"

"I did," she murmured.

"But I never thought you didn't know how much I *wanted* to touch you."

Their gazes met. Sara almost stopped breathing.

"I was thinking about myself so much," Ryan said, "that I didn't even see that you worried you weren't . . ." He closed his eyes and made an angry sound. "Attractive enough. Sexy enough." When he re-opened his eyes, they were full of regret. "Lots of women feel that way. It's common. It so damn deadly common. But it never occurred to me that you felt that way." He shrugged. "I've spent so much energy just trying not to touch you, I never realized. But I should have known better. It's a rare woman who isn't insecure, and I shouldn't have forgotten that when I was with you. I'm sorry." He nodded. "So let me be clear. I *really* wanted you just now. And for weeks before this."

She couldn't have looked away even if lightning struck her. "You're not just saying that because—"

"Sara, tonight was the first time I've acted like a randy, clumsy kid . . ." He shook his head. "Well, since I *was* one. And that was such a long time ago."

Sara didn't comment. She was starting to realize that, young as he was, his youth may nonetheless have ended long ago.

"I don't lose control," he said, "not sexually. Not like that—all over you and crazy and not even knowing what I was doing . . . I don't *ever* do that."

Her hurt was fading. Her humiliation seeping away. But her confusion remained. She edged closer to him now, wanting to understand. Wanting more. "But you did tonight."

He let his gaze drift over her face. "I did tonight."

"Why?" she whispered.

Their gazes locked and held. Her heart pounded, drumming in her ears, driving her towards him. He came closer, driven by the same thing. Their lips met in a slow, warm kiss. Tender. Erotic. Honest.

Sara shuddered and slid her arms around his waist. His hand found her neck and held her to him, deepening the kiss with his tongue until her head was reeling.

"That's why," he breathed against her mouth.

"Then why did you stop?" Their lips brushed again. "Tell me what's wrong. What you're hiding from me." Sensing his lingering hesitation, she said firmly, "Ryan, you can't *not* tell me. Not after this."

He rested his forehead against hers. After a moment, he sighed. "I know. I have to tell you. I should have told you before it came to this."

When he didn't say anything else, she urged, "Go on."

"Just give me a minute," he murmured, still holding her close.

She'd give him all the time in the world. She didn't want to leave anymore. Not now. Not tonight. Not ever. She waited.

When he finally pulled away from her and turned his back, she knew from his stiff posture that he was genuinely afraid of what the truth would bring to their relationship.

Feeling shaky, Sara took a seat.

"Whatever it is," she said, "it doesn't—"

"Don't say that, Sara. It matters."

His face, when he turned towards her, was serious and so unhappy. What secret tormented him so? AIDS? A drug habit? A wife?

"Ryan is my real name," he said, "but . . ."

She waited.

"But a lot of people know me by my working name." He paused. "Kevin."

"Kevin?"

"Yeah." He took a deep breath. "And I'm not a model."

CHAPTER SEVEN

He stood before her, his stomach churning so badly he was afraid for a moment he'd be sick right in front of her.

Oh, that would be smooth.

The flickering lights of the candles cast subtle shadows across Sara's face, bringing out those strong cheekbones which he'd often thought made her look a little exotic, as did the colorful clothes she wore, the artsy earrings she liked, and the rich darkness of her eyes.

Those curious, thoughtful, expressive eyes . . . which were gazing at him right now with such intensity and tender concern.

His heart contracted, just looking at her. He'd learned all too well by now that she could do this to him—make his insides quiver just by meeting his eyes.

"You're not a model," she said, trying to get the ball rolling. "Okay."

Say it. Get it over with. Tell her.

She said, "Is that why you told me that your face doesn't photograph well, that you only model below-the-neck stuff?"

He nodded. "I almost always include that in the story."

"Because . . . you need a handy reason," she said, "that no one ever comes across a photo of you modeling?"

He nodded again. Of course she would figure it out right away. He knew by now how smart she was.

She continued, "You could just say they *had* come across photos of you, but they didn't realize it because—"

"My body looks like anyone's body."

"Not quite," she said with a touch of dryness.

Rain continued drumming gently on the roof. Ryan's gaze shifted to Sara's mouth. Her lips were a little swollen now, and he realized how hard he must have been kissing her before. She looked so . . .

God, he wanted to kiss her again.

And once she knew the truth, she'd never let him do it again.

He shouldn't have done it in the first place. That's what she'd think, too, once he told her.

"Ryan?" she prodded.

"Um . . ."

Jesus, just tell her, would you?

Her thick, dark hair was a tangled mess now. From the rain. From his hands. From that sudden tumble to the floor he'd inadvertently given her when he realized what was happening and shot out of that chair and her embrace only seconds before he'd have taken off all her clothes and made love to her.

His body was still crying out for her.

"So if you're not a model," she said, "then what do you do for a living?"

Say it. Say it. Say—

"I'm an escort."

Finally! Thank you.

"An escort," she repeated.

His breath came rushing out. "Yes. I'm an escort."

There. It's out. Done.

He should have told her weeks ago. When he realized how he was starting to feel about her. When he suspected how she was starting to feel about him. He should never have let things come this far between them without telling her.

He'd wanted to slit his own throat when he saw how he'd hurt her tonight. Her tears and humiliation. The wounded look in her eyes before he'd explained himself. He didn't deserve to live, hurting her like that.

And now he wanted someone to beat him up for the way he'd been unwittingly hurting her before this. She'd thought he didn't want her? That she didn't attract him? Christ, he'd been pacing his cage for weeks because of her!

He'd been going so crazy lately, unable to give her up and unable to try to claim her, it had turned him into an idiot. How could he, of all people, not have realized that she needed to know he found her desirable?

Maybe I was a little preoccupied with lying to her.

Or maybe he'd just been trying to avoid this moment as long as he could. He knew that once the lid was lifted on his desire, he couldn't continue hiding the truth from her. That was the line he'd drawn for himself somewhere along the way: He wouldn't touch her without her knowing exactly what he was. And since he didn't want to tell her . . .

"An escort." Sara shrugged, a slight frown on her face. "Like . . . a PR escort?"

He blinked. "A what?"

"A public relations, um, escort. You know." When he just stared at her blankly, his blood pounding through his throbbing head, she elaborated, "When a writer gets sent on tour to promote a book, for example . . . Are you saying that you're the person who would take her around to her interviews and autographings while she's here in San Francisco?"

Shit. She didn't understand what he meant.

"No," he said hollowly, "that's not what I do."

"Then what do you do?"

She sat with her hands folded, looking patient, intent, and encouraging.

"I, um . . ."

"Go on," she urged.

"I spend time with people."

"You spend time with people?"

"With women."

"You spend time with women." She still didn't understand.

He looked away. "Maybe at a party, or a restaurant, or on a trip . . ." *Come on, spill it.* "Maybe in bed."

"In bed? Are y . . ." Now her voice was uneasy. "I mean, when you say . . . Is this—"

"I get paid for it." He took a breath, seized hold of his resolve to give her the honesty she deserved, and met her eyes again. "Usually by the hour or by the day. I get paid to be good company. In bed, out of bed, whatever the client wants." Seeing her jaw drop slightly, he added, "That's my job. To be whatever the client wants."

She looked stunned, confused, a little upset. "You mean you . . . Women pay you to have sex with them?"

"Actually," he mumbled, "they pay Catherine."

"Who's Catherine?"

"She's, um . . . I guess you could say she's my boss." He shrugged. "Whenever my cell phone rings, it's her."

"Calling you to . . ."

"To schedule me for an appointment."

"An appointment." Her voice was faint. "To . . . have sex? With other women?"

"Sometimes. Sometimes, I just spend time with them."

"Spend time," she repeated.

"Uh-huh."

"Being good company."

"Yes," he said, lowering his gaze.

"And you get paid for this."

"I do." He wished this conversation could be finished now.

"Paid by Catherine."

"Yes."

"And they pay her," Sara said. "They pay . . . to be with you."

"With me. Or with someone like me."

"Are you telling me . . ." Sara sounded like she was sure she must be mistaken when she said, "Ryan, that sounds like prostitution."

"Oh, no," he said ironically. "It's only prostitution if you get paid for sex. If you just get paid for your time . . ." He met her eyes, wincing at the dawning shock he now saw there. "Well, then it's all strictly legal."

"You just . . . get paid for your time?"

"That's how it works."

"So . . . I mean, if you don't want to have sex . . ."

"It doesn't matter what I want. It's whatever the client wants."

"But . . . if you don't want sex, and you do it because someone's paying you . . . Then, well, they *are* paying you to have sex, and that *is* prostitution."

"Yeah." She understood it now, all right. He could hear it in her voice, see it in her expression. "It is."

"You're telling me . . . You're telling me you're a prostitute." When he didn't respond, she prodded, "Ryan?"

"Yes. I'm a prostitute." And he was discovering that telling her made him feel even worse than he had anticipated. For no particular reason, he added, "A very expensive one."

"Expensive?" she repeated weakly.

"Oh, yeah." He sank onto the couch and rubbed his brow. "I'm a pricey item. Top drawer. A first-class fuck."

"Ryan!"

"It's true, Sara."

"Don't talk about yourself like—"

"I usually say 'escort,' because that's what Catherine taught me to say." He had to be candid with her, no matter what it cost him. "But it's just a nice way of saying that I'm a high-priced whore."

"But what—"

"I work for an exclusive agency. You couldn't even afford the so-called membership fee that most people have to pay just to see my photos, never mind meet me." If anything ever happened between the two of them after this, he didn't want it to be because he'd glossed over the facts. "It costs a client a lot of money to have sex with me, and even more to spend the night with me. It's not so cheap for someone to have me on her arm at dinner or a party, either."

"Stop!" Sara was shaking her head. "What are you saying? What are you *talking* about?"

"You wanted to know what happened to me today?" He recalled her questions and how he'd tried to avoid answering them. "I spent most of the day in the lock-up."

"The lock-up? What's the l—"

"A holding cell. Awaiting arraignment."

"You were in *jail* today? You've been *arrested?*"

"For the third time." His chest hurt as he held her gaze. "I've got a rap sheet, Sara."

"What?" She looked sick from this succession of shocks. "What were you arrested for?"

"Which time?"

"I . . . I . . ."

"Today I got up, walked Macy, bummed a cup of coffee from you, went to the gym . . ." He made himself tell her. It was wrong to keep hiding this from her. "And then I did a two-hour trick."

"A tr . . ."

"We're not supposed to call it that—"

"We?"

"The escorts who work for Catherine. But I have bad habits. You can take the boy off the streets, but you can never completely wipe the streets off the boy."

She just stared at him, stunned and distressed.

Now that he had started, he couldn't seem to stop himself. He felt compelled to strip everything, to be more naked with her than he'd been with anyone in years. "Anyhow, it was a two-hour trick, like I said. Easy work. A massage and sex. We finished early, I got dressed—"

"You had sex with another woman today?"

"Yes." He held her gaze. "And two days before that, with someone else. And last week—"

"You've been . . ." She squeezed her eyes shut briefly, then said, "You've been sleeping with other women. All this time."

"Yes."

"All those times you said you were working . . ."

"I was working. Just not the kind of work I told you I did."

"You've been lying to me?"

The betrayal in her voice cut into his heart, but he wouldn't try to escape his punishment. "Yes. I've been lying to you. Ever since we met."

"So . . . so last week, when I took care of your place and your pets while you were out of town, you weren't on a photo shoot." A little anger was starting to join the betrayal. "You were . . . doing *this?*"

"Yes," he admitted, not shying away from her bewildered and accusing gaze.

"And what *is* 'this?' " she demanded. "What exactly were you doing?"

"I don't think details are a good idea, Sara." There was a difference between honesty and stupidity, after all.

"No, I want to know," she said, some more anger creeping in now. "How many women were you sleeping with on your trip last week while I was here, walking your dog, and feeding your fish, and taking your cat to your vet, and—"

"One," he said. "One woman. I was hired to put her in a generous mood."

"What does *that* mean?"

"Someone is trying to attract new capital for their failing luxury resort. So they invited a few potential backers there . . . and made sure they had a good time."

Sara gaped at him. "The people who hired you thought that a hot affair with a dream lover at their resort would influence this woman's financial judgment in their favor?"

"I never talked to the clients," he said, avoiding her gaze, "but that was my impression from Catherine's instructions to me."

"Did it work?"

He shrugged. "Maybe. Catherine says they were pleased with me."

"So you went along with this travesty?" she demanded.

He'd expected her outrage, but that didn't make it easier to bear. "I did what I was paid to do."

"Which entailed what?" The contempt in Sara's voice hurt him, sparking defensive anger and an unworthy impulse to hurt her back. "Flirting with the woman, complimenting her, listening to her . . . being *good company?*"

"And fucking her," he added, feeling a dark satisfaction when Sara flinched. She wanted details? *Fine,* she could have them. "Don't forget fucking her until she was limp."

"I suppose that was in the job description?"

"She invited me to her room, and my job was to be whatever she wanted me to be."

"But didn't she want you to be *real?* Didn't she want your home phone number or something?"

"She's married, Sara."

"Married? Oh."

"I wasn't supposed to be a new love interest. Just a temporary perk."

"A perk?" she repeated, clearly appalled.

"Yeah," he said, wishing they could stop now. "A perk."

Sara paused a moment before saying, "But even so, how do you know *she* didn't think you were more than that? Maybe she thought you *were* a new love inter—"

"Since she tipped me before she left, I think she kept her perspective."

"She *tipped* you?" Sara sounded scandalized.

"Pretty generously."

"So she *knew* you were a hired . . . hired escort?"

He shrugged again. "I don't think so. She was just showing her appreciation to the golf instructor who'd shown her such a good time."

"She thought you were a golf instructor at the resort?"

"It seemed a safe story, since she didn't know anything at all about golf."

"Do other women tip you, too?"

"I don't think we should talk about—"

"*Do* they?"

He sighed. "Sometimes. Now can we just stop this?"

"What about this morning, after your . . . your 'easy'

two-hour trick?" Sara was glaring at him now. "Did *she* tip you?"

"Actually, if she *hadn't* handed me money," he said wearily, "I suppose they wouldn't have even tried to bust me."

"What happened?" When he hesitated, she prodded, "Well?"

"Vice grabbed me in the hallway, as I leaving." If this was the way Sara wanted it, *fine.* She could have so many details, she'd despise him. It was what he deserved, after all. "They said they had a tape of me doing the client, right there on the massage table. I got her off three times—"

Sara made a stifled sound and put her hand over her mouth.

"—and she never even looked at me. I think she was pretending I was someone else." He shrugged indifferently. "Anyhow, the cops caught the whole show on camera. Including the part where I accepted payment from her. They said I was screwed. But it was a bad bust, so they let me go this afternoon."

She was staring at him in horrified silence.

"Sara . . ." He made an awkward gesture. "I told you that details weren't a good idea."

She looked as if she'd never really seen him before.

"I told you I wasn't who you thought I was." When he saw tears gather in her beautiful dark eyes, he said desperately, "I *told* you the truth would make a difference between us, Sara."

Tears started to roll down her cheeks, glinting in the golden candlelight.

"Aw, Jesus, *don't.*" He rested his elbows on his knees, put his aching head in his hands, and stared at the floor, unable to look at her anymore. "*Please* don't do that."

She tried to speak, but she choked on a sob.

"Please, stop," he whispered.

"Wh . . . Why?"

"Because I can't stand it," he said desperately. "I can't *stand* making you cry."

"No, I mean . . . I mean, why do you do it? Why do you sell yourself like . . . like some . . ."

"Like a whore?"

"Like some *thing!*"

He kept his gaze on the floor. "This is the way things worked out."

"What are you talking about?" She made an angry noise and shifted in her chair. "Worked out? How do things just *work out* this way, Ryan?" When he didn't answer, she added sharply, "Or, now that I've had my hand inside your pants, should I call you Kevin?"

His head snapped up at that. *"No."*

"Why not? Isn't that the name you use when you're *working?*"

He was stung by her comparing what happened between them to what he did on the job. "Almost all escorts work under a phony name, Sara. For privacy, for protection." He didn't know the legal names of any of Catherine's employees, and they didn't know his, either. When he was in that world, he *was* Kevin. "But I don't use my working name here. I don't use it with *you*."

Sara glared through her tears. "So do I owe you anything for your *time* this evening? What's the fee?"

"You couldn't afford me, Sara," he snapped.

"Oh, is that why you threw me on the floor a little while ago?" she snapped back. "Because if we'd gone through with it, you knew I couldn't have *paid* you?"

"Jesus, Sara!"

She rose to her feet and demanded shrilly, "Was that a *business* decision?"

He rose, too. "You're the one who insisted on knowing the truth!" he shouted. "You're the one who had to have *details!*"

Their agitation again disturbed the dog, who now rose to his feet, too, and started whining. They both ignored him.

Sara shouted back, "How could you keep lying right to my face every single day since we met?"

"Goddamn it, Sara, do you think I ever wanted you to know *any* of this?" He was angry and hurt and bitterly ashamed. "Do you think I haven't been going crazy trying to figure out how to tell you, or else how to give you up so I'd never *have* to tell you? So you'd never look at me the way you're looking at me right now? *Right now,* Sara!"

She gasped, then closed her eyes and pressed her hands to her face. "Oh, my God. I can't believe this is happening. Oh, God."

He watched her shoulders shake. Longing to touch her, and knowing he shouldn't try, he said in quiet despair, "I'm sorry."

She tried to speak, swallowed, then lifted her tear-streaked face to meet his eyes. "I'm sorry, too."

Their gazes locked, acknowledging the hurt they'd inflicted on each other, sharing their regret over it. Connecting exactly the way they'd become so accustomed to connecting with each other.

"I should never have let this happen," he whispered to her. "Getting this close to you."

"It wasn't just your choice to make," she said on a watery sigh. "I knew I'd probably get hurt. And I knew there were things you weren't telling me—possibly important things. But I couldn't . . . Didn't want to . . ." She gazed at him for another moment. "I couldn't stop."

"I couldn't, either," he admitted. "But I should have, and I knew it."

"But whatever I imagined you were hiding . . ." She shook her head. "Well, I never imagined anything like *this*."

"I know."

"I don't think I knew anything like this really happened."

"I wish you still didn't know," he said. "But Sara . . . We nearly became lovers tonight. And I couldn't do that without telling you what I am."

"What you are . . ." She shook her head. "But, Ryan . . . or Kev—"

"Don't."

She looked at him.

"Please, don't," he said. "Don't ever call me Kevin."

"I . . . All right."

"Promise me. Not even if you get really mad at me again. Just . . . promise me you'll always say 'Ryan,' okay?"

"Okay. I promise."

"Because I . . ." He looked away for a moment, trying to find a way to say it. "I've never *worked* you, Sara. And I promise I never will. I know I haven't been honest, but I swear I've always been sincere with you."

"Then . . ." Her eyes overflowed again as she asked brokenly, "Then is this real?" She made a gesture indicating the two of them. "What's between us. Is it real?"

He wanted to touch her so much. "It's so real it's eating me up." He closed his eyes. "It feels like the only real thing in my life."

She made a little sound, twisting the knife in his heart. After a long moment, she said, "Well, I understand why you didn't tell me the truth when we met. This isn't really the sort of thing you can tell a new neighbor. But—"

"I don't tell anybody. Ever. I mean, not anybody who knows me as Ryan. This is a separate life. In this life—Ryan's life—you're the only person I've ever told."

She glanced at the chair where they'd come so close to making love. "Because you had to tell me."

"Yes." He folded his arms over his chest, because that made it easier to control the impulse to reach for her. "But I guess I'd have had to tell you sooner or later, anyhow, Sara, even if we never wanted . . . what we wanted tonight. Even if there was no risk of me hurting you that way." He tightened his arms against his own body. "Because I've never liked anybody as much as I like you, and I guess you're also the person I respect most—and trust most—out of everyone I've known."

"Ryan . . ." She sounded so surprised, he realized she hadn't known just how much he treasured her, even if they hadn't known each other that long.

"So I didn't like lying to you. I didn't want to keep doing it. It already felt like a violation of our friendship. Of your trust in me. Apart from the way it's made me . . ." He drew a shaky breath. ". . . try to keep my hands off you. Because I knew if I touched you, I'd have to tell you the truth. And then you wouldn't want me to touch you again."

She gave a little start, as if she'd forgotten what his revelations meant in terms of where their relationship had been about to go; where they'd both been longing, for some time, for it to go.

"So I didn't touch you, but I wanted to," he said. Her gaze softened, and he felt a foolish hope unfurl inside his chest. "And I still want to."

"Oh." Her voice was barely audible.

His heart was pounding so hard he wondered if she

could hear it. "Now that you know the truth, and maybe we're both kind of tired of talking . . . I'd really like you to come into the bedroom with me and stay the night." He heard her startled breath and saw her gaze shift uneasily from him, to the bedroom door, and back to him. "But if you don't want to do that," he added, "now, or next week, or *ever* . . . I understand."

"Um . . ." She nervously started trying to smoothe her tangled hair. "I don't . . . Um, I don't know, Ryan. I . . ."

His heart sank.

Come on, what did you expect? he chided himself.

"It's okay, Sara," he said.

She glanced over her shoulder at the balcony door, as if longing for escape now. Then she turned back to him. She looked uneasy and unsure of what to say.

You knew it would be this way, he told himself. *You knew.*

Sara suddenly hugged herself and gave a bitter puff of laughter. "Lately, I'm not sure there's anything, not even success, that I've wanted as much as I've wanted you to invite me to bed."

"And I don't remember the last time I wanted anything as much as I want you in my bed."

He saw the effect his words had on her and felt guilty. He knew exactly the right things to say to get what he wanted now. Just as he knew how to *do* things to coax her into his bed. She was very smart, but he was an expert at this. He'd been taught very well, and he had excelled at his lessons. One way or the other, even against Sara's better judgment, he could seduce her if he wanted to. Especially in her current state of emotional confusion.

But, as truthful as that line about wanting her in his bed had been, saying it to her right now was unfair. And saying or doing anything that would be deliberately calculated to manipulate her . . . No, that wasn't the way he wanted things to be between them.

She said, "Everything's different now, Ryan."

"I know."

He wanted the affection and the warmth. He wanted the heat. He couldn't even remember when he'd last wanted sex as much as he wanted it now, with her.

"I'm just really . . . pole-axed by this," she said.

To sink inside of her, to melt and meld with her, to give her pleasure, to feel her touch everywhere, to know every inch of her skin, to share himself as he never did . . .

He said, "Of course you are."

That might be worth eternity in hell . . . But it wouldn't be worth losing whatever regard she had left for him. Even if not touching her was starting to feel like starving, he was pretty sure that it was nonetheless better than losing her friendship or not being worthy of her trust.

He had never worked her like a client, and he never would. He had promised her that, and he meant it.

She said, "I never thought I'd say this if you asked, Ryan . . . but, um, no. I . . . I don't think I can stay."

You knew it would be this way.

He nodded, suddenly unable to speak.

She said, "I'm sorry."

"D . . ." He pressed his lips together and got control of his voice. "Don't apologize. You're right. You shouldn't . . . I know this wouldn't be right for you, Sara. I knew it from the start."

Her face crumpled a little. "But, Ryan, I d . . . I don't underst . . ." She lowered her head, sniffed, and wiped impatiently at her eyes. "I don't understand why you . . ."

His throat hurt so much it was hard to say, "I'll get you some tissues." For the first time since they'd met, it was a relief to leave a room while she was in it. He fled to the bathroom, which was wedged behind the bedroom, and leaned against the sink there for a minute, trying to pull himself together.

After a few long, dark moments, he lit the candle he kept on the vanity for nights when the power went out. He nearly flinched when he saw his reflection in the bathroom mirror. He'd forgotten about the damage from the fight with Derrick. The fresh bruises combined with the emotional stress to make him look like an improbable specimen for an expensive hired lover.

"You had to know a woman like her wouldn't want you," he said to his reflection. "And you knew the longer you didn't tell her the truth, the more it would hurt her when you finally did. You're a shit."

He picked up the box of tissues from the top of the toilet tank and headed back to the living room.

When he got there, the room was empty. Sara was gone.

The French doors were ajar, and Macy stood with his head sticking outside, letting the drizzle hit his nose. Ryan pushed him aside and stepped out into the light rain. In the faint glow of the city lights, he could see the tread of Sara's shoes on the wet surface of the balcony, going from his apartment to hers. Her French doors were closed. There was no lock, and she knew he knew it; but her silent departure was enough to bar him from pursuit, and she probably knew that, too.

He tried to stifle the sudden flood of despair.

Come on, what did you expect?

He'd known it would be this way.

Re-entering his apartment, he stumbled a little as Macy suddenly turned and pushed past him. The dog went to stand by the front door, then turned his head to look at Ryan expectantly.

"Right," Ryan said wearily. "Time for your walk." As he went into the bedroom to get a shirt and some shoes, he said over his shoulder, "But I am *not* carrying you back upstairs tonight."

CHAPTER EIGHT

Ryan wasn't surprised when he found the young pickpocket in Cow Hollow the next afternoon. While watching the kid work the crowd outside of Catherine's townhouse yesterday, Ryan had noticed that he had more guts than brains. So it wouldn't occur to the boy that it was a mistake to come back here right after having lifted a wallet in this neighborhood; he thought that success here yesterday promised success here today.

Ryan wore sunglasses, a baseball cap, an old sweatshirt, and even older jeans. He felt sure the kid wouldn't spot him, but he maintained his distance, even so, as he kept the boy under observation. After a while, he felt downright embarrassed that this kid had been able to frisk him; the boy was about as deft a pickpocket as Sara was an electrical engineer.

Sara . . .

He had tried not to want what he wanted, but he couldn't help it. Ever since meeting her, he'd fallen under her spell. Tumbling into the colorful warmth of her nature was so natural, so inexorable, he hadn't known how to stop. Hadn't really wanted to stop. Because, when he was with her, for the first time in years, he was happy.

He sort of remembered happiness from his childhood. So long ago. But until meeting Sara, he hadn't realized that he'd given up expecting to feel it again. And he'd forgotten how powerful it was. Even more powerful than sex, which Catherine had always told him was the most powerful force in human experience.

Happiness. Yes, he'd given up thinking of it in relation to himself. Until Sara made it float inside of him like a water lily surfacing above all the muck.

He certainly never saw happiness in his work. Not among the other prostitutes he knew. And not among the women who, each for reasons of her own, paid for an ideal companion. He gave his clients pleasure; that had become easy by now. But not happiness, which he'd learned long ago couldn't be bought and sold.

He thought sometimes he gave it to Sara, but now . . .

Now he had ruined it. He was bound to ruin it, of course; he'd known that from the start, and *still* he hadn't been able to leave her alone. Because she gave him happiness; and he wanted it more desperately than he'd ever realized.

And if he'd been anything else but what he was, maybe they'd be together right now, sharing a meal after hours of satisfying sex. They'd be sitting together on her living room floor, or maybe holding hands at the neighborhood café . . . Sara making him laugh, Sara delighting him with the way she saw things, putting the world into perspective, or pulling it way out of perspective and somehow making sense of it that way. Sara laughing at his jokes, because such a funny woman thought he was funny, too. Sara listening intently to him, because such a smart woman nonetheless seemed to find his thoughts worth hearing.

Maybe they'd be with each other, right now. Happy . . .

If I'd really been just a model. Or . . .

He should stop dwelling on it. He'd already spent all night on it. At times angry and hurt, at other moments disappointed but resigned. And wondering if there was a better way he could have explained things.

Oh, like what?

There was no good way to explain what he was to a woman like Sara.

"*But didn't she want you to be* real?" she had asked him.

How could Sara, to whom sincerity meant everything, understand that the whole point of someone like him was that he wasn't *supposed* to be real?

Years ago, Catherine had taught him that a *real* man belched at the table, farted in bed, scratched his crotch in public, wanted sex when a woman didn't, or didn't want it when a woman did, interrupted a woman and looked bored when she talked, made her feel self-conscious about her breasts or her thighs or her stretch marks (even if she'd gotten them bearing *his* child), ridiculed her opinions, second-guessed her financial decisions, was rude to her friends . . . and was the reason that a woman who could afford it came to someone like Catherine to procure someone like *him*.

Even if Catherine was unduly cynical about men in general, the comments of various clients over the years had revealed to him that she was at least partially accurate about *their* men.

He wasn't supposed to be real; he was supposed to be ideal.

Women who hired someone like Kevin rarely mistook an escort for the real thing. They almost never *wanted* the real thing. And it usually got messy if they did.

What Ryan had with Sara, though—whatever it was . . . *that* was real.

It might also be over.

Feeling morose and tired, he continued shadowing the pickpocket, casually following him around the elegant neighborhood where Catherine ran her business, watching him make bold and clumsy tries for another score. Finally, a woman standing on a street corner and wearing a leather backpack purse felt the kid fumbling with its clasp behind her. She whirled around, shrieked, and clobbered him, drawing the attention of a dozen people.

Ryan shook his head and wondered how in the world he had let someone this sloppy take him yesterday.

Well, I'd had a hard day. I guess I was a little distracted.

The kid started backing away from the woman and several other people who were now crowding around, too. He was shaking his head in denial and holding up his hands in pretended innocence. The woman didn't buy it. She advanced on him angrily, seized his sleeve . . . then reached into her jacket pocket and pulled out a cell phone. The kid started struggling, and the woman clung to him fiercely as she started talking into the phone.

Calling the cops, no doubt. After all, that's what normal people did when someone tried to steal their wallets.

Ryan waited, wondering what would happen. The kid, obviously in a panic now, finally succeeded in twisting roughly out of the woman's hold and escaping her grasp. He dodged past someone trying to stop him, then ran down the street as if he had wings on his feet.

Ryan started after him, pleased. If, as he suspected, the kid would respond to this scare by retreating to his rabbit hole and hiding there until he regained his nerve, that would make Ryan's day considerably shorter. He'd anticipated having to tail the kid for many hours before finding out where he holed up; so this unlucky break for the pickpocket was a lucky one for Ryan.

As Ryan reached the small crowd gathered around the woman who had grabbed the boy, he heard the woman, still on her cell phone, telling 911 what the kid looked like and which way he was going. Ryan shifted his direction just enough to grab the woman's cell phone as he ran past her.

"Hey! *Stop!* Someone stop him!"

Ryan disconnected the call, then tossed the cell phone to another pedestrian, who gaped at him in astonishment. "Sorry!"

The kid hadn't taken anything from the woman, and Ryan saw no reason for her to make the cops interfere in his own business with the boy. Who was, Ryan noticed as he pursued him, pretty damn fast for someone his size. Which was good. Being smart was the best way to survive on the streets, but being fast was a good back-up plan.

After a while, though, the kid started wearing out, his fleet-footed run turning into a trot. Knowing what would come next, Ryan soon paused to slip into a doorway, letting the boy create an even bigger distance between them. Sure enough, now that he was going slower, the kid started looking over his shoulder to see if anyone was after him. He didn't spot Ryan, who continued to hang far back at this slower pace. In time, the boy evidently decided he wasn't being pursued, and he slowed down to a walk.

Since it seemed unlikely he'd be noticed now, Ryan closed the distance between them a little, just enough to be sure he wouldn't lose sight of him when they finally reached the kid's home turf. Which was far away, a long walk from where they had started. The hilly streets ensured that it was a tiring walk, too. Ryan wasn't surprised that they were covering a big distance on foot. Unless someone had taken it away from him, the kid still had Ryan's cash; but if his scores were as few and far between as Ryan suspected, then experience had probably taught him to save the cash for food and other necessities rather than to waste it on public transportation. When you had youthful energy and nothing to do with your time except try to stay alive, a long walk didn't exactly cut into your busy day.

They eventually passed through the sleazy area on the southern stretch of Polk Gulch. They went past a lot of bars, liquor stores, leather shops, and "adult entertainment" outlets. Ryan started seeing the familiar stuff of street life: a couple of obvious drug addicts, a probable dealer, a homeless adult, some teen runaways.

They kept on going, Ryan always about a hundred yards behind the kid—who hadn't looked over his shoulder for quite some time. Whereas it had once taken Ryan a long time to lose the habit of looking over his shoulder every few minutes.

"Hey, honey, you lookin' for a good time?"

Ryan shook his head as he passed a couple of working girls.

"We're runnin' a special," the other one said, stepping into his path. "Two for one."

"Thanks, but that much pleasure would kill me." He stepped around her and continued on his way.

The next one he encountered said, "How about a date?"

"No, thanks."

"Come on, man, why not?"

He didn't acknowledge her again. It would just make her think he was opening negotiations, and she'd waste her time pursuing it.

There were only a few hookers hanging out on the street at this time of day. Come sundown, this neighborhood—which Ryan had once known all too well—would be thick with them. They'd spend hours on their feet, and hours on their knees in dark doorways, in alleys, and in cheap rooms that rented by the hour and stank of urine, disinfectant, and fast, graceless sex acts between strangers. Men passing these women in the streets regularly insulted, threatened, and even spit on them. The customers who paid for hookers usually used them hard and contemptuously. Most of these women were raped often—and most of them were back on the street, working again, twenty minutes after being beaten, sodomized, or violated by a john who balked at paying for it and thought nothing of brutalizing a hooker. At the end of the night, if a girl's pimp wasn't happy with her earnings, *he'd* probably knock her around, too. Many of the women were drug addicts, some had AIDS, and very few of them would live long a time.

On average, women who worked the street were raped and killed far more often than their male counterparts. No one in the life was lower than hookers.

Except for kids.

That never changed. Kids in the life were the lowest of all. They were the weakest and the most naïve. And they were in the most danger from everyone.

The kid whom Ryan was now trailing at a fairly close distance was hugging the buildings, keeping his shoulders hunched and his head low. Trying to disappear, to make himself invisible.

So he's learned that much, at least.

A kid survived on the street by being a ghost, a shadow. It was dangerous to risk crossing anyone, or even annoying them. It was best not to come to anyone's attention. But if they did notice you, then you had to hang tough. You could never back down, no matter what. Nothing would be more dangerous for a kid here than showing weakness or fear.

Even after having been off the streets for ten years, Ryan could still feel the mingled dread and despair start seeping through his blood as he absorbed the sights, sounds, and smells which had comprised his whole world back in the day.

As the kid turned another corner and Ryan followed, he

supposed it was a blessing that circumstances had forced him to come here today. Being on these streets reminded him—with the force of a hard kick in the gut—that his life had turned out so much better than it would have done if Catherine hadn't taken him in and made him what he was now. Though he had spent last night choking on his own bitterness after Sara had rejected him, being here now made him made him realize that he had no business feeling sorry for himself just because he couldn't have what he wanted most. In fact, being here forced him to remember he was lucky just to be alive. If Catherine hadn't saved him that night . . .

Rounding another corner, he paused when he saw a small group of adolescents hanging out there. All street kids—grubby, tough, hungry, lonely, living on nerves and will. Ryan knew the look. He studied them for a moment and realized with some consternation that none of them was the boy he'd been following. Apart from them, there was hardly anyone else on the street. Ryan looked around. *Shit.* Had he been so absorbed in his own thoughts that he'd lost the kid? Or let the kid spot him?

On the verge of being really annoyed with himself, Ryan leaned one hand against a dilapidated building and looked around, wondering how the kid could have disappeared so fast.

Across the street, there was a Dumpster backed up against a high fence surrounding an old warehouse. Ryan went over to it, wondering if the kid could have hidden behind it. As he got closer, he thought it unlikely the kid had hidden *in* it—the thing stank to high heaven! Was someone throwing out a *corpse,* for chrissake? Trying not to breathe, Ryan looked behind the Dumpster, and—

"Ah."

There was a small space between the Dumpster and the

fence, and a fairly big hole in the fence, low down.

Broad scuff marks on the sidewalk around the Dumpster made Ryan suspect that, each week after it was emptied, someone pushed it back towards the fence again to conceal the hole there. Ryan glanced over his shoulder and saw, sure enough, that a couple of the boys on the street were watching him with obvious suspicion. They knew the hole was here, all right. The camouflage of the Dumpster wasn't for hiding the hole from other people on the street; it was for hiding it from strangers—and The Man, of course. No one around here trusted cops any more than Ryan did.

Turning his back on the boys, Ryan removed his sunglasses, squeezed behind the Dumpster, and crouched down to see if he could fit through the hole in the fence. No problem, he decided. Directly on the other side of it, though, there was a huge, dirty puddle. He saw no way to avoid winding up in it unless he just didn't go through the hole at all.

"Of course," he said with resignation.

He reached through, grimaced as his hands squelched in God-only-knew-what, and dragged himself through the hole. Then he stood up, shook his hands, wiped them on his sweatshirt, and looked around. There was a small parking lot full of rusted machinery parts and a warehouse with many broken windows.

"Why didn't I know about this place back when it would have come in handy?" he muttered.

Well, it *had* been ten years, after all. Maybe back in those days, this warehouse had been a going concern instead of a tax write-off inhabited by homeless people. Ryan peered through one of the broken windows and saw evidence of habitation inside. Separate little areas where individuals had set up their personal campsites with blankets, shopping carts, and cardboard boxes.

It was a far cry from his cheerful, cozy apartment in Glen Park, let alone Catherine's comfortable townhouse in Cow Hollow; but it was nonetheless better than most places Ryan had slept when he was living on the streets.

No wonder some care was taken to hide the hole in the fence from outsiders' eyes. The various people who used this flop certainly wouldn't want the cops to discover it and evict them all. Sooner or later, whoever owned this property would find out about its habitants, though, and the end result would be the same. It always was.

Ryan heard a noise around the side of the building. He stepped away from the window and, hugging the wall, peered around the corner.

Coming around the corner the other way, the kid bumped right into him.

The boy let out a startled shout and flinched. Ryan snorted in surprise and took a reflexive step backwards.

"Jesus fucking Christ, mister!"

"Watch your language," Ryan snapped, then realized what a stupid comment that was, under the circumstances.

The kid tried to dodge around him, obviously eager to be on his way. Ryan grabbed his collar. The kid panicked, of course—every kid in the street knew that *nothing* good came of a stranger putting his hands on you—and started struggling.

Ryan grabbed a handful of his hair, parried the fist which swung at him, then used his free hand to squeeze the boy's right biceps so hard the kid gasped and tears of pain appeared in his eyes.

"Remember me?" Ryan said.

"No!"

"Try."

"No! Let me go! I don't know you!"

He shoved the kid up against the wall. "We met yesterday."

"What? *No!* You're thinking of someone else! Let me go!"

"I want my wallet back."

"No! I don't know who—who—" Apparently something clicked, because the kid stopped struggling and stared at him. "Your wallet?"

"Uh-huh."

"It ain't your wallet!"

"Ah, so you do have it."

"It ain't *yours!*" The kid actually sounded a little outraged.

"Yes, it is."

"No! I took it from some rich guy!"

"I'm not rich, I just have great taste in clothes," Ryan said. "And I want my wallet back."

"That wasn't you!"

"That was me." He was amused at the way the kid studied him, as if having the right to demand proof of his identity before returning his wallet. "You've looked at the driver's license, right?"

The kid frowned. "I *guess* it could be you . . ."

"Thank you. Now can I have my wallet back?"

Wondering what would happen, Ryan eased up on the boy's biceps. He immediately tried to escape. However, Ryan was still holding his hair. The kid gave a little cry of pain and went still again.

"My wallet?" Ryan prodded.

"How'd you find me?" the boy demanded.

"Well, you're making quite a name for yourself in the neighborhood where you frisked me."

"They don't know my name!"

"Figure of speech."

The kid looked spooked. "They know who I am?"

"You're getting to be a familiar face around there." After today, it wouldn't be smart for the kid to go back there any time soon, so Ryan hoped his words discouraged the boy.

"Fuck." The kid scowled.

"Now about my wallet . . ."

The boy's glance flickered briefly to the junk-filled parking lot behind Ryan. "I don't got it no more."

"Ah." Ryan made sure he had a good grip on the kid, then pulled him away from the wall and turned so they were both facing the parking lot now. "Of course. You don't keep your stash inside the building. There are always people in there. Someone would see you hiding it. So you hide it somewhere in this mess out here, and you only go to it when no one's around. Much safer."

"I don't keep nothing nowhere! Leave me alone!"

"I'm guessing that you didn't think of it right away, though," Ryan continued. "I'll bet someone cleaned you out at least once before you figured out a good place to hide things."

"I—I *sold* your wallet!"

Ryan didn't think so. This wasn't a smooth pro. This was a scared kid who had no gift for stealing.

"Get me my wallet right now," he said, "and I'll forget this ever happened."

"I told you, I don't *got* it."

"You've got thirty seconds. Then I'm calling the cops," Ryan lied smoothly.

"No!" The kid started struggling again. Ryan squeezed his biceps so hard, the boy's back arched with pain.

"Goddamn it! You bastard!"

"Twenty-five seconds." Ryan let go of the kid's hair and pulled his cell phone out of his back pocket to make his point.

"All right! Jesus, man! All *right,* already!"

Ryan slipped his phone into his pocket and, keeping hold of the boy, said, "Good. Let's go get it."

The kid dragged his feet. "No, wait! You have to wait here."

"Yeah, right, that's going to happen." He tugged on the boy's arm. "Come on."

"No, man. I swear I'll get your damn wallet! But . . . you stay right here."

Ryan sighed. "I don't care about whatever else you've got in your hiding place. I just want what's mine."

"Oh, right, you say that *now.* But as soon as I show you where it is—"

"I don't need your stash, kid. I'm a rich man, remember?"

"Yeah, well, *yesterday,* maybe. Today you look like a wino."

"I do *not* look like—"

"What the hell happened to your face?"

"I had this face yesterday." Ryan glanced at the boy, who was shaking his head. "Well, no, maybe not. I guess it took a little time for the bruise to start coming out." He knew his black eye looked pretty scary by now, though it hurt less than it had yesterday.

"And your clothes are all different, too."

"Somehow, I had a feeling yesterday's clothes might stick out in today's neighborhood. Now can we please get my wallet?"

The kid regarded him with mute suspicion and hostility.

"My wallet or the cops," Ryan reminded him.

Clearly convinced Ryan meant to rob him, the kid glowered and, with Ryan still attached to his arm, led the way through a tortuous maze of twisted metal and rusted machinery parts. Just as Ryan began to suspect he was being taken for a ride, the kid stopped, got down on his belly, and reached beneath an unidentifiable object which was so rusted that orange-red flakes fell off it as the boy's shoulder bumped it. He seemed to be reaching as far underneath it as he could, his face contorted as his fingers sought, found, and then grasped what he sought. He pulled it out, frowned, and quickly put it back.

"Wrong thing," he muttered.

The second object he grasped, however, was indeed Ryan's wallet. Ryan took it from him and started examining it. His credit card was still inside it. He held it up. "Did you use it?"

The kid shook his head. When Ryan just stared at him with raised brows, he said, "I figured you'd report it right away. People like you do. And then I'd get caught as soon as I tried to use it."

"Did you learn that from experience, too?"

The boy scowled.

Ryan's driver's license, his membership card to the health club, and various other things it would have been a nuisance to replace were all in there. Of the two hundred dollars that had been in the wallet yesterday, one hundred sixty were left. He extended his hand and said, "Give it to me."

"Give you what?"

"You were back here right before I found you, and you weren't here to *visit* my wallet. You were getting some cash."

"No, I wasn't!"

"You don't lie any better than you frisk people."

"I frisked *you,* didn't I?"

Ryan almost grinned, kind of liking the kid's bravado. He saw resentment in the boy's face, and some renewed fear—perhaps not so much of him as of the future.

Shit.

Now that he had his wallet in hand, he considered what his two hundred dollars had meant to this kid.

After a moment, Ryan said, "Here's the deal. If you tell the truth, I'll just take the missing cash out of your finder's fee. But if you—"

"My *what?*"

"—keep lying to me and pissing me off, you don't get anything."

The kid glared at him in surly silence.

"Well?" Ryan prodded.

The boy looked away. "You can count. I took a little."

"I guess that's my penalty for being careless enough to let you steal my wallet."

The boy shrugged and continued to avoid his eyes.

After a moment, Ryan said, "And for giving it back to me with everything else in it, you get . . . Here." He held out sixty dollars.

The kid saw the money and went very still. After a long moment, his eyes met Ryan's and he asked with dark suspicion, "What do you want for it?"

Ryan understood the question. "Nothing."

"No one wants nothing."

"That's usually true. But not this time."

The boy continued to stare at him, radiating tension as he looked at the hand extending the money to him. Ryan realized he'd demonstrated that he was faster, stronger, and ruthless, so the kid had some reason to suspect Ryan was toying with him—planning to pounce and take what he wanted when the boy reached for the cash.

Ryan shook his head. "You've already earned it, kid." He put the money down on the ground and backed away from it. "It's yours." He turned and left.

Ryan came awake suddenly in the dark, hauling in air on a long, tortured gasp. His throat constricted as a stifled cry of pain and fear rose from his chest, from his belly, from his soul.

He kicked away the damp sheet, sat up, and swung his legs over the side of the bed so his feet could touch the floor. So he could feel it there, solid and real. So he could know that he was here, awake, and safe.

He was shaking. He hunched over, hugging himself, and rocked back and forth for a moment. Then he turned on the bedside lamp and started trying to steady his frantic, shallow breathing.

Jesus. Oh, Jesus.

He hadn't had that nightmare in a while. And it had been particularly vivid tonight.

It had been years since he'd been back in that environment. He hadn't realized it would affect him so much. He supposed he shouldn't be surprised by it, though.

You could take the boy off the streets, but you could never completely wipe the streets off the boy.

The mind was a strange thing, Ryan thought dimly. He could swear he smelled old urine in a garbage-filled concrete lot, even though he was in his clean, comfortable bedroom. Probably the worst odor that ever invaded this apartment was Macy after he came in from a walk in the rain. Wet dog hair. Not a smell most people enjoyed in close quarters. Ryan didn't mind, though. It smelled homey to him.

Not like the sour, corrupted smell filling his senses right now, even though he knew it was only his imagination.

He got out of bed wearing only his boxer shorts, padded out of the bedroom on bare feet, and went into the kitchen. He got a pitcher of cold water out of the refrigerator and drank from it. Even after all this time on his own, drinking straight from the pitcher still felt rebellious. Catherine had forbidden it, like so many other bad habits, when he lived with her. He recalled that his mother had forbidden it, too, years earlier.

He wondered if Sara would also have asked him not to do it, if they'd ever . . . No, he shouldn't think about that.

She hadn't been on the balcony this morning before he left to go in search of his pickpocket, and she hadn't been there when he returned home in late afternoon, either. Her living room was empty the couple of times he gave in to the temptation to peer through her French doors. He thought he'd heard her front door close this evening and so he had looked out into the hall, but she wasn't there.

She was avoiding him.

It didn't surprise him; but it did hurt. It wasn't as if she didn't have her reasons, of course. Apart from whatever she thought about him being an escort—which, in fact, she clearly thought was appalling—she was bound to be both hurt and angry that he had lied to her for so long. That he had let her grow to care about him without telling her the truth.

Hell, who was he kidding? *Let?* No, he had *tried* to make her care about him. He'd known it was wrong, known that with all his heart. But he'd done it anyhow. He'd wanted her affection, and he'd gone after it. Even knowing how she'd be hurt.

Even knowing how I'd be hurt, too.

No, given his behavior, it wasn't surprising that Sara was avoiding him. And in addition to whatever guilt he felt about how long he'd waited to tell her the truth, he now *also* regretted he hadn't done it sooner because if he'd gotten it over with a while ago, she might be talking to him again by now.

Based on the optimistic assumption that she was ever going to talk to him again, that was.

If he could just talk with her about today . . . Then maybe his subconscious wouldn't be tormenting him tonight. Maybe he could exorcise the old despair and fear that rose up out of nowhere now. If he could just talk about the day with Sara, perhaps his memories wouldn't be assaulting him now as if they were from last week rather than from ten years ago.

Maybe, if he and Sara talked, she'd be able to help him decide if he'd done the right thing when he gave the boy that money.

Or if I should have given him more?

It wouldn't have killed Ryan to let the kid keep all the cash. Whereas *not* having the cash might kill the kid.

Living in the street, anything *might kill that kid.*

The boy had spirit, the streets hadn't destroyed that in him yet. But they probably would.

If he lived.

He seemed so vulnerable to Ryan. So young. He wasn't stupid, but he had more guts than brains. Being brave probably led him to make many mistakes; and mistakes were deadly for a street kid. He learned from his mistakes but, if his behavior as a pickpocket was any evidence, he learned slowly, through trial and error.

In a normal life, that would be fine. On the street, though . . .

What if I were *someone dangerous? What if I* had *intended to hurt him?*

It would have been so easy. If Ryan had been the wrong sort of man, the boy would have become a victim today.

Ryan snorted. Become? As if that kid wasn't already a victim.

He couldn't stop thinking about the boy. And by the time Ryan was asleep again, fragments of his life layering abstractly in his dreams over fragments of what he imagined about that boy's life, he had already decided what he was going to do in the morning.

CHAPTER NINE

Ryan went to the warehouse at dawn, too early for most people here to be up and about. He wore yesterday's jeans and a ragged blue shirt that he left open over a gray T-shirt. He didn't want to look like "some rich guy." Not in this neighborhood.

He crawled through the hole in the fence behind the smelly Dumpster, then crept up to the warehouse. A rusted padlock secured the main doors. Rather than wasting time searching around back for an easy entrance, Ryan climbed up onto one of the broad cement windowsills and entered the building via a huge and mostly-missing window, taking care not to touch what little glass still remained. He jumped down to the floor, glad his sneakers prevented the drop from being noisy, and then crouched there for a moment, looking around.

As he'd anticipated, there were a number of people sleeping in here. Walking softly, he searched the entire warehouse. A few people were starting to wake up; but since Ryan looked innocuous despite his black eye—and perhaps even because of it—and wasn't making any trouble, they pretty much ignored him.

He found no sign of the boy anywhere, but Ryan believed he was bound to be in the vicinity. He wouldn't want to flop far from his stash. Deciding it was time to narrow the search, Ryan approached a couple who were emerging from beneath an old sleeping bag that they had unzipped and spread out to cover them both. The young woman had heavy, smeared eye make-up and oily hair. The young man was dirty and tattooed. There was a crack pipe by their makeshift bed.

When they noticed Ryan standing in front of them, he said, "I've been hired to find someone." This produced no reaction, of course, so he continued, "A kid. He hangs out here. About so tall." Ryan gestured with his hand to indicate that the kid's head came up to his nose. "Black hair, brown eyes, looks Hispanic. No visible marks or tattoos." Ryan thought for a moment. "His nose has been broken and healed a bit crooked."

"Oh!" After making this sound of recognition, the girl caught her boyfriend's hard glance and lowered her gaze.

"Dunno who you're talkin' about, man," the guy said to Ryan.

Ryan looked at the girl. "You know him." When she didn't respond, Ryan said, "He has relatives who want to help him. They're spending money on my services to find him."

"Well, they ain't spending money on *us,*" said the guy.

"Actually," Ryan said, reaching into his pocket, "they've authorized expenses in exchange for information."

"Huh?"

"Tell me where the kid is, and I'll give you fifty bucks," Ryan clarified.

The couple looked at each other again. Ryan could tell he'd sparked their interest with that offer, as expected.

"How much do they want this kid?" the guy asked.

"Tell me where he is, and the fifty is yours," Ryan said.

"I can't say nothin' for under two hundred."

Ryan sighed. "That's too bad. Fifty is all I've got. Oh, well, thanks for your time."

He turned around and left them. Not surprisingly, the

girl caught up with him about twenty yards later.

"I know where he is," she said. "The kid with the crooked nose. I can tell you."

He held up the money, but drew it back when she reached for it. "*Show* me."

She nodded. "This way." She led him through the warehouse and then outside via a small door—the easy access he hadn't bothered to find earlier. There, in what appeared to have been a loading area once upon a time, sat an old delivery truck that looked like it hadn't functioned in years. "In the cab," she said.

"Thanks." Ryan gave her the cash and waited for her to go back into the warehouse, then he approached the truck and looked inside. Sure enough, the boy was asleep, his dark head sticking out from under a ratty blanket. Ryan tried the driver's door; it was locked. He assumed the other one was, too.

It was a good flop. Off the street. Unknown to the cops. The kid could lock the doors for safety, and the windows and mirrors let him see if anyone was nearby.

On the other hand, it was isolated enough that the kid was dead meat if someone got into the truck, or if he got out when it wasn't wise to do so.

Thoughts like these felt so familiar now, Ryan wondered if he'd ever really stopped having them every day. He'd thought he had, thought he had adjusted to the comfortable and mostly-safe lifestyle he'd been leading for years . . .

But you can never completely wipe the streets off the boy.

He sat down near the truck, out of the kid's line of vision and waited. After a while, he was sorry he hadn't brought *The Architect of Time* with him—another of Sara's mystery novels, which he was in the middle of reading now. Sara's writing was good company when he couldn't be with her. Really good reading, too. Who'd have guessed that a bunch of imaginary medieval people could be so interesting, or that Ryan would care so much what happened to the recurring characters from book to book? When he remembered how many times he'd bought a novel that he wound up considering a waste of his money, it really burned him that some idiot publisher had decided to stop publishing Sara's books when they were so good.

Tired from his restless night and early morning, Ryan was dozing a bit when he heard the door of the truck cab click open. He shook his head to clear the cobwebs and braced himself, suddenly wishing he'd spent a little of these past two hours planning what he would say.

The kid slid out of the cab feet first, rubbing one fist sleepily against his eyes.

"Good morning," Ryan said.

The kid gasped, flinched, stumbled backwards, hit his elbow on the truck door, cried out, and hopped around a little.

"Not a morning person?" said Ryan. "Well, most teenagers aren't, I guess."

The kid's expression turned to one of unconcealed horror as he recognized Ryan. "What the fuck are *you* doing here?"

"Watch your language," Ryan said.

"What the *fuck,* man?"

"Okay, forget I mentioned your language."

"What are you *doing* here?"

Good question.

"I was in the neighborhood."

"Yeah, right." The boy regarded him with open suspicion.

Wishing he'd thought of a smoother lead-in, Ryan asked, "Are you hungry?"

"Huh?"

"Are you hungry?"

The kid glowered.

"Would you like some breakfast?"

No response.

"I'm offering," Ryan said, "to buy you breakfast."

"Why?"

"You look hungry."

"What are you, a fucking good Sumerian?"

"Samaritan."

"Whatever."

Ryan remained seated on the ground, attempting to look unthreatening. But when you were a kid on the street, every adult was a threat—especially a man who kept tracking you down in isolated spots like this—so he knew the attempt probably wasn't working.

To break the silence, which was starting to grow tense, Ryan said, "What's your name?"

"You don't need to know my name."

"Mine's Ryan."

"So what?"

"So . . ." *Just be honest,* he advised himself. "You're living in this shit hole—"

"Watch your language," the boy said snidely.

"—you steal money, and you're a kid." Ryan shrugged. "That sucks. I was thinking about it, and it bothered me."

The kid looked wary and said nothing.

"So I thought I'd buy you breakfast."

"Where do I have to *go* for this 'breakfast'? You got a car waiting on the—"

"I'm not going to ask you to get into a car with me. Or

go anywhere private with me." Ryan held his gaze. "We'll just walk up to the main drag and find a coffee shop."

"What do you want from me for this breakfast, man?" the kid said coldly. "Just tell me."

For some reason, Ryan suddenly heard his mother's voice in his head. He repeated what he heard there. "I want some good manners from you, young man."

Sara didn't see him for two days. During that time, she tortured herself to the best of her ability.

She couldn't sleep. She couldn't eat. She couldn't work or concentrate. She couldn't believe what Ryan had told her, yet she knew he was telling the truth. It explained so much—the secrets, the strange hours, the sudden assignments, the exquisite clothes and impressive accessories, his loathing of the police . . .

She'd thought she was falling in love with him, but, in fact, she didn't even know him.

Yet she *did* know him, because the man who had tenderly asked her to go to bed with him, and was then so gentle in his understanding when she refused, was precisely the man who'd become so dear to her that going two days without talking to him now was like going that long without food and water.

Ryan . . .

The charming, considerate man who'd practically been living in her pocket in recent weeks, the warm and generous friend whom she'd grown to trust and rely on . . .

"I've never liked anybody as much as I like you . . ."

. . . the man whom she fantasized about as a lover . . .

"I really *wanted you just now. And for weeks before this."*

. . . was actually a high-priced male prostitute who'd been having sex with other women practically every day since they'd met! All the while that Sara had been mooning over him and wishing he might become her lover.

"They had a tape of me doing the client, right there on the massage table."

Sara held her head in her hands, trying to block out the memory, trying to banish the images Ryan's word invoked.

"I got her off three times, and she never even looked at me."

Who *was* that guy? Surely he wasn't the same man who'd called Sara long-distance last week from his out-of-town assignment—

"I was hired to put her in a generous mood."

—because he was so worried about out how his hysterically shy cat had survived her appointment at the vet's office in his absence.

"The cops caught the whole show on camera. Including the part where I accepted payment from her."

Could this be the same man who companionably puttered around the kitchen with Sara several times a week? The same man who was trying to teach her some exercises to help ease the knots in her back caused by hunching over a hot keyboard all day? Who slavishly carried his fat, lazy dog up the stairs of this building whenever Macy balked and refused to keep climbing? Who'd accepted with enthusiasm when Sara had invited him to her private video marathon of old *Thin Man* movies two Sundays ago?

"I get paid to be good company. In bed, out of bed, whatever the client wants."

Was that the same man who'd already read three of Sara's novels and liked to talk about her work?

Well, sure, she thought bitterly. *He's been perfect company to* me, *after all.*

But he'd known her mind would travel in that direction, and so he had made a point of telling her he'd always been sincere with her . . . And she believed him.

Sara curled up on the couch, picked up the TV remote, and started channel surfing.

Yes, she believed him, damn it. And it made her miserable and confused.

If he had made a fool of her, played her—"worked" her—then she'd be mortified, wounded, and devastated now. But at least she would have some clarity. It would be over between them—whatever "it" was. He would just be the enemy now, the deceitful shit who had humiliated her. A man whom she would regard as a painful and embarrassing mistake, but a finished episode.

Instead, now she was chasing her tail and losing sleep as she tried to reconcile Ryan with . . . Kevin.

"And fucking her . . . Don't forget fucking her until she was limp."

Sara clicked the remote over and over, scarcely seeing the images that flashed past her on the television screen.

Now, instead of regarding Ryan as a former obsession to be forgotten as quickly as possible, Sara found herself wrestling with unbearable temptation. He wanted her—the way she wanted him! And the memory of his hands on her body, eager and possessive and recklessly demanding, the dark honey of his kisses, the smooth heat of his skin and the tickle of his breath, the way he groaned when she touched him, the way he knew exactly how to touch her . . .

Forget it, forget the way he felt, the way he tasted, the sound of his whispers . . .

But she couldn't forget it. She knew she wouldn't forget it if she lived to be even older than her Great Aunt Minnie—which was pretty damn old.

God, I want him. I want him so much.

She'd nearly locked herself in the bathroom last night to

make sure she wouldn't go to him.

Because she didn't want *Kevin,* and she couldn't separate the two lives as cleanly as Ryan apparently could.

She shouldn't have left his apartment that night like a coward, fleeing the moment his back was turned. But she was weak with desire and afraid to let him see it. If he had asked her once more to stay, she might have done it. If she had looked into his tender gaze again, he might not even have needed to ask.

But she was disgusted, too, and so she fled.

My God, Sara, his dick was inside someone else only that morning. It's probably inside someone else right now.

She'd also fled because she didn't want Ryan to *see* her disgust. He'd gone far out on a limb to be honest with her, she'd already been hurtful in her initial reaction, and she didn't want to make things worse.

And now, for two days, ever since escaping his apartment while he was getting tissues for her, she'd been avoiding him: She waited until she heard him leave the building before she went out the door to run her errands; when she came home, she slipped in quietly and quickly, praying not to bump into him; when they were home at the same time, she stayed in her bedroom, so he wouldn't see her in the living room if he went out onto the balcony.

It was immature and absurd, and she had to stop acting this way. It was also unfair to Ryan. As well as unkind. He'd been honest with her, he'd trusted her—and, in response, she was treating him like a leper.

He wasn't a serial killer or a child molester. He just had sex with women for money.

A *lot* of women, apparently.

For money.

Why? Why does he do it?

Well, she wasn't going to find out by hiding in here. She had to pull herself together, face Ryan, and move forward.

Just as she was embracing this resolution, her recently-fixed doorbell rang. Lost in her thoughts, she nearly jumped out of her skin.

She wasn't expecting anyone. Ryan presumably wasn't, either, since he wasn't home. So, wondering who could be at the door, she found her slippers and, wearing yesterday's sweats, made her way downstairs to open the outside door.

Ryan had been so anxious to see her and so depressed over the way she was avoiding him, he actually did a doubletake when he opened the downstairs door to enter the building, late that afternoon, and found her sitting right there in the stairwell, on the third step.

"Sara?"

She looked up at him, her expression so morose he felt a terrible stab of guilt. Had he done this to her?

"Ryan." Her voice was distracted.

"Hi," he said cautiously.

"Mm." After a moment, her gaze drifted back down to the floor.

"Are you okay?" he asked, coming a little closer.

She shrugged. "I guess."

Her hair was a mess, there were dark circles under her eyes, there was a coffee stain on the leg of her sweats, and she was in her slippers. She was wearing her glasses instead of her contacts, which was rare. He thought she looked cute in her glasses, sort of a prim librarian sex fantasy; but he knew she disliked them.

"I don't mean to sound argumentative," he said, "but you don't look okay."

She looked up at him, her expression tired and defeated.

She made a noncommittal sound and shrugged again.

He risked taking a seat next to her. If she noticed, she evidently didn't mind. "Are you sitting here dressed like a bag lady and staring at the floor because of me?"

"What?" she said without looking at him.

"Because of what we talked about the other night?"

"Huh? Oh! That."

"Yes, that." When she didn't reply, he added, "You've been avoiding me ever since we talked about *that*."

"Yes." She nodded slowly. "Yes, I have. I'm sorry."

"Sara . . ."

She turned her head and held his gaze. "It was wrong to disappear the way I did that night. I was just . . ."

"I know. It's okay."

"It's not okay." She shook her head, closed her eyes, and rolled her shoulders around a little as if they were aching. He wanted to rub them for her. Instead, he clasped his hands together. After a moment, she said, "And avoiding you after you told me, um, your secret . . . That was no way to treat a friend."

Relief started to flow through him. "*Are* we still friends?"

"Of course!" She met his eyes again and put one of her hands over his clasped ones. "Of course, we are, Ryan. I mean . . ."

"What?"

"If the part of you I've known, the part you've always shown me . . . If that's real—"

"It is," he said. "Except for lying to you about what I do when I leave here, everything has been real between us." He unclasped his hands and turned one over to lace his fingers with those of the hand she had extended to him.

"Then I guess you really are who I thought you were," she said. "After all, I knew there were things you weren't telling me. Things I might not like, that might even hurt me." She looked at their joined hands. "Now you've told me, I don't like it, and it hurts. So, in a way, everything's going according to plan."

That startled him into a puff of laughter. She did that to him all the time. He loved the way she put things.

"Then what's the next stage of the plan?" he asked.

She smiled wryly. "I guess we just go forward."

Hoping it would be okay, he raised their joined hands to his lips and brushed a kiss across her knuckles.

She added quietly, "But being friends is as far forward as I can go."

He'd expected that. "Then I won't ask you to go any farther."

"I can't be lovers with a man who's busy beings lovers with everyone else."

He shook his head. "I'm not lovers with any of them, Sara, not like that. I just—"

"Have you slept with someone today?"

"No." After an awkward moment, he gestured to his black eye. "I'm off for a few days. I can't go back to work until this stops looking so scary."

"Right. Because a woman paying a whole lot of money for you to be the perfect lover doesn't want to see—"

"I'm not supposed to look like a street boy or a bruiser," he said a little irritably. "I'm supposed to look smart and respectable, like someone they might meet at the country club or a fundraiser."

"In a couple of days, you'll look that way again, Ryan. And as soon as you do, you'll be in bed with another woman."

He couldn't deny it.

She added, "Or at least having dinner and flirting with her."

"Yes, I will," he admitted.

"I can't live like that," she said.

He closed his eyes and took a breath. "I know."

"I don't want to wake up next to you and wonder who you'll be having sex with that day, or just a romantic dinner, or how many of them there'll be that week, or—"

"I know."

"—what they're like, or what *you're* like when you're with them—"

"Sara, I understand."

She seemed as if she wanted to say more—*lots* more—but, for the moment, she dropped the subject of his working life and merely said, "But I'm still your friend."

"Thank you." He gently rubbed his free hand over hers while he continued holding it. "Your friendship is the most important thing to me. I don't think I could stand to lose that, Sara."

"Well, you haven't." She squeezed his hand. "And I don't think I could stand to lose yours, either."

"You never will. You couldn't."

She smiled softly, then frowned a little and raised her free hand to brush her fingertips across his black eye. "You said you were arrested that day, and . . . Ryan, my God, surely the *cops* didn't do this to you?"

"No. I got this after they released me."

"Who did it?"

He explained briefly, keeping the details down to a minimum.

She spent a moment digesting his tale before she asked, "Are you in any more danger from this guy?"

"Derrick? No," he said dismissively. "He'll have problems of his own to worry about for a while."

"I don't know, Ryan. If he set you up for an arrest just

because he was annoyed about, er, losing that client, how much more angry is he going to be now that you've humiliated him and physically hurt him?"

"Oh." Ryan sighed. "When you put it that way, I guess he *will* be pretty pissed off at me for a while."

"Even more so than he was when he informed on you to the vice squad and got you arrested."

He shook his head. "Don't worry about Derrick. I doubt he'll try anything—"

"I hope not."

"—and I can handle it if he does." When she continued to look concerned, he squeezed her hand. "Really. He's dumb and he's clumsy. I can handle him, and I don't want you to worry about him. All right?"

"All right."

"So . . . we're okay, then? Things between you and me, I mean?"

"Yes. We're okay."

When she went back to staring morosely at the floor, he asked doubtfully, "Feeling better now?"

"Huh? Oh. Actually, I wasn't sitting here brooding about, um, that stuff."

"Oh?"

"No. We're already back to my regularly-scheduled self-absorption."

He almost laughed again. "Why? What's wrong?"

"This." She leaned forward a little to reach for a large manila envelope that was under her feet. Ryan hadn't even noticed it before. "I thought stomping on it a few times might make me feel better," Sara said as she handed it to him, "but it hasn't helped."

Puzzled, he looked inside the envelope. It contained a single sheet of paper.

"It came as certified mail. I had to sign for it," Sara said. "That's why I had to come downstairs. And after I read it, I didn't feel like climbing all the way *up*stairs again."

Ryan pulled the letter out of the envelope and read the return address. "It's from your literary agent?" When she nodded, he prodded, "That's the person who markets and sells your work, negotiates your contracts, and advises you about the business?"

"Yes. Only she is now my *former* agent."

He frowned and began reading the letter. Within moments, he made a disgusted noise. He read aloud: " 'I feel that relaunching your career will require more time than I am able to commit, especially as I have serious doubts about the viability of the new novel which you have described to me. So I am regretfully ending our association.' " He looked at Sara. *"What?"*

"Funny, that's exactly what *I* said when I read it: *What?*"

"I thought you wouldn't tell anyone anything about the book you're working on," he said, though that probably wasn't the most important point right now. "You won't tell *me* anything."

"Mm."

"What did you tell *her?*"

"What I've told you: It's sort of a historical thriller."

"And?"

"That's it."

"And on the basis of that, she decided it's not 'viable'?"

Sara shrugged, looking downcast.

"She's *dumping* you?"

Sara nodded. "Just like my publisher."

Outraged, Ryan finished reading the rest of the letter, which simply mentioned a couple of bureaucratic details which would need to be tied up and then wished Sara "the best of luck" with her future.

"Oh, for fuck's sake," Ryan said, furious on Sara's behalf. "What a lazy, short-sighted bitch!" As if Sara weren't under enough pressure, now her agent was abandoning her? Jesus! "What's *wrong* with the people in your business?"

Sara sighed and took off her glasses. "Publishers have become pretty unforgiving in this tight market. So, given my circumstances, she thinks I'm done, finished, old news." Looking suddenly exhausted, she bent over and put her head in her hands. "She thinks I'm a washout, and she'd just be wasting her time trying to sell anything else I write."

Angry at the agent and distressed to see that Sara was taking this very hard, Ryan put his arms around her and rested his cheek on her bowed head. "She *didn't* say 'washout,' Sara."

"It's in the subtext." Her tone was irritable.

"Look, the way I remember it," he said, "you told me that you couldn't get an agent to represent you when you were an aspiring writer, so you spent two years submitting to publishers on your own, until one of them made you an offer. And *then,* after *you'd* done all the legwork, this chick finally got interested in your career, and that's when you hired her to negotiate that contract."

He heard Sara sniff. He suspected she was starting to cry.

"So she's not saying you're a 'washout'," he continued firmly. "She's saying that she's had a nice, easy ride with you, just sitting around collecting her commission on the seven books you've sold to the publisher *you* found without her help. But now that you're actually going to need her to *work* for a living, to market and sell your new manuscript, to find a publisher for it . . . Forget it! That's just more than she's willing to do for you, after five years of you being such an easy trick for her."

For a split second, he wondered if Sara would be offended at his making the comparison to turning tricks; but then he heard her make a mildly amused sound, and he was relieved.

"I don't know," she mumbled. "Maybe she's just sizing up the situation and making a smart decision."

"What's 'smart' about this decision? You've sold seven books already—"

"Writers disappear from the business all the time, Ryan, even writers who've sold a bunch of—"

"—you're incredibly talented—"

"Talent is cheap."

"—you're dedicated, you don't give up—"

"Maybe it's time."

"Don't even say that. I'm not going to listen to that."

"Ryan, I—"

"And you're working on a new book that's going to turn your career around."

"That's just a lot of bullshit," she muttered. "You're just saying that because—"

"Damn it, Sara." He dragged her upright, made her face him, and shook her gently. "If you want to be depressed about this, you're entitled. I can tell it's a big blow to your confidence. But don't you ever accuse me of bullshitting you! At work, I say whatever I think people want to hear. But when I'm with you, I'm sincere—and I've *told* you that."

"Oh, for God's sake!" She scrubbed a hand across her tear-streaked face, which was a little pink and puffy now. "If I say you're bullshitting me because you're trying to make me feel better, Ryan, I'm not accusing you of *working* me! I'm just saying that—" She made an exasperated sound. "—that you're sugarcoating this because you don't want me to feel so—"

"I don't *have* to sugarcoat this. It's what I believe."

She scowled at him for a moment, and then her expression changed to reveal such unhappiness that it broke his heart. "It's what *I* want to believe, too," she said brokenly.

"Oh, sweetheart." He hugged her as she wept. His arms around her, her head on his shoulder, her curly hair tickling his neck and jaw . . . It felt so good to hold her like this. And it felt so awful to be unable to protect her from the blows of her profession.

"God, I've turned into such a watering pot lately," she said in a weepy, disgusted voice.

"Well, between me and your career, you've taken some hits below the belt lately," he murmured, stroking her back.

Sara let out her breath on a long sigh. "Well. My agent had sort of a patronizing manner. On the bright side, I guess I won't miss that."

"Plus, she was a lazy, short-sighted bitch." When Sara made a watery, amused noise, he added, "Besides, you probably should have fired her, anyhow. So maybe she's relieved you of that decision by just leaving."

"Why should I have fired her?"

"Whenever you talk about being dumped by your publisher, you always blame yourself for not having seen it coming. But you're the artist. It would be a big advantage if you were savvy about business, but it's not your job. Writing is your job. Being savvy about business is your agent's job." He rubbed his cheek against her hair. "So why didn't *she* see the trouble coming? Why didn't she talk about it with you, maybe come up with a game plan? And now that it's happened, why is her best plan for *her* career to dump a longtime client who's hard at work on a new book?"

"Well . . ."

"She's reacting to the past, not planning for the future. That's bad business."

"Maybe . . ."

"She hasn't read your new book. Not one page! She doesn't even know what it's about. What was it going to cost her to read it when it was done and *then* make her decision about whether or not to keep being your agent?" He made a dismissive sound. "But she didn't do that because she doesn't want to *work*. She was only interested in you as long as you kept her on Easy Street." When he stopped talking, he realized Sara was breathing evenly now. Not crying anymore. Just listening to him and thinking about what he was saying. "Am I right?"

"I don't know. Maybe," she murmured. "I hope so."

"Will you try to pretend I'm right?"

"I guess I can try."

"Good. Because I think it'll work out better than your plan, which was to pace around the apartment thinking about what a washout you are."

"Yes, that *was* my plan," she admitted.

He smiled and kissed her hair. He felt her arms tighten around him. She rubbed her cheek against his shoulder as her palms moved slowly over his back—a guilty pleasure that made him close his eyes and call on his self-control.

After a long, warm moment, she whispered, "I have to tell you . . ."

"What?" he whispered back, feeling sort of dazed as they continued clinging to each other.

"I'm having . . . those feelings again." When he didn't reply, she added, "You know the feelings I mean?"

"Oh, yeah. I know." His hands tightened on her. "I'm having them, too."

"I can't do this," she whispered.

His chest started to hurt. "Okay."

She shuddered a little. "We have to let go."

"Right." *Just one more second.* "Okay." *No, just give me a second.* "Let's let go." *No.*

Her hands tightened on his shoulders, and when she turned her head, he felt her warm breath against his neck.

Oh, I want this. Please, please . . .

She shifted her weight, and he was instantly, hotly aware of her breast pressing against his biceps, and her knee nudging his thigh, and her . . .

Remembering he had assured her he wouldn't do what he was on the verge of doing, he found the strength to shove her away, and he scooted backwards until he hit the banister. His breath was coming a little too fast and shallow, and he knew the flush in her cheeks now wasn't from crying.

She shuddered again, clasped her hands, and looked away from him.

"Sorry," he said gruffly.

"No, I'm sorry. I was a mess, and you were just comforting me, and I—"

"No, you were upset. But then I got sort of, uh . . ."

"So did I."

"Well. Yeah. I guess we both did."

She cleared her throat. "We probably shouldn't . . . um . . ."

"Shouldn't touch," he said.

"Not like that."

He should be honest with her about this. "Maybe not at all." When she looked at him, he said, "It'll just keep leading to this, Sara. It's the way I feel about you. And if it's the way you feel about me, too—"

"You know it is."

"—then every time we start out touching as if we were friends—"

"We *are* friends."

"—we'll just wind up right here again."

"We *are* friends," she repeated.

"We're friends whose bodies want to be a lot more than just friends."

Their gazes locked. After a moment, she said, "It's not just my *body* that wants it."

"No. Me, neither," he admitted. "If my body was all that wanted it, I wouldn't . . . I mean, I could control . . ." He lowered his gaze and hoped she'd understand when he said, "Look, sex doesn't really mean anything to me."

"No, I guess it doesn't." Her tone was guarded.

"So this is different. What's between us." He folded his arms across his chest and turned a little away from her, feeling exposed. "And if I could find a different word for it . . . Then *that's* what I'd say I want when I touch you." He shrugged uncomfortably. "I guess it looks the same from the outside. But it feels like something different to me."

"Ryan . . ."

Out of the corner of his eye, he saw her lean towards him and extend a hand. He turned away a little more and said quietly, "Don't. Not unless you want to go upstairs together. Right now."

When he didn't feel her touch upon him, he knew what her answer was. There was a long silence between them.

"I want you to tell me," she said at last, "why sex means so little to you. I need to know why you keep company with lots of other women. For money. I want to know how you became . . ."

"An expensive whore?"

She didn't protest his choice of words. "Yes."

"It's a long story, Sara."

"I think I can spare the time," she said.

"You want to know how I wound up like this—"

"Yes."

"—from the promising start that I had in life?" he said with a twinge of bitterness.

"What *was* your start in life? You never tell me anything about your past."

How could he make her understand his past? "I should take you to meet that kid," he mused.

"What kid?"

"This kid who stole my wallet."

"You know him?"

"I do now. I found him. Since the last time I saw you. I tracked him down."

"Did you get your wallet back?"

"Yes. With my I.D. and stuff still in it."

"Oh, good! So that's where you've been all day?"

He shook his head. "Yesterday. Oh, and this morning. I went back to buy the kid breakfast."

"You bought him *breakfast?*" When he didn't reply, she said, "Why? And how'd you find him? What's his name?"

"I don't know his name. He wouldn't tell me." The boy had followed Ryan to a diner in hostile silence and maintained it while waiting for his breakfast to be cooked. He wolfed down the food without even looking at Ryan, and then bolted for the door. "Not that he would have given me his real name," Ryan added absently to Sara. "Not if he was smart."

"Why not?"

"He should be using a street name."

"Why?"

"Everyone's got their reasons."

She drew in a sharp breath. There was a pause before she said, "What were your reasons?"

He glanced at her, a little surprised.

"The other night," she reminded him, "you said something about being able to take the boy off the streets, but not the—"

"Oh. Right." He should have realized she'd catch that. She caught everything. And made the connections.

"What was your street name?" she asked. "Kevin?"

"No. Catherine named me Kevin. Because it sounds . . ."

"Smart and respectable."

"Yes."

"How old were you when she named you Kevin?"

He drew in a breath and let it out slowly. "I was sixteen."

"*Sixteen?* My God! You were just a *kid,* and she turned you into a prostitute!"

"And I was glad," he said. "Grateful."

"Grateful?" She sounded stunned.

"So grateful that it took me years to figure out I was trapped and wanted to escape."

"Why were you *grateful?*"

He met her eyes. "If she hadn't found me and turned me into Kevin, I'd be long dead by now. Hell, I was *nearly* dead when she did it."

"How? Why?"

"Life on the street is pretty brutal."

"But why were you on the street in the first place?"

He hesitated for a moment, then said, "Do you want to get dressed and go get a drink? This is a story that really needs a drink to go along with it."

CHAPTER TEN

He was raised by his mother, who worked full-time as a housekeeper for a wealthy family in Tulsa, Oklahoma. She and Ryan lived in a small apartment above her employers' garage. The two of them had a tight budget but a stable lifestyle. The employers' home was in an excellent school district, so Ryan was getting a good education—supplemented by the religion classes, which his mother, a strict Catholic, insisted he attend without fail.

"In fact," Ryan said dryly, "I was an altar boy."

"That isn't how I see you," Sara admitted.

The employers were kind people. Their children were considerably older than Ryan, and so they gave him old furniture, toys, books, records, and sports equipment that their kids didn't want anymore. Rather than letting him resent his hand-me-down status, Ryan's mother made sure that he appreciated the opportunity to own things that she couldn't have bought for him. And she was so strict that she insisted he offer courteous and effusive thanks even for the occasional item that he really didn't want.

"Then she'd quietly go and give it to someone with even less money than we had," he told Sara.

His mother was strict about everything, in fact: his manners, his schoolwork, his tidiness, his language.

"And, oh, my God, the *guilt* that woman could inflict if I didn't do my chores or didn't get a good grade on a test."

"Now she sounds like *my* mother."

He grinned. "If I was rude or got into a fight, then she'd

assign me some really awful chore. One time, I had to go around the neighborhood collecting money for some charity, and I wasn't allowed to come home until I had fifty dollars."

"That's a good punishment," Sara said, clearly impressed.

Ryan took a sip of the beer he had ordered at this bar, which was several blocks away from where he and Sara lived. He'd never been in here before and doubted he'd return. He hadn't wanted to be alone in private with her, not right after they'd nearly jumped each other's bones on the stairs; and he didn't want to be overheard in their neighborhood café, where people knew him. So this place had seemed a good choice.

Now he and Sara sat in a shadowy corner at the back of the establishment. Her elbows were propped on their little table as she listened to him. Catherine had trained Ryan never to put his elbows on a table, and he didn't break the habit now. Sara had a glass of wine in front of her, and he knew she probably wouldn't finish it, no matter how long they sat here. She wasn't much of a drinker.

"Where was your father?" Sara asked.

"Well, I thought he was dead. That's what my mother told me. In fact, it was the *only* thing she'd tell me about him."

"I take it he wasn't really dead?"

"No. One day, when I was eight, he just showed up."

"That must have been weird."

"Very."

Ryan was outside playing one Sunday afternoon when a strange man pulled into the driveway, got out of his car, and, upon seeing Ryan, came over to talk to him.

Ryan knew he wasn't supposed to talk to strangers, but

the man knew his name, knew his mother's name, and kept his distance, so Ryan didn't run inside right away.

"Then, suddenly, my mother was shouting at me from the window of our apartment. 'Ryan, get away from him! Come inside! Right now!' So I did—but he followed me. My mother blocked the doorway and wouldn't let him in. She was shouting and making threats. I'd never seen her like that."

The man argued with her, growing very angry. Ryan's mother threatened to call the police, and the man dared her to do so, shouting at her, "He's my son, too! I'll get a court order if I have to!"

After the man's departure, Ryan's mother was extremely upset, wouldn't talk to him, and got angry when he asked questions about the man.

"But he did get a court order," Ryan said. "So she had to let him see me. Which meant she had to tell me who he was."

"Why didn't she want your father to see you?" Sara asked.

"Well, she didn't put it this way at the time, of course," Ryan said, "but he used to knock her around when he got drunk. When he started knocking *me* around, too, she left him. I was less than two years old. Don't remember anything about it."

"And you hadn't seen him since then?"

He shook his head. "My mother never divorced him. I don't know why. That's the sort of question you only think of when you get older. Maybe it was because she was so religious. Or maybe she couldn't afford a divorce lawyer, or my father wouldn't agree to get divorced." Ryan shrugged.

"But now he was back and tried to establish a relationship with you?"

"Not quite. He saw me for two weekends that first month, which was evidently what the court order stipulated. Both weekends were incredibly boring and awkward, I might add. And then he disappeared. The next time he was supposed to come pick me up, my mother and I sat waiting for two hours. He never showed, never called. My mother said she didn't care what the court said, she wouldn't let him see me again. The next time he tried, about a year later, she stuck to that. He made some threats about going back to the courts again. But I guess he never did."

"Was he drinking again?"

"Probably."

"So you never saw him again?"

"Oh, if only that were the case." Ryan took a long swig of his beer. "When I was thirteen, my mother died."

"Oh." Sara conveyed strong sympathy in that one syllable. "How? She must have still been pretty young."

"Not even your age yet," he said, remembering that day. "Aneurysm. It happened instantly. Mrs. Ferguson—the Fergusons were her employers—came home from shopping that afternoon and found her dead in the kitchen. Just like that." He paused. "I came home from school to find an ambulance and a squad car in the driveway. I thought maybe Mr. Ferguson had had a heart attack. Mom always worried that he would. But . . . then they told me."

"Oh, Ryan. I'm so sorry."

He took a breath. "A few days later, I was sent to live with my father in Oklahoma City."

"That must have been very hard for you."

"Actually, the hard part came when he started beating the shit out of me."

"What?"

"He was drinking a lot by the time I moved in with him. He slugged me occasionally, but—"

"Oh, Ryan!"

"—it was about a year before he really started beating me in earnest."

"Oh, my God."

"So, finally, after the old man passed out one night, I called Mr. and Mrs. Ferguson and asked them to come get me. They'd always been nice to me, and I didn't know what else to do."

The Fergusons were nice to him again. They drove a long distance through the night to rescue the incoherent adolescent who had phoned them for help. Appalled by what he revealed about his life with his father, the Fergusons took Ryan home with them and consulted a lawyer.

"I stayed there for a few days," Ryan said. "But I was taken away from them, and then I was sent back to my father."

"Why?"

"Since my mother had never divorced my father, or filed for separation, or anything like that, my father had a lot of rights over me. There was no record of my mother ever filing any kind of complaint against my father; and there *was* a record of him having had the court force my mother to let him see me after she'd refused, so it made him look like a *concerned* and *responsible* parent." Ryan could have choked on the words.

"Didn't the authorities care that he was an alcoholic who was *beating* you?"

"My father said it had happened just the one time, and it would never happen again. His lawyer said the Fergusons had colluded with my mother to deny my father his rights as a parent and were involved in this out of spite." He made a disgusted sound. "The Fergusons had no legal right to help me, and I was just a kid, so the system didn't give a shit what *I* said or thought. So I got sent back to my father."

"What happened?" Sara asked.

"I guess the brush with the law made an impression on my father. It was a few months before he started beating me again. I had to see a social worker once every two weeks. I guess she was supposed to be my 'protection' against him. But when I showed up one day with a fat lip and told her who'd given it to me, she went and bitched to him, and that just made him even madder at me. So I never told her a thing again."

"I feel sick," Sara said. "Ryan, why didn't an adult help you?"

"The Fergusons tried, but . . ." He shook his head. "They couldn't help. There was no one."

"What about relatives?"

"My mother was an only child and her parents were dead. I didn't know how to contact any of her other relatives. And I never met anyone in my father's family."

By now, Ryan seldom attended school and was failing. He couldn't sleep, he was depressed and scared, losing weight. He'd made no friends since moving in with his father. He had no one and nothing.

"And then my father got sloshed again one night, and this time he tried to kill me."

"Ryan!"

After all these years, the memory of that night still made his back sweat with fear. "He was chasing me around the house, knocking over furniture, hitting and kicking me. He was screaming that he was sick of me, he wanted me dead, he was going to kill me." Ryan clenched his fists. "I was so scared, I couldn't even speak. I really thought he was going to do it. I really believed I was going to die."

There were tears in her eyes as she reached for one of his clenched hands, ignoring the "no touching" rule they had established earlier.

"I ran outside, trying to get away from him. But he was right on my heels, screaming that he'd break both my arms, he'd teach me to talk back, he'd kill me." His father's enraged, terrifying bellows filled his head again. The curses and the threats. The screaming, irrational violence. " 'You're dead, boy!' he kept shouting at me." Ryan rubbed his brow, feeling shaky as it all came back to him. "There was all sorts of equipment in the yard. I don't know why. I never saw him use any of it. It was all rusty and ruined. I picked up this piece of machinery . . . I guess it was about the size of a toaster. I don't know what it was for."

When he fell silent, she prodded gently, "What happened?"

He took a breath. "I turned around, and when he lunged at me, I smashed it into his face as hard as I could. He screamed and staggered back. His hand was over his face, like this." Ryan demonstrated. "In the light coming from the porch, I could see blood start trickling down his face, from underneath his hand." Ryan paused for a moment. "And then I hit him again."

"That may have saved your life," she said quietly.

"That's what I thought," he agreed. "He passed out. I got his wallet and took all his money. Then I went into the house and threw some of my stuff into a duffel bag as fast as I could. I don't even remember thinking. I was like a machine or something. No thoughts, just actions."

"You were in shock."

"I guess I was. All I knew was that I had to get out of that house forever, and *quick,* because when he woke up, he'd kill me, for sure. When I looked out the window and saw him start moving, I stopped packing, just took what I already had, and ran."

"Where did you go?"

"Bus station. I walked all the way there. It took me until dawn. I looked at the schedule when I got there, to see which buses were leaving in the next hour. And I bought a ticket for the one that was going farthest."

She closed her eyes and lowered her head. "That's how you wound up here."

"I had this idea in my head that I had to get out of Oklahoma. That he'd be able to find me or they'd be able to send me back to him if I stayed in the state."

"How old were you?"

"Fourteen."

She made a distressed sound, "What did you do when you got here?"

"The usual. I slept in the bus station until the cops bothered me. Then I started sleeping in lobbies, public bathrooms, alleys, a cemetery, wherever. I tried to look for a job, but you can't get one when you're underage, dirty, and have no home and no I.D." He shrugged. "I became a street boy. I figured out how to survive. I ate out of Dumpsters. I waded into traffic to wash windshields." He wondered uneasily how much to tell her. "I shoplifted . . . And I picked pockets . . . And I, uh . . ."

"You were a thief?"

"Yes." He added, "And I was better at it than the street boy who stole my wallet the other day."

"Did you look for help? Until you went to live with your father, you had a normal life and a good education. But you were so young, of course . . . Did you know there were social agencies and shelters?"

"My experience of social agencies was that they'd send me back to my father. And shelters were worse than the streets, Sara. At one, I had to strip, let them check me out, treat me like dirt. It was filthy and crowded, and, uh, I had to stand, sleep, and shower with my back to the wall. So to speak."

"Oh," she said faintly.

"At another, some guys regularly smuggled in weapons—a knife, a club, a pipe—and beat up anyone they felt like beating up." But they'd learned not to pick on *him*. He'd survived his father's assaults, and he certainly wasn't going to let some street punk kill him—or take away what few belongings he possessed.

"It's like *Lord of the Flies* or something," Sara said bleakly.

"I've never read it."

"I suppose this explains why you don't like cops."

"Living on the street, you learn fast to avoid them. They don't help you. They just move you along or try to lock you up." He thought back and said, "There was a church that sent its members around to give us—kids on the street—food, some clothes, and these kits that had things in them like toothpaste, deodorant, and combs. There was another church where we could go for hot meals . . . but I wouldn't go unless I was really hungry, because some adult would bother me as soon as I sat down there."

"Bother you?"

"Ask for my story. Ask how they could get me off the streets."

"Why was that bad?"

He sighed. "Different reasons. For the first year, I was always afraid my father would find me."

"Do you really think he was looking?"

"Not hard." Ryan shrugged. "Maybe not at all. But I was a scared kid who thought that every social worker and cop in the country had my photo and would send me back to him as soon as they recognized my face or learned my real name."

"Oh. That's right. You used a street name."

"Mo." He rolled his eyes. "I thought it sounded tough. And being tough mattered a *lot* back then."

"But after the first year, you didn't think your father was still looking for you?"

"Not really. But I still wasn't going to take the chance of being returned to him. I wasn't even going to let him find out what state I was in." He added, "Anyhow, by the time I'd survived a year on the streets, I knew to be wary of *all* adults."

"All? Why?"

"Well, apart from the ones who might send a kid back to the home he ran away from, I heard stories from kids who'd run away from foster care, and I didn't want to wind up there, either."

"But I have a friend who's a foster parent, and she and her husband are wonderful—"

"But that wasn't the kind of story I heard from other runaways," he explained. "Because kids with foster parents like your friends don't usually run away to live and die on the street." When she nodded, he continued, "And then there are a lot of adults who prey on homeless kids."

"Such as?"

"Such as perverts and sadists whose tastes and habits I refuse to describe to you, Sara. They and their customers get off on practices which a lot of kids don't survive, and so they need a steady supply of them."

He'd nearly been taken by someone like that his first

month on the street. He'd also known a girl who simply disappeared one day; and then her body turned up months later. Ryan had trouble sleeping for a long time after learning the details of what had been done to her. Kids disappeared off the street all the time that way. People talked about it, people wondered. And once in a while someone would survive to tell the tale—or would leave behind a corpse which did the same.

"I can't imagine how you stayed alive," Sara said, still holding his hand. "I can hardly imagine the strength, courage, and brains it took for you to survive."

In fact, he had done things to survive which he'd much rather she didn't *try* imagine. Things that were best left in the dark shadows of his past.

"How long did you live on the streets?" she asked.

"It was a little over two years. Then I met Catherine."

Sara withdrew her hand. "How?"

"I was . . ." He thought back. "Picking pockets in the neighborhood where she used to have a condo. I liked working prosperous areas. They were clean and pretty, and they felt safe. Catherine noticed me before long. She could tell I didn't belong there—which made her wonder what I was doing there." After a moment, he added, "I noticed her, too. Very beautiful. Very elegant. Her clothes looked so good, I wanted to eat them. After a while, I started flirting with her whenever I saw her. She always acted like a lady, but I could tell she sort of liked me. Eventually, she started paying me to do odd jobs for her once in a while. Deliver a package or wash her car. Errands like that."

"And then she hired you to have sex with a client?"

"God, no," he said. "I was a scrawny, dirty, foul-mouthed, street boy. I definitely wasn't ripe for her kind of clients."

"Then how did it happen?"

He wondered how to tell her. He wondered if he should tell her at all.

"Ryan?"

He decided to tell her the relevant part. "I got raped and beaten."

"What?" Her hand covered his again.

"Yeah. And it was pretty bad."

"Ryan." She looked horrified.

"I thought I was going to die. I'd never been in so much pain. Catherine had once given me her phone number, when she wanted me to call her about an errand I was doing for her. So I'd memorized it. Probably because I had a terrible crush on her, of course. So I went to the nearest phone—crawling most of the way—and called her collect. She accepted the charges, and . . ."

He paused as the waitress came over to collect his empty glass and ask if he'd like another drink.

"No, thanks." Apart from Catherine's strict rules about alcohol, seeing what booze did to his father ensured that Ryan always chose to stop at one.

The waitress said to Sara, "Are you still working on yours?"

"Um, yes." Sara looked at her wine as if she hadn't known it was there. To Ryan's surprise, she suddenly picked up her glass and downed half its contents in one long swallow. Then she made a horrible face—which made him smile. That was her way. She could make him smile, even in the middle of *this* story.

When they were alone again, Sara prompted, "So you phoned Catherine . . ."

He nodded. "I could hardly talk, and I was very confused—couldn't really tell her where I was. She kept asking me questions, trying to locate me. I passed out in the middle of the call and just lay there in the dark."

"Oh, Jesus." Sara covered her mouth with her hand and kept gazing at him, her eyes sparkling with tears.

"She got one of her boys, a guy called Jason, and they got in her car and came looking for me. It took her until after dawn to find me, but she didn't give up. She just kept looking. For *me*—a street kid she barely even knew."

"My God, I would think any decent human being would have kept look—"

"That's because you don't know how dangerous it was to spend the night searching that neighborhood. But she knew. And she did it, anyway."

"But—"

"When she finally found me, she and Jason put me in the car. She didn't leave me there to die—"

"How could anyone have left you th—

"—or dump me in some clinic, or drop me off at some emergency room. She didn't call the cops, or social services, or anyone else that I didn't want messing with me." He held Sara's gaze and tried to make her understand. "She took me home and took care of me. She got a doctor to come see me, and she gave him my street name—she wouldn't even let him ask for my real name. She got blood tests done on me, got pain pills and antibiotics for me, cleaned me up, and poured fluids into me. I'd have died if it wasn't for her."

"But—"

"Catherine saved my life, Sara."

"Ryan, you were a kid, and you'd been brutally—"

"I asked her for help, and she gave it. She saved my life. And she took me off the streets forever."

Catherine never actually suggested Ryan live with her

permanently. But, after more than two years in the streets, he suddenly had enough to eat, a clean bed in a room of his own, and a safe home with someone he trusted. So he had no intention of leaving until she told him to; and she never did.

"She took care of me," he said. "Maybe, at first, she thought I could be like a son to her. Or maybe, for a little while, she wanted to do something charitable. I don't know. Maybe she just cared what happened to me."

"Or maybe she'd noticed, even under the dirt, how good-looking and charming you were, even at that age," Sara said, "and she realized you could become a profitable employee in her business."

"I don't know," he repeated. "But I don't think so, Sara. In those days, I didn't remotely resemble anyone's idea of an expensive date."

"*I* can imagine what she saw in you back then, even if you can't."

He decided to move on rather than argue about it. "When I was all healed, Catherine started, uh, renovating me. I wanted to be whatever she wanted me to be, so I tried hard to please her. Jason started taking me to the gym to build up my body, and Catherine started teaching me how to talk, how to dress, how to act like I belonged in an expensive restaurant or at the theatre. She gave me books and magazines to read, because women like her don't enjoy talking to someone who's ignorant. I'd been a working class schoolboy, then a grubby, sly street kid. She started training me to be . . ." He shrugged. "Someone who doesn't seem at all out of place with wealthy women."

"What else . . ." Sara paused, as if about to change her mind, but then said with resolve, "What else did she train you to do?"

"I think you know the answer to that," he said quietly.

"So what did she do?" Sara's tone revealed her distaste. "Just hop into bed with the underage kid in her house and relieve you of your virginity?"

"I hadn't been a virgin for almost two years, Sara."

"Oh. I guess there were girls living on the street, too."

"Yes," he said.

"So you already had some experience."

"And I was completely infatuated with Catherine. Sexually obsessed. I was also young enough that, uh, my hormones were always eager for exercise."

Despite that, he had never made a move towards her, and maybe he never would have. He knew from having stolen a peek at her driver's license that she was nearly twenty years older than he. She had an air of cool, firm authority that didn't readily invite audacity. And she could kick him out of her home and send him back into the streets the moment he irritated or offended her. So he just fantasized about her. A lot.

She knew it, of course. In retrospect, he realized that she had encouraged his infatuation and deliberately teased his sexual appetite for her.

"But I was living with her for almost a year before we finally had sex."

He'd realized fairly soon after moving in with Catherine exactly what kind of business she was running out of her elegant condo. The world had changed him too much since childhood for Ryan—whom Catherine now called Kevin—to be shocked by this; he was just shocked to discover, living here, how much some people would pay for a fuck.

He also knew that Catherine didn't fuck for money herself, she just procured. Very successfully.

Not that she was celibate. Ryan knew that she slept with

Jason sometimes. There was also an older man who came to the house every once in a while. Catherine wouldn't even tell Ryan who he was; she just told Ryan to clear out whenever the guy came around. He smelled like The Man, so Ryan was happy to disappear on those occasions. Jason once told Ryan the guy was "an important friend" who helped Catherine out sometimes. In exchange, she treated him like a lover when he came calling.

Then one night, while Ryan was lying on the couch in the living room with a book, Catherine came into the room dressed in elegant lounge clothes, sat down to talk to him, and . . . slowly, artfully seduced him.

"The main event was over in less than a minute," Ryan recalled wryly, staring at Sara's half-empty glass. "I wasn't a virgin, but I had an awful lot to learn."

"And she taught you," Sara said in a brittle voice.

"Yes."

Over the next few months, during which time he turned eighteen, he and Catherine lived as lovers. Sexual pleasure took on dimensions and qualities he had never previously dreamed of as a scared kid seeking a moment of human warmth in his occasional, desperate couplings with girls on the street. Catherine taught him to make love, to indulge the senses, to drown in pleasure . . . and then she taught him to control his own needs in favor of ensuring the sex was sensational for a woman. She also instructed him in a thousand details of intimacy related to sex, molding him into her image of an ideal lover.

"One for whom she can charge high prices," Sara said.

"Yes."

"Did you know that's what you were being prepared for?"

"I'm not sure," he said vaguely.

"You didn't wonder? You didn't *ask?*"

"I wasn't going to do anything to rock the boat. Turning eighteen only meant no one could ever send me back to my father again. Legally, I was free. In reality, though, I was the same helpless, ignorant, homeless kid I'd been the night Catherine had scraped my bloody carcass off the ground and taken me home."

"When did you find out what she intended to do with you?"

"Around the time she started sleeping with another of the escorts."

"That must have hurt."

In fact, it hurt him so much that, for once, he talked back, created a scene, and made melodramatic threats. He was stunned at Catherine's firm assertion, in response to his wounded fury, that she couldn't keep devoting all her time to him anymore. The business was growing, she was bringing in some new escorts to keep up with the demand, and she was buying a bigger place in which to live and work. She had done so much for Kevin already, didn't he appreciate it? Was this jealousy and possessiveness how he repaid her generosity and kindness to him?

"Oh, good grief," Sara said.

Catherine moved into the townhouse in Cow Hollow and let Ryan continue living in the condo. One of her other boys was usually living in the other bedroom. Catherine started setting up dates between Ryan and some of her girls.

"Why?" Sara asked.

"So I'd get used to a variety of women. And she wanted some of them to, uh, teach me skills that I have no intention of describing to you."

At Catherine's request, Jason also got involved in Ryan's education, giving him tips on maintaining an erection when he was tired or bored, teaching him how to groom and take care of himself, advising him in detail about condoms and other products.

"Condoms . . ." Sara clearly struggled for a moment with what she wanted to ask. "Ever since you told me what you do, I've wondered, um . . ."

"Safe sex. Every time. No exceptions," he said succinctly. "Ever since Catherine took me in. No client has ever asked me to forego it, but I'm supposed to refuse if they do—even if that means losing their business. Catherine has no intention of being ruined by a massive lawsuit because one of her escorts gives someone an infection or a disease, let alone a fatal one."

"So you're not . . . I don't have to worry that you'll get sick?" she asked tactfully.

He shook his head. "And I get a blood test every month." He added in a bland voice, "Company policy. No exceptions."

Sara nodded and closed her eyes. After a long moment, she said, "So you had all this *preparation*—"

"Also three meals a day," he said quietly, "a lot of nice clothes, and a very nice place to live. And Catherine was paying for all of it."

Sara put her hands on her head as if it were throbbing.

"When she turned me out . . . er, put me to work . . . It was okay, Sara. Really. Not awful or a nightmare, or anything like that." He wanted to be honest about this with her. "I didn't mind it. In fact, compared to where I'd been in life, I usually liked it. The only thing that really hurt me was that Catherine and I weren't lovers anymore." After a moment, he added, "Well, not exclusively, I mean. We still had sex sometimes. But I knew she slept with other boys, and it bothered me for a long time."

"Boys?" she said scathingly, her head bowed and her hands still pressed against her forehead.

"Men," he amended. "In the life, prostitutes are called things like 'working girl' and 'rent boy.' Catherine's other boys were all five, ten, even fifteen years older than I was when I started out. I was the only . . . youngster."

"And women just pay for a boy's—a man's—company?" She sounded dazed. "Why? Why would someone *do* that?"

"To get exactly what they want." After a moment, he added, "And some people just like to feel they're buying something that other people can't afford."

"It just seems so weird for a woman to do that."

"Male clients are a lot more common," he admitted.

She lowered her hands and lifted her head to meet his gaze. The question in her candid face was obvious.

So he said, "When I was young, Catherine would send me to these private parties with a few other escorts. We were supposed to be whatever the guests wanted us to be." The first time he'd attended one of those parties, Ryan had paired off with a young woman who described herself to him as an up-and-coming rock musician, and they'd fucked their brains out. Hot, energetic sex in a luxurious place, and he got paid for it. It sure beat eating out of Dumpsters. "At the second or third party I went to . . ." He shrugged. "A man wanted me. That wasn't unusual. Especially when I was younger."

Sara kept staring at him, clearly upset. "You . . . You . . ."

He hesitated before saying, "I was polite, as I'd been taught, but I refused. The client—who ran these parties—complained to Catherine. I told her I wouldn't do it. I didn't care that most of the other boys did—"

"They do?"

"Not all of them, but a lot of them. Even if they're

straight. It's just business, Sara."

"Oh, my God." She put her head back in her hands.

"Because men buy it—sex—a whole lot more often than women do."

"That's what I thought. I didn't know *any* women bought it."

"Anyhow, Catherine and I argued about it—"

"She *argued* with you about it? She tried to make you—"

"But because of what had happened to me in the street the night she took me in . . ." He shrugged again. "She agreed, in the end. And she never deliberately put me in that position again."

"Gosh, what a Good Samaritan."

"Or a good Sumerian," he muttered.

"Sumerian?" She lifted her head and blinked at him.

He waved a hand. "This kid said that this morning. I keep thinking about him."

She studied him for a moment. "You identify with this kid, don't you?"

"I *was* this kid. Only a little smarter and more street-wise." He frowned. "And if I could barely survive for the two years I was on the street, what chance has *he* got?"

"Then why don't you help him?"

He met her eyes, and he was stunned to see her looking at him as if she thought he, of all people, *could* help that kid.

When he didn't reply, Sara said, "Despite all your touching gratitude to Catherine—"

"Sara, that's—"

"—the one plan I won't go along with is getting this kid involved with her, too."

"*Jesus,* Sara! What do you think I am?" he snapped. "I'm not going to drag a *kid* into . . ." He remembered they were in a public place and lowered his voice. "I am *not* dragging a kid—or anyone else—into prostitution. This is the hand I got dealt, and I've had to play it. I'm not sitting here *recommending* it to you as a way of life—"

"I know that." She tried to put her hand over his again, but he withdrew it and glared at her.

"—let alone as something I'd lure a kid into—"

"Ryan, I'm sorry."

"—or as a great solution to a runaway's problems!"

"I didn't mean—"

"Yes, you did, Sara."

She sighed. "Maybe I did. I don't know. I'm sorry."

"I'm a whore," he said tightly, "but I'm not a sleazy bastard—"

"I know that."

"—and I don't prey on kids."

"I'm sorry."

He looked down. After a moment, he asked, "Did you really think I'd do that?" When she didn't answer, he said, "I've been honest. You have to be honest, too. Is that what you think of me?"

He felt a little sick when she didn't answer immediately.

After a heavy moment, she finally said, "I understand why it seemed . . . No, to be fair, why it *was* the best option in your life once upon a time." She paused. "But I don't understand why you're still doing it." When he didn't reply, she continued, "Ryan, you have everything going for you—"

"No, I don't."

"You're intelligent, good-looking, charming—"

"A great escort," he said with grim irony.

"You could do something else with your life. Something you wouldn't have to hide from people or lie about."

"Like what?" He shook his head. "Sara, I have no work history, no skills, and I have an arrest record."

"You could get out of this life," she insisted.

"I *tried,*" he snapped. "It didn't work. I'm stuck, Sara."

She stared in surprise and waited for him to say more.

He reached for his wallet, threw some money on the table, and stood up. "Macy will be standing at my front door with his legs crossed by now."

Sara rose, too, and followed him out of the bar.

CHAPTER ELEVEN

Now *he* was avoiding *her.*

Sara sighed despondently and stared at the blinking cursor on her computer screen.

When she'd been miserable in her day job . . . When her comfortable but unsatisfying relationship with her boyfriend, Nathan, had ended after two years . . . When her mother was dying . . . Sara had coped with those hard times by throwing herself into her work and disappearing into the world of her novels. Immersing herself in the fiction she created, and which often controlled her as much as she controlled it. Writing was not only Sara's passion and her obsession, it had also been a solace to her in times of grief. It was a healthy, satisfying, productive means of exorcising her demons and focusing her energy when the rest of her life was going to hell.

And now, when she needed her concentration so much, when her career was on the line, when her very identity as a writer was in question . . . She had produced a grand total of two paragraphs all day. And they were both crap. She'd probably have to scrap them.

Damn Ryan!

The one good thing she could say about his behavior lately was that it had taken her mind off being dumped by her literary agent last week.

Sara peered into her coffee cup, saw nothing but congealed dregs there, and scowled.

Ryan had been so sweet, so supportive, and so intelligent

in his reaction to her agent dumping her. How could he be such a comfort to her sometimes, and drive her so nuts at other times?

Ever since bringing her home from the bar so he could take Macy for his walk that evening, he'd been ducking her company. When he couldn't avoid her, he kept the conversation superficial. This had been going on for five days now.

How could he tell her such personal things . . . and then behave since then as if none of that had occurred between them?

She wondered if her reaction had hurt him, if she'd offended or distressed him that evening in the bar. She'd tried to broach the subject since then, but—on the rare occasions when he deigned to be in her company—he kept shifting the conversation, evading the topic, and avoiding another serious discussion.

How could he do this to her?

Sara wiped some dust off her monitor, realized she'd have to do some cleaning before her housewarming party on Saturday, and went into the kitchen.

Ryan was intuitive, intelligent, sensitive, kind, funny, attractive, and personable. Sara thought that he was surely the strongest and bravest person she'd ever known, and she could scarcely imagine how resourceful he'd needed to be to survive the challenges he'd encountered as a boy.

How could a man like that think he had nothing better to do with his life than prostitution?

Whenever she was with him, she felt simultaneously more excited and more comfortable than she'd ever felt with anyone in her life. Didn't he feel it, too? And if he did, how could he simply trot off to more dinner dates and sexual encounters with other women?

For God's sake, stop thinking about him, and think about your damn book, *would you?*

She was about to pick up the coffee canister, but she paused a moment to consider how tense she was, then picked up the canister of decaf, instead.

The story of Ryan's life was a nightmare that began the moment his mother died. Sara thought about what a loving, nurturing parent she must have been, to have raised a boy who could survive what Ryan eventually survived with his soul, his sense of humor, and even his sense of honor intact.

Oh, yes, he was honorable. He could have continued lying and gotten anything he wanted from Sara, emotionally and sexually, and he knew it. But, instead, he had chosen to be honest with her, even knowing how she might react.

How I have *reacted.*

She poured water into the coffee machine, turned it on, and stood there watching it brew as she wondered if she should just go ahead and sleep with Ryan, despite what she now knew.

He had said what was between them was different. That he felt he needed a different word for it.

If it's not the same as what he does at work . . .

Regardless of how many women he'd had sex with in his life—or how many women he'd had sex with in the last *month*—Sara accepted that it didn't mean anything to him. Not only because she chose to believe what he told her, but also because of the way his loneliness reached out to her. As hers, she supposed, reached out to him.

She wondered if his loneliness had intensified beyond bearing since the two of them first met, as hers had.

He found unwanted animals, adopted them, and spoiled them. They were something for him to love, someone for him to come home to. They were the family he'd lost in childhood and so far hadn't replaced in adulthood. They were something he could protect and tend. He rescued them as no one had rescued him.

Until Catherine.

Oh, man, I can't believe that woman!

She had a hell of a hold over Ryan. He was so grateful to her for getting him off the streets, he couldn't see how she had exploited a helpless adolescent. He was actually *loyal* to her. He felt he owed her his life. And that he *deserved* the existence he was stuck in.

What can I do for him?

He could have chosen to maintain a casual distance from Sara ever since she'd moved into this apartment. He could have retreated from their friendship rather than let it lead here, to this stark exposure of all that he chose to hide from people who knew him as Ryan. But he hadn't. He had continued moving forward with their relationship, knowing full well that he might lose her affection and respect after being truthful with her. He was that brave.

She wished she knew what to do. How to respond to the naked honesty he'd shown her. How to give him the kind of support and confidence he had such a talent for giving her. Good God, how would she ever have gotten through the past couple of months without Ryan's friendship?

What could she give him in return for all that? How could she help this lost man, this abandoned soul, this wayward altar boy fallen so far from grace?

What can I do for him?

She thought back to their dizzying embrace in the stairwell last week, after her tears had faded. When she recalled the tension in his touch, the hunger in his gaze, she knew perfectly well what she could do for him, though it seemed an absurd paradox, given what he did for a living.

Was Sara, by rejecting him sexually now that she knew the truth, merely confirming what Ryan thought about himself? That he wasn't good for anything besides prostitution, that he was just a cleaned-up street boy, that he had nothing real to offer a woman—only the façade which Catherine had created?

Or maybe Sara was just trying to rationalize a choice she increasingly wanted to make despite her better judgment.

Gosh, no, I just think it would be so good for him *if I went to bed with him.*

What a good Sumerian she was.

Because he doesn't get nearly enough sex.

She felt like beating her head against the wall.

It wouldn't be just sex. It would mean something to him. He had said so. And that made it different for him. It would mean something to her, too, and that made it . . .

"It would mean something to me," she murmured.

And it would mean something to him.

Sara sat staring at the coffeepot and suddenly couldn't remember why anything mattered beyond those two facts.

"Sara?" he called from the living room.

"Yagh!" She jumped in startled fear and dropped her coffee cup, which crashed to the floor and shattered into a million pieces.

"Sara?" Ryan came into the kitchen. His gaze took in the broken cup and Sara standing there with her hand over her pounding heart. "Did I startle you? Sorry."

"Where did you come from?" she snapped.

"The balcony," he said. "You left your doors open, so I—"

"I've been leaving them open so you'd know you could come in if you suddenly felt like lowering yourself to spend some time with me."

He looked a little wary. "Is the writing going badly?"

"What makes you think that?" she said defensively.

"Oh, your mood."

"My mood is *your* fault!"

"And you're on the same page you were on the last time I looked, which was two days ago."

"You looked at my computer screen?" she demanded. "You *looked?*"

"It's sitting right out there in the open, Sara."

"I live alone!"

"You left the doors open for me."

"I didn't think you'd come in!"

He lifted one brow. "Do you want me to leave?"

"No," she said quickly. "You should help me clean up. You made me drop the cup, after all."

His lips twitched. "Okay. I'll help. But do me a favor and lay off the caffeine."

She handed him a broom. "Where have you been?" she demanded.

"Today? I took Adam for a meal again."

"Adam? Oh! That kid?"

"Yeah."

"He finally gave you a name?"

"Yes." He added wryly, "After I'd fed him four times and let him keep a hundred dollars of my money. Trust doesn't come cheap."

"He trusts you now?"

"No, I guess 'trust' would be an exaggeration. But today was the first time he came over to talk to me when he saw me, instead of panicking or trying to bolt."

"So he's decided you're not a sadistic pervert who wants to torture and kill him?"

"Actually, no, I don't think he's decided that yet. But

he's getting a little closer to it."

"I hate to imagine what that's like. To be so helpless. To be a kid all alone in a hostile and dangerous world, with no rights and no protection."

He nodded and continued his task. Sara folded her arms and watched in silence as he swept the floor thoroughly. She noticed the final faint discoloration had faded from his eye since the last time she'd seen him. That meant he'd be going back to work any moment. In fact, maybe that's why he'd been so scarce lately; maybe he was *already* working again.

He gave her an amused look. "When you said I had to help, you really meant I had to clean it up *for* you, didn't you?"

"Why won't you quit this life?"

The plaintive question was out of her mouth before she even knew she was thinking it, let alone contemplating saying it aloud.

He sighed and rested his forehead against the broom for a moment. "I tried. I can't. That's why I've been avoiding you ever since you asked about it. Because this . . ." He made a vague gesture indicating the two of them. ". . . this will only hurt you. And I don't want to hurt you."

"Too late now."

He met her eyes. "I'm sorry."

"What do you mean, you tried? How? What happened?" When he didn't reply, she said querulously, "Try *harder.*"

He gave a startled puff of laughter. Then he bent over to sweep the little pile of rubble into the dustpan. "A few years ago, I decided I wanted to quit. Catherine didn't take me seriously at first. Then she was angry. We fought about it a lot."

"She inflicted guilt, of course," Sara said with a sneer, sitting down at the kitchen table.

"Well, she did a lot for me, Sara." He emptied the dustpan into the garbage can then sat down at the table, too.

"Ryan, I believe you when you say she saved your life that night." It still made her feel dizzy with horror to think of him brutalized, alone, and lying unconscious in the dark street at the age of sixteen. "And, given the things that happened to you, maybe she saved your life twice over by taking you off the streets for good." She shook her head as she added, "But if you did that for Adam, would you think it entitled you to turn him into a prostitute and make him work for you?"

"No. But if you did that for Adam, wouldn't you wind up one day encouraging him to become a writer?"

"Ryan," she said sincerely, "I wouldn't encourage *anyone* to become a writer."

He chuckled, his mood shifting suddenly. Then he asked, "Have you thought over what we talked about a few days ago?"

"Constantly."

"So are you going to do it?"

Go to bed with you?

"Sara?" he prodded.

Am I going to do it? Maybe I really am. What do I say now?

"Well?" he asked. "Are you going to write to some of those agents?"

"Huh?" She blinked. "Oh! *That* conversation."

"Yes, *that* conversation, Sara."

On one of the few occasions they'd spoken in recent days, she'd been trying to decide whether or not to query a couple of literary agents now, or wait until the book was done. Although Sara had dark superstitions about discussing a work-in-progress with anyone, let alone showing it to them, she nonetheless felt it would be smart to hire a new agent before she completed the manuscript, so that the agent could start marketing it as soon as it was done. That would be a more economical use of her time than searching for an agent only *after* the book was finished. On the other hand, agents tended to respond more intelligently to a completed novel, since partial books and book proposals were only shadows of what they would become when finally completed. So Sara had been having trouble making up her mind.

But after talking it over with Ryan, and considering his sensible opinions, she had decided to start looking for a new agent now rather than waiting.

"Yes, yes," she said absently, "I've sent queries to a couple of agents. Don't change the subject. Catherine took advantage of you when she turned you—"

"Catherine doesn't think of prostitution—or sex—the way you do, Sara." His briefly improved mood flattened again as they returned to this subject. "It's just business to her. A lucrative one. She probably thought she was doing right by me when she started training me to—"

"Oh, good grief, Ryan! You don't know nearly as much about women as you think you do. She knew *exactly* what she was doing."

He held up a hand to forestall further argument about it. "Anyhow," he said, "when I told her I was getting ready to quit, we fought about it. Meanwhile, I decided I wanted to put aside a pile of money, so I wouldn't wind up in the street again as soon as I stopped working for her. I'd spent every penny I'd ever earned. On clothes, a car, dining out, a nice apartment I'd moved into a couple of years earlier, other stuff . . . I didn't really know where it went. I'd been stupid about money—"

"You hadn't had anyone to teach you. And I'm sure *she* encouraged you to spend it as fast as you earned it. It would have been a way for her to maintain control over you."

"So, with an eye to leaving the life altogether, I started doing tricks on the side, in addition to my tricks for Catherine. To make extra money."

"That had to be a little . . . tiring."

"I was young, and I ate lots of protein." His voice was dry. "Before long, she found out I was free-lancing. I'd never seen her so mad at *anybody*. I agreed to stop it—but I was lying. And when she found out I was still doing it, I thought she'd have a stroke, she was so enraged."

By then, their fights were legendary among the rest of the employees. The two of them went round and round in circles, and he supposed people listened outside the door while he and Catherine shouted at each other. He didn't understand why she wouldn't let him quit working for her. She had let Jason leave, she let other people leave. So why wouldn't she let *him* leave?

Sometimes she'd flatter him: There was nobody else like him, he was her number one boy, there were clients whom only *he* was charming and smart enough to satisfy. Sometimes she'd make it personal: He was her favorite, there was something special between them. And sometimes she'd get straight to the point: She had saved his goddamn life, she'd taught him everything he knew, she'd made him what he was, and now he *belonged* to her.

"Well," said Sara. "At least she was frank about it."

"I drove her crazy," Ryan said. "I pushed her, I lied to her, I challenged her, I goaded her. I decided I'd either make her let me go or I'd make her kill me. I wanted *out,* and I'd do whatever was necessary to get there."

Sara could see that he'd brought the same determination

to his escape from Catherine that he'd brought to his escape from his father or his survival in the streets. However, unlike those earlier challenges, Catherine was clever. She also, Sara could tell, had an emotional hold over Ryan that made her a more powerful foe. Yes, there was loyalty, gratitude, and guilt mixed with Ryan's resentment and disillusionment. Even he knew that. There was also, Sara suspected, a more primal connection, too. Ryan had been infatuated and sexually obsessed with Catherine for a long time; and she was the woman who had taught him to make love, after all.

All of that put together, Sara guessed, ensured that, however determined Ryan was, it had nonetheless been a complicated and difficult decision for him to leave Catherine.

And that amoral, opportunistic bitch had done everything she could to make it even more difficult and complicated, Sara thought angrily as Ryan told her about their fights and Catherine's attempts to manipulate him.

"And then I got arrested," Ryan said wearily. "For the second time. I was doing a free-lance trick in . . ." He paused and shook his head. "It's pretty sleazy, Sara."

"It's all right, just tell me." It wouldn't do either of them any good for her to be squeamish. She was the one who'd insisted on talking about why he was still escorting for a living.

"Okay." After a moment, he continued, "The client and I were having sex in her car. It was her idea—and she was the customer, after all. The cops caught us at it, figuring it would be just a public lewdness charge. Which would have made me feel stupid enough, since I knew better than to risk that. But that was the least of my worries," he said darkly, "because there was a big bag of blow right there on the seat with us. I didn't snort any of it—I don't do drugs, not ever—but, like an idiot, I had let her hand it to me before I knew what it was. So my fingerprints were all over it. Which gave some credibility to her story when she told them I was a dealer."

"Oh, *no*."

"They hauled us in. I was twenty-four, I had no visible means of support, no education, and I was wearing designer clothing and had a lot of cash on me."

"So they figured you had to be a drug dealer, as she said."

"She was married to a wealthy man, and her lawyer made me the fall guy. The record of my previous arrest didn't help, either."

"For soliciting?"

He said grimly, "Rape."

"Rape?" Her jaw dropped. "Ryan, whatever secrets you've kept, I know you're no rapist. How on earth did you get a rape charge?"

He sighed. "Well, some rich girl in Marin had two friends who decided to buy her an escort for her eighteenth birthday."

"You were someone's *birthday* present?" When she saw him shift uneasily in response to her appalled tone, she added more mildly, "How could girls that age even find an escort?"

"Oh, that's easy enough, Sara. Especially these days, with escorts advertising on the Web. Even Catherine's agency is on the Web—though her website is so discreet, you might not realize what she's selling if you just stumbled across it by accident."

"So these teenage girls found her on the Web?"

"Oh, them? No. One of them had a stepmother who used Catherine's agency, and I guess the stepdaughter pried a lot." He shrugged. "Anyhow, Catherine sent me to the appointment. I was nineteen, and she thought the girl would like someone her own age. Well, it turned out that the best thing this nice Catholic schoolgirl could say about two years of regular sex with her boyfriend was that it didn't hurt after the first time." He tilted his head. "So she found our date pretty mind-blowing. Not exactly a big recommendation—she'd have found a date with a *vibrator* pretty mind-blowing. But she hired me a few more times."

"How do kids get that kind of money?"

"They have filthy rich parents who give them credit cards and don't pay much attention to what they're doing with them," he said. "Anyhow, we met in her car, or else in her house when her parents weren't there."

When he paused, Sara realized what was coming. "The girl's parents caught her with you?"

He nodded. "They came back from a party hours before she expected them. We had the stereo turned way up and didn't hear a thing—until we heard them enter the room and start screaming." Ryan's expression was resigned as he recalled what happened next. "The girl saw how furious her parents were. She panicked and told them I'd threatened her and forced her. They chose to believe her.

"I got cornered, arrested, and hauled off, scared to death. The following morning, Catherine sent a lawyer to explain the situation to the parents. He showed them a record of their daughter's credit card charges at the agency. He pointed out to them that I had nothing to lose in the scandal I would make if their daughter continued accusing me of rape, but *they* might not find the public embarrassment so easy to bear." He added, "I was released when the charges were dropped."

Sara digested this for a moment before saying, "Then

there you were, five years later, with a rape arrest on your record, a bag of cocaine with your fingerprints on it, and a charge of drug dealing."

"Don't forget public lewdness," he said sourly. "And I didn't think it would help my situation to say, 'No, officer, I wasn't dealing drugs, I was just turning a trick.' I didn't figure they'd drop the drug charges just because I admitted to prostitution."

"What happened?"

"Well, they locked me up. I got arraigned, and my bail was high because I had no job, no family, no ties. The judge considered me a flight risk. My lawyer wasn't cheap, and he wasn't very encouraging, either. I thought I was going to go to prison on drug charges, and I was terrified." He met her eyes. "*Terrified,* Sara. I'd been raped and beaten within an inch of my life once already, and I didn't want to repeat the experience. I couldn't get locked up for a couple of years with guys who do that for fun. I just *couldn't,* Sara."

"You asked Catherine for help."

He nodded. "She said she knew people, she could make the whole mess go away. But the first time I got arrested, I'd been working for her, so her protection was automatic. This time, though, I'd gotten in trouble while free-lancing, even after she'd told me half a dozen times to stop."

"So in exchange for her help," Sara guessed, "she wanted you back where she thought you belonged."

"Yes. She told me I would have to work for her, and only for her. No more free-lancing, and I'd have to give up the idea of quitting or leaving."

"And you agreed?"

"No, I told her to go to hell. I told her I'd find a way out of this mess without her." He closed his eyes briefly and shook his head. "But I couldn't. I was screwed. The more clear that became, the more scared I got. I fired my lawyer and hired another, but he said the exact same thing the first one had: I should cop a plea in exchange for a reduced sentence, because they'd just put me away for a longer time if I made them go to the trouble of prosecuting me."

Sara waited for him to continue.

"I couldn't go to prison," he said. "I knew what would happen to me there. So I went back to Catherine and agreed to her terms. Including the new one she named then, which was that, because of the 'cost' of helping me out of this mess, she'd be taking a bigger cut of my earnings in future."

"That sounds perfectly in character," Sara said with disgust.

"But she kept her word, Sara. She got the charges dropped. It was over."

"And you were under her thumb again. Just as much as you'd been when you were younger." After a moment, she asked, "Is that why you moved to this apartment? Because you had to reduce your expenses?"

"That, and also . . . I moved into this apartment because I thought it looked like someplace a happy person would live." When she gave him a questioning look, he said, "After that whole mess, I knew I couldn't get out, but I wanted some part of my life to be separate from . . . from Kevin's life. From Catherine's boy." He looked down. "I split myself into separates parts. Kevin is an expensive whore with a police record. Ryan Kinsmore is a decent guy who lives quietly in a friendly neighborhood and pays taxes on his 'modeling' income."

"You pay taxes on your earnings?"

"I do now. When I got arrested that second time, I realized what a tight corner I'd put myself in by having no visible income and not even the fiction of a normal lifestyle."

"So you made up the story about being a catalogue model."

"I figured that it explained my strange work schedule and my trips out of town, and that my lack of education wouldn't matter."

"And keeping yourself in such good shape and having such nice clothes—that fits most people's idea of a model, too."

"I also decided that, even if I couldn't get out of the life, it didn't do me any good to have no education. So I got my G.E.D. about six months before you moved in."

"The equivalent of a high school diploma?"

He nodded. "I just wanted to be . . . Different than I was. Better. When I'm here, using my real name. I wanted to be . . ."

Sensing his insecurity, she said, "I never would have guessed that you had no education. You read all the time—"

"It's a habit Catherine got me into."

"Your mind is quick, you're a problem solver, you're computer literate."

"Well, compared to you, *Macy* is computer literate."

She smiled. "You know, there are professional novelists who don't have college degrees."

"Really?" Like so many people, he seemed surprised by that. "Writers?"

"Really. And I've certainly met *plenty* of college graduates who don't strike me as better educated than you. Or as intelligent as you are."

He smiled, clearly pleased. "If that's true, it means a lot to me. That someone like you . . ." He grinned. "Likes me for my mind."

She smiled back. "Now that you have your G.E.D., if you wanted to study for another career, you could go to college and—"

He sighed. "I've just told you, Sara. A career change isn't possible."

It broke her heart. "Ryan." She put her hand on his cheek. "How can she do this to you? What kind of a person is she?"

"It's business, Sara."

"No, it's not! She's ruining your life! I think she's ruining *my* life now, too."

She regretted saying that when she saw how it pained him. He took her hand from his cheek, and pressed it against his mouth. "I think *I'm* ruining your life."

"No." After a moment, she admitted, "The jury's still out on that."

"I'm hurting you," he murmured. "Upsetting you. And interfering with your work."

"Well, I guess I'm hurting you, too." He closed his eyes and kissed her hand again. "Upsetting you. And as for interfering with your work . . ."

"Actually . . ." He opened his eyes. "That's what I came to talk to you about."

"Yes?" She sank into the feel of his breath against her knuckles, his thumb caressing her as he held her hand.

"I have to go away tomorrow."

That startled her out of her pleasant distraction. "You're going away?"

"I'll be back Friday," he assured her. "So I won't miss your party."

She pulled her hand out of his. "Work?"

"Yes." Aware of her withdrawal, he sat back a bit. "I wasn't even going to ask you to take care of the animals.

Under the circumstances, it seemed too . . ." He shrugged. "But I knew you'd be hurt—and maybe really worried—if I just left without saying goodbye. And then I wondered if you'd feel hurt if I *didn't* ask you to take care of them, because they're the same as always, even if you and I . . ." He rubbed his forehead. "I'm babbling."

"Where are you going? What are you going to be doing?" she demanded, frowning at him.

"Details aren't a good idea, Sara."

"No, if I'm going to be walking your dog while you're—"

"I'm going to the island," he snapped. "Catherine leases a villa in Mexico. A luxury retreat for clients."

"And what'll you be do—"

"I'm not telling you, Sara." He rose to leave. "I just wanted you to know I'll be gone for two—"

"I'll take care of them," she said as he walked past her.

He paused. "You don't have to. Not if this is too much to ask. If taking care of them is just going to make you think about me and what I'm doing, then it's better if I hire my old pet sitter again, or else take them to stay at the vet's."

"Your cat's so insecure she gets sick when you do that, Macy gets depressed, and only someone very fond of you would *ever* agree to look after that demented bird of yours," Sara said grumpily. "I'll take care of them. Don't worry about it."

"Thanks." He paused in the doorway and met her eyes as she looked over her shoulder at him. "*Are* you still very fond of me?"

"Yes." She felt as if he had thrown cold water on her, but she wouldn't toy with his emotions or make him doubt her regard for him. "What about Adam? Does he need looking after, too?"

He shook his head. "I don't want you going into that neighborhood without me."

"Oh. Okay."

Their eyes held. Sara's heart was bursting with things she wanted to say, but her brain felt numb and unable to herd the rampant feelings into coherent thoughts.

"When I get back," he said, "I'll help you get ready for your party." He shrugged. "Move furniture or carry groceries upstairs. Whatever. Okay?"

"Okay."

"Uh . . . Macy threw up today. But I think it was just because he ate my socks. It probably won't happen again."

"All right."

He couldn't seem to leave, and she couldn't look away. Miriam was right, the two of them had trouble saying goodbye in less than a half-hour.

She wanted to kiss him, hug him, touch him, *something*. But it wasn't wise. And, considering where she knew he was going tomorrow, she also wanted to hit him, shout at him, weep.

"Sara, I'm sorr—"

"Don't," she said. "Don't keep saying that to me."

He lowered his head. After a moment, he said, "I'll see you when I get back."

And until then, he would be . . . Sara pressed her fists against her temples, which were starting to throb.

Don't think about what he'll be doing until then. Just don't.

But the writer's imagination was a powerful thing, and Sara found she couldn't simply shut it off at will.

CHAPTER TWELVE

By nine o'clock Saturday night, Sara's little apartment was so crowded that the latest arrivals to her housewarming party couldn't even *enter* it. So they started partying in the hallway, their festive spirit undiminished by this minor inconvenience.

Ryan decided that he and Sara should discuss accommodating the overflowing guests more comfortably. So he sought her in the laughter-filled throng, where her friends and relatives were eating, drinking, talking, gesticulating, mingling, searching for the bathroom, and (in a few cases) guessing what Lance's murals were trying to say.

"I think he's saying he hates Sara!"

"*I* think he's trying to inspire Sara to write horror."

"It reminds me of township art."

"What the hell is township art?"

"Are we positive that Sara didn't paint this herself and is just trying to cast blame elsewhere now?"

Lance had been invited to the party, though he hadn't yet made an appearance. If he did, Ryan had a feeling that Sara's friends would be delighted with her wild-eyed, eccentric landlord.

As Ryan passed the drinks table he had set up this afternoon, he checked to make sure it didn't need replenishing. A quick glance revealed that, in fact, it probably wouldn't need replenishing until the following century. So many of the guests had brought wine, Sara might wind up with more bottles at the end of the night than she had started out with.

Nearby, a thin young man in glasses and conservative clothes was saying to a redheaded woman, "Wait! How could they pay him for the rewrite of a script that didn't exist in the first place? There was nothing *to* rewrite!"

"*See?* See what I'm saying?" the redhead said. "This is why we ought to go to Hollywood. It's like stealing!"

A fat, middle-aged man with glasses, long hair, a beard, and a strange hat snorted. "You mean it's like prostitution."

Ryan glanced curiously at him for a moment.

"Okay, that's a good story, I admit," said the younger man. "Nonetheless, it's *generally* true that Hollywood shits on writers even worse than New York does."

Ryan squeezed past three men and a blonde woman engrossed in a passionate discussion about Macintosh computers, then passed several people whom Sara had introduced to him earlier as old college friends. Then he spotted Sara herself.

She looked wonderful. Her hair was piled atop her head, with wispy dark curls escaping to lie against her fair skin. Her dangly earrings swung gracefully with every turn of her head. She wore some simple but exotic-looking outfit with tiny gold threads scattered throughout the fabric; they caught the light and gleamed subtly whenever she moved. She was clearly enjoying herself tremendously, reconnecting with the people in her life now that she had settled into the apartment well enough to take this break from her work and welcome them all into her home. Her face was prettily flushed, her eyes sparkled, and she was laughing a lot.

She was happy. And Ryan hadn't seen her look happy lately. It made him feel guilty. What the hell was he doing, clinging to her as he did? What could he possibly offer her that was worth the pain he was causing her?

The scratches on his back, which he'd gotten during his

stay on the island, suddenly seemed to burn. If Sara knew everything, would she even want him in her home, let alone in her bed?

And she was indeed on the verge of inviting him into her bed. He could see it in her eyes, in her body language, in the thoughts that drifted across her candid face when silence fell between them. She was leaning heavily towards it by now. Ryan knew that with the slightest nudge from him, she would open her bed, her arms, herself to him, and he could crawl inside and get warm there.

It was tempting. So tempting. But the scratches on his back burned in silent accusation. He didn't deserve to touch her. He should leave her alone.

He knew that. Yet, even so, because it was safe tonight, because they were surrounded by people and nothing could happen, when he came up behind Sara, he put his hands on her waist and squeezed affectionately. He knew he shouldn't, but he couldn't help it.

She paused in her conversation with her Great Aunt Minnie, a tiny, fierce, and immensely old lady whom Ryan had already met and found frightening, and smiled over her shoulder at him.

As someone elbowed past him, Ryan leaned into Sara, melding himself against her back and bottom, pressing closer to her. She snuggled back against him, inviting the contact. He lowered his head, resisted dropping a kiss on her neck, and said into her ear, "I'm going to open my balcony doors and my front door, so people can just circulate through both apartments."

She put her hand over one of his as it rested on her waist and turned her head, her cheek brushing against his. "Oh, are you sure? Somebody might spill something or—"

"If they do, I'll just make you clean my place tomorrow." He added, "I cleaned yours this morning, after all."

"Well, if you really don't mind . . ." She squeezed his hand and pressed it more firmly against her. "Opening your apartment would be wonderful, Ryan." She looked around. "I had no idea so many people would turn up."

Aunt Minnie asked, "How many did you invite?"

"Um . . . I'm not sure. I just kept inviting people as they came to mind."

Aunt Minnie made an exasperated gesture then announced she was going to check on the little pork-sausage appetizers she was heating up in the oven.

"I thought Jews didn't eat pork," Ryan said, sliding his arms around Sara's waist as Aunt Minnie abandoned them.

"Aunt Minnie is violently opposed to keeping kosher," Sara said. "She thinks it's a foolish custom invented by a misogynist patriarchy in primitive times and now clung to by credulous sycophants."

"I'm afraid of her," Ryan said.

"So is my father. Where is he, anyhow?"

"He was in the bedroom the last time I saw him. It sounded like he had found a Republican in there."

"Oh! Well, that'll keep him busy for hours, then."

He rested his cheek against her hair. "It looks like everyone you've ever met must be here."

She laughed. "No, no. Just everyone I *like*."

A tall, heavy, and lushly voluptuous black woman in a tight, floor-length, low-cut dress overheard this and said in a warm, earthy voice, "Just everyone she likes in the *Bay* area, she means." The woman grinned beautifully at Ryan and added, "Sara's parties are so famous, people in Portland, L.A., and Denver were thinking of coming!"

"How do you know people in all those places?" he asked Sara.

"Writers' conferences. Writers' e-lists. Writers' organizations," Sara said. "We meet each other everywhere."

"And so everyone hears what good parties Sara throws."

"Ryan," Sara said, "this is Delia. She runs an incredible bookstore in Berkeley, and she knows even more writers than I do. Delia, this is Ryan. He lives next door and keeps me from shooting the computer."

"Oh?" Delia smiled as her glance flickered over the two of them, Sara wrapped possessively in Ryan's embrace. "What else does he do for you?"

Suddenly aware of the impression he was creating, Ryan released Sara. "I'm guessing the crowd will keep getting bigger?"

Delia made an affirmative noise. "There are people I don't see here yet who told me they were definitely coming."

Sara added, "And the San Jose crowd isn't even here yet."

Ryan smiled at Sara and gestured towards his apartment. "Then I'll go open my doors, before you have to start making your guests wait in the street."

"I'll ask Miriam to bring some napkins and some food over there," she said as he left.

He pushed his way back through the crowd and out into the hall. Macy, attracted by all the commotion outside Ryan's front door, was lying with his head so close to it that Ryan accidentally hit him upon opening it. Macy yelped in protest, and several guests were inside comforting the dog before Ryan even finished inviting them to enter his apartment.

"He'll drool on you," Ryan warned.

The three women who were fawning on Macy waved aside this comment. One of them asked Ryan where he'd gotten Macy, then started telling him about the cats she'd adopted from various shelters.

"Cat," he said suddenly. "Excuse me for a minute."

He went into the bedroom, crouched down, and found her hiding under the bed, distressed by the sound of strangers in the living room. Realizing that all the company would be too much for her, and fearing that she might flee out the front door if startled by a well-meaning animal-lover trying to touch her, Ryan picked up his cat, put her in the bathroom with her sandbox, brought her water bowl from the kitchen, and then stuck a note on the closed bathroom door telling people to keep out. By the time he finished this task, a short, plump, dark-haired woman with glasses was looking over his shoulder at the note.

"Broken toilet?" she asked.

"No, it's Alley. My cat. She wants to be alone."

"Alley? As in, cat from the alley?"

"That's where I found her."

"That's perfect! I love it!"

She patted him companionably on the shoulder. Then she joined two other people who were sitting on his bed and arguing about "the princes in the tower," whoever *they* were.

Ryan went into the living room to make sure none of the guests there were foolish enough to disturb Mrs. Thatcher, whose cage sat covered in one corner. The three women who'd been fawning on Macy were now examining the fish in the tank. Sara's father was already sitting in Ryan's leather chair, as if he had preternaturally sensed its sudden availability all the way from Sara's bedroom and hastened here in response. Macy sat next to the chair, leaning his head against its arm while the old man scratched his ears with one hand and gesticulated with the other.

Abel Diamond was saying to an earnest-looking man of about thirty, "Why? Why would I have *three* books on this desert island? Why not two? Or ten? Maybe I could have one hundred classics on a CD ROM!"

"The point of the—"

"What am I doing on a desert island anyhow? How did I get there? It's a ridiculous premise!" Professor Diamond, who had earlier insisted Ryan call him Abel, saw Ryan and said, "Do *you* worry about getting stranded on a desert island with only three books? Is this likely to become a problem in your life?"

"I don't stay awake nights fretting about it," Ryan admitted.

"Who does? That's my point!"

"Ryan!" said Miriam, upon entering the open door with a large platter in her arms. "Sara told me you've offered to sacrifice your apartment to the cause. I come bearing food for the horde."

"Miriam!" Abel cried. "Do *you* ever worry about being stranded on a desert island?"

"In fact, Dad, I think about it constantly."

Her father made an exasperated gesture.

"Here, I'll take that," Ryan said, reaching for the platter of little party sandwiches which Miriam carried.

"No, no," Miriam said, "I've got it, Ryan. But why don't you help Jan?" She nodded over her shoulder to the woman entering the apartment right behind her. "Have I already introduced you? Janice Lieberman, Ryan Kinsmore."

Ryan took one of the two dessert trays balanced in Jan's arms. "Yes, you've already introduced us."

"Oh, okay. There's so many people here," Miriam said,

"I can't keep track. How many people did Sara invite, for goodness sake?"

"She doesn't know."

Miriam rolled her eyes. "Of course not."

Jan Lieberman met Ryan's gaze and smiled. "The second introduction is handy, though. I'm afraid I can't remember all your names."

"I can't remember all our names, either," Ryan said. "Just put that on the coffee table, Miriam."

He followed the two women to the coffee table and chatted with Jan as Miriam arranged the food. Jan, who had come to the party with Miriam, was about thirty, of average height, and had light brown hair styled in an attractive cut. She seemed a little shy, but very good-natured, and she was clearly interested in the eclectic crowd flooding the two apartments.

"Are you a writer, too?" she asked Ryan.

"No, I'm just the neighbor. You?"

"No, I'm a physical therapist."

"Napkins! I forgot to bring over napkins," Miriam said, hands on hips. "I'll be right back."

"Want help?" Jan asked.

Miriam absently reached out to squeeze the other woman's hand, and they laced their fingers together for a moment. "Don't be silly. How heavy are *napkins?* Stay here and talk to Ry—Hey!" She let go of Jan and moved to block Macy's path as he ambled over to examine the food that she had so thoughtfully placed within easy reach. "Ryan, Jan, you are both on duty now. Keep this damn dog away from the food."

"Macy, *no,*" Ryan said.

The dog gazed back at him with beatific innocence, as if wholly unaware of the sandwich tray sitting only six inches away from his nose.

"Macy," Ryan said warningly.

"Can't you lock him in the bathroom or something?"

"Miriam!" Jan chided. "He can't do that!"

Since Macy would whine and Alley would have hysterics, Ryan didn't contradict her.

"Miriam doesn't like dogs," Jan said to Ryan. "Not even mine."

"Oh, your dog is okay," Miriam said placatingly to her. "I'm getting used to him."

"Okay? My dog is the *best."* Jan said to Ryan, "Present company excepted, of course."

He smiled. "Oh, I love Macy, but even I have to admit he's an acquired taste."

"He's *drooling*. Ryan, he's drooling near the food!" Miriam said. "*Do* something about this."

"Macy," Abel called, noticing his daughter's irritation. "Come here, Macy. Good boy, Macy. *Goooood* boy."

"Okay, Dad, you're in charge of the dog. Ryan, you keep an eye on the food. And I," Miriam said, turning on her heel, "will go get some napkins."

Smiling with fond amusement, Jan said to Ryan, "Sorry. She can be a little bossy."

He smiled back, wondering what Sara was going to make of this. He was certain she didn't already know. She'd have talked to him about it, or at least been so distracted by it that he'd have noticed her mood.

"Young woman," Abel said to Jan.

"It's Jan," Ryan reminded him.

"Jan," Abel said, "what do *you* think?"

"About what?" she asked, smiling at Miriam's father.

Ryan listened to the subsequent conversation while his mind wandered. When two people habitually touched each other in affection, and apologized for each other, and started learning to compromise over things like pets . . .

Sara stuck her head in the door and looked at Ryan. "How's it going in here?"

"Fine," he replied. "Who are the princes in the tower?"

"Good grief, someone's on *that* riff again? Here, I brought wine." Sara came over to him and unloaded the three bottles in her arms. They stood close together for a moment, smiling into each other's eyes. Then Sara looked over Ryan's shoulder at Jan and said to her, "I've come in the nick of time. You need a top-up."

Jan replied, "Oh, no, thank you, Sara. I'm fine."

"Well, no one's allowed to leave until we've gone through more of this food and drink," Sara said.

Sara was sexually conventional, perhaps even more so than she herself realized. Ryan suspected that Miriam knew this; and she was probably anxious about it, given how close the two sisters were.

Sara put a hand on Ryan's arm and started to say something to him, but Miriam exclaimed from the doorway, "Did you bring napkins? I thought *I* was supposed to bring napkins! I've got napkins here."

Sara turned slightly, still holding onto Ryan, and said to her sister, "Yes, you're in charge of napkins. I've got to get back to my kitchen to help Aunt Minnie. When I left, she was doing something athletic with a bowl of whipped cream."

"Thank you for *that* mental image," Miriam said, arranging the napkins by the food.

There was a burst of uproarious laughter from the stairwell, and then a shrill whoop. Sara chuckled and leaned against Ryan as she looked up at him. "*That's* the San Jose crowd. Here at last."

"Maybe I'll go hide in the bathroom with my cat."

"Courage!" She kissed his cheek and then trotted out his front door.

Miriam was looking at him with a speculative expression.

"The corkscrew is in the kitchen," Ryan said, turning to leave the room and escape that piercing stare.

When he reached the door of his kitchen, though, he found his way blocked by more people. He glanced over his shoulder and saw Miriam whispering into Jan's ear.

"Hi, there!" A pale, dark-haired man in the doorway of the crowded kitchen said to Ryan, "I think Sara pointed you out earlier. Is this your kitchen?"

"Yes. Can I get pas—"

"Thank God!" cried a blonde woman with wire-rimmed glasses. "We're looking for a corkscrew."

"It's in the drawer below the microwave," Ryan said. "Yes, there, that's right."

"I'm Joe." The dark-haired man tried to shake Ryan's hand. "Oh . . . Here, let me help you with those bottles. Look, guys! *More wine.*"

"Any beer?"

"It's in Sara's apartment," Ryan said.

"I thought *this* was Sara's apartment."

"No, next door. I live here."

"Oh, I thought you lived with Sara!"

"No, I—"

"They're just dating, dummy."

"But Delia said—"

Ryan said, "Actually, we're not—"

"Oh, now you guys are embarrassing him," said Joe.

"No," said Ryan, "but we're not—"

"I'm sorry!" Joe exclaimed. "I didn't even get your name!"

"Ryan."

"Well, Ryan, I'm not going to pry." Joe rolled his eyes at

the derisive noises his friends made. "I'll just say that Sara is the best."

Ryan smiled. "Yes. Sara is the best."

"Hear, hear!" The blonde woman waved the corkscrew in the air and said, "Let's drink to Sara!"

Joe grinned at Ryan. "Any excuse will do."

"Oh, Mir, you don't have to do that," Sara said as she entered her kitchen to find her sister washing dishes.

Miriam waved a soapy hand at her. "It's okay. Just clearing up a few things."

Sara crossed the floor and gave Miriam a hug from behind. "Thank you so much for all your help tonight!"

"No problem. It was a good party." Miriam finished rinsing a serving platter. "How many people are left out there?"

"Apart from Jan and Ryan, there are only three people left in my living room. And they're on their way out the door." It was after two o'clock in the morning. Sara was happy but exhausted. "Aunt Minnie finally got Dad and Lance out of Ryan's apartment about ten minutes ago." Lance had arrived shortly before midnight, and he and Abel had soon fallen into an animated discussion.

"Yeah, Jan said that Dad had bonded with your crazed landlord. Figures." After a moment, Miriam added, "And it looks to me like you've been bonding with Ryan."

"We've become close," Sara said as she got some plastic containers out of a cabinet, preparing to put away the leftover food.

"Is that a euphemism?" Miriam asked, wiping her hands on a towel and turning to face Sara.

"No." She met her sister's inquisitive gaze. "We're not sleeping together."

"You're kidding me!" Miriam put the towel aside. "I mean, when I saw you two together tonight, I was a little surprised you hadn't told me. But, well, it seems so obvious, now I'm *really* surprised by *this*."

Sara started packing away the olives. She wasn't sure what to say. Miriam's comment didn't surprise her. By now, too many party guests had already revealed their assumption that she and Ryan were a couple.

Clearly impatient with Sara's silence, Miriam said, "The two of you can't be within three feet of each other without touching. And you're telling me you're still just friends?"

"Yes." They'd been affectionate tonight because it felt deceptively safe with her guests all around them. "We're just friends."

"Why?"

Sara was tired and wished Miriam would drop this painful subject. "Do you think I should save these sandwiches? They'll probably be soggy tomorrow, won't they?"

"Sara, what's going on?"

She sighed. "It's complicated, Mir, and I don't feel like—"

"My God, was I wrong? *Is* he gay? Because if he is—"

"No."

"—then it's pretty shabby of him—"

"He's not gay."

"—to keep stringing you along—"

"He's not gay!"

"—just because he likes the companionship—"

"Would you stop?"

"—or likes the way having you on his arm makes people think he's straight."

"Are you listening to me? He's not gay!"

Miriam paused for a moment, then said more mildly, "I guess I'm just con—"

"Would you get off this?" Sara felt irritated and defensive now. She was annoyed with Miriam and . . . yes, sexually frustrated and, because of that, suddenly angry at Ryan, too. "Would you get *off* this, once and for all? God, Miriam! I'm sick of this! Why does it matter to you so much if—"

"Because *I'm* gay," Miriam said in a rush.

"—I sleep with Ryan or just stay friends with . . . with . . ."

"Oh." Miriam put her hand over her mouth.

". . . with . . ." Sara's brain was working slowly.

"I thought you were going to ask—"

"What?" Sara said.

"—why it matters so much to me if he's gay, not why it matters to me—"

"*What* did you say?"

"—if you sleep with him."

Sara stared at her. "What did you *say?*"

Miriam took a breath. "I'm gay."

"What?"

"Jan's not a friend. She's my girlfriend."

"Huh?" Sara said.

"My lover, actually."

"What?" Sara couldn't believe her ears.

"Do you like her?" Miriam asked hopefully.

"She's your *what?*"

"Sara—"

"Tell me I didn't hear you right!"

"She's my lover!" Miriam snapped.

Sara stared at her sister, aghast. "What do you *mean,* she's your 'lover'?"

"You know what I mean."

"But you're . . . you're not . . . not . . ."

"I just told you, Sara. I am."

"No, you're not!" Sara insisted.

"I'm gay!"

"But you're . . ." She fumbled for a rational thought. "You were married!"

Miriam made an obvious effort to regain her composure. "I know this is a big surprise, and I wanted to tell you in a more—"

"You're telling me that you and *she*—"

"Her name is Jan."

"—are . . . a couple?"

"Yes. We're a couple. A serious couple. I'm in love with—"

"Oh, my God. No wonder you were asking me all those questions a while ago! Was I prejudiced about gays, what did I think of lesbians?" Sara threw up her hands. "Well! I might have thought through my answers a little more carefully if I'd known my own *sister* was a lesbian!"

"Oh, do you really think you might have, Sara? That certainly would have been a nice surprise!"

She took a breath. "Okay, I'm sorry. I guess I'm not taking this very well."

"Gee, y'think?"

"But you've really kicked my legs out from under me," Sara said.

"Right. Because God forbid *you* should have a sister who's a lesbian!"

"I didn't mean it that way."

"*Didn't* you?" Miriam challenged.

"What did you expect me to say?"

"Pretty much *this,* in fact! You are so uptight, Sara!"

"Miriam, that's not f—"

"But I guess I hoped that because *you've* found someone," Miriam said, "you'd be happy that *I've* found someone."

"Look, I just really never expected—"

"Of course, that was before I knew—"

"—that your 'someone'—"

"—that you don't even have the guts to tell Ryan how you feel about him!"

"—was another woman!"

Frustration welled up in Sara. "I *have* told him!"

"What does it *matter* that she's another woman?"

"But it's complicated, Miriam!"

"Why does anything about this matter to you except that I'm in love and I'm happy?" Miriam said.

"I'm entitled to be a little shocked when my sister suddenly turns around after more than thirty years of being normal—"

"Don't you *dare* say this is 'abnormal!' Anyhow, *look* who's talking!"

"—and tells me she's a lesbian!"

"What's so *normal* about being in love with a man you can't keep your hands off of," Miriam said, "and still being 'just friends' with him, because you're too afraid to risk—"

"You have no idea what you're talking about!"

"Well, why don't you just explain it to me, Sara? *I* had the guts to go out on a limb, acknowledge what I really wanted out of life, and go after it! Why don't *you?*"

"*You're* talking to *me,* of all people, about going out on a limb?" Sara said. "*You,* who've been discouraging me from my dreams ever since I lost my publisher?"

Miriam looked stunned. "What? No! I have never! *Never* discouraged . . . *No.* I . . ." She ran a hand through her hair. "Have I?"

Sara hadn't even realized how much she'd resented Miriam's lack of support until the words came out of her mouth. "Well . . . yes."

Miriam stared at her in consternation.

Sara tried to pull her thoughts together. "So you and she . . ."

"Jan."

"You and Jan . . ."

"We've decided to move in together."

"You . . . sleep together?"

"Yeah, Sara. When I said she was my lover, that's what I meant. I didn't think the word was ambiguous. Then again, I'd forgotten how long it's been since you had a lover—"

"Don't be a bitch."

"Sara, I see the way he looks at you. And I'm not the only one. What the hell is going on here?"

"I don't want to talk about—"

"He loves you," Miriam said.

"*Please,* don't."

"Why not?"

Pushed beyond her limit, Sara blurted, "Because he's a prostitute!"

Miriam's eyes bulged. *"What?"*

"There! Now you know! Happy?"

"What are you talking about?"

"He's an expensive male prostitute who sleeps with other women—dozens of women, maybe even hundreds of women!"

"He's a *prosti—*"

"And I'm so *uptight,*" Sara said, "that I'm having a little trouble with that, go figure."

The kitchen door swung open. Ryan and Jan came into

the room, carrying food trays and chatting.

Jan was saying, "Which is why I decided to get a Labrador. Because they have that . . . that great personality . . . which . . . uh . . ."

The two of them drifted to a halt, their expressions growing uneasy as they saw Sara and Miriam's faces. Given that the room was practically vibrating with emotion, Sara supposed they sensed the tension.

After a moment, Ryan asked Sara, "Is everything okay?"

Jan asked Miriam, "Are you all right?"

Sara saw the way the woman looked at Miriam, who tersely replied: "Fine."

"Miriam?" Jan prodded, clearly not convinced. Her gaze shifted to Sara, and her eyes widened. *"Oh."*

Sara opened her mouth, wondering what to say to her sister's lesbian lover.

Miriam said, "Don't say a word, Sara. Not right now." She said to Jan, "We're leaving." Jan looked distressed, and Miriam made an obvious effort to be more reassuring. "Everything's okay, but it's time to go."

Now Sara saw the way her sister looked at this woman. The way they looked at each other. What they shared.

Miriam said to Sara, "We'll talk later." Then she crossed the floor to Jan and took her hand. "Let's go."

Jan looked at Sara, then back to Miriam. "Are you sure? If you two want to talk now, I'll wait—"

"No, I've had enough of my family for one night," Miriam said. "Let's go home."

Jan looked at Sara again, her expression worried. "It was a lovely party, Sara. Thank you for having me."

"Mm."

Stepping into the breach, Ryan said, "It was nice to meet you, Jan."

"Oh, it was *very* nice to meet you, Ryan."

"Drive safely."

"Come on." Miriam tugged her girlfriend's hand, eager to leave. She paused in the doorway, though, glanced at Ryan for a moment, and then looked at Sara. "I guess we've both got bad news for Dad, Sara. But at least mine's Jewish." She started laughing.

The kitchen door swung shut behind them, Miriam's slightly hysterical laughter still floating on the air.

Sara avoided Ryan's gaze and slumped into a kitchen chair. He came over to the table and sat down, too.

He said, "So she told you."

Sara gaped at him. "You *knew?*" When he nodded, she demanded, "How long have you known?"

"Only a few hours." He put his hand over hers. "It was sort of obvious when I saw them together."

She made a rude noise. "Well, obvious to a *sex professional,* maybe, but I had no id—"

"Come on, Sara." He withdrew his hand.

"What?"

He seemed to be sorting through a multiple-choice list of possible comments. Finally, he settled on, "I thought you might be caught a little off guard by this."

"Well, *yeah.*" She threw her hands up. "My stable, conventional sister, who's always been the normal one, is suddenly a lesbian, and I—"

"You mean, she's suddenly *told* you she's a lesbian."

That gave her pause. "Well . . ."

"Their relationship seems pretty serious."

"It is." Sara's head started to throb. "They're moving in together."

"If Miriam's got a serious partner now," he continued, "it's probably not because dumb luck struck her one day last week."

Sara remembered a phone conversation she'd had with her sister only days after moving in here. "No. They met months ago."

"And assuming that Miriam had to date a while, like most people, before meeting the right person . . ."

She held her head in her hands. "You mean she's been hiding this for some time. Keeping secrets from me." Feeling cranky, she added, "Like you."

"I don't think she'd like the comparison."

Realizing she had a confession to make, Sara said, "Ryan, I'm sorry. I told her. What you do. For work."

He drew in a sharp breath. "Oh?"

"We were fighting, she was goading me. About you and me. I was angry, and I just blurted it out. I'm sorry."

"Oh. Well." After a moment, he said, "I guess I'm not that surprised. She was giving me some 'If you hurt my sister, I'll castrate you' looks tonight. So I suppose she was bound to push you about what's going on between us."

"What *is* going on between us?" she asked plaintively.

He lowered his gaze and went very still. Sara watched his jaw muscle work tensely. When he didn't reply, she gave in to what she longed for and could no longer bear not to have. "Ryan, I want to make l—"

"Does it bother you?" he asked abruptly. "Two women together in bed?"

Surprised by the question, she admitted, "Yes. In fact, I'd rather we change the subject. I don't want to think about—"

"This trip I just took. To the island," he said. "I screwed one woman while her lesbian lover watched. Then I did a three-way with them."

She covered her eyes with her hands. After the initial, mortifying shock passed through her, she ground out,

"*Damn you,* Ryan. You're the one who keeps saying that details aren't a good idea!"

"Still want me in your bed?"

She didn't answer. She was waiting for the flood of revulsion to subside.

"So Miriam was always the conventional sister, the normal one," he said, "and I guess you were always the artistic one, the oddball."

Her blood was roaring in her ears. Unwanted images thundered through her mind.

Ryan. Fucking two women at once. Fucking one woman while another watched.

"In a way," Ryan said, "you and Miriam are like mirror images of each other. The normally conventional sister became the oddball in her sex life, in the desires that pumped through her blood and made her want something other than what she'd always thought she was supposed to want."

Ryan, performing. Like some kind of live porn show. In private. For two women.

"You're the unusual one—the original—in the other areas of life, but sexually," he said, "you *do* want exactly what you always thought you were supposed to want. You want a monogamous relationship with a sexually conventional man—"

"I want *you,*" she said miserably.

"—and you're repulsed by the idea of anything else. For yourself. Or for others." He paused. "So if you thought about Miriam going down on Jan after they get home tonight—"

"Stop it!"

"—you'd be disgusted."

"I don't want to think about my *sister's* sex life! Or *anybody's* sex life! Sex is private!"

"Then *don't* think about it, Sara," he said. "Think about Miriam being happy, being satisfied with her choices, making a life together with someone she loves. I mean, it's not Jan *personally* that you mind, is it?"

"I hardly talked to her," Sara mumbled. After a long moment she admitted, "She seemed nice. Ten times better than David, in fact."

"David?"

"Miriam's ex-husband."

"Oh. Your father says he was a schmuck."

She choked on a startled laugh. "He was."

They were silent for a few minutes, Ryan sitting patiently with her while she pulled herself together. Finally, Sara scrubbed her hands across her face and looked at him. "You and two women."

His expression didn't change. "Yes."

"I suppose a lot of men fantasize about that."

"It was just a job, Sara."

She felt exhausted and depressed. "I don't understand."

"I know." He folded his arms across his chest. "And, well, there's something else you should know."

"I'm not ready for another shock, Ryan."

He ignored that. "You remember, I told you that when I first started out escorting, I told Catherine I wouldn't do men?"

"I don't think I want to hear this," she said.

"You remember, I told you we argued about it?"

"And she gave in because of what had happened to you."

He nodded, keeping his face inexpressive. "But the reason we argued about it, the reason she thought I might do it, is that . . ." He met her eyes. "She knew I had done it before. That's why she hadn't thought it would really be a problem for me, on occasion."

Sara said nothing. Just stared.

"To survive on the streets, I shoplifted, I picked pockets, I washed windshields, I even begged . . . And when I was desperate enough, I got down on my knees." Ryan must have thought her blank-faced shock indicated a lack of comprehension, because he added, "Oral sex, Sara. I gave blow jobs for cash."

"Oh, Jesus." She leaned over and rested her forehead on the kitchen table, feeling sick. She couldn't look at him. Couldn't stand this. Could barely find the words she wanted. "As a *kid?* A teenager? When you were, what, sixteen? *Fourteen?*"

"Uh-huh."

"Ryan . . ." She wanted to cry, but tears didn't come.

"Not often," he said. "Not if I could find money any other way—but sometimes I couldn't. And it was always easy to pick up cash that way."

"No. No . . ." She was *trying* to cry, but her eyes were dry.

"Just stand around and wait. In the right place. With the right attitude. Someone would walk up, or drive up. And for fifteen minutes of my time, I'd get enough money to eat for a couple of days." He added very quietly, "I didn't think about it while I was doing it. I didn't think about it afterwards. I turned off my mind."

"Oh, God . . ." She heard herself breathing in short, distressed pants.

"If I could just *not think,* then it was easy. Too easy, I guess. That's why so many street kids wind up doing it."

"Please . . ."

"They figure, hell, I could spend all day busting my butt and risking getting picked up by the cops for stealing or panhandling, and I might wind up with seven dollars to show for my trouble. But if I can just turn off my mind once or twice a night, just for as long as it takes for some pervert to get off—"

"Ryan."

"—I can get twenty, thirty, maybe even fifty bucks, just like that." After a moment, he said, "I know it doesn't make any sense when you're sitting here. But back then and there, Sara, sometimes it made perfect sense to me. And so I did it."

With her eyes closed, she took a shaky breath. "Wasn't it terribly dangerous?"

"Of course. That's how I got hurt so badly."

She finally lifted her head to look at him.

"One night," he said, "I went with the wrong customer. He decided he wanted more than I was willing to sell. When I wouldn't give it to him, he beat the shit out of me and took it."

Sara felt her face crumple, but she still couldn't cry. "If he'd had AIDS or something . . ."

"I know." He said with bitter irony, "Aren't I a lucky sonofabitch?"

"Oh, Ryan." Her throat ached and her chest hurt. "I wish I had known you back then."

That startled him. "What?"

"I was an adult. I could have helped you. Looked after you." Her eyes ached dryly. Why couldn't she cry? "If only—"

"Shhh. I don't do if-onlys and what-ifs, Sara. I learned a long time ago it does no good and hurts too much. So let's not start now, okay?"

"Okay." Her voice was faint, her head spinning with sorrow and fatigue.

Ryan rose from his chair. "It was a great party, Sara. You have nice friends."

"I do, don't I?" Her head was muzzy, and her heart felt raw.

"Most of them seem a little eccentric." He smiled. "I've learned that I really like that in a person."

"Ryan . . ."

He leaned over and kissed her forehead. "Get some sleep."

Then he was gone.

CHAPTER THIRTEEN

Ryan wasn't surprised that he didn't see Sara for the next three days. Despite his parting suggestion, he doubted that she'd been able to sleep in the hours after Miriam had dropped her bombshell and then he'd delivered one or two of his own. He supposed Sara had spent much of Sunday either dozing or puttering around the apartment in a half-hearted attempt to start cleaning up the post-party mess.

He also supposed she wasn't at all eager to see him. Her feelings for him were probably a little confused right now. Or maybe they were crystal clear: revulsion and rejection.

Ryan tried not to be upset about it. This was exactly why he had said what he'd said, wasn't it? He didn't have the will to let her go, so he'd given her a reason to let *him* go. If knowing that he bedded other women for money appalled her, it was easy to predict how she'd react to knowing that he had worked men in the street. And if her sister's unconventional sexuality disturbed her, he could guess how she'd feel about his own unconventional sexual experiences.

He had told her because it was the right thing to do. And because it was the only thing which was going to stop this train from moving forward. She'd have invited him to her bed—the words were tumbling out of her mouth at that very moment—and he'd have entered it, knowing full well that it was wrong. She'd be hurt by anything more that happened between them, and he didn't want that. So he'd sought a way to put a stop to this.

Besides, the truth would be even worse if she only discovered it after she'd let him into her bed. He hated to think of how disgusted she'd be, how betrayed she would feel, if she found out later instead of now.

It was good that he had told her everything. It was good that he'd been fair to her.

And since it was good, he wished it would stop feeling so awful.

He went about his business and tried not to think about her. But he hated not seeing her, not knowing how she was feeling, not talking with her, not even having a superficial chat so he could spend some time in her company. Initially, it made him lonesome, unhappy, and distracted. By today, he missed her so much it was making him cranky. He'd snapped at Adam this morning, who was so offended that he refused to let Ryan buy him a meal. For a hungry street kid, that was *seriously* offended. Ryan knew he'd have his work cut out for him tomorrow, trying to regain some of the ground he'd lost with the kid today.

Ground for what? What am I going to do?

He tromped morosely up the long, steep stairs to his apartment, unlocked his front door, greeted Macy, and was closing the door behind him when he heard Sara's door open.

"There you are!" Evidently unaware of his startled expression, she stalked across the hall, pushed past him, and entered his apartment. "Hello, Macy."

Ryan stared at her. "Hi."

She finished patting Macy with one hand, using the other hand to clutch a big pile of paperwork to her chest. Then she turned on him with an exasperated glare. "It's late. Where have you been?"

"Um, working."

She rolled her eyes. "Lovely."

"Sara . . ."

"I've been waiting for you for hours!"

"Uh . . . Sorry."

Her gaze flicked over him, and her expression changed as she noticed his expensive suit. "Why don't you change? Then we'll talk."

"O . . . kay."

When he came out of the bedroom in sweatpants and a T-shirt, she was sitting on his couch. He hesitated until she patted the place beside her and said, "For God's sake, Ryan, I'm not going to bite you. What on earth is the matter with you today?"

He sat down a couple of feet away from her. "Well. We had a pretty frank talk. And then I didn't see you for three days. I thought—"

"Is it three days?" She looked surprised. "Oh, you're right. Well, I had a difficult night after the party was over. I fell asleep about two hours after dawn, and I slept through most of Sunday. Yesterday I was busy all day with this." She indicated the paperwork she was spreading out on the coffee table as she talked. "Today I was busy with this again, but you haven't been around much today, anyhow. And I've spent all evening waiting for you to come home." She frowned at him. "I can't keep doing that. You have to give me your cell phone number."

Right. So she could phone him while he was with other women. Great idea. "No one has the number but Catherine," he said. "And it's not really my phone. It belongs to her."

"Oh, good grief."

He looked at the paperwork spread out on his coffee table. "What have you been doing?"

"Well, as you probably expected, the things you told me

the other night had a pretty heavy effect on me."

"Yeah. I figured."

"I started out thinking a lot about you. About what it must have been like for you. Alone on the streets, with nothing in the world but your guts and your wits." She was silent for a minute, her expression somber. "Then, eventually, I got round to thinking about this kid."

"Adam?" he said in surprise.

She nodded. "You've told me his name. You've said enough about him to give me a sense of who he is. So he's become a person to me, even though I don't know him. He's real to me. And he's in the same position you were in, all those years ago." Her shoulders slumped. "I wasn't there for you—"

"Sara—"

"—and I can't go back in time to help you. But I can help him. Or, I can help *you* help him, because I know you want to."

He touched her hair, not knowing what to say.

"I know you think about him. Spend time with him," she said. "He has a hold on you. So he has a hold on me, too."

A glow was spreading through him, warming all the cold places. This was what she did to him. All of the time.

"Ryan, I don't want this kid to go through everything you went through. To make the choices you had to make."

He put his hand on her shoulder and squeezed gently.

She said, "And I don't want him to wind up dead. Or as a prostitute, or a crack addict, or whatever else is likely if he stays on the streets." She gestured to the piles of paperwork in front of them. "If there's one thing I know how to do, it's research. So I got up early yesterday morning and started researching what we could do to get Adam off the streets."

"You did?" He stared in surprise at the papers covering his coffee table.

"I went to the library. I looked up information on the Web. I e-mailed some people. I made some phone calls."

"Sara." He looked at her in amazement. "Wow. You did all this? For Adam?"

"Yes. And for you. But, well, the truth is, Ryan," she said, "it's almost certain that you won't be granted any kind of legal supervision of Adam."

"You looked into that?" He picked up one of the piles of paper and leafed through it, noticing her handwritten notes in the margins of some articles she'd downloaded and printed.

She said, "As long as you're working as a prostitute, you can't get custody of him."

"I suppose I knew that."

"And your lies about being a model won't hold up under any kind of responsible scrutiny."

"No." He'd known that, too.

"Even if you quit right now," she said, "you have no legal work history of any kind. You've also got three arrests on your record. No convictions, I know. But the first two charges were very serious—rape and drug dealing—and the third charge, when you got picked up for prostitution, is so recent. Plus, you're a young, single male. So without a family connection between you and Adam . . ." She shook her head. "The bottom line is, Ryan, it's not going to happen. Even if you changed your life tomorrow, Adam needs help much sooner than any legal authority is ever going to allow you to give it to him."

He nodded, surprised to realize that he was disappointed. Nothing she said was unexpected, after all.

She continued, "So if you were thinking of taking Adam in . . ."

"Was I thinking of it?" he mumbled to himself, again a little surprised.

"I think you were."

"Yeah. I was, wasn't I? I just hadn't really . . ." He met her eyes. "I've been taking it slow. One day at a time. Because I know that's how he thinks. How he *has* to think. I've been matching myself to his pace, because I know how easy it would be to spook him and make him disappear."

"Because Adam knows enough to get away from a grown man trying to convince him to come home with him."

Ryan nodded. It made his blood run cold to think of what could happen to Adam if he accepted an invitation like that from someone else, or failed to elude such a person before being snatched. "Maybe he's only alive," Ryan said, "because he's so slow about growing to trust me."

"How did he wind up on the streets?" Sara asked. "Has he told you yet?"

"He told me yesterday," Ryan said with a nod. "His mother died three years ago, while his father was in prison for manslaughter. But Adam says his dad was okay, didn't knock him around or anything like that."

"Unlike your father."

"Uh-huh."

"Actually . . ."

"What?"

She cleared her throat. "Well, since I was in research mode, anyhow . . . I got a friend in Oklahoma—another writer—to help me."

"Oklahoma? Help you do what?"

"Was your father's name John Michael Kinsmore?"

That stunned him. "How'd you know that?"

"My friend found his obituary."

"His *obituary?*" His jaw dropped. "He's dead?"

"Six years ago. Fell off his back porch, hit his head, and lay there until someone found the body. He died of the head injury. There was so much alcohol in his bloodstream, it wasn't surprising that he fell, just surprising that he'd been conscious enough to walk."

Ryan stared at her in dumb surprise for a long moment. Then he said, "Well, doesn't that just figure?"

"I'd had a hunch," Sara said, "so I asked my friend to look at Oklahoma City area obituaries for the past dozen years and find white males, over thirty years old, named Kinsmore."

"That was a hell of a hunch."

"Not really. A violent drunk? I thought there was a fair chance he might not make it to a ripe old age."

"Oh. When you put it that way . . ."

"My friend faxed me the obituary, and also a very brief article about his death. I've got them both in here." She tapped a file folder. "If you want to read them."

He stared at the folder as if it were a snake. "Maybe later."

"Would you rather I keep them with me for a while?"

He took a breath. "No. You can leave them here." After a moment, he added, "Thank you, Sara."

"There's a photo with the article. Obviously not recent. He died at forty-eight, but he looks about your age in the photo. That's how I knew he was your father—there's a resemblance."

Ryan grunted. "Only skin deep."

"Obviously." She shrugged. "I wonder if his good looks were what attracted your mother."

"Maybe so," Ryan said. "She was very young. Maybe her hormones were stronger than her judgment."

"Are you all right? I didn't think you'd mind finding out that he's dead, but . . ." She shrugged.

"I'm fine. I'm . . ." He thought about it for a moment. "*Relieved.* I'd reached a point where I never expected to have to see him again, but even so . . ." He nodded. "Yeah. It's a relief. He's finally where he belongs. Six feet under. If only it had happened twenty years ago."

"Then I'm glad I decided to check. I wasn't sure you'd want me to."

"I probably would have told you not to," he said, "so I guess it's a good thing you didn't ask. I thought I didn't want to know anything about him. But, honestly, I'm glad to know he's dead." He shook his head. "That's a hell of a way for a father to make his kid feel about him."

"Which brings us back to Adam. Whose father is in prison, you said?"

"Oh! Right." Ryan pulled his thoughts back to a much more important subject than his own father. "Well, when his mom died three years ago, there wasn't anyone to take Adam in, and his father wouldn't be eligible for parole for at least five more years. The first foster family didn't keep Adam. He doesn't know why. With the second family, he started getting into a lot of trouble. Then he got sent to some juvenile facility. Where two other kids molested him."

"Oh, God." Sara put her hand over her mouth.

"He ran away the first chance he got. Adam is his real name, he's fifteen, and he's been on the street for five months. He figures if he can just stay out of the system until his father gets out of prison . . ." Ryan shook his head. "But he doesn't know when that'll be, and he doesn't know how to find out. And *I* don't know if he can stay alive that long, Sara."

"Plus, his father might not get out the first time he comes up for parole."

"Good point."

"The thing is, Ryan, if you took Adam in, he'd be safer

than he is now, but he'd still be a non-person."

"What does that mean?"

"He couldn't have any legal identity. Because as soon as he did, he'd be taken away from you. In that respect, it would be like your life after Catherine took you in. He couldn't go to school. He couldn't go to a hospital if he got injured. You probably couldn't take him to a doctor for check-ups."

"That's not his biggest worry right now, Sara."

"No, but my point is—"

"Yeah, I see your point," he said wearily.

"—that it's not the best choice for him. Not even if you were thinking of sheltering him just until he can be reunited with his father. Even if we had any real idea when—or if—that will happen."

He ran a hand through his hair. "So what do you suggest I do?"

She picked up a pile of printouts. "I was losing heart, to be honest, until this afternoon. That's when I found this place called Safe House. It seems different. Better than the other possibilities I researched, though I've got those here, too, if you want to discuss them. Anyhow, Safe House is an outreach organization."

He didn't touch the papers, though she tried to hand them to him. "Outreach?"

"It was founded five years ago by an ex-prostitute."

"A prostitute?" he blurted.

"Some people actually get out of the sex trade and do something worthwhile with their lives, Ryan."

Her tone stung him. "Don't start with me, Sara. Not right now."

She held up her hand. "Okay. I agree. Let's focus on Adam."

He shook his head. "Look, I know you mean well, but I remember what 'outreach' meant back when I was—"

"They're not going to send him anywhere he doesn't want to go, Ryan, and they're not going to report him or turn him over to anyone. They do counseling, advocacy, drug treatment, job training, placement—"

" 'Placement' means sending him back into the system. No way, Sara."

"Not necessarily."

"He doesn't want that. I don't want that for him."

"This woman I talked to there, Isabel, says they don't *make* anyone go anywhere. They'll go over Adam's options with him—"

"You *told* them about Adam?" he demanded.

"No. I told them you had taken an interest in a street boy and wanted to help him, but didn't know what to do. I told them that you'd go there first, and if you liked the place—"

"You said *I'd* go there?"

"—then you would talk to the kid about going in to talk with them."

He insisted, "I'm not turning him over to anyone, Sara."

"Of course not. And they won't ask you to. That's why I thought you would consider this. They'll talk with you, and if Adam goes in, they'll talk with him. If he wants to walk away, they'll let him walk away." When he looked at her in mute suspicion, she said, "This woman I talked to today, Isabel, is expecting you tomorrow at two o'clock."

"You made an *appointment* for me?"

"It seemed like a good idea at the time," she said with a touch of exasperation.

He said the first thing that came into his head. "I can't go tomorrow afternoon. I have to work."

He could tell from her expression that it was very much

the *wrong* thing to say. "God forbid," Sara said, "that saving Adam's life should interfere with your Wednesday afternoon trick."

He sighed. "It's not that."

"Then what is it?"

He shook his head. "Places like this . . ."

"You don't know anything about this place, Ryan! It didn't exist when you were a street kid! Isabel took ten minutes out of her busy day to tell me about it, and I believe her when she says they're not going to seize Adam and force him into juvenile detention, foster care, or any other situation he doesn't want. Now do you think I'm such a naïve idiot that you can't trust my judgment—"

"Sara, I didn't mean—"

"—or do you think you could take an hour out of your busy day of well-paid sex to keep this appointment for Adam's sake?"

He lowered his head, embarrassed and confused. "I'm sorry. I just . . ."

"Right now, you're thinking like a street boy—and like a prostitute, I guess," she said gently. "But I happen to know that when you put that attitude aside, you're an intelligent and sensible adult."

"Thanks."

"So now you have to put that attitude aside for Adam's sake. You can't really help him if you're only willing to help him outside of the laws and structures of society." After a slight pause, she added, "Which was the only way Catherine was willing to help you."

He let his shoulders slump. "Two o'clock tomorrow?"

"Yes."

"You have the address?"

"Right here." She waved her printouts at him again.

He nodded. "Okay. I'll go."

"Good. I'm going to leave this pile with you. It's some information I downloaded from Safe House, and some articles I found about possibilities that may apply to Adam. You can read them tonight. In case you want to ask about them tomorrow."

"Uh-huh."

"I'll take the rest with me." She got up and started gathering her papers. "But I've got them if you decide you want to read them, too."

"Sara . . ." When she turned to look at him, he tried to think of what to say. Feeling inadequate, he settled on, "Thank you. For everything."

She smiled and gave his knee a quick, affectionate squeeze.

Somewhat encouraged by this, he added, "You really are the best."

"No. Just trying to do better than I've been doing." She hesitated before saying, "Now that this is done, I should go call my sister."

"You haven't talked to her yet?"

She shook her head. "You managed to knock her off the front page for a few days, go figure."

"I'm sorry."

She touched his cheek. "But now that I've got you doing as you're told . . ."

He grinned wryly and nudged her with his knee.

"I need to make peace with Miriam."

"Yeah, I guess you do." He stood up and walked her to the door. "I'll let you know how it goes tomorrow."

She nodded. "Goodnight, Ryan."

He watched her leave, wanting to keep her here or to go with her.

Until he realized that the first thing he had to do now was phone Catherine to say he needed to cancel or postpone tomorrow's appointment with Alice Van Offelen. Then he was glad Sara was gone.

He picked up his cell phone, hit the autodial, and waited for Catherine to answer. He took a quick glance at the clock and realized it was probably too late for her to notify the client tonight. She'd have to do it tomorrow, only a few hours before he was supposed to show up. Alice was a nice woman who was unlikely to make a fuss. But Catherine would chew him out for this.

"I've been talking with Jan about what happened . . ." Miriam's voice sounded hesitant on the telephone.

"I talked with Ryan," Sara said. "He said I'm sexually conventional. I think he's too tactful to actually *say* 'uptight.' "

Miriam made a dismissive sound. "I dumped this on you out of the blue at two o'clock in the morning, without any warning or preparation. I was confrontational and defensive."

"Look, I wish I could be someone who wouldn't have *needed* preparation for you to tell me the truth, Miriam," Sara said. "But, it's true, I did. So I was shocked and reacted badly. I admit it."

"I didn't want it to be that way. I've been worrying so much about how to tell you—"

"And I guess I said things that made you worry even more."

"I didn't want you to think of me differently."

"But, Miriam, you *are* different."

"No, I'm the same."

"You're in love, and that makes you different than you

were. You're gay, and that makes you different than I thought you were," Sara said. "Both of these important things about you are completely new to me, and they're big changes."

"Are you freaked out by it?"

"I was when you told me," Sara admitted. "But once I calmed down, sometime in the middle of Saturday night—Sunday morning?—I realized Ryan was right. I never wanted to know what you did in bed with David, so there's no reason for me to think about what you do in bed with Jan. And the truth is, Miriam, if you change personality so much that you start trying to force your sex life down my throat, we'll fight, because I don't want to know about it."

"I don't want to force anything down your throat, Sara." Miriam's tone was again defensive and confrontational as she said, "But I also don't want to feel you judging me if I hold Jan's hand or kiss her in front of you."

"To be honest, that'll be awkward for me at first," Sara told her. "I'll get used to seeing you be affectionate with a woman, Miriam, but you have to allow me *time* to get used to it. It's not fair to expect me to turn on a dime when *you* obviously didn't. You hid your sexuality from me until you were comfortable with it, didn't you?"

Miriam sighed. "Even longer than that."

"How long *have* you been hiding this from me?"

"In terms of a lifestyle," Miriam said, "about eighteen months. But there are things I've hidden from you for years because *I* didn't want to acknowledge them."

"So . . . Now don't get mad at me for asking a fair question," Sara said. "You mean, you didn't start dating women just because your marriage to a man had been so disappointing?"

"Sara," Miriam said, "that is *such* a stereotype."

"Sorry, it's how we straight girls think about these things," Sara shot back.

Miriam sighed. "Okay. Sorry. You're trying. I'll try, too."

"That would be good."

"I didn't start dating women because of David. I started dating David because of women."

"What?"

"I slept with another woman once in college. I told myself it was because I wasn't used to wine, and so I never touched the stuff again until after I graduated. To make sure it wouldn't happen again."

"So this goes back a long way," Sara said in surprise.

"Then I met a woman when I was working in the city, between college and grad school. I slept with her twice—and I was sober the second time. I totally freaked out about it. I was so sure I couldn't be *that* person. *I* was a 'normal' person who wanted normal things, including normal sexuality and a normal family . . ." Miriam sighed. "Well, this woman wanted a relationship with me. She pursued me. I wanted her, too, but I wasn't ready to see myself that way, to accept what I truly wanted."

"Oh!" Sara's jaw dropped as she put the pieces together. "The year you were working in the city—the year you got engaged to David."

"Yeah. David was right there, and he was convenient—for hiding behind, I mean. He'd been at the law firm for two years and was ready to invest in a wife and a house. I saw an opportunity for all the 'normal' things I wanted so much—"

"I'm sorry I used that word the other night."

"—and an easy escape from the 'abnormal' thing that was so tempting to me. So I threw myself into getting David to marry me, and I rejected this woman."

"Wow. I never had any idea." Sara was shaking her head, stunned at the emotional difficulties Miriam had faced without ever confiding in her. "Mir, I'm ashamed you felt you couldn't tell me. I'm so sorry."

"No, don't, Sara. It wouldn't be fair for me to let you blame yourself. I never even considered telling you. Or *anyone*. I pretended to myself that I just had a strange, unique attraction to this one sole woman, and that *she* was my only problem." Miriam added softly, "I hurt her when I rejected her. Hurt her a lot. In fact, I *tried* to hurt her."

Hearing Miriam's guilt, Sara said, "Six years of marriage to David seems like punishment enough for any unhappiness you may have caused her."

"To be fair to David—"

"Oh, let's not bother."

Miriam laughed. "Granted, he was not the most supportive or sincere husband."

"He screwed around on you!" Sara added, "I thought that was why you divorced him."

"I thought so, too. But, really, finding out about his adultery the second time, after he'd promised it would never happen again, was an escape hatch. All those tears I shed weren't because I cared about losing him. They were because I was scared of the future. And also because I felt guilty."

"Guilty?"

"I know you don't want to be fair to David, but I have to," Miriam said. "Our marriage was no picnic for him, either, Sara. I never really wanted him sexually. Not the way a person needs to be wanted by a spouse or lover. Even someone as self-centered as David had to find that hurtful. And I didn't love him, which couldn't have been easy for him to bear, either, once he realized it."

"I didn't like him and I don't have to feel sorry for him," Sara said, "but I understand what you're saying."

"Since I had made a mess of my personal life by denying what I wanted," Miriam said, "a few months after David and I split up, I tracked down and apologized to the woman I'd rejected and dumped so I could marry him. And she was incredibly nice to me about everything. She has a partner whom she's been with for five years, and I became friends with both of them. They started introducing me to people . . . And I started dating."

"Dating women, you mean."

"Dating women."

"And keeping big secrets from me."

"Yeah. Which I did for too long, I know. I'm sorry."

"Well, I can understand that telling me wasn't easy." She switched the phone to her other ear and shifted in her chair. "Look, what I didn't like about David was that he didn't deserve you and didn't make you happy. I've decided that's what still matters most to me in anyone you choose. Not what gender the person is."

"Well, in this case, I'd say it's a question of whether *I* deserve *her*. And Jan does make me happy, Sara. I've been *so* happy since we met. So I knew that I couldn't keep hiding this from you. Besides," Miriam added wryly, "I was getting sick of Jan nagging me to tell my family about us."

"Then I'm glad you're happy, and I'm glad you told me about you and Jan."

Miriam asked, "So you're okay with this?"

"Yes, I am." She was only lying a little. "But it would help if I actually knew Jan, Miriam. Right now, she's just sort of a theory to me."

"I thought you could get to know her at your party. It

seemed like a no-pressure way to introduce her to the family." Miriam made an amused sound. "But I should have remembered what your parties are like and realized you'd have no time to get to acquainted with her."

"I had no idea so many people would show up."

"It was nice of Ryan to let them into his home. I wouldn't have done that."

"Well, he's a pretty brave guy."

There was a brief silence before Miriam said, "I have to ask."

"I know. Don't bother. I'll tell you." The things Ryan had confided to her were private, so Sara only gave Miriam a quick outline of how he had become an escort and why he felt he couldn't give it up.

When she was finished, Miriam said, "Well, you can see how he'd be good at it. I mean, I'm finished with men and happy about it, and even *I* think he's sexy. In a classy way, too."

"But he's more than that, Mir. A *lot* more than that." No matter how appealing Ryan's packaging was, it wasn't what made Sara love him.

"So," Miriam said, "the problem between you two has never been that he doesn't find you sexually attractive, or that he cares about your age—"

"I'm only nine years older," Sara said irritably.

"If you recall, that's what I kept telling you—"

"Yeah, yeah."

"And it sounds to me as if, now that you know the truth, you still want him, and you don't care where he's been."

"It would be more accurate to say that I don't *blame* him for where he's been." Sara felt the familiar frustration start welling up again. "But I do care that he still keeps going there."

"Yeah. That's not something you can just . . ." Miriam sighed. "Well, I don't fault you for being 'uptight' about this, Sara."

"He doesn't, either."

"What are you going to do?"

She brushed her hair behind her ear. "I don't know."

"Well, whatever you do, I swear I'm going to be supportive. Because, well, you're right. I haven't been supportive of your choices lately. And I'm sorry about that, Sara. Jan says I always think I know best, and so I just steamroll over other people sometimes."

"Wow, she really *does* know you well."

"Yeah, yeah. Anyhow, I'm sorry. When it comes to your career problems the past few months, I've been someone you had to fend off instead of someone you could talk to."

"Thanks, Miriam. I guess I've had so much trouble believing in myself lately, I didn't even realize how much I minded *your* not believing in me."

"I do believe in you! I'm just worried about your impractical and risky . . . Uh, never mind."

Sara chuckled. "But I've been okay, Mir. Ryan has been there for me. Ever since we met, he's been incredibly supportive."

"Well, *sure*. Your life probably looks pretty stable to a homeless kid turned prostitute. But I've got a good professional job with a regular salary and benefits."

"And if that mattered to me as much as it matters to you," Sara said, "things might be different. But my passion for my work is much more important to me than the stability you need."

"Sometimes I envy you that," Miriam said, surprising her. "But I definitely don't envy you what you endure for your work."

Sara smiled. "I can't argue with that." After a pause, she asked, "When are you going to talk to Dad?"

"Oh! I didn't tell you. I've talked to him."

"You already talked to him? When?"

"Yesterday. I told him I was going to bring some Chinese food over to his place so we could have dinner, because I needed to tell him something important."

"And?"

"And I did it, Sara," Miriam said. "I told him that you're in love with a Catholic."

Sara sputtered with laughter. "Bitch."

"Okay, no, I didn't waste my breath on it. He knows."

"He does?" Sara bleated.

"Yes. After he got over his shock about me and Jan—and, I have to tell you, he was so shocked, he didn't speak for about two minutes, which is the longest I've ever known him to be silent unless he was asleep."

"Was it very awkward?"

"At first. But then he recovered and focused on the important point, which is that Jan is—"

"Jewish."

"—and a liberal."

"You sycophant. You knew as long as you found someone with those qualifications, you could slip this 'and we're lesbians' thing right past him."

"Yeah, it worked out pretty well. Anyhow, then he got on this riff about grandchildren. He said at least he could hold out hope that you'd provide them, because you've been considerate enough to find a companion who's a member of the impregnating gender, even if he is a goy."

"Oy vay," Sara said.

"I thought you'd say that." Miriam was obviously enjoying herself. "Does Ryan vote Democrat?"

"We've never discussed it. You know I don't care about politics. But if I had to guess, I'd say he doesn't vote."

"Then just lie to Dad and *say* he's a liberal."

"Yeah. And then I'll just breeze past Dad with this 'by the way, he's a prostitute' thing."

"Oops."

"Look, I've got to go. I'm wiped out," Sara said, feeling depressed again. "I'm going to hit the sack."

"Wait. Tell you what. So that Jan won't keep being just a 'theory' to you, why don't you come for lunch on Sunday? About one o'clock? I'll invite Dad and Aunt Minnie, too. Jan can start getting used to the family, and you can start getting used to us."

"That sounds good. I'll be there."

"Sara?"

"Hmm?"

"Well. I love you."

"I love you, too, Mir."

CHAPTER FOURTEEN

"Any involvement in prostitution?"

Ryan nearly flinched before he realized that Isabel was asking about Adam, not him. "I haven't asked, but I don't think so."

She gazed at him inquisitively, waiting for him to say more. Isabel was a no-nonsense woman, roughly Catherine's age, and she looked a bit like his cleaning lady. There was a gentle patience in her manner, but Ryan could tell she was also shrewd and observant.

"Does it matter if he's been hustling to survive?" Ryan asked, bristling a little. "If he has, does that make him less worthy of your help?"

"No," Isabel said, "I'm just wondering why you haven't asked."

"So that he doesn't think he has to answer the question to keep my friendship. Or think he has to *lie* to keep my friendship."

Isabel nodded and then returned to asking more questions. She was particularly persistent in discovering all the details of how Ryan had initially tracked down Adam and started winning his grudging trust. Getting tired of her interrogation after a while, Ryan said, "Look, I didn't go to that neighborhood cruising for boys, if that's what you're wondering. I don't do that."

"I believe you."

"Then what's with all the questions? How did I find him, how did I know his patterns, how did I convince him—"

"Why did you track down your stolen wallet yourself instead of notifying the cops the way most people would?"

Ryan met her gaze. "Oh. Well . . ."

Isabel tilted your head. "Those of us trying to understand street kids so we can help them know that there are two kinds of people who understand them better than we do, Mr. Kinsmore."

"Oh, call me Ryan."

"There are the people who prey on street kids. And the people who are—or *were*—street kids."

Ryan held her gaze for another moment, then nodded.

"How long were you on the streets?" Isabel asked.

"A little over two years."

"Then someone got you off the streets?"

"When I was sixteen." Ryan took a breath. "I don't think Adam can wait that long. And I don't want the things that happened to me to happen to him."

"What happened to you?"

"I didn't come here to talk about me."

"I'm sorry." Isabel smiled. "I got a little ahead of myself. I wasn't asking because I want to pry, or even because I want to hear your life story and make sympathetic noises."

"Then let's get off the subject."

She overlooked his chilly tone. "I'm asking because I think you could help Safe House."

"Me?" He blinked.

"As your friend Sara may have told you, Safe House was founded by a former prostitute. She wanted to get women off the streets. She's been doing incredible work, helping many women, getting a lot of attention for them, and for Safe House."

"That's good," Ryan said, thinking about Sara's exasperation with him. Because some people quit turning tricks and did something worthwhile with their lives.

"I joined Safe House two years ago," Isabel said. "I got the job by convincing the boss that this place should help kids, too. Now I direct our outreach, placement, and counseling services for youth."

He didn't jump on the word "placement" as he had with Sara. He'd been firm and direct at the beginning of this meeting; and Isabel had already assured him at length that Safe House would not detain Adam, report him to anyone, or coerce him in any way. Being convinced of that was the only reason Ryan was staying to discuss the specifics of Adam's situation with Isabel.

She continued, "I have the education, training, and experience to help these kids once they come in and *ask* for help. What I don't have is the ability to convince them to do that. Outreach begins in the streets, Ryan. It's incredibly hard to get these kids to take that first step and come here."

"Try offering free food."

"We do. They eat and leave. If we try to talk to them while they're eating, they brush us off, leave faster, or just stop coming."

He was nodding. "Of course."

"You understand that, don't you? You could even have predicted it."

"I did it myself, Isabel."

"That's why I think you can help here."

He shook his head. "I'm not going to go around your soup kitchen pestering homeless kids while they're eating."

"That's not what I have in mind."

He frowned. "You have something in mind?"

"Do you think you could do for other kids what you've been doing for Adam?"

Ryan made a frustrated sound. "What have I been doing

for Adam? I feed him a little, I give him a little cash, and the moment I leave, he's alone on the street again, with no future and no protection. And that's all I've been able to do for him. At least, until Sara thought of doing more."

"You did what you had to do when that was all you knew," Isabel said. "And when you knew better, you did better."

"That sounds like a quote."

She smiled. "It's the motto around here."

"Look, I haven't really done anything for him," Ryan said. "That's why I've come here."

"You're not viewing this clearly," Isabel said. "You've done a great deal for Adam. Just letting him know that you care what happens to him is more than anyone's done for him in a long time. You've shown him undemanding and unconditional friendship. You've been forging a bond of trust with him, and you've let him accept the relationship at his own pace."

"Well." Ryan looked down. "I remember that pace."

"You also remember what it would have taken to win *your* trust. You know how to talk to him, you understand his fears, even the ones he won't talk about, and you know exactly what can happen to him out there." She looked Ryan over and, after a pause, said, "It also looks like you learned to make a better life once you got off the streets."

This conversation was moving onto shaky ground. "In a way."

"You got an education—"

"Just my G.E.D."

"That's an education, Ryan. You can go on to college if you want—"

"Now you sound like Sara," he grumbled.

"Even without college, you obviously earn a decent living."

Cut to the chase, he thought.

"Isabel, I'm an escort."

"Oh." She nodded. "I see."

"You know what that is?"

"A nice word for prostitute." She didn't look shocked. Not even surprised.

"Did you suspect?" he demanded. "Is that why you're pushing?"

"Actually, no. But I'm certainly not surprised. As I'm sure you know, it's not at all unusual for a street kid to wind up as a prostitute. What *is* unusual is that you're evidently making good money at it, based on those nice clothes and that expensive wristwatch."

He said, "Because of escorting, and because of the arrests on my record, I can't help Adam myself. That's why I'm here, why I want *you* to help him."

She hesitated, looking as if she still wanted to pursue Ryan's own story, then said, "You're right. Let's focus on Adam. Are his parents alive?"

Relieved not to be talking about himself anymore, Ryan told her everything he'd been able to learn from Adam. After they had talked a while longer, Isabel said, "Considering his age, that he still has a living parent, and what his past experiences are, I do have a couple of ideas to consider for Adam's remaining years as a minor. I want to make some calls, and then I can talk to Adam about this. Or talk to you again, if you don't think he's ready to come in yet."

"Not just yet." Ryan wondered whether it was Adam or *he* who needed a little more time to adjust to this new idea.

"But you will convince him." It sounded more like a statement than a question.

"I will."

Isabel nodded. "I'll talk to you again. Maybe even by tomorrow. I have your home phone number here. Meanwhile . . ." She beamed at him. "Do you have a little more time? I want to show you around the center. That way you can answer any questions Adam might have about it when you discuss it with him."

"Sure, I have a little time." He needed to keep an eye on the clock, though. Catherine had been unpleasant about his request last night, but she had rescheduled his appointment with Alice for later this afternoon. "I'd like to have a look around."

"Good!" Isabel rose from her desk and led him out of her office. "This way."

Physically, Safe House was not particularly impressive. It was in a characterless building on a dreary street not all that far from where Adam lived in a truck cab behind an abandoned warehouse. Although handmade and hand-me-down decorations tried to cheer up the place, the real cheer, Ryan noticed, came from the staff—counselors, administrators, a nurse, a number of volunteers. They were mostly women, and their ages and ethnic groups were varied. They bustled around with smiles, energy, and an obvious sense of purpose.

There were also a lot of women who were clearly clients. Ryan saw several hookers who looked like they were dressed for work. A dozen women were going into a group discussion. A hollow-eyed woman sitting outside an office was smoking with furious dedication and repeatedly checking her watch. Although the woman was within three feet of a "No Smoking" sign, Isabel didn't admonish her. Ryan saw track marks on the woman's arm, which didn't surprise him. A lot of hookers were addicts.

In addition to two group meeting rooms, there were

several private counseling rooms, a small clinic, a conference room, a modest soup kitchen, some storage rooms, and some simple showering facilities for clients.

"No dormitory," Ryan observed.

"We're here to get people off the street permanently, not to warehouse them for a night." She added, "But I can recommend a shelter if Adam needs a place."

"I don't know," Ryan said, uneasy with the idea.

"Maybe not today, then. If you change your mind, you'll tell me." When they reached the reception area, she asked the secretary for some documents, then handed them to Ryan. "This tells you more about Safe House and our work. This is a list of names and phone numbers; you can reach us twenty-four hours a day. And this is some information about volunteer training, in case you—"

"Volunteer?" he repeated.

"Well, we do have some paying positions. If you'd like a job application—"

"That's not what I meant." Ryan waited until someone passed them, then said in a low voice, "You don't really want a prostitute volunteering here, do you?"

"Well, we do have a strict policy about that," she admitted.

"No kidding?"

"None of our staff or volunteers can be working prostitutes."

"So I don't need information about vol—"

"We want to protect kids from prostitution, not teach them how to make top dollar at it. The way someone evidently taught you."

"Could you just lay off me and—"

"So, like everyone else here, you'd have to give it up if you wanted to contribute to our work."

"Everyone else?"

"Well, almost everyone else. I am one of the few people on our staff who *wasn't* a prostitute before working here, Ryan. I'm also one of the few people on staff here with no rap sheet, whether we're talking about arrests or convictions."

He didn't try to hide his surprise. "Everybody working here was in the life?"

"*Almost* everybody. Including, as you may recall, the boss."

"Oh. Right."

"Nobody here condemns a person's past, Ryan."

"Yeah, well, it's not my *past.*"

"But you could quit it, turn it into the past," Isabel said, "and do important work here."

"Are you trying to save my soul or something?"

"I don't care about your soul. I care about the kids I think you can help. You've developed some trust with Adam and will get him to seek our help. Having talked with you, I think you can do that with a lot more kids."

"Let's just see if I can help this one," he said.

"You're a potentially valuable resource, and you're wasting your life turning tricks for a rich clientele." Her gaze flicked over him. "I mean, you're obviously not selling it in the streets for fifty bucks a pop."

He checked his expensive wristwatch. "No, I'm certainly not, Isabel. And, if you'll excuse me, I've got an appointment on Telegraph Hill. Mustn't be late for work."

"Ryan."

He walked away, angry and defensive. "I didn't come here for this. You have no right to—"

"Ryan, I'm sorry."

He looked over his shoulder at her.

She smiled. "Occupational hazard, I guess."

He shrugged. "I guess so."

"We'll get Adam off the streets. *Then* we'll talk about what you could do to help around here if you'd just apply yourself."

A puff of laughter escaped him. "I think you just spoiled your apology."

She called after him, "I'll make those calls I mentioned, and I'll be in touch very soon."

He waved over his shoulder in acknowledgement.

"No, Kevin, you're *not* canceling!" Catherine snapped over the phone at him two days later. "Not *again.*"

"Oh, come on," he said into his cell phone. "I didn't cancel last time, I just postponed." After his appointment at Safe House, he'd dutifully bedded Alice Van Offelen for the rest of the afternoon, even though he was so distracted by thoughts of his conversation with Isabel that his performance was a trifle erratic. He'd apologized and claimed he had injured his back during a game of squash; Alice had believed him and expressed sympathy.

"Don't mince words," Catherine said. "Just get your ass to your damn appointment on time, Kevin."

He knew she only swore when she was really angry. "Catherine. I'm sorry, I know this is inconvenient—"

"Inconvenient? It's *outrageous,* and I won't put up with this, Kevin! Not twice in once week!"

"What do you want me to do?" he said. "I'm almost a hundred miles from the city, stuck behind an overturned eighteen-wheeler, with traffic at a standstill all around me. I'm not getting back in time for this evening's appointment, Catherine, and there's nothing I can do about it."

"What are you doing that far out of town on a day when you knew you had to work?" she demanded.

"I had some personal business to take care of."

"*What* personal business?"

He closed his eyes and clung to his patience. "It was *personal,* Catherine. I'm not free-lancing. I wasn't out here doing a job."

"What's going on, Kevin?"

"Nothing that you need to know about."

"You're becoming unreliable. You're letting me down."

Oh, the hell with patience. "It's not my fault I got stuck behind an accident blocking the whole goddamn highway, Catherine! Go find a traffic report if you don't believe me!"

"I want to know what you were doing out there."

"My personal life is none of your goddamn business," he said.

"It is when it interferes with your work!"

"Oh, right, because the world will certainly come to an end if I don't show up tonight."

"This is an important client, Kevin, and I won't have you fucking up."

"What an interesting choice of words."

Her voice dark with fury, she said, "If you don't get there on time and do exactly as—"

"It's not going to happen, Catherine. I won't be there. Call Trevor or someone to replace me."

"I will not tolerate this, Kevin!"

"Fine. *Fire* me."

He hung up without waiting for her reply.

Ryan tapped on Sara's French doors, then opened them. "Sara?"

"Ryan?" she called from the bedroom. "Is that you?"

He strolled into the living room, tired from his long

drive. "No, it's the other man who's always entering your home without warning."

She came out of the bedroom a moment later, buttoning a pretty blouse. Her hair looked nice and she had on a pair of earrings he hadn't seen before. She said, "I thought you weren't going to be home tonight."

"Change of plans," he said. "Going somewhere?"

"Dinner with friends." She glanced at the clock. "I have to leave in a minute. But since you're back, tell me! What did you think of the place?"

He sat down on the couch and watched while she started searching for something. "You were right."

"I love those words! Say them again."

He smiled. "It was worth the trip."

Isabel had called yesterday to tell him that there was a space available for someone Adam's age at a place called the Bernice Village Foundation. Since it was a juvenile facility a hundred miles from the city, Ryan had instantly rejected the very idea, knowing how Adam would view this suggestion. After an hour of arguing about it, Sara had convinced Ryan to call Isabel back and make arrangements to go see the place himself, the sooner the better. So he'd gone this morning.

"So," Sara said, nudging him aside to search the cushions behind him, "it wasn't a concentration camp?"

"I never said that. You said that."

"Yes, when you were accusing me of colluding with Isabel to lock Adam up in a bleak juvenile detention center in the middle of nowhere."

Ryan shifted so she could search on the other side of him. "I've already apologized for that. I've already said I overreacted. Could we not go over this again?"

She smiled. "So what was it like?"

"Actually . . ." He watched the way her pants stretched across her bottom as she bent over to look under the coffee table. "It was nice. I liked it."

The Bernice Village Foundation was named after a woman, Bernice, who had been the foster mother of an orphaned girl who eventually grew up to star in a popular television sitcom for nine years. It was a private foundation that mostly relied on the TV star and wealthy donors for its funding. The "village" consisted of several group homes in a peaceful rural setting.

"There's a short-term shelter for kids who need a temporary place to stay while permanent placement is found for them," Ryan said. "But what we're looking at for Adam is one of the permanent group homes, where he could stay until he turns eighteen. Or until his father is able to take him back, *if* that happens before then."

Sara put her hands on her hips and looked around the living room with a frown. "And what did you think of the permanent homes?"

Ryan rose from the couch and looked under her desk. "Here, Sara." He handed her purse to her.

"Oh, there it is!" She looked surprised. "Thank you."

He watched with fond amusement while she checked its contents. "Well, in fact," he said, "the group homes were nice. Clean. A little impersonal, but pretty cheerful. The kids are very well supervised, so it seems unlikely that another kid would have an easy time harming Adam in this place."

Clearly dissatisfied with the contents of her purse, Sara started searching again. "What did you think of the staff?"

"Very earnest. Dedicated. Pretty strict."

"That's good, right?"

"Adam would have to follow the rules, or he couldn't

stay. But it means that dangerous kids definitely don't get to stay." He started walking towards her kitchen.

"How would you feel about Adam living there?"

"Much better than I thought I would." He looked on the kitchen table and, sure enough, found her keys. He picked them up and went back to the living room. "The staff spent two hours answering every question and showing me everything. Here, Sara."

"Oh! Thank you!" She accepted her keys from him, put them in her pocket, and said, "I need my shoes."

"And the people there think ahead to the future," Ryan said, raising his voice as she disappeared into the bedroom for a moment. "They'd get him back on track with his education. They'd even do what they could to help if he wanted to attend college after he leaves."

"That's wonderful!" She came back into the room and sat down to put on her shoes.

He nodded. "I think . . ."

"Go on."

"I think I'm going to talk to him about it."

"That's great, Ryan." She finished buckling both shoes and looked up at him. "It sounds like a very good opportunity. I didn't even know a place like that existed."

"It's new. And there are very few places like it. There's just one spot available there at the moment, and once it's filled, they don't know how soon another will open up."

"So you need to talk to Adam soon?"

"Yes."

"And see if you can convince him to meet with Isabel?"

"Uh-huh."

As if sensing his restless emotions, she paused in her preparations and fixed him with a concerned look. "What is it?"

He shook his head. "Nothing really. Just . . ."

"Ryan?"

"Isabel and I had a long talk today. This time on my cell phone. While I was stuck in traffic and couldn't escape her."

"You could have hung up," she pointed out dryly. "Or just not called her."

"She, uh . . ." It was on his mind so much, he couldn't *not* talk about it with Sara anymore. "She keeps trying to talk me into volunteering at Safe House."

"Yeah? Doing what?"

"Act as a pipeline between her staff and homeless kids. Start building trust, convincing kids to come to Safe House and find out how they can get off the streets."

"That's a great idea!"

He looked at her. "I don't know . . ."

She caught his shifting gaze and held it. "Would it bother you? To spend a lot of time on the streets, I mean?"

He shouldn't be surprised at her perception. She was sharp, and she knew him well by now. "Yes. No. I don't know anymore. It bothered me a lot the first couple of times I went to hunt up Adam. It made me feel like I was that kid again—that helpless, scared, ignorant kid living on the razor's edge." He folded his arms across his chest. "But I'm not."

"No, you're not. Even though, sure, you sometimes feel like it. The way I sometimes feel like that bespectacled, dateless nerd whom the boys all snickered at."

The vibrant colors of her blouse brought out the contrast between her dark hair, fair skin, and dark eyes. Her breasts pushed subtly against its fabric, and her hips and thighs filled out her trousers just right. Sara's face was alive with enthusiasm, concern, and good humor.

"Well," he said, "the boys aren't snickering now."

She smiled, pleased. "Then if being there again isn't what bothers you . . ."

"I would just feel like a fraud. I'm no outreach worker, Sara. I'm . . ." He shrugged uncomfortably. "You know what I am."

"Isabel knows, too," she reminded him. "So why not just assume that she knows what she's talking about when she says you can help?" She glanced at the clock. "Damn! I have to go, Ryan. I'm late." She jumped up and picked up her purse. "I'm sorry. We'll talk more later."

"Will you be out late?" he asked, following her to her door.

"Hmm? Oh!" She looked frustrated. "Yes, I will. I'm sorry. I didn't think you'd be home tonight."

He put his hand on her back and steered her toward the door. "I didn't, either. Go have a good time with your friends."

"Do you want to come?"

"No, I'm beat. I'm going to sack out."

"Oh! Wait. I knew there was something I wanted to tell you. I heard from one of the literary agents I queried."

"And?"

She waved a hand. "It's probably nothing."

"And?" he prodded.

"Well, we had a really good talk. About my career, about the business. About my work—she's read one of my books. And she's asked to see the first six chapters of the new book."

"Do you have that much done?"

"Yes." She added, "I'm not getting my hopes up or anything, of course. But, well, she's sort of my dream agent. I know her reputation, and I'd be thrilled if we could work together."

"Who are you trying to kid? Your hopes are *up*."

"Okay, yeah, they are." She smiled. "Thanks. You know. For the moral support. For listening to me babble and obsess. And for the good feedback and sensible advice."

He gave her a hug, closed his eyes, and held on to her for a long moment. His body knew what it wanted, and so did his heart, so it wasn't easy to let go. Judging by the flush in her cheeks as she stepped back, it wasn't so easy for her to let go, either.

"Will you be around tomorrow?" she asked softly.

"No," he said. "I have to work, and I also want to go s—"

"Oh. Never mind." She turned to leave. "Goodnight."

"Sara."

"No," she said over her shoulder. "You don't get to put your arms around me and then tell me that you're 'working' tomorrow."

He saw the anger in her eyes and felt stricken. "Sara, can we jus—"

"No, *don't*." She shrugged off his hand. "Even if what you do means nothing to you, it means something to me. It cuts me to ribbons, Ryan. Every single goddamn day."

She slammed the door behind her, leaving him standing alone in her apartment.

The following morning, Ryan wrapped his hands around a cup of bad coffee while watching Adam eat a huge, greasy breakfast.

After a long silence between them, Adam said, "What's with you? You seem all wound up today."

He didn't bother denying it. If the kid smelled insincerity, it would chip away at the trust. Ryan understood. He'd been the same way. He supposed he still was. That didn't wash off, no matter how clean he got. One of the many things that drew him to Sara was her inability to be anything *but* sincere.

He said to Adam, "Yeah, I guess I am pretty wound up today."

"You have a fight with your girlfriend or something?" When Ryan looked at him in surprise, Adam said, "With you, it's always 'Sara this' and 'Sara that.' But you ain't said her name once today."

Ryan made a wry face. "That's not exactly what I was thinking about. But, yeah, good call. She got mad at me yesterday."

"What about?"

"Personal stuff."

"Like what?"

"Like personal stuff."

Adam rolled his eyes. "Whatever."

Ryan had never told Adam that Sara was his girlfriend, but it was a natural assumption for the kid to make, and Ryan didn't bother to correct him. It was the way he felt about her, after all, even if it wasn't the way they were living.

Now he said to Adam, "But there's something else on my mind. Something I want to talk to you about."

Adam stuffed half a sausage into his mouth and looked expectantly at Ryan.

"I don't think it's safe for you to be living on the streets."

Adam snorted and said, with his mouth full, "Y'think?"

"So I've been thinking about where you could live instead."

That got his attention. He stared at Ryan for a moment, then swallowed his food in such a huge gulp that Ryan winced a little.

"The thing is," Ryan said, "you can't live with me."

The kid looked so hurt for a moment that Ryan was surprised. Adam still shifted so easily into hostile suspicion, Ryan hadn't realized the boy had been entertaining the possibility of living with him. Or even, in fact, of getting into a car with him.

Then Adam looked down at his food and said, "No *way* would I live with you."

"Of course," Ryan said, "if you'd visit me, I'd like that. You could come to my place." Seeing the familiar frown of wary suspicion creep across Adam's face, Ryan added, "You could watch TV. Raid the fridge. Play with my dog."

"I'd like to see your dog," Adam admitted. "I like dogs."

"I should warn you, Macy's idea of playing is just sleeping while you scratch his belly. He doesn't fetch. Or run. Or even walk much. I thought he had a thyroid problem, and Sara kept nagging me until I took him to the vet. But the vet did some tests and said, no, Macy's fine, he's just lazy, and I spoil him too much."

He was babbling. However, Adam seemed to find this an amusing story and asked a lot of questions about Macy.

"You can come see him any time you want," Ryan said.

The kid surprised him by saying, "Today?"

Ryan checked his watch. "Today's not good."

Another mood shift. "Oh, well. Forget it."

"It's just that I have to go to work soon." He'd told Adam he was a model.

"Whatever."

"What about tomorrow?" When Adam shrugged, Ryan said, "I could come get you in the morning." Seeing Adam puzzle over whether or not that sounded potentially dangerous, he added, "We could go by bus, if you want. So you'd know the way by yourself after that."

"Bus?"

"It's too far to walk."

"Do you come here by bus?"

"I usually bring my car and park it in a garage." He wasn't careless enough to leave his Infiniti sitting out on the street in this neighborhood.

Adam pondered this. "The bus sounds okay. Then I could leave whenever I want to."

"Okay. And once you know the way, you can come over whenever you want to, too."

"So I could see Macy tomorrow?"

Ryan smiled. "Yeah. And you can meet Sara . . . Oh, no, she won't be there tomorrow. She's going to her sister's for the day. But you can meet her next time." Struck by inspiration, he added, "Actually, I'd really like you to come over tomorrow, because it's my birthday."

"Yeah?"

"Yeah."

"So how come your girl won't be there, then?"

"I forgot to tell her. And she wasn't my girl last year, so she doesn't know."

"Your birthday, huh? Well, I guess it sucks to be by yourself on your birthday."

"It totally sucks."

"I guess I could come over," Adam said.

"But the thing is," Ryan said, trying to get back to the discussion he wanted to have, "although you can visit me, there's a lot of reasons you can't live with me."

"I don't wanna live with you."

"Well, I wanted you to."

"You did?"

"So Sara tried to find out how we could do that. I've

told you how smart she is. She's really good at finding out about things. And what she found out is that there's no way they'll let you live with me."

Adam shrugged and poked at his food.

"So then we started to look at other places you might be able to live."

Adam went still and gave him a dark glare. "Like what?"

"Well, there's this place I went to see yesterday . . ."

"What *kind* of a place, man?"

Ryan started describing Bernice Village. He was only a few sentences into his speech when Adam started protesting. And if Ryan had been negative when Isabel first suggested the place, Adam was positively livid.

"You're not putting me into another one of those places! No way!"

"It's not like that, Adam. I went to see it, and it's nice."

"Fuck you, man!"

"And I promise, no one is 'putting' you anywhere. We can just talk about this."

"*Fuck* your talk!"

"I won't ever try to make you do anything you don't want to do—"

"Why are you doing this? Why don't you just leave me alone?"

"—and I won't let anyone else make you do anything you don't want to do."

"Why don't you just stay *away* from me?"

"Because I'm worried about you."

Adam started sliding out of the booth where they sat. "Well, I don't need you worrying about me. And I sure as hell don't need you trying to put me away somewhere, where they can—can—I won't go!"

Ryan threw some money on the table and followed him

out of the diner. "It's not safe for you, living on the streets."

"Yeah, well, so far it's better than the last place they put me!"

"No one's putting you in a place like that again."

"Bullshit, man!"

"Adam, you have no future on the streets. It's dangerous, you're not getting any education—"

"Just stay the fuck away from me!"

People were staring. Ryan ignored them as he pursued Adam down the street. "Will you just *talk* with me about this? I'm just asking to talk. Nothing more."

"Get away!"

Realizing that crowding and hounding Adam now would just make things worse, Ryan said, "Okay, I'll go now." He had to get ready for work, anyhow. "But I'll be back tomorrow."

"Don't bother, man!"

"If you don't want to talk about this anymore, we won't."

"I don't want to talk to you at *all*."

"And if you want to talk about anything—not this, just anything—before then, or if you need help or something, you've got my phone number, right?" When Adam didn't respond, Ryan said, "Can I give it to you again?"

"I don't need it again," Adam snapped.

"Well, say it back to me, so I know you know it."

Adam made a rude gesture, turned around, and stalked away.

"Oh, that went well," Ryan muttered to himself. "Yeah, I could really make something worthwhile out of my life by doing *this*."

CHAPTER FIFTEEN

Sara felt cranky and morose when she got home on Sunday a full hour later than anticipated. Traffic coming back into the city had been awful, and the sun was low on the horizon by the time she opened the door to her apartment, came inside, and kicked off her shoes.

She immediately glanced out onto the balcony to see if Ryan was there. When she saw that he was, her heart gave a little skip. She opened her French doors and stepped out into the early evening breeze, longing to be with him.

He was leaning against the balcony rail, gazing out across the gradually darkening expanse of the park. The soft wind stirred his hair, ruffling it so the fading light could find the gold hidden somewhere in its dusky depths if only he'd favor the sun by turning his head just the right way. He wore old jeans, ragged around the cuffs, and a white shirt that he hadn't bothered to tuck in. He looked as carelessly beautiful as a wild animal, a wary creature willing to take food from her hand because he had grown to trust her.

She saw him stiffen a little when he heard the doors open, then turn his head slightly to acknowledge her presence.

"Hi," he said.

"Hi."

The shifting shadows emphasized the slant of his cheekbone, the slight hollow beneath it, the firm line of his jaw, the breath-stealing good looks which she knew by heart. His shoulders—straight, square, and smoothly muscled beneath the cotton of his shirt—moved with a single deep breath.

Then he raised his arm to take a sip from the drink in his hand.

Sara came forward to stand beside him, looking in the direction of his gaze as she rested her hands on the balcony rail. Her heart pounded with sudden awareness. Drumming heavily in her ears. Echoing through her blood. Aching with anticipation inside her chest . . . because it knew what she had decided even before she acknowledged it in her mind. Even before she admitted to herself why she had come out here to join him in the seductive apricot light that turned him into a fawn, a golden panther, something both innocent and feral. Something she couldn't leave alone or turn her back on.

She heard the ice cubes click together in his glass, and she glanced sideways as he took another sip.

"Scotch?" she asked as he drank the last of it.

"Yeah." After a moment, he added, "I don't suppose you want any." His voice, soft as sand, sent a shiver through her.

"No."

"How was lunch at Miriam's?" he asked.

"Well, Jan's a better cook than Miriam is, thank God."

His mouth quirked. "That's not exactly what I meant."

"If you'd ever tasted Miriam's cooking, you'd realize how important that is."

"I meant," he said, "how was it, seeing your sister playing house with her lady love?"

"A little weird." She started chuckling, her mood shifting a bit now that she could finally share the day with him. "Of course, my father made it even weirder by doing his best to casually work the names of famous lesbians into the conversation."

Ryan's shoulders shook with silent laughter. "Of course."

"Mostly literary figures. Aunt Minnie got into the spirit

of things and started mentioning Hollywood lesbians, but Dad had never heard of any of them." Smiling at Ryan, Sara admitted, "Jan bore up very well. But Miriam got a little short-tempered after a while."

"Go figure." He asked, "Do you feel better about Jan and Miriam now?"

"Yes, I do. Jan seems very good-natured, and it's obvious that she loves Miriam. They seem very happy together. So happy they're almost giddy." Sara folded her arms on the railing and rested her chin on them. "I felt a little uncomfortable, and I'm sure Miriam knew it. But, in fact, as 'meet the family' meals go, it was much better than when Miriam first brought David home."

"Well, he was a schmuck, after all."

She smiled. "I'll get used to the two of them together."

"You will."

"Miriam's happy. That's what matters."

"Right."

"I think that's what my father has decided matters, too." After a moment, she added, "He kept talking about my mother today. I guess because Jan can never meet her." Sara turned her head a little and watched the breeze toy with Ryan's hair. "To tell the truth, today would have been much more awkward if my mother had been there. But, of course, Miriam and I didn't contradict Dad when he kept saying he wished Jan could have known her."

He nodded absently. "I'm glad the day went all right."

Silence fell between them. After a while, she asked, "What did you do today?"

He frowned. "Tried to get Adam to talk to me."

"About Bernice Village?"

"No, I tried that yesterday. And he was furious about it. Today I just tried to get him to talk to me at *all*. About anything." Ryan shook his head, his expression bleak. "No dice."

"I know you're worried, but you knew it would be tough," she said. "You knew he'd reject the idea at first. I mean, Ryan, *you* rejected the idea at first." When he didn't respond, she put her hand on his arm.

He pulled away from her touch and stepped out of reach. "I know. I'm just a little . . ." He shrugged.

Sara straightened up, her heart starting to drum heavily again. "Are you going out tonight?"

"I'm off work today," was the bland response. After a moment he made a sound which might have been amusement—or might not. "It's my birthday. Catherine never makes me work on my birthday."

She turned to him. "Today? Your birthday?"

He looked into his empty glass. "Twenty-seven."

"Ryan! Why didn't you say something?"

He shrugged. "Just did."

"Before now, I mean," she chided.

He shrugged again. "What for?"

"So we could celebrate." When he didn't reply, she added, "We still can. Let's go out."

"Nah. Don't feel like it."

It hurt her to see him looking so downcast. She put a hand on his arm again.

He moved away as if she'd burned him. "Don't."

"Ryan."

"Just *don't.*"

"But I—"

"I've just had a big shot of really good scotch on an empty stomach, Sara," he said. "Don't test me now."

"I'm not."

"If you touch me, you're testing me," he snapped.

"That's how it is. So just back off, okay?"

He certainly hadn't intended that as a seductive speech, but his outburst made her head spin with desire.

"I don't want to go out, either," she said. "I have a better idea."

He caught the suggestive note in her voice and looked at her suspiciously. She held his gaze as she came toward him, tingling with nerves and excitement and the glow of passion finally let out of its cage. He went tense all over when she took his glass out of his hand. She delicately licked the rim where his lips had touched, then took a sip of the scotch-flavored melting ice. Their eyes met again, hers telling him what she wanted. He drew in a swift, sharp breath.

"No." He shook his head. "You said—"

"I don't care what I said."

He took a step back. "You'll regret it later."

She took a step forward. "I don't care about that, either."

He took his whiskey glass away from her. "I'm going inside now," he said, retreating as he spoke. "And tomorrow, you'll thank me for it."

As he turned away from her, she said, "Ryan, I love you."

He stopped in his tracks, lowered his head and made a choked sound. "Not fair, Sara."

"Not fair?" She pressed her body against his back and wrapped her arms around his waist. "My sister is so happy in love she's practically levitating. I felt so lonely, seeing the two of them together. You know what's not fair? I'm in love—"

"Sara . . ."

"—and I'm so lonely I wanted to cry all day. Why don't I get to be happy now that I've found someone, too?"

"I never wanted to hurt you like this."

"My father kept talking about my mother, and he misses her so much, his eyes got misty and his voice got choked." She felt Ryan's ribs moving in and out with his breath, felt his tension and his wary indecision. "I drove home all the way thinking, what if I died in a pile-up on the highway this afternoon? When I took my last breath, what would be my favorite memory? What would be my biggest regret?" She whispered, "They would both be you."

She felt a shudder go through him as she slid her palms across his stomach. One of his hands covered hers convulsively, gripping too hard. She closed her eyes and rubbed her cheek against his shoulder. He didn't even breathe for a moment, and then he started breathing too hard.

Sara murmured, "And I couldn't even bear to think about how I'd feel if you died. It would be worse than pain, worse than grief, to lose you." She stroked his torso, her palms moving over the flesh-warmed fabric of his shirt. "Especially without ever having loved you the way I want to love you. It feels like criminal stupidity, like mortal sin to squander this, Ryan."

"If we make love . . ." His voice was dark and husky.

"Yes, let's make love," she urged, swamped with longing. "I want to feel you inside me and wrapped all around me."

"Sara." He dropped his glass, which clunked hard on the wooden balcony. "Everything will be different."

"I *want* it to be different."

He turned his head to rub his cheek against her hair. She heard him swallow. "You know where I've been."

"I don't care where you've been," she told him, meaning it. "I just want you to be with me."

"Don't change your mind afterwards," he whispered, turning in her arms.

"Don't change your mind now," she whispered back.

She met his kiss as his arms came around her. He was rough for a moment, squeezing the air from her body, grinding his lips against hers, shoving her back against the door to his apartment so hard that she grunted as she hit it with a thud. And then suddenly he was gentle, nuzzling her as his hands stroked and squeezed, murmuring her name and pressing soft, warm kisses upon her forehead, her cheek, her neck, and upon the flesh which he bared as his fingers worked at the buttons of her blouse.

She clutched his shoulders when she felt his breath on her cleavage, and then his hot, tender lips. He unfastened her bra, pushed it out of his way, and sought her breasts with his mouth. She sagged in his arms as her knees gave way and dark heat flooded her senses.

"Mmm, let's go inside," he murmured, breathing hard as he fumbled for the door handle. "Come to bed with me, Sara."

It gave her an absurd thrill that his eagerness made him clumsy. He laughed shakily because he couldn't get the door open right away, and then he apologized in horrified tones for accidentally whacking her with it when he yanked on it.

"I'm so sorry!"

"Come inside," she insisted, tugging on his hand.

"Are you okay? Does it—"

She kissed him. "Mmmm, that's better."

He forgot his earnest apologies and kissed her again, his tongue hot and sweet inside her mouth, his hands moving over her with possessive urgency. They stumbled across the living room together, their mouths clinging ferociously while they fumbled with each other's clothing. She made a frustrated sound as his buttons confounded her, and she stopped kissing him to look at what she was doing. He seized her chin and brought her mouth back to his again, then dealt with the buttons himself. He shrugged out of his shirt as he backed her towards the bedroom, his mouth still moving hungrily on hers. His back and shoulders were naked under her hands, his skin smooth and warm and satiny. The tender fuzz of his chest brushed against her breasts as he tugged off her blouse and her bra.

They bumped into a wall and he pressed her against it, moving his hips snugly into hers, letting her feel the effect she had on him. She arched her back, rubbing her breasts against him, and cupped his bottom to pull him even closer.

He drew in a breath through his teeth and pulled his head back, putting his hands on either side of her face so he could look into her eyes.

"Tell me again," he said.

Dazed with passion, it took her a moment to realize what he meant. "I love you."

He kissed her, his lips soft, his breath hot.

"I love you, too," he said. "You know that, don't you?"

"I guess I do."

"Don't guess." He burrowed his fingers into her hair and pressed his forehead against hers. "You're the best thing in my life. The best thing that's ever happened to me."

She smiled, her heart melting. "You're the best thing in my life, too."

He shook his head. "No."

She kissed him.

He said, "No, I cause you so much—"

"Shhh. You don't even know how good you are for me, do you?"

"I know how good I want to be for you." His hands moved from her hair to her shoulders, then down to her breasts, which he stroked and cupped. "I know how good I want to be *to* you."

Sara's breath rushed out of her lungs as he lowered his head to be very, very good to her. His lips toyed, his teeth teased, and his tongue tickled and massaged.

"Oh!" She quivered in startled response when his hand slid between her legs to tease, tickle, and massage there, too.

She made desperate, guttural noises as he took his time with her, being so good to her she thought she might dissolve into putty if he didn't stop tormenting her. Before this, she had imagined that even with Ryan, whom she loved, she would feel awkward the first time they were naked together. Now, however, she was just eager and relieved when he finally stripped off her trousers, shed his jeans, and pulled her against him, their naked bodies straining together as they kissed and clung. She couldn't imagine how she had endured the barrier of clothes between them for so long.

He took both her hands and backed away from her, pulling her into his bedroom, his eyes glowing with pleasure as he studied her body in the dying light coming through the window. As she came into his arms again, he sank back onto the bed, sprawling across it with her. They laughed in surprise as his cat, startled out of her nap, leaped off the bed and left the room. And then the two of them were all over each other again, ravenous and tender and greedy. They rolled over and over on his bed, drowning in the taste and feel of each other, exploring, discovering, and lingering on their discoveries while the last of the sunlight faded and the room gradually turned dark.

Eventually, Ryan reached over to turn on a bedside lamp. "I want to see you."

She was breathing so hard she could barely speak. "I want to see you, too."

"Just a minute," he whispered, pulling away from her.

She held onto him. "What are you doing?"

"Wait," he panted, "wait." He dragged himself out of her arms.

"Where are you going?"

He grinned at her tone and slid off the bed, pointing mutely at the dresser while the sound of his breath gusted through the room.

"What?"

He opened the top drawer, reached inside, and pulled out a handful of condoms.

"Oh!"

He smiled again and came back to the bed, still breathing like he'd just run all the way up their stairs. He tossed all but one of the packets onto the nightstand, then seized her by the shoulders and drew her up for a hard kiss.

The room spun dizzily when he pushed her onto her back and fell into the rumpled covers with her. She felt his hand between her legs, moving with familiarity now that they had spent time exploring each other so thoroughly. Then she felt something new exploring there—

"Oh."

—and closed her eyes to concentrate on the sensation of Ryan pushing gently into her body. She spread her legs wider and tilted her hips, welcoming him. He put his hand on her knee and nudged, and she shifted in response to his silent urging. Then she felt his arms on either side of her, bracing himself to thrust harder, and she stroked her palms along his torso, her whole body hot and tingling and yearning for him.

The world fell away as he started moving. Sara knew she wouldn't notice if the building collapsed on top of them. All she could feel was the way they fit so perfectly, the way their bodies danced in such hungry harmony, the way she kept soaring and plunging with him as his deep groans shivered through her and his hips ground desperately into hers.

His skin gleamed with sweat and his muscles strained under her seeking hands. He pressed his forehead against hers and said in a tight, breathless voice, "You wanted . . . to feel me . . . inside you . . . and wrapped . . . all around you?"

She couldn't answer, couldn't speak, and couldn't control the rhythmic moans tearing through her. She bucked against him and focused on his sweetly murmuring voice as hot, glorious spasms washed through her, shaking her with delicious violence and forcing the surrender that she had been begging to give.

As she lay beneath him in a mindless, sated daze, she felt him kissing her face, her shoulder, her neck. She opened her eyes to meet his glittering gaze and raised a trembling hand to touch his flushed face.

"Hold me while I come," he whispered.

She moaned softly with a different kind of pleasure and wrapped her arms and legs around him.

Her contented body accepted every hard, deep thrust with stirring interest, warming to his dance again when his back arched, his hips jerked, and he plunged desperately into her with a soul-deep groan as his eyes squeezed shut and his body shook with powerful tremors.

After he collapsed on top of her, he rubbed his cheek against her breast and murmured, "I promise I'll move in a minute."

"Don't move." She tightened her arms and legs around him.

"I must be heavy."

"Don't move." She kissed his tousled hair. "Ryan?"

"Hmmm?"

"Happy birthday."

She felt his puff of laughter against her breast. "And many happy returns." He tugged on one of her arms until she stopped hugging him with it and instead let him hold her hand. "I love you."

She kissed his hair again and lay with him in limp, contented silence for a while.

After some of her energy returned, she asked, "Why do you keep the condoms all the way over there?"

"I've never needed them by the bed before," he answered. "You're the only one besides me who's ever been in this bed." He paused, then added, "Well, except for the people sitting on it during your party. Who are the princes in the tower?"

Sara started laughing. "No *way* are we spoiling this moment by talking about a five hundred year old murder mystery."

"A real one?"

"Yes."

"No kidding? Tell me about it."

"That does it. I'm going home."

He laughed and wrestled her as she tried to get up. "Okay, okay. No questions about dead princes. Just lots of sex. I promise."

"You'd better mean that."

After so much sex that Sara felt as if her bones had melted, she lay on her side in satisfied exhaustion, drowsing under the covers. Ryan lay snuggled up against her back, his arm draped over her waist.

She murmured, "I thought I'd be more nervous. I mean, you know, shy."

He nudged her with his knee. "About what?"

"My body."

"Your body?" He started moving his hand over it, as if seeking the source of her shyness. "I love your body."

"Well . . ." She closed her eyes as he lazily touched and caressed her. "You're younger, you work out, and your body is in great shape. I'm older. I'd actually rather clean house than go to a health club—and you *know* how I feel about cleaning house."

"Yes, I do."

"And gravity has been taking its toll for years."

"Hey, you don't get to say mean things about this body." He wrapped his arm around her waist and squeezed. "This is my girlfriend's body, so I have to throw down with you if you disrespect it."

"Wow, I guess I'll be quiet, then."

He moved his hand to cup her breast and kissed her shoulder. "Sara, looking at you and touching you turns me on. Like nothing else. I love what this body does for me."

She reached back to touch him. "Then we're even."

"So I'm glad you aren't shy."

"I always have been before. Just not with you."

He shifted so he could kiss her mouth. Then he lay his head back down on the pillow and made a contented sound as he snuggled more comfortably against her.

Sara's thoughts drifted pleasantly for a while, until she noticed the remaining packets on the nightstand. Half a dozen of them. She smiled. "That's so ostentatious, Ryan. Putting that big pile right next to the bed."

He lifted his head and looked over her shoulder. "I just don't want to make multiple trips across the room. Especially now that my legs are so wobbly."

"We don't need all those tonight."

He slid his hand over her hip. "Oh, yes, we do."

"No, I can tell. You're fading fast."

He gave her bottom a light slap. “Only because I haven’t eaten all day.”

“All day? You must be starving by now.” She started to sit up, but he tightened his hold on her, stopping her.

“I’ll bet you’re impressed with my stamina.”

“Ah, but if I don’t feed you, how much longer will it last?” She nudged him to make room, then rolled onto her back so she could look at him. “A girl’s got to plan ahead.”

“Hmmm. Good point.” He brushed a kiss across her lips, then propped his head on his hand. “Want to go get something to eat?”

“It’s late.” She stroked his calf with her foot. “The café might still be open, but we should go right away. It’s probably closing soon.”

Sara turned her head when she heard Macy’s footsteps in the doorway. The dog came to the side of the bed, looked at the two of them as they lay snuggled together, and burped.

“He wants his walk,” Ryan said.

“You know this because he burped at us?”

Ryan kissed her, sat up, and threw the covers aside. “I know this because he’s awake and on his feet.” He rose and went to the dresser to find some clothes. “But you’re so demanding, I don’t have any strength left to carry him up those stairs.”

“Demanding?” Sara sat up. “Look who’s talking.”

Grinning at her, Ryan pulled on a pair of briefs. “Let’s go out first, and I’ll walk him after we get back. I can probably manage the stairs after I’ve had something to eat. And then . . .” He nodded at the pile of condoms on the bedside table. “We can work our way through those.”

CHAPTER SIXTEEN

Whenever he had been weak enough to let himself imagine what it would be like, it had been just like this: Sitting close together in their neighborhood café, talking, laughing, and holding hands. Sharing a meal after hours of satisfying sex. Winding down companionably as fatigue caught up with them, and looking forward to sleeping together in the same bed.

They'd been too excited by each other to sleep earlier. He hadn't been able to get enough of her. Now he felt pleasantly tired, his belly was full, and he looked forward to curling up with her in his arms when they got home.

They walked back to their building arm-in-arm, their heads close together while she finished telling him about the princes in the Tower of London, the young sons of Edward IV who may or may not have been murdered on the orders of their uncle, Richard III, in the fifteenth century.

Still talking, they entered his apartment. Ryan closed the front door, ignored a clearly impatient Macy, and started pushing Sara's jacket off her shoulders as he backed her towards the couch.

"Are you listening to me?" she said.

"Yeah, yeah." He dropped her jacket on the floor and went to work on her blouse. "Henry . . . some number."

"Henry VII." She brushed away his hands. "Pay attention."

He shifted his attention to her trousers. "They should have come up with some names . . ." Unbuttoning and unzipping. ". . . besides Richard, Edward, and Henry. It's confusing." He slid his hands under her blouse and kept herding her towards the couch. "Using the same names over and over."

She was laughing. "So Henry VII—"

"I'm tired of history," he whispered against her mouth. "Let's move on to biology." He slid his hand inside her pants.

"Hey, you're the one who insisted on talking about . . ." She gasped and closed her eyes. *"Oh."*

He smiled, enjoying the way she shuddered when he touched her just right. Then he pushed her backwards until she fell onto the couch.

"It's been at least ninety minutes." He tugged at her trousers. "I want you again."

She lifted her hips to help him, her breath coming faster now. "You said you wanted to sleep when we got home."

"Just changed my mind." He stripped off his shirt.

"You said you were too tired to do this again."

"Food revived me." He unzipped his jeans and joined her on the couch.

It was fast and hot and intense, and he could hardly move when it was over.

He was dozing with his head next to hers when something poked him. He opened his eyes to find Macy staring intently at him.

"Oh. Sorry," he mumbled to the dog. "I know. Walk."

Sara lifted her head sleepily, then gasped and went stiff all over. "Ohmigod! We did this in front of him?"

Ryan shook a little with silent laughter.

Her tone was horrified. "He's been *watching?*"

When he started laughing aloud, Sara poked him.

"Stop that!" she said.

"It's all right, he doesn't look shocked."

"He *saw.*"

"Sara, he's a dog."

"I thought we were alone." She buried her face in the couch cushions. "Oh, my God. I'm so embarrassed."

Grinning, Ryan patted her bottom and then made the monumental effort of hauling himself to his feet. He went down the hall and ambled through the bedroom to the bathroom to get rid of the condom and to have *his* walk. Then he came back into the living room, scooped his shirt off the floor, slipped into it, and grabbed Macy's leash.

Sara was dressed again and making a futile attempt to straighten her hair. "I'm going to go have a shower."

"You're sleeping here tonight." He pulled his jacket back on, then realized he still needed to button his shirt. As Sara came over to do that for him, he said, "God, I wish he could walk himself. I'm exhausted."

She smiled and kissed him. "Don't be long."

He watched her hands moving on his buttons. "Keep your ears open. I may call for help if he won't come upstairs. I really don't think I can carry him." He nodded toward the couch. "Not after that."

She finished her task and shook her head. "I'm *not* helping you carry him upstairs."

He pulled her closer. "Hey, it's your fault I'm so weak now."

Macy, who saw the leash in Ryan's hand, started whining with impatience.

"You spoil him," Sara said. "He's perfectly capable of climbing those stairs without help. The vet said—"

"If you start quoting the vet to me, you definitely won't get any more sex tonight."

"Oh, as if you *could,* anyhow."

He grinned and nudged her. "*I'm* still well under thirty, you know."

She rolled her eyes. "I don't want any more sex tonight."

"Well, you say that *now* . . ."

"I can hardly walk." She wriggled away from his roving hands. "You're going to come back to find me sound asleep."

"In my bed," he reminded her.

"Yes." She kissed him lightly. "Now go walk your dog. His whining is driving me nuts."

His cell phone rang. He stiffened as he heard its discreet jingle coming from the shelf by the door, where he usually kept it when he didn't have it on him.

Their eyes met.

All the laughter and affection faded from her face, taking his glowing happiness with it.

After a heavy moment, as the phone continued to ring, Sara said, "It's awfully late for a business call."

"Yeah. She almost never calls so late."

You knew, he wanted to say to her. *It's not as if you didn't know.*

"Then it must be important." Sara's tone made the final word sound like an insult.

He nodded. "I'd better take it."

Her jaw dropped. "You're going to take it?"

You knew, *Sara.*

He crossed the floor to pick up the ringing phone. "Hello?"

"Kevin. Did I wake you?" Catherine asked.

"No."

Sara looked at him with stunned anger for a moment, then headed for the door. Ryan didn't try to stop her.

"I apologize for calling this late, Kevin. And on your

birthday, too. It's an emergency."

"Right."

Sara didn't slam his door, just closed it quietly without a backward glance. But he heard *her* door slam, across the hall. Oh, yes, he heard that, all right.

This isn't fair, he wanted to say to her. *You knew.*

He could smell Sara on his pillow, and the scent of sex lingered in the dark bedroom, haunting him. He closed his eyes and inhaled, remembering the details. Remembering her smiles, her sighs, her warm affection, and her hot passion for him. Remembering what it was like to share himself as he never did. To surrender everything. To touch a woman with total honesty, and to accept her touch with complete trust.

I trusted you, he thought. *I didn't hold anything back.*

In his head, he again heard her door slamming.

He rolled over and kicked irritably as the sheets tangled around him. His lover's scent rose from the rustling bedclothes and clouded his mind. For a moment, he could feel himself snugly inside her again, with her arms and legs wrapped around him, loving him, warming him all the way through. For a moment, he felt again the powerful lust that consumed him as she climaxed in his arms, as well as the shattering tenderness that shook him to the core as she gave herself up to him.

But in his head, he saw the stunned fury in her expression before she walked out on him.

How could she do this to him?

You're not being fair to me, he wanted to tell her. *You knew the truth. You knew, and you came to my bed, anyhow.*

After a couple of hours, he decided that lying here in the dark, silently fuming at Sara, feeling sorry for himself, smelling sex on his sheets, and wishing Macy would stop snoring was going to make him crazy before long. So he pushed his purring cat off his head, wincing when she used her claws to cling to him, and got out of bed.

He stepped around Macy's prone body, went to the dresser, and got dressed in a T-shirt and some cotton pajama bottoms. Angry, hurt, and frustrated, he left his bedroom and stalked through the living room. He was ready for a big fight. And if his girlfriend found the late—or, rather, very early—hour for their quarrel a little inconvenient, that was too damn bad.

He went out onto the balcony, pushed open her French doors, and made his way through her darkened living room.

"*Ow!* Goddamn it!"

He gritted his teeth and lifted the aching foot he had just smashed into something lying on the floor. Why the hell couldn't Sara put things away once in a while?

He turned on a light to see what had attacked him. It was a laser printer. He remembered that a writer who didn't need it anymore had given it to Sara the other day as a back-up machine, since her own printer was so old.

"And the middle of the living room floor is *such* a good place to leave it, Sara," he muttered.

"Who is that?" she called anxiously from the bedroom.

"Who do you think?" he snapped at her.

As he made his way past the front door and down the hall, he saw a light go on in her bedroom. He paused when he reached the doorway. She was sitting up in bed and putting on her glasses. Her hair was in a ponytail and she wore crimson pajamas made out of some silky material.

"Ryan." She looked groggy and a little confused.

"Well, at least one of us didn't have any trouble getting to sleep," he grumbled, coming forward.

"I did." She put a hand on her forehead. "So I took something."

He paused. "What did you take?"

She waved away his question. "Just some homeopathic thing that Delia gave me a while ago. You remember my friend, Delia? From the party?"

"Yeah, I remember."

"Homeopathic," Sara repeated. "I didn't really think it would do anything." She shook her head as if trying to clear it.

"Oh, don't bother trying to wake up." Tired and annoyed, he put a knee on her bed. "Just move over."

"What?"

"Move over." He scowled at her.

"What are you doing here?"

"For fuck's sake, Sara, would you just make some room in the bed for me?"

"But . . . um . . ." She looked around in confusion. "Do you think we should . . ."

"Should what?" When she just looked at him, he challenged, "Should do *what?* Sleep together?"

"Can you get me a glass of water?"

He closed his eyes for a moment. "Okay."

When he came back from the kitchen, he sat down on the edge of the bed and waited while she drank her water. Then she scrubbed her hands over her face, adjusted her glasses, and gave herself a brief shake.

So much for the dramatic quarrel he'd been planning.

She looked at him, clearly feeling more like herself now, and said, "Okay. We have to talk."

"Yes. We do." He looked at the floor and let his shoulders slump. "You can't do this to me, Sara."

"I don't want to—"

"I'm not just a hired boy you can fuck and forget."

"Ryan."

"I'm your lover, goddamn it. You don't get to count your orgasms and then just go home."

"That's not what happened!"

"That's *exactly* what happened."

"No, what happened is that your *pimp* called—"

"You knew what I was."

"—and five minutes after you'd been on top of *me*—"

"You knew everything about me."

"—you were answering her tug on your leash—"

"And you wanted me, anyhow."

"—to go have sex with another woman!"

He raised his voice. "But now that you've had enough sex to keep you happy for while—"

"Don't you *dare*—"

"—you're back to thinking—"

"—accuse me of using you sexually!"

"—that I'm not good enough to touch you!"

She gaped at him. "I have *never*—You *know* I don't . . . *What* are you . . ." Her dark brows swooped into a furious frown, and she looked as if she wanted to slug him.

So when she lunged for him, he flinched in surprise and tried to get out of the way. She flung herself against him and used all her weight to shove him onto his back. Startled, he sprawled across the bed, then struggled to sit up again. "Sara—"

She kissed him, and he went very still.

Her mouth was warm and generous, and her breath was soft on his cheek. Her legs slid against his as she sought a less awkward position. After a moment of stunned immobility, he started kissing her back, snared by her passion and drawn helplessly into the flame. He forgot about the additional furious accusations he'd been so eager to hurl at her.

She made an impatient sound and stopped kissing him just long enough to take off her glasses and toss them aside, and then she was all over him again. Her hands stroked his shoulders and his arms, then slid under his T-shirt to caress his stomach and his chest. Her tongue sought his, gentle and sweet, and her legs squeezed him affectionately as they bracketed his hips.

He wrapped his arms around her, his eyes closed, his head spinning. He could drown in her. He could go under forever, just like this, and die happy, without a fight. He shifted his hips, snuggling against her, trying to get even closer to her as they continued kissing, their clinging lips making up for the angry words they had uttered moments ago.

She sought his hands with her own, laced her fingers with his, and raised their joined fists to rest on either side of his head. Then she pulled away from his kisses to look at him. They gazed into each other's eyes for a long moment, both of them breathing fast now.

Finally Sara said, "Okay. Are you done now?"

He nodded.

"You're sure?"

He nodded again.

"So we can actually *talk* now? Instead of you just flinging your insecurities around the room?"

He was startled into a puff of laughter. "Yes. We can talk now. I'm done."

"Good."

"Sorry."

"That's okay. I guess you were pretty wound up."

"Uh-huh."

"You were spoiling for a fight."

"I sure was." He squeezed her hands gently. "I was hurt when you just left like that."

"I know. I'm sorry. But I had to leave. I was so angry, I couldn't even speak. I needed a little space. Time to clear my head. I had to think. Because this is too important for me to—"

"But you *knew,* Sara. You knew when you went to bed with me—"

"I love you," she said. "You know that, don't you?"

He nodded, still holding her gaze.

"I will *never* think that you aren't good enough to touch me." When he didn't say anything, she asked, "Do you believe me?" He just looked at her uncertainly, and she sighed. "You don't believe me, do you?"

"I don't think you're lying," he hedged.

She tried to pull her hands away from his. "Can I let go of you now?"

"No." He held her fast.

"You said you were ready to talk sensibly."

"I'm not ready for you to stop touching me."

"I don't want to stop, but, uh . . ." She nudged her hips against his. "I can feel what's happening down there—*again*—and it's distracting me. Man, you really *are* well under thirty."

He loosed his grip on her hands. "Okay, yeah, if I'm going to concentrate on talking, I guess you should get off me."

She rolled off his body, found her glasses, and put them back on as she arranged herself to sit cross-legged next to him. He stayed lying on his back and stared at the ceiling.

She began, "I don't think I can ever really understand your attitude about sex, your attitude about what you do.

But I trust you when you say you feel differently about me—"

"I *love* you."

"—than you do about the other women you have sex with."

He turned his head to look at her. "Don't bring them in here. Not into your . . . *our* bed, Sara."

"I believed you when you said that sex with me would mean something to you—"

"It does!"

"—and that it would be different with me than it is with anyone else."

"It *is*." He rolled towards her and rested his arm on her leg. "Jesus, Sara, how can you not know that? Do you think I ever give myself up the way I did with you tonight?"

"I just want to be clear about this. I want you to know, it's not that I doubt you. If you tell me that what you do with other women means something totally different to you than what you do with me, I believe you."

"What I do with Catherine's clients doesn't mean *anything* to me." He hauled himself upright and sat opposite her, his legs touching hers. "Hell, it didn't mean anything to me the last dozen times I did it with Catherine, either. By then it was just . . ." He shrugged. ". . . habit."

"So even if it looks the same, I believe you when—"

"It doesn't, Sara. I thought it would, but that's because I didn't know any better." He held her gaze. "Do you think that with anybody else—with a *paying customer,* for chrissake—I ask for what I want in bed, and say when I'm too tired to do it again, and just lie there in a sweaty, panting heap on top of a woman because I know she loves me and will overlook the lack of finesse?"

"You didn't lack finesse."

"Well, then, that's where *you* don't know any better." He took her hand in his. "Do you think I ever tremble and get clumsy, beg and lose my head during sex with anyone but you? I don't. When I was seventeen, Catherine started making sex my *job*. Ever since then, even when I've done it for fun, that's been my way. I stay in control, I keep my head, I'm slick. Exactly the way she taught me." He held her hand against his cheek. "But I don't do that with you. I don't want to. When I'm with you, I just want the free-fall that any other guy in love wants. I just get lost in you the way . . . the way you get lost in me." They gazed at each other in tender silence for a moment, and then he leaned forward, longing to kiss her.

But she put a hand on his shoulder to stop him. "I believe you, Ryan. But, even so, I can't share you. Not with Catherine, not with clients, not with anyone. Not like that."

He let his breath out and lowered his head. "You're talking about me quitting."

"Yes." When he didn't respond, she said, "Why did she call you so late?"

"Oh. One of the escorts got arrested. Drugs." He added, "He wasn't on the job. He was just in some club. On his own time. Being a jerk. He did some property damage, too."

"Was it that guy who set you up for an arrest and then fought with you?"

"Derrick? No. He's an idiot, but he doesn't do drugs. No, this was a new guy. Trevor. I don't really know him. He's only been around a few months." Ryan tilted his head. "Long enough, though."

"For what?"

"He's trying to get the D.A. to let him off by telling the cops everything he knows about Catherine's business."

"Will that get her in trouble?"

"Maybe. It's drawing attention to her, anyhow, and attention is bad for someone like her."

"Will this get *you* into trouble?"

"It depends."

"Is that why she was calling you?"

"Oh. No." He knew how Sara would react, but he wouldn't lie to her. "She was calling to tell me I have to take over a job that Trevor was supposed to do."

"Oh, good grief!"

He said nothing.

Sara's eyes narrowed. "Tomorrow?" When he didn't immediately answer, she said, "Of course. Why else would she call so late at night?"

"Yeah. Starting tomorrow. I have to go meet someone at the airport."

"Don't go."

"Sara . . ."

"Ryan, I can't stand you doing this to me. I can't stand you doing this to *us*."

"It's not about us."

"It is now, Ryan. There's not just you, anymore. There's me, too, and *I* can't stand this."

"I understand, but—"

"But what I can't stand most of all is what you're doing to yourself. I cannot bear to see you treating the person I love most in the world—"

"Sara." He tried to touch her cheek, but she evaded him.

"—like a commodity, like a thing, like a—a—"

"Whore?"

"Yes!" They stared at each other for a moment, then she said, "Kevin is an expensive whore with a police record. But you're the bravest, strongest, most wonderful man I've ever known."

His heart started thudding heavily against his ribcage, as if trying to escape his body and go to her.

"I want to spend the rest of my life with you," she said. "If you want that, too . . ."

"The rest of our lives together?" He felt a little dizzy.

"Yes."

"Is that really what you want?"

She nodded. "More than I want anything. Even more than I want to sell another book. Even more than I want to *write* another book. I want to wake up every day with you."

He just stared at her and listened to his heartbeat. He felt a bit like he was floating. Then, finally, he realized that she was waiting for him to say something.

"You have to let me put my arms around you," he whispered, reaching for her.

He dragged her onto his lap and she came willingly. He kissed her, hard at first, then more gently. Then he buried his face in her neck and asked, "Are we really going to do that? Spend our lives together?"

She stroked his hair. "Only if you quit. That's what I needed time alone to think about after I left tonight. Whether it was worth it to me. To give you an ultimatum. To draw the line and honor it."

He lifted his head and looked into her dark eyes.

She said, "I love you, I believe in you, and I will give you the rest of my life. But you have to quit. If you don't, what kind of life can we have together? 'Hi, honey! I'm home from my trip to the island, where I did a three-way with two other women.' " He closed his eyes. She continued, "Will you have to skip dinner with me because you've got a date with another woman? When you come home to me, will you have to shower off the smell of sex with someone else before you touch me?"

"Shh." He opened his eyes. "Don't keep talking about it."

She nodded. "We can't go forward if you don't quit. And since we can't go back . . ."

"Yes?"

"If you don't quit . . ." She paused and made an obvious effort to control her voice. "Then one of us moves out of this building, as soon as possible, and we agree not to see each other anymore."

"*What?* Sara! No! What are you talking about?"

"We tried being just friends. It wasn't enough. After tonight, it'll *never* be enough for me." She put her hand on his cheek. "I want you to be my lover. My partner. I guess I want you to be my husband."

"Husband?" She would *marry* him? Knowing what she knew?

"But whatever we decide, I can't keep sleeping alone while you keep sleeping right next door. I can't bear that anymore. Not after tonight."

"No, I can't, either."

"So you either sleep with me from now on, or else I don't even want to know where your bed is anymore." She took a breath. "Which means, either you decide that I'm the only woman you'll ever have sex with again, or else you decide that you'll never have sex with *me* again."

He just stared at her, his blood roaring in his ears as he realized she meant it. He had to leave the life or else give her up completely.

He tightened his hold on her, clinging to her solid form as he felt the world shifting around him. "I can't give you up. I tried. I couldn't do it before. And I sure as hell can't do it after tonight."

"Then you have to break with Catherine," she said quietly.

He lowered his head to rest his forehead against her shoulder. "She saved my life."

"You've given her ten years of it, Ryan. That's enough. More than she should have taken."

"I'd have gone to prison two years ago if it weren't for her."

"But you'd probably be out of prison by now, free to live your own life. So she's gotten her time out of you."

His stomach churned as he held onto her and considered her words. After a while, he said, "This is it, isn't it? The rest of my life. I'm standing at the crossroads, and everything that comes after this will be because of which way I turn now."

"Well, I wasn't going to spring this on you in the middle of the night," she said. "I thought we'd talk tomorrow. That's why I was trying to get some sleep. So my head would be clear when I saw you." She added wryly, "But then you came bursting in here in at three o'clock in the morning, looking for a fight."

"Sorry about that."

She kissed his hair. "Look, think it over for a day or—"

"No." He felt her stiffen in his arms, and he lifted his head. "I mean, no, I don't need a day or two." It was suddenly so clear to him, he couldn't understand why it had seemed like such an impenetrable maze until this moment. "Choosing a life with you, or else giving you up so I can keep whoring for Catherine?" He took her face between his hands. "I don't need more time to think. I know what I want."

Her eyes started to get misty. "Are you sure?"

"Yes." They kissed, and then he hugged her, rocking her

in his arms as they laughed together, giddy with relief and new-born excitement. "I'm sure. I'm so sure, I've already forgotten why this seemed like such a big decision."

She tightened her arms around him as he pressed his face into the silky fabric covering her breasts. "Big decisions are always like that," she said. "I can't remember why it was so hard to decide to sleep with you. But I know I agonized about it over and over."

"My God, I'm *quitting*." He was amazed at the prospect.

"And becoming monogamous," she said pointedly.

"Monogamous, yes. But not celibate." He pulled her silky top over her head and then lowered her into the pillows.

"You'll tell her right away?"

He took off his T-shirt. "Yes. I will."

"First thing tomorrow?" Her breath caught as he bent to kiss both her breasts.

"No." He started peeling her pajamas down her hips and over her legs. "First thing tomorrow, woman, I get all the sex I want, any way I want it."

"Well, I suppose just this once . . ." She laughed when he pinched her.

He tossed her pajamas aside. "After that, we're having a really big breakfast." He shouldered his way between her thighs and pressed an open-mouthed kiss on her stomach. "And *then* I'll go quit my job."

"Sounds like . . ." She gasped when he licked the crease of her thigh. ". . . like a plan."

He turned his head, nuzzled the dark curls he found there, and decided he wasn't interested in further conversation right now.

"Ryan?"

"Hmmm?" He pressed a quick kiss between her legs.

"I don't have . . ." She gasped when he kissed her there again, much less chastely this time.

"Have what?" He blew softly on her sensitive flesh and ignored the restless shifting of her legs.

"Um . . ."

"What don't you have?" he asked.

"C . . . *Oh.* Con . . . Condoms."

"Oh. Don't worry. I have some here." He patted his pocket.

Her thighs tensed against his arms and she propped herself up on her elbows. "You *brought* some?"

"Only two." He grinned. "I'm pretty tired, you know." He slid his hands under her hips to pull her into a better position for this.

"You *brought* some?"

"Well, I figured we'd have a big fight, and then we'd have sex. Stop wriggling."

"You brought condoms." She shook her head.

"There's no law against foolish hope. Besides, here we are, so I was right." He grasped her hips firmly and lowered his head.

"Um, Ryan . . ." She was shifting restlessly again.

"Now what?"

"I, uh . . ."

He looked up and met her embarrassed gaze. "Ah. You're shy about this?" When she nodded, he smiled and nuzzled her thigh. "Well, I'll just have to help you get over that, won't I?"

CHAPTER SEVENTEEN

When Ryan arrived at the townhouse in Cow Hollow, Catherine was talking on the phone. Her assistant, Jolie, was feeding the contents of client files into a paper shredder.

Catherine's hair was swept into an elegant chignon, and she was wearing a dark green suit that complemented both her figure and her coloring. Ryan had always thought her the most beautiful, stylish woman he'd ever known, and his being in love with another woman didn't change that.

Nonetheless, he *was* in love with another woman, and he couldn't lose her. So despite what he owed Catherine and despite what bargains they had made, it was time for him to quit the trade and start a new life.

He was practically quivering with fatigue now, after having made love so many times since yesterday's sunset. He was still young, but no one was *that* young.

As he caught Catherine's eye, he admitted to himself that some of his near-quivering state was also due to nerves. He expected a big thunderstorm from her when he broke the news, and he wasn't looking forward to it.

She glanced at the clock, frowned at him, and finished her call. Then she said, "What are you doing here? You're supposed to be on your way to the airport right now."

Shit. He'd been so tired, happy, and nervous, he hadn't even thought about the time. The fact that he was screwing up a big job for her at this very moment was going to make this conversation go even worse than he'd anticipated.

"What's going on here?" he asked, watching Jolie feed

more paper into the shredder.

"There may be a search warrant," Catherine said, looking tense. "Possibly as early as tomorrow."

"Oh. Because of what's-his-face. Trevor."

"Trevor," she agreed. "He's talking a *lot.*" With a coldly furious expression, she added, "He's inventing half of it, but that won't protect me from an unconscionable invasion of privacy."

"Oh. I'm sorry." Well, he'd picked just a *great* day to come in and tell her he was quitting. With an inward sigh, he decided he might as well get it over with as quickly as possible. "Can we talk, Catherine?" With a glance at Jolie, he added, "Privately?"

Catherine's expression grew a little colder. She said, "Jolie, would you mind leaving us alone for a few minutes?"

Jolie nodded, her expression full of open curiosity as she made a quick exit. Ryan wondered if she'd listen at the door.

Catherine leaned against the desk and folded her arms. "Well? Explain yourself."

He glanced at the clock. "I'm sorry about today's job. I kind of forgot all about it."

"You *forgot?*" She made an obvious effort to control her already-frayed temper. "Then you'd better get in your car right now and go take care of it. This is *important,* Kevin."

"I know it's worth a lot of money to you. If I had remembered, I would have called early and told you to get someone else."

"I'm not getting someone else!" she snapped. "*Go,* Kevin."

"I'm not going."

Her expression would have chilled him to the marrow in earlier years. "I've had it up to *here* with your nonsense!

This is the third time lately that you've tried to cancel or postpone an appointment at the last minute! Whatever your problem is, sort it out on your own time, Kevin! I will not tolerate—"

"Catherine, I'm quitting."

"What?" She stopped her tirade. "*Oh.* So that's what this is all about. You're thinking about quitting again?"

"I'm not 'thinking' about it. This is it. My resignation. I quit. It's over. I'm done."

She headed for the door. "I don't have time to waste on this today. We are *not* opening this old subject again. Go to the airport. *Now,* Kevin."

"I just wanted to tell you in person," he said, not moving. "I thought I owed you that much."

She paused by the door and looked over her shoulder. "You owe me a lot more than that, as you well know."

"Yes. I owe you my life," he said. "I'd be dead if it weren't for you."

"Yes, you would."

"But I've given you almost ten years, and that's enough."

Her eyes narrowed. "If it weren't for me, you would also have spent the past two years getting butt-fucked every day."

"Nice language, Catherine."

"No, but it's accurate. You know exactly what happens to a beautiful young man in prison, Kevin. Much the same thing that happened to you on the streets."

"Thank you for keeping me out of prison. I served you instead of serving time." He relied on Sara's argument. "But it's been more than two years. They'd have released me by now. So you should do the same."

"Don't you *dare* try to tell me what I should do!" She

stalked back to the center of the room. "I saved your life! I taught you everything you know! You were *nothing* when I met you! A starving, ignorant, scabby street urchin! I taught you how to talk, how to dress, how to walk, how to make love, what to read, what to do! I *made* you, Kevin! Are you listening to me? Stop! Where are you going?"

"We've had this conversation before," he said wearily. "Far too many times."

"We certainly have!"

"This is the last time."

"What do you think you're going to do if you leave me now? How do you expect to survive?"

"I'll manage."

"Oh, really? Doing what?" she asked. "You know how to do *one* job, Kevin. The job I taught you."

"Maybe so, but I've got a job interview later." He'd phoned Isabel earlier today, a little while after slow, tender, late-morning sex and right before a really big breakfast.

"You can't be serious."

"I am."

"Where?"

"It's called Safe House." He smiled involuntarily, feeling excited and a little self-conscious. "I think I'm going to try to help kids get off the streets."

"*You?* Working with kids? They'll never let you, Kevin. You're a prostitute with an arrest record."

"I just became an *ex*-prostitute. And they know about my record."

"What are you playing at?"

"I'm serious, Catherine. I've quit. If I don't get a job at Safe House, then, somehow or other, I'll find something else."

"You're not fit for anything else! I pay you very well

for the one thing that you do very well."

"I'm leaving."

"No, you're not!"

He sighed, feeling no desire to shout back or to convince her, though he always had in the past. "I suppose we fought so badly about this whenever we discussed it before because I always wanted you to agree. To let me go. To forgive me." He shrugged. "To give your permission."

"Well, it won't happen. So give it up, Kevin!"

"I'm sorry it won't happen. I would have liked it better that way. But, even so, I'm finished with this life. If you can't forgive me for that now—"

"You're not finished until I say you're finished!"

"—maybe you'll be able to forgive me later. After you've gotten used to me being gone."

"You promised you would give up the idea of leaving! When I saved you from prison, you *promised* me."

"I'm asking you to release me from my promise."

"No!"

He didn't bother to ask why she wouldn't let him go the way she'd always let others go when they decided to leave. They'd had *that* conversation far too many times, too.

"I didn't come here to fight about this."

"What's going on?" she demanded.

"I just thought that, after everything that's been between us over the years . . ."

"*Something's* going on," she said. "You've been acting strangely for weeks. Even before you got spooked by that arrest."

"How *is* Derrick?" he asked dryly. "Did that lip heal all right?"

Her gaze flickered to the door. "He's fine."

"He's here now?" When she didn't reply, he snorted

with sudden amusement. "Ohhh. He's upstairs. So that melodrama we all performed together brought you two closer together, did it?"

"He's eager to please." She added, "The way you once were."

"Comparing me to *him* really undermines any nostalgia I might have had about our past, Catherine." He shook his head. "Look, you've done a lot for me, and once upon a time, you *meant* a lot to me."

"You're not leaving me."

"So I didn't want to just do this over the phone. I thought . . ." *Phone.* He closed his eyes in momentary exasperation as he realized, "I forgot my cell phone. I'm sorry. I meant to give it to you today." He'd been so upset about Sara last night when he put the phone down, he wasn't even sure where he'd left it. "I'll drop it off another time."

"You don't know what you're—"

"It's yours, after all. But I'm not. Not anymore."

"Where do you think you're—Stop! Kevin!"

He opened the door. "I'll always be grateful—"

"Close that door! We're not through!"

"—for everything you've done for me."

"Close the goddamn door!"

"Tell my regulars whatever you want to tell them."

"Don't you dare walk away from me!"

"Goodbye, Catherine."

"Kevin! Come back here!"

He left the room and encountered Jolie's wide-eyed stare.

"Kevin!" Catherine shouted, following him out of her office.

He crossed the floor and headed for the front door. As he was reaching for the handle, Catherine startled him by throwing herself in front of the door.

"You're not really leaving. This is a bluff! What do you want? More money? Is that it?"

He took her by the arms and moved her out of his way.

"I know the sixty-forty split has been hard on you," she said. "We'll go back to fifty-fifty."

He opened the door and kept her from blocking his way again.

"Fifty-fifty, Kevin!"

He shook her off his arm.

"You want forty-sixty?"

He walked through the door and down the path.

"What is it, then? What do you want?"

When he reached the street, he heard her shout, "Kevin! Goddamn you, *come back here!*"

He took a shaky breath and kept on walking.

Sara awoke with a start when the phone next to her bed rang. She picked it up and mumbled, "Hello?"

"Sorry, did I wake you?" Ryan said.

"Mmmm." She smiled and sank back into the pillows. "Hi."

"Hi."

"What time is it?" she asked sleepily.

"Almost six o'clock."

"Omigosh! I've been sleeping for four hours!"

"You needed it. Actually, *I* need it."

"When are you coming home?"

"Not for a few hours."

"So how did it go?"

"Well. Telling Catherine I quit was almost as much fun as getting a major dental procedure."

"Oh." She bit her lip. "Are you okay?"

"I'm just glad it's over."

"Was she awful to you?"

"I left before she could get as awful as she really wanted to get. But it was pretty grim, even so."

"But it's over, right? You're done?"

"I'm done."

Something in his voice bothered her. "What's wrong?"

"Nothing." After a pause, he said, "I'm done, and I was very clear about being done. I'm just not sure she accepts it yet."

"She'll have to, though."

"Yes, she will." When she didn't say anything, he said, "I'm really finished with her, Sara. It's over."

She smiled again. "I love you."

"So . . . what are you wearing?"

She laughed. "Where are you now? Safe House?"

"Yeah. Actually, I went looking for Adam first, before I came here. I'm kind of worried. I couldn't find him."

"He's avoiding you?"

"I don't know. Maybe. Or maybe . . ."

"You said he was still very angry at you yesterday."

"Yeah."

"So he's probably avoiding you."

"But when a homeless kid avoids you, he can really *avoid* you. I mean, he can disappear forever."

"You think he would do that?"

"He might. If he thinks I'm trying to put him back in a place like the one he ran away from."

"What are you going to do?"

"Well, after I leave here later, I'll go looking for him again. And if I don't find him . . ." He sighed. "Just keep looking, I guess. Could you walk Macy for me tonight, in case I'm out late?"

"Sure. But, Ryan, I don't like the idea of you looking for Adam after dark."

"Honey, I lived on those streets for a long time when I was smaller and a lot weaker. I'll be okay."

She didn't like it, but she supposed he had a point. "So you'll be at Safe House for a while?"

"Oh! Yes. That's what I called to tell you. I've just gotten my very first real job."

"Ryan! That's wonderful!"

"Yeah. I told Isabel that her lectures to me about giving up prostitution and doing important work with Safe House had such a huge effect on me that I quit the trade today."

"But you quit because of *me*."

"Yeah, well, I wasn't going to tell *her* that. I really need a job."

"Ah. So you applied a little leverage."

"You bet."

"Smart."

"I get by. I also told her that I don't want to wind up homeless again now that she's convinced me to go straight."

"Nice touch."

"I thought so. Anyhow, I said I'd throw myself into the work, but I needed to be paid."

"I gather it worked?"

"I start tomorrow."

"I'm so proud of you!"

"You won't be so proud when you see my first paycheck. They're starting me out at less money than Adam makes picking pockets."

"I'm *proud* of you."

"Isabel says that if I do good work, they'll even pay me a real salary some day. She just needs to get more funding, or juggle resources, or something like that. When she got into the administrative doubletalk, I kind of lost her."

"Well, we can reduce our expenses for a while."

"We?"

"I'm pinching pennies, too, you know."

"So what do you have in mind?"

She rolled onto her side and cradled the phone. "We could cut down on rent, for example."

"You mean, live together?"

"Uh-huh." She waited for his response.

"Before you make that offer definite, you should know that I have some bad habits."

She smiled. "Such as?"

"I drink straight out of the milk carton. And the water pitcher."

"I hate when men do that! What's wrong with a glass, I ask you?"

"And I use all the hot water."

"I already know that. We share a water tank."

"Oh, right. You do know that."

"Anyhow, I have some bad habits, too."

"Such as?" She could hear the smile in his voice.

"Well . . . I'm not very tidy."

"Now you're shocking me."

"And I can be a little moody," she said.

"You don't say?"

"Especially when my work's not going well."

"I never would have noticed," he said.

"Plus, my family's a little annoying."

"Oh, they're okay."

"So what do you think?" she asked.

"I think one of us should give notice to Lance."

"Really?"

"Yeah. Really."

"Okay," she said. "You do it."

"Hey, why me?"

"Because I'd rather hit myself repeatedly in the head with a brick than move again this year."

"Oh. Okay. That's a good reason. I'll be the one to give up my apartment, then."

"Good."

"So we're really going to live together?" he said.

"Yes." She squeezed the phone. "I'm glad."

"So am I." After a moment, he said, "I'll talk to Lance tomorrow."

"We have too much stuff for this apartment," she warned.

"*You* have too much stuff for that apartment."

"We'll have to figure out what we're going to put into storage until we're able to afford a bigger place."

"Well, I think it's obvious that we have to keep my leather chair with us, or your father will never approve of me."

She grinned and was about to reply when she heard him talking to someone else.

"Sorry, honey," he said after a moment. "I've got to go."

"They want you to work now?"

"They want me to fill out a million forms now. And then they want to test me."

"Test you?"

"For drugs. And nasty diseases."

"Oh!"

"Don't worry. They're not going to touch anything that belongs to you now."

"Well, that's good."

"I've got to go."

"I'll see you when you get home," she said.

"I love you."

"Be careful tonight."

When Sara heard rain hit the roof and the windows, she turned off her computer, found her flashlight, and got out some candles and matches. She had learned her lesson well.

Then she remembered that Mrs. Thatcher was out on the balcony. So she went into Ryan's apartment, found his welder's gloves, and brought the mad bird's cage inside.

Macy woke up, noticed Sara, and came over to demonstrate his affection by drooling on her.

"Hello, Macy." She scratched his ears, suddenly realizing that he was going to be living with her soon. "Wow, I *must* be in love."

As long as she was here, she figured she might as well feed the fish, clean Alley's sandbox, and make sure everybody had enough food and water.

"*Hopelessly* in love," she muttered.

Macy followed her into the kitchen, obviously hoping that she'd be as weak-willed as Ryan and give him a dog biscuit. She was avoiding his eyes and pretending to be unaware of his mournful stare when the phone rang.

Sara turned her head towards the sound—then froze when she realized it was Ryan's cell phone.

He had told her that the only person who had that number was . . .

Why was *she* calling him?

The ringing continued.

She's calling to lure him back into her web, of course.

Maybe she intended to inflict guilt. Or maybe she'd threaten him with something he found as terrifying as prison. Maybe . . .

Sara snatched up the phone and answered the call. "Hello?"

There was a long pause. "Er, hello. I'm calling for Kevin."

That startled Sara. It was the first time she'd actually heard anyone call him that. "He's not here."

Another pause. "This *is* his phone?"

"Yes."

"Oh." There was a world of comprehension in that single syllable. "So *you're* what's going on."

"He told me this phone belongs to you."

"Yes."

"So I guess you want it back."

"No. He'll be needing it."

"No, he won't. He quit today."

"Ah. He's told you a few things, I gather?" Catherine's voice was smooth and cultured. She sounded like an educated woman, a professional.

"Yes."

"That's not like him." When Sara didn't reply, Catherine prodded, "Do you know what he does for a living?"

"Yes."

"*Everything* he does?"

That was obviously a leading question. Sara didn't want to hear Ryan's secrets from this woman, so she said, "He doesn't do it anymore."

"You sound like you believe that."

"Why don't *you?* He told you. Weren't you listening?"

"But I know him. Far better than you do."

"I don't think so."

"This isn't the first time he's quit, my dear."

"I think you mean, this isn't the first time he's *tried* to quit, my *dear*."

"It's not easy to give up . . . a certain way of life."

"He's given it up. Why can't you accept that?"

"I can tell you're very concerned about him."

"I'm very concerned about you bothering him."

"I think it would be better if I just call back when he's there. When will that be?" When Sara didn't reply, Catherine said, "Of course, if you're *afraid* to tell me . . ."

"I'm not sure when he'll be back."

"He didn't tell you?"

"He's got things to do."

"Where is he?"

"He didn't tell you?" Sara said a little nastily.

"That place he mentioned? Safe House?"

Surprised, Sara said, "Yes."

"Perhaps I'll call him there."

"Oh, that'll be good. His pimp calling Safe House. I wish I could be there to see hear his language when he finds *you* on the other end of the line."

The silence was thick with tension. Then Catherine said, "I don't think you and I have anything to discuss. Good—"

"Catherine, wait!" There was no reply. "Hello?"

"I'm still here," was the chilly reply. "He told you my name?"

Sara said, even as she realized it, "Only your first name."

"What else has he told you?"

"A lot. Probably not everything yet."

"Yet?" That single word positively dripped with skepticism.

"I want to know why you won't let him go."

"Perhaps for the same reasons you hope to keep him."

That surprised Sara. "I doubt that."

"Do you really?"

"Yes. I don't think you have any idea what I see in him."

"Oh, I know exactly what you see in him. I know, because I *put* it there."

Sara said, "What, his sexual skills?"

Catherine made a dismissive sound. "No, I don't mean his sexual skills. My God, if that's what's got you clinging to him, I'll be happy to send over someone to take his place. Do you honestly imagine that sexual skills are so rare that *that's* why I've put up with the trouble Kevin has caused me over the years?"

Increasingly interested in Catherine's comments, Sara said, "Well, he seems pretty skillful to *me*."

"If that's why you want him, then you don't deserve him."

"If that's what you think, then maybe you really do see the same things in him that I do," Sara said. "His intelligence."

"Yes."

"His charm. His sensitivity."

"Yes."

Sara tried to think of which other attributes Catherine was likely to admire. She doubted that Ryan's courage and honesty were high on the list, so she tried, "His style."

"Yes."

"He's a class act."

"Of course he is." Catherine added gently, "I can understand your attraction to him."

Gosh, we're really bonding *here.* "And I can understand yours."

"Can you also understand that Kevin and I have shared things that he will never share with anyone else? That I know him in a way that neither you nor any other woman ever can?"

"I think you overestimate your influence on him."

"Or perhaps you overestimate yours."

Sara deliberately injected defiance into her voice as she said, "He loves me!"

"He's enjoying a temporary change of scenery, that's all."

"You really think he'll come back to you?"

"What I think," Catherine said calmly, "is that you have no idea who he is or what he needs."

"And you do?"

"I understand him very well."

Sara listened with dawning comprehension to the possessive tone and the obvious attempts to assert a superior relationship with Ryan.

So that's what this is all about—what it's probably always been about.

All this time, Ryan had thought it was business. And all this time, it had been exactly the opposite.

"And *I* understand," Sara said, having learned all she needed to know, "that you took a homeless kid and seduced him, used him, and then exploited him for money."

"I have *never* ex—"

"I understand that you are an amoral, opportunistic bitch who has manipulated him for years, and who has never hesitated to use emotional blackmail, threats, and extortion to get her way."

"You have no idea what you're talking ab—"

"And what *you* don't understand is that Ryan is through with you. Forever. So get used to it, and get over it." She paused. "Hello? Hello?"

Sara put down the phone and looked at Macy. "She hung up. Gosh, do you think it was something I said?"

Well, isn't that interesting?

Whatever had initially drawn Catherine to the grubby,

foul-mouthed street boy Ryan had once been, she had ultimately, like the sculptor Pygmalion, fallen in love with her own creation.

If you could possibly call what she did to Ryan "love." Sara certainly couldn't.

But sex didn't mean anything to Catherine, so the relationship had followed a strange and sordid course. Catherine didn't care who Ryan slept with—on the contrary, she *sold* him to women. No, Catherine cared who influenced him, who had emotional power over him. Who *controlled* him, as she saw it. She couldn't bear for that person *not* to be her. So she had furiously stomped on his attempt to seek his own life, free of her influence, two years ago. She had succeeded then, but she wouldn't succeed this time.

And that, Sara could tell, would really gall her.

Macy whined at Sara, his soft brown eyes conveying a life of unspeakable deprivation.

Feeling rather glad that she'd had the opportunity to give that appalling woman the earful she deserved, and only sorry that she hadn't worked the words "demented control freak" into her tirade, Sara relented and gave Macy a biscuit.

Having given blood, urine, and several hours of his time, Ryan shrugged into his jacket, said goodnight to a few of the Safe House staff members whom he had met today, and left the building. The exhilaration of so many major events in a short span of time was being replaced by bone-melting, mind-numbing exhaustion. He would give anything to go home right now, snuggle up to Sara, and sleep for a week.

But he was worried about Adam; and Isabel had agreed that it would be a good idea to make sure that the boy was safe and still in the vicinity. She didn't seem at all disappointed by Ryan's initial failure to convince Adam to come here, and her calm perspective renewed his confidence that he would eventually succeed with the kid.

As long as he could find him, that was.

Ryan rounded the corner, thinking he might as well go back to the warehouse and start his search from there.

With fatigue dimming his senses and slowing his reflexes, he noticed the rapid footsteps directly behind him a second too late. He was only just starting to turn around when the blow hit his skull.

He grunted and stumbled forward, his head whirling with pain and crazily flashing images. Someone grabbed his hair. He moved to defend himself, but he was disoriented and clumsy. The next blow hit his face, and then everything went black and silent.

Lights flashed in his eyes with dizzying speed. He heard a continuous, deafening roar. It seemed to be both far away and very near, screaming through his brain.

Someone grabbed his hair and yanked his head up, hurting his scalp, jerking his neck. He grunted, and immediately gagged. It felt like he was smothering.

There was something stuffed in his mouth. To keep him from screaming.

Fear flashed through him with a dark, bitter chill.

He panicked, trying to spit out the thing which was in his mouth.

Someone slapped him. Hard.

Tears stung his eyes, and his nostrils moved with rapid, panicky breaths.

Whoever had him by the hair let go suddenly. His head hit the pavement with a thud, nearly sending him back into the dark well of unconsciousness. He fought it, confused and afraid.

Pavement?

He was outside . . . He'd been coming out of Safe House . . . and someone had jumped him . . .

Pain exploded in his body as someone kicked him. When he rolled away, he felt the rough pavement scraping the bare skin of his stomach and thighs.

He was naked?

Holy shit.

A horrible sense of familiarity flooded him. Naked, on the pavement, surrounded by the stench of urine and garbage, with a gag in his mouth . . . He had been here once before.

Oh, God, no . . .

He heard heavy breathing. With his heart thundering madly, he held his own breath and listened. He still heard the breathing. Very near. Someone breathing hard. Directly over his naked body.

Panic swept through him. He tried to get up. But he couldn't move. Why couldn't he move?

That's when he realized his arms were tied behind his back.

It was the only thing that was different from his memories. Maybe he'd been tied this time because he was bigger and stronger now, not as easy to subdue as he had been all those years ago.

No, no, no . . .

The lights in his eyes flashed even faster. What *was* that?

A pair of strong hands grabbed him and forced him onto his back. One hand roughly toyed with his cock.

No!

Grunting and strangling on the cloth in his mouth, he kicked out at his attacker and tried to squirm away.

Another blow sent him sprawling, and then he was on his stomach. He tried to get up, using his head for leverage in place of his arms. A knee in his back forced him down again. He collapsed and nearly blacked out from lack of air.

He felt a hand fumble between the cheeks of his butt to explore his anus.

No! No! Oh, Jesus, God, dear God, please, no!

He heard himself screaming, the noise trapped in his throat, in his chest. He was strangling and screaming and so scared, so fucking scared.

He felt fingers there, intruding, testing him.

No!

He was going to vomit. Vomit into his gag and drown.

And he *wanted* to. If it meant he could die before he was raped again, then, yes, he wanted to die drowning in his own vomit.

Tears were streaming down his face, and his nose was running. He'd suffocate any minute, he knew he would.

God, no, please, not this, not THIS, I can't, I can't stand it again, no, no, no . . .

Then the knee in his back was gone. He was dragged up to his knees. Then to his feet. His legs wouldn't support him, and his weight seemed to hang from his head as his captor dragged him by the hair across the pavement . . . and then shoved him into a wall.

He tried to think, tried to use his head, to stop wallowing in blind animal panic. He tried to kick. But he was weak and sluggish, and his attacker punished him by banging his head into the wall.

Dazed, terrified, and reeling with pain, he sagged against the wall, limp and helpless, as a bigger man's body pressed up against him.

Stop, no, no . . .

He wanted to die. Right now. He couldn't endure what he knew was about to happen.

Please, just let me die.

"Does this seem familiar?"

His lungs burned. He could feel blood on his face.

"You've been here before, haven't you?"

What?

He tried to speak and choked on the gag.

What did you say?

"It was a lot like this, wasn't it?"

How do you . . . know that?

"Or did you forget?"

That voice . . .

Your voice . . .

He knew that voice.

"And did you forget who saved you? Who took you away from this shit?"

Is that you?

The man moved away from his body. A moment later, Ryan felt his legs kicked out from under him. He hit the ground so hard he nearly passed out again.

Derrick?

"She thinks maybe you forgot what you owe her. What can happen to you without her protection."

The lights were flashing madly, making him dizzy. He focused on that hideously familiar voice, feeling sick and weak.

He felt hands working behind him, and his panic returned until he realized he was being untied. Freed. Then the gag was yanked out of his mouth.

Some big, flapping things flew into his face. He flinched and whimpered like a child.

"Relax. They're your clothes, asshole."

He made a pathetic sound, then lifted his head and tried to see who it was. But by the time he realized that the rapid flashing he saw was caused by the fluttering of his eyelids and he willed them to stop doing it, it was too late to see his attacker. The man was gone. Ryan lay naked and alone in a garbage-strewn concrete lot. Corrupt odors stung his nostrils and pain flooded his battered body.

He clutched his clothes to his chest and curled up into a fetal position.

He'd been spared this time. But he still wished he was dead.

CHAPTER EIGHTEEN

Sara ate dinner, walked Macy, changed into her pajamas, and was reading a book in her living room when she heard Ryan come up the stairs and enter his apartment. Glad he was finally home, she opened her front door and crossed the hall. She knocked on his door, then tried the knob. The door was locked. Habit, she supposed. She knocked louder.

"Ryan?" she called.

No response.

She knocked again. "Ryan?"

Sara went back to her apartment, through the living room, and out onto the balcony. She opened his French doors. "Ryan?"

She turned on a lamp in the living room. Moving towards the bedroom, she turned on the hall light and called his name again. She found Macy blocking the doorway of the darkened bedroom.

"Come on Macy, move. What are you . . . Oh! Ryan." She could see him faintly in the light coming from the hall.

He lay sprawled across the bed, fully dressed. He was even still wearing his jacket. "You really *are* tired," she said in amusement.

Nonetheless, she wanted to find out what had happened this evening. She switched on the overhead light. He groaned and turned his head towards her.

"Sorry, but I want to know . . ." She gasped when she got a good look at him. *"Ryan."*

He groaned again and put a hand over his eyes. "Turn that off," he muttered.

Sara rushed forward. "Ryan! Oh, my God! Ryan, what *happened?*"

His face was bloody and battered. His clothes were dirty and only partially fastened. His hands were filthy, and there were abrasions on them.

He turned his head away from her.

Tears of horror and panic misted Sara's vision, but she forced herself to use her brain. She sat on the bed, turned his head back towards her, and examined his face. Despite the blood, abrasions, and initial swelling, she was relieved to see that the damage was superficial. Nothing was broken, gouged, or disfigured. Ryan looked even worse than he had after his fight with Derrick, but he wasn't seriously injured.

"Did you find Adam?" she asked, thinking about where he had intended to spend the evening.

"Adam?" He frowned a little. "No."

"How did this happen?" When he didn't answer, she prodded, "Ryan? What happened?"

"Go away," he said wearily.

"Is Adam all right? What happened to you?"

"Just go away, Sara."

She put her hands on his shoulders. "I'm going to get some first aid stuff. I'll be right back."

He made a weak attempt to shrug out of her grasp. "Leave me alone."

"Who did this to you?" When he just looked away from her, his eyes dull, she wondered if he was in shock. "I want to take you to a hospital."

That got his attention. *"No."*

"To a doctor, then."

He closed his eyes and shook his head.

"Then I'm calling the cops."

"No!" He suddenly sat up and shoved at her. "No cops! Goddamn it, Sara, if you call the cops—"

"Okay, I won't. I won't. But—"

"Go away! Just go away!"

"Shh. Ryan. Calm down. I won't—"

"I said *go away!*"

She blinked, shocked and confused.

"I don't want you here," he ground out.

She shook her head, dazed. "Ryan . . ."

"Go! *Get out!* Get *away* from me!"

She slid off the bed and stumbled past a whining Macy, ran through the living room, and was back in her apartment before she even remembered to breathe. By then, her head was spinning and her cheeks were streaked with tears.

What in the name of God had happened to him?

She risked entering his apartment again an hour later, thinking he'd probably be asleep now.

Although she wanted to phone the police, it was obvious that he'd feel betrayed if she did so. She couldn't drag him literally kicking and screaming to a doctor, and she didn't know any doctors well enough to ask them to come here. She had called Safe House and tried to find out if anyone there knew anything about Ryan's evening; but he had evidently left in a good mood, without incident, and that was all that anyone on the night staff knew. Sara told them he had been injured and wouldn't be able to start work the following day as planned. She promised to update them tomorrow.

Creeping through Ryan's apartment now, Sara saw that he had turned off the bedroom light since her stumbling departure. With the hallway light as her guide, she entered his bedroom and, as hoped, found him sleeping. She watched him, feeling sick with anxiety and helplessness. What should she do? That combination of dirt and blood was bad, she knew that much; those cuts and abrasions might get infected. And what if there was damage beneath his clothing that she couldn't see, such as cracked ribs?

He was breathing evenly, though, and his skin didn't feel unusually hot when she touched him.

Whatever had happened, perhaps rest was the best thing for him right now. She sat down on the chair in his bedroom. It didn't mater that it wasn't very comfortable. She didn't think she'd get much sleep no matter where she spent the night.

When she opened her eyes in the morning, he was gone.

After a moment of panic, Sara saw his dirty clothes on the floor. An instant later, she heard a splash in the bathroom.

Groggy and stiff, she pushed herself out of the chair and staggered towards the bathroom. She found Macy lying next to the bathtub, and Ryan lying in it. His knees were up, his head rested against the wall, his eyes were closed, and his skin was flushed as he soaked in the hot water. The mirror was fogged and a thin blanket of steam filled the little room.

She must have made a noise, because he suddenly flinched and opened his eyes. He saw her and, after a tense moment, lowered his gaze.

"It's good that you're soaking." Sara heard her scratchy voice and cleared her throat. "You were so dirty."

"Hm."

His face looked nasty, but not horrifying. It undoubtedly hurt, but it would heal.

She said, "Do you want some ice? That might make it feel better."

"No." His voice was soft.

She came forward and sat on the edge of the tub. It puzzled and distressed her that he seemed to shrink away from her. She could see abrasions on various parts of his body now. How could that have happened? He'd been wearing jeans and his jacket.

Then she remembered: His clothes had been only partially fastened last night, his shirt barely buttoned at all, his pants zipped but not buttoned. Had his clothes been *off* when this happened to him?

"What happened last night?" she asked quietly.

He closed his eyes. "I don't want to talk about it."

"Yes, I've noticed. But, Ryan, you can't come home like this and just not tell me what happened."

He didn't open his eyes. His jaw muscles worked tensely for a moment. Then he said, "I'm sorry I yelled at you last night."

When it became clear he didn't intend to say any more, she said, "It's all right to yell when you're upset. It's not all right to shut me out like this."

He turned his head away from her. "Why don't you go home, Sara? I don't feel like talking." His voice was flat and dull.

"I'm not leaving you like this."

"I'm fine. Nothing's broken."

"You look like hell, and you're acting like a stranger."

He opened his eyes. "I want to be alone. Go home."

"*No*. I think you may be in shock or something."

He looked at her with a touch of exasperation—which was a reaction, at least. "I didn't give you the right to push like this."

"Yes, you did. And you gave *up* your right to treat me like this."

He closed his eyes again. "Lay off. I'm tired."

"Tell me what happened."

He ignored her.

She looked at the scrapes on his knees and, when he shifted, she noticed one on his belly, too. "Christ," she muttered. "How's your backside?"

His eyes flew open and he stared at her with a sudden, glittering tension. Since it was the first sign of real emotion he'd shown, she said, "Turn around. Show me."

"Get out." The words were like bullets.

"No. Show me the rest. What exactly has happ—"

"This is *my* apartment!" He gripped the side of the bathtub and pushed himself into a standing position, grimacing a little as he did so. "And I don't want you bothering me!"

He got out of the tub and seized her arm. Naked and dripping water everywhere, he dragged her out of the bathroom, through the bedroom, and down the hall to the door. She felt sure this sudden surge of anger was healthier than his dull apathy, but she was nonetheless distressed by it. Still, as long as he was on his feet and interacting with her, even angrily, she thought it would be best to keep pushing.

"I'm not leaving until you tell me what happened!"

He yanked open his front door and thrust her into the hallway.

"Who did this to you, Ryan? *What* did they do to you?"

"God, stop! Stop!" He slumped and put the heel of his hand against his forehead. "Would you just *stop,* Sara?"

"No, I won't stop. What's going on?"

He started breathing hard. "I *can't* . . . Please, I can't . . . talk about it."

"Ryan, let me help you. Let me—"

"Don't," he said in a rough voice. He slammed the door in her face.

She stood there staring at the closed door, feeling lost and helpless. What could she do for him?

Should she leave him alone for a bit? Would that really be the best thing?

A tear rolled down her cheek. Whether or not it was best, that was clearly what he wanted right now. What he insisted on, in fact.

Her shoulders slumped with fatigue and distress, Sara returned to her own apartment to shower and change. While she was in the shower, the phone rang. Of course. That was when it always rang.

When she went to her desk a little while later to check the answering machine, she found a message from the literary agent to whom she had sent six chapters of the new book.

After casting another worried glance in the direction of Ryan's apartment, Sara picked up the phone and returned the call.

"I don't know what to do, Miriam," she said into the phone late that afternoon, her voice ragged with worry. "I've tried knocking on his door a few times since he threw me out. He doesn't answer. And he's locked the balcony door."

"Oh, right, and that door is so sturdy, you could never get in that way now that he's *locked* it."

"Oh. You think I should break in?"

"How worried about him are you?"

"Physically, not so much. He's obviously uncomfortable and sore, but that seems to be all. Emotionally, though . . .

Very worried. Something's terribly wrong."

"Do you think that woman is involved in whatever has happened to him?"

Due to Miriam's acid tone when she said the words "that woman," Sara—who had broken down and told her a great deal during the past half-hour—didn't have to ask whom she meant. "I don't know. I hadn't even thought of that."

"That's because you're crazy with worry. If you weren't so emotional over Ryan right now, it would have occurred to you before this."

"He was going into a very bad neighborhood after dark, Mir. Maybe he was just overconfident about his ability to take care of himself there. It *has* been a long time since he had to survive at night in places like that."

"I guess that's possible, but . . ."

"You really think Catherine did something to him?"

"Well, look at the big picture, Sara. At the start of the day, he ends a longtime association with a woman who has been possessive of him to the point of ruthlessness. A woman who lives outside the law and who . . . well, I agree with you, we really can't call it 'love.' Let's say she's obsessed with him."

"Uh-huh." Sara nodded. "He told me that their scene had been grim, that he'd left before it could get even uglier, and that he didn't think she really accepted that he had quit."

"And then that same night," Miriam said, "he comes home physically hurt, emotionally distraught, and possibly suffering from shock." There was a brief pause. "That's a pretty big coincidence, don't you think?"

"My God, you're right." Sara's heart pounded as she considered this. "I didn't even think of it like that."

"Like I said, you probably would have, if his emotional

trauma wasn't traumatizing *you*."

"I could tell when she called him yesterday, when I answered his phone, that she didn't accept his leaving. I thought she was going to bother him. Maybe make trouble for him. But it never occurred to me she might *hurt* him." She put her hand over her mouth. "Oh, no! I wonder if that dressing-down I gave her had something to do with—"

"Sara, don't even go there. If she hurt Ryan, it's because she *is* an evil bitch, not because you called her one."

"But what if I pushed her over the edge?"

"Stop. You're not responsible for her behavior," Miriam said. "But do you have any idea what she could have done that would send Ryan round the twist like this?"

"I don't know. I don't have the impression that she could beat the shit out of him, but *someone* obviously did."

"So maybe she found someone to do it for her. That couldn't have been a big challenge for a woman who has a bunch of male prostitutes on her payroll."

"I wonder . . . Maybe it was Derrick."

"Who's Derrick?"

Sara explained.

"Okay," Miriam said. "So we know she's got at least one employee who's already gotten violent with Ryan, and who'd probably like to do it again. Maybe it *was* him."

"But Ryan is so contemptuous of Derrick, it's hard to believe that a fight with him could upset him this much."

"Maybe it was more than a fight. I don't want to distress you, Sara, but if you think Ryan's clothes were off, or at least partially off, during whatever happened to him . . ." Miriam drew in a sharp breath. "Oh. *Wait.* You said . . ."

Sara realized what her sister what thinking. A dark chill swept through her. She suddenly remembered Ryan's reaction to her question about his "backside." Maybe there was physical damage she just couldn't *see*. "Oh, no."

"You said the rape and beating nearly killed him ten years ago," Miriam said. "That's a huge trauma. That stays with a person for a long time. Especially if they don't get counseling. Which, I gather, Ryan never did."

"No, he . . . *Jesus,* he went from being a rape victim, to being Catherine's toy boy, to being a prostitute in her stable."

"It's a rather common pattern, though we usually associate it with women. The only thing that's really surprising about it is the *kind* of prostitution Ryan wound up in—the style and self-education he had to bring to his role." After a pause, Miriam said, "I think Ryan may have been raped again last night, Sara. I think that evil bitch may have arranged it to put him in his place."

Sara's eyes filled with tears. "Well, it would explain his behavior. Two years ago, the thought of another rape was so terrifying, he was willing to do anything to avoid a prison sentence. Even give up the idea of quitting prostitution, which he was desperate to do by then."

"So, yesterday, maybe Catherine thought that if she could again reduce him to a helpless, terrified, traumatized boy—"

"The boy who'd been so *grateful* to her," Sara said through tight lips.

"—she could end this new rebellion of his and get him back where she wants him. Under her control."

"How could she *do* something like that to him?"

"He told her he was leaving her. He told her about Safe House, revealed that he was headed in a new direction and didn't need her anymore. She discovered that he has a woman, one to whom he's told a great deal and whom he's kept a secret from her." Miriam blew out her breath. "I'm guessing she freaked out. Panicked. Blew her stack. Did the most extreme, desperate thing she could think of to rein him back in."

"I still don't understand how she could do it."

"That's because you're a decent human being with a conscience."

"If we're right," Sara said, "then I *am* calling the cops. I don't care what Ryan thinks. She has to be arrested."

"You'll only know if we're right if you can get him to talk to you about this."

Sara made a weepy, frustrated sound. "How am I going to do that?"

"Think of something that will break through the shell of shock that's cutting him off from you right now."

She started thinking. "You're right. I've got to get him to talk to me. Okay. I have to go."

"Will you be all right?"

"Yes." She had to use her head. Had to figure out how to get through to Ryan.

"Call me again if you need to. No matter how late or early."

"I will. Miriam?"

"Yes?"

"I love you."

"I love you, too."

"Go be with Jan now."

"I will. Good luck."

An hour later, dressed for the role she had mentally written for herself, Sara took a hammer wrapped in a towel and shoved it through a glass pane on one of Ryan's French doors. Then she reached inside, turned the lock, and entered his silent apartment.

Macy was lying on the couch, as he sometimes did when

he thought no one would catch him there. He lifted his head, waited for her to scold him, and then sighed and went back to sleep when she didn't.

Sara made her way through the apartment to the bedroom, where she found Ryan lying on his side, bare-chested and dozing. The cat, upon seeing her, skittered past her and out the bedroom door. Sara closed the door behind her and turned to face Ryan. In the golden light of the sunset spilling through the bedroom window, he looked like a fairytale lover awaiting the kiss that would end his enchanted, centuries-long sleep.

Until she got close enough to see his bruised face and scraped flesh. Then he looked like *her* lover, bitterly beaten down and suffering wounds of the soul.

As if suddenly aware of her presence, he opened his eyes and flinched.

"It's just me," she said.

He swallowed. "Oh."

"How do you feel?"

"Okay." He pulled the sheet a little higher and closed his eyes.

"I need to ask you a question."

He didn't open his eyes. "How did you get in here?"

"This will just take a second."

"I thought I locked the doors," he muttered.

"Do I ask for the money before sex, or after?"

His eyes opened. "What?"

"You've told me some things about the trade," she said, "but I realized on my way out the door just now that I never asked you about that."

He squinted at her, a little surprise registering on his face as he finally noticed her appearance. "You're all dressed up."

"How do I look?"

She was wearing a dress she'd bought on a whim at a consignment shop a few years ago. It was a little, black, beaded garment with a push-up bodice that did remarkable things for her breasts. She had never worked up the nerve to wear it in public, but it was so pretty that she kept it anyhow.

To reinforce the purpose of the dress this evening, she'd put on eye make-up and lipstick, and she'd taken some care with her hair.

"Ryan?" she prodded as he stared dumbly at her. "How do I look?"

He lowered his gaze and mumbled, "Beautiful."

"Oh, good. I guess the dress works, then."

"Mm."

"So, about the money. Do I ask for it before or after the sex?"

"What are you talking about?"

"And how much do you think I should ask for?"

"Huh?"

"Two hundred? Oh, maybe not. I'm new at this. And I suppose I'll be older than the other women. Er, girls."

He frowned up at her. "What the fuck are you talking about, Sara?"

She sat down on the bed. "Well, you know, money's a little tight. I've been thinking I should go look for a job. At least part-time. But you know how that depresses me. I hated every job I ever had, and I hate anything that takes time or energy away from my writing. And then—" She snapped her fingers. "—it finally occurred to me. I can't imagine why I didn't think of it before. If I spend one or two nights a week in hotel bars, maybe I can make an extra few hundred dollars here and there."

"What?" He sat up.

This was progress.

"So, I look okay?" she asked. "I don't want to look cheap or too obvious, but I do want to attract some attention. The right kind of attention, I mean. I thought I'd aim for business travelers. Spend some weeknights at first-rate hotels—"

"What?"

"—and see how it goes. Obviously, there'll be some stiff competition for that business—"

"Sara, what the fuck are you talking about?"

"—and the other girls will probably be younger and prettier than me."

"Stop," he said. "Just stop."

"Plus, I have no experience at this," she said. "Which brings me back to my question. Do I ask for the money before I go into a guy's hotel room—"

"This isn't funny, Sara."

"—or as I'm leaving his room?"

She was pleased to see him looking angry.

He said, "Why don't you just shut the fuck up?"

"Jesus, Ryan. Take it easy. Forget I asked."

He grabbed her arm as she rose to go. "What the hell are you playing at?"

"I told you. I need money."

"You have money! You've got . . . Don't you?"

"I've run through twice as much as I thought I would spend by now. You know I'm no good with money."

He let go of her and shook his head. "You are *not* thinking of turning tricks. Whatever the hell you're—"

"I've got to go." She checked her watch. "I thought the tail end of happy hour would be a good time to start."

"Oh, really?" he said. "And where am I supposed to believe you're going?"

"I've made a list of hotels. Tonight, I'll try the first two on it."

"Bullshit!"

"See you tomorrow, Ryan." She headed for the bedroom door, her heart pounding. *Please, please, please . . .*

Her hand was on the knob when he leaped out of bed, his lower body clad in sweat pants. She opened the door. He seized her arm and slammed the door. "Sara, you are *not* on your way to some hotel to turn tricks. I know you."

She said, "Tell me what happened to you last night."

He staggered back as if she'd hit him.

"Did Catherine do something to you?" she asked.

He started breathing too fast. "Wherever you're going, just go."

"I've told you where I'm going."

"I don't believe you."

"I got the idea from *you*." She opened the door.

He slammed it shut again. "What are you *doing?*"

"Did Derrick do this to you?"

He put a hand to his head as if it was pounding.

She opened the door. "I'm going to fuck the very first man who's willing to pay."

He made a furious sound, slammed the door shut, and pushed her away from it. "*Stop* it. You won't do that. Not you."

"I will do anything to make you talk to me," she said. "I'll go out on the street right now and give a blow job to some stranger in an alley if it will—"

"Don't you even *say* that to me. Not to *me*." His eyes glittered with wild anger.

"Were you raped last night?"

He made a terrible sound and turned his back on her.

She tried to touch him, but he jerked away from her, breathing hard.

"What do I have to do for you, Ryan?" she asked. "Get down on my knees for some man in a dark doorway?"

"*Don't* talk about this. Please, don't talk about it."

She circled him. "If I get on my back for men at a hundred bucks a pop, will you stop thinking you're not good enough to touch me, to talk to me?"

His expression was awful. "What are you doing?" he asked despairingly.

"Because if that's what it takes, then that's what I'll do." She headed for the door again.

"Sara!"

She shook him off. "I won't let you shut me out like this."

"Sara." He grabbed her again.

"What did they do to you?" she demanded, trying to pull away from him.

"Don't make me . . . *Please,* don't make me."

She whirled to face him. There were tears in his eyes. She was so close to breaking the ice encasing him.

"You tell me what happened to you," she said, "or I swear on my mother's grave, I will go whore myself in a hotel bar tonight."

"Oh, God, Sara, don't, *God,* don't, please, I don't want you to know what it's like, *please,* just stop this."

She took him by the shoulders. "Were you raped last night?"

He backed away from her, stumbled into the bed, and sank down upon it. He bent over and covered his face with his hands. After a moment, a sob escaped him.

"No," Ryan choked out. "He didn't *need* to rape me."

She knelt before him, pressing herself against his knees,

and stroked his hair. "What do you mean?"

He sniffed and his shoulders shook. Sara wrapped her arms around him and pressed kisses into his hair. "I love you. Please, let me comfort you. What happened?"

Gradually, with much coaxing from her, the whole story poured out of him, along with his tears. She listened in horror and compassion as he told her how the attack last night had mimicked the rape which still haunted him: He'd been stripped naked, gagged so he couldn't scream, and silently brutalized in a dark concrete lot which stank of urine and garbage.

"Oh, Ryan," she murmured, stroking and hugging him, kissing his neck, his damp cheek, his rumpled hair. "Oh, my love."

"It wasn't the pain last night," he said brokenly. "He didn't hurt me that much. Nowhere near as bad as the night it happened." He choked on a watery hiccup. "It was the fear. *God,* I was so scared. Even more scared than when it really happened, because this time I knew what was coming. I remembered." He sniffed and sighed wearily. "Only it didn't happen this time."

"She didn't want the merchandise damaged," Sara said. "She just wanted to freak you out. Make you weak. Make you give up and do as you're told."

He nodded. "It had to be her. She had to have told Derrick what to do. He knew the details. Knew what had happened to me, what would scare me. And Catherine is the only person I ever told."

"Will you at least *think* about going to the police?"

"No!"

"Ryan . . ."

He shook his head. "You don't understand."

"Explain it to me."

"I was picked up for prostitution just a few weeks ago, Sara. The cops will assume this was just a trick gone bad. At best, they'll ignore me. Maybe they'll humiliate me. That's just how it is for a rent boy."

"But I'll tell them—"

"What? That my madam got mad at me for quitting her stable and sent another of her boys to knock me around a little? A boy who had a grudge because I knocked *him* around a few weeks ago? You think the cops are going to care about a squabble between a couple of prostitutes?"

"He assaulted you, Ryan. That's illegal, no matter what you do for a living."

"In the real world, Sara, I can't go to the cops about this. It'll just be worse for me. Please, drop it," he said, his eyes pleading with her.

She sighed and relented. The one thing she could agree with was that he didn't need any more emotional trauma or humiliation. She kissed his damp mouth. "I'm glad you're telling me about this. I wish you had talked to me before now."

"I couldn't. I'm sorry. I know I've been awful to you."

"Shhh." She kissed away another tear slipping from his eye. "It doesn't matter now."

"I just couldn't talk," he said. "Couldn't think. Didn't want to feel. I thought an avalanche would fall on me if I looked at you, or talked to you, or let myself feel anything." He made a self-deprecating gesture. "And now my avalanche is here."

"But I'm here, too."

"Thank you."

"I *want* to be here for you."

He scrubbed at his eyes, then looked at her in sudden surprise. "Your questions really hit the mark. How did you know what happened last night?"

"Call it a lucky guess."

He made a sound that might have been amusement. "A guy can't hide much from a smart woman."

She stroked his hair again. "I wish you had talked to me about the rape before. I mean, actually told me what you went through."

He groaned in protest. "I *don't* talk about it, Sara. I try not even to think about it. Not ever. And I *hate* dreaming about it."

"*Do* you dream about it?"

"Once in a while."

"Maybe that's because you never talk about it. Maybe the memory wouldn't be so powerful if you talked to someone who could help you recover from it. Like a rape counselor." Although his sharp intake of breath indicated he didn't like the idea, she said, "After all, *not* talking about it to someone hasn't worked out very well for you. Catherine was able to use the rape as emotional extortion two years ago and as a weapon last night. And if you still dream about it sometimes . . ." She raised his flushed face so she could meet his eyes. "It would be a good idea for you to confront what happened to you. Because, in your new job, you'll be helping kids who've had similar experiences, and they'll need guidance."

He was shaking his head. "*I* can't do that job, Sara! I'm just . . . I'm not . . . I have nothing to offer—"

"You can do it. You're just shaken right now."

"I can't even get Adam to listen to me!"

"It's only been a few days. You just have to keep trying. And I know you will. It's not in your nature to give up. If it were, you wouldn't be the man you are now. You wouldn't even be alive."

He sighed and pressed his forehead against hers. "What are you doing with me? Why are you here with a guy like me?"

She smiled and caressed his naked shoulders. "Because I love you. Because I respect you more than anyone I've ever known." A startled breath escaped him and brushed her face. "You make me happy. You make me laugh. You listen to me, and you make me want to listen to you. You make me feel loved. You make me feel sexy."

His knee nudged her. "You *are* sexy."

"Actually," she whispered, "I'm starting to feel pretty sexy right now."

"*I* don't feel sexy. I've been blubbering all over you, and I must look like something from a horror movie."

"Shhh. I can make you feel sexy." She nudged him backwards on the bed and started kissing him, gently so as not to hurt his bruised face. "How's your back? Can you lie down?"

"Um . . ." He met her kiss. "Yeah. I can." He gave in to the urging of her hands and lay back upon the bed.

"I'll take care of you." She followed him down to the mattress.

He took a long breath, trying to relax, and put his hands on her. "Yes," he whispered. "That's what I want. Take care of me."

"Mmmm. Leave everything to me."

She pressed her mouth against his chest, his stomach, the thin trickle of hair trailing towards his groin. She caressed and massaged him with her hands, tended and adored him with her mouth, worshipped him with her body. His hands were on her back, her thighs, her face, her hair . . . and then he found and enjoyed the bountiful cleavage created by her push-up bodice.

"This is a great dress," he said. "Why haven't I seen this dress before?"

"It's uncomfortable. It pinches."

He pressed one more hot kiss into her cleavage, then whispered, "So take it off." He found the zipper, pulled it down, then lay still, breathing deeply and watching appreciatively while she peeled off the dress and her underthings.

Naked and comfortable now, she slid along his body, exploring and enjoying him, being extra gentle with his cuts and bruises. She gave her attention to his hard chest, his taut buttocks, his smooth belly, his loins. When she took him in her mouth, he made a wonderful sound as his thighs tensed and his hips moved reflexively. His sighs and groans were free of the sorrow and shame that had tormented him, and he let her see, without shyness or restraint, how helplessly enthralled he was with her tender loving care.

There were no shadows between them, and they had no thoughts of the outside world as they twined together and sated each other with love.

CHAPTER NINETEEN

Dawn was just starting to paint the sky pink when Ryan rang the doorbell at Catherine's townhouse the following day. He'd awoken in the dark with Sara snuggled warm and soft against him. The feel of her sleeping so trustingly in his arms made him feel strong and clean, as if he were brand new; and he'd decided he wanted to get this over with immediately. The sooner he dealt with Catherine, the sooner he could turn his back on the past and start living the life he wanted—the life which Sara had even convinced him he deserved.

After a good night's sleep, he was starting to feel like a human being again. He'd left his lover sleeping in his bed, oblivious to his pre-dawn departure. He'd written her a note saying only that since he was feeling much better, she shouldn't put on any clothes, because he'd be back soon. Ryan figured that Sara would be very worried if she knew where he was going, so he'd decided not to tell her until after he returned home.

He rang Catherine's bell again. Then, since he felt like hitting something anyhow, he pounded on the door a few times.

After making love yesterday evening, he and Sara had talked for a while. Then he'd slept while she walked his dog and fed his pets—God, he loved that woman!—and then he'd woken up, and they'd talked some more.

Ryan was uncomfortable with Sara's proposal that he spend some time talking with a counselor about what had happened to him; but he had finally agreed to it, because when he considered how he'd lost his head the other night, he knew she was right: The rape, though ten years in the past, still held too much power over him. He needed to conquer the terror, banish the shame, and turn it into just a bad memory.

In truth, he'd always secretly feared that he deserved what happened to him that night. Because he'd been turning a trick. Because he was a dirty, unwanted street boy who'd offered to suck that guy's dick for money. Because he hadn't been smart enough or quick enough to escape.

And the experience had been so brutal, so terrifying and painful and humiliating, he'd lived in fear of it ever since.

As Sara said, if he was going to work with street kids who'd been through such an experience or who were in danger of it, then he had to triumph over it. And he *was* going to work with them, damn it. He wasn't going to let Catherine change the decisions he had made or stop him from turning his life into something worthwhile. So if talking with a professional would help him, then he'd do it. As Sara pointed out, he could probably talk with someone right there at Safe House, or else get a referral from them.

"Eventually," Sara had said, "*you* might even think about becoming a counselor for kids who've been through something like that."

That would probably require additional education. She'd suggested he consider college. *Him.*

"Why not?" she'd said. "If it's what you decide you want, of *course* you can do it."

God, he loved that woman.

He rang the bell again and muttered, "Come on, Catherine, get your ass out of bed."

The door opened. She stood there wearing a gorgeous

cream-colored floor-length robe, with her hair down around her shoulders and her face as beautiful as usual despite its lack of make-up.

"Finally!" He brushed past her and went inside. "I'm returning your cell phone." He set it down on the exquisite table in the foyer.

"Do you have any idea what time . . . *Kevin.*" She stared at him in horror.

"Looks pretty scary, doesn't it? I actually flinched when I saw myself in the mirror this morning."

"My God!" She put a hand up to her mouth, her expression stricken. "Oh, Kevin . . ."

"Save the act, Catherine. I know you put him up to it. You're the only person I ever told the details to. He got them from you."

Tears misted her eyes, surprising him. She shook her head. "He was just supposed to remind you. Make you remember. He wasn't supposed to . . . to do *this.*"

"Oh, come on, what did you *think* would happen? Derrick's bigger than me, he's got a grudge against me, and he's an idiot."

"I told him not to hurt you! He was only supposed to go far enough to make the point!"

"Jesus, Catherine, I was stripped naked, gagged, beaten to a bloody pulp, raped, and left for dead. You really can't reiterate a point like *that* without doing a little damage."

"Are you badly hurt?"

"No," he said. "My girlfriend's going to have to watch what she kisses for the next few days, but I'll live."

"Your girlfriend." Catherine frowned. "Look, Kevin, if you're interested in someone and want more personal time for a while—"

"I'm not 'interested' in her," he said. "I'm in love, and

we're going to get married."

That clearly shocked her. "You're *marrying* her?"

He smiled wryly. "Well, I used to be a good Catholic, you know. We talked about it last night, and I realized I feel like it would be wrong *not* to marry her. And she wants me for a husband, even knowing what she knows about me."

"She *doesn't* know you. Not the way I do."

"She knows everything, Catherine. And I mean *everything.*"

Catherine shook her head. "No. I talked to her, I know what kind of woman she is. She doesn't—"

"No, you don't know. You couldn't. But it doesn't matter."

"You don't have to leave because of *her.*"

"I want you to listen to me very carefully. If I get home today to find a note saying she's left me, and I never see her again, I still quit." He recalled the phrase he'd heard at Safe House and felt he understood it in his bones now. "I did what I had to do when that was all I knew. But now I know better, and I'm going to do better. I'm moving on with my life, Catherine. I'm done being your rent boy."

He thought her hand was shaking a little as she brushed her hair away from her face. "I didn't want it to be this way, Kevin. What happened with Derrick . . . you forced me to do that."

"Oh, for fuck's sake."

"What is it that you want?" she asked with a touch of desperation.

"I want you out of my life. Completely. Forever."

She drew in a breath. "Maybe . . . maybe you're right, you've worked long enough."

"Finally! Thank you for seeing it my way. Goodbye, Catherine."

She blocked his path. "You could quit escorting, and—"

"I have quit."

"—we could just . . . be together. You and me."

"What?" He wondered if she'd heard anything he'd said.

"You could help me run the business."

"No."

"No more client work, Kevin. Maybe you could train some of the boys—"

"No." He tried to brush past her and she grabbed him.

"All right then, you wouldn't have to be involved with that side of things at all. You'd just . . . handle the money."

"Handle the money?" he repeated.

"Yes. I'd leave it in your hands."

"You'd trust me with your money?"

"We'd be partners."

He almost laughed. "No, thanks."

"You've earned it. And I've been doing very well lately."

He tried to get past her again. "God knows you've made plenty off *me* lately."

She stopped him again. "Now you can have it all. And more. Everything I've got. We'll share. We'll be . . ."

"A couple?" he said.

"Yes. Why not?"

He was surprised, Sara had told him about the telephone conversation which had convinced her that Catherine was obsessed with him—or, as Sara had put it, in love with him in a totally deluded, abusive, and narcissistic way. But he was surprised now, even so. He hadn't really agreed with Sara's interpretation. Now it seemed so obvious, he felt like a fool for never having realized it before. Maybe Sara was right when she said he didn't know as much about women as he thought he did.

"We can't be a couple, Catherine."

"Why not? We could—"

"After what you did to me the other night," he said, holding her gaze and trying to make her understand, "I'd go back to working the streets before I'd ever let you touch me again."

She blinked and took a step back.

He said, "For years, all I've felt for you is gratitude. And now you've destroyed even that."

"Kevin, I can make it up to you."

"No, you can't. What you did to me the other night can never be taken back or forgiven. And it made me realize what you've done to me for years."

"What I've *done?* I've paid you well and treated you well!"

"You whored me out, used me, and manipulated me," he said. "I'm really glad I didn't die ten years ago. But I wish to God that anyone but *you* had found me that night."

"You don't mean that."

"I'm not your boy anymore, Catherine. And I never will be again. The thought of touching you . . ." He shook his head. "I've fucked plenty of women I didn't like or want, but the thought of ever touching you again actually sickens me."

She gasped. "I can't believe, after everything I've done for you, that you're speaking to me this way."

"I'm not going to do anything about what happened the other night. Derrick's had his revenge, so he won't bother me again if I don't bother him," he said. "And all I want from you is your word that you'll stay completely out of my life. Forever."

Her eyes glistened. *"Kevin."*

"I guess you're headed for some trouble with the law, thanks to Trevor."

She blinked hard and took a breath. "Yes."

"I want you to know, I won't talk. Not to the cops or to lawyers, not to the press, not to anyone. I owe you that much. But that's *all* I owe you."

"I can't believe you're doing this to me."

He said, "I will never touch you again, I will never work for you again, and after I walk out that door, I never want to see you or speak to you again. I can't make it any clearer than that."

A chilly bitterness swept across her face. "Fine. *Go,* then. We're through. I've put up with far too much from you already."

He released his breath and let his shoulders relax a little. "Goodbye, Catherine." He headed for the door.

"See how well you do without me," she said nastily. "The world is a cold place, Kevin. You'll find that out."

Borrowing a phrase from Adam, he said, "Whatever." And he left. For good.

When he didn't find Sara in his bed, he went looking for her. They bumped into each other on the balcony.

"Hi! I thought I heard you come in," she said. "Where have you been?"

He stared with open exasperation at her pants and shirt. "Oh, thanks, Sara."

"What?"

"I ask you to do *one* little thing for me . . ."

"Huh?"

He grabbed her. "You were supposed to stay naked and in my bed. Now I've got to go to all the trouble—"

She was laughing. "Stop!"

"—of hauling you back there—" He suited the action to the words.

"Hey, let go!"

"—and taking your clothes off. As if I don't have enough things to do today!"

"Were you getting groceries or something?" she asked as he dragged her towards the bedroom. "I walked your dog. He was whining."

"He was playing you. I don't usually walk him this early."

"Where *did* you go so early?"

He pulled her down to the rumpled bed and rolled over with her. "Okay. Straight up. I went to Catherine's."

"What?" Stunned, she sat bolt upright. "Why? What happened? Are you okay? Ryan!"

He folded his hands behind his head and looked at her. "I had to make sure she knows it's over, that nothing will ever get me back. I didn't want her bothering us, let alone trying something even more extreme than she did the other night."

"I can't believe you went there without telling me!"

"You were sleeping."

Now *she* was the one staring with open exasperation. "Ryan."

"Okay, I'm sorry. I didn't want you to worry. Or try to stop me. Or insist on coming with me. I woke up and just wanted to finish it. Right away. This morning."

She took his hand. "What happened?"

He told her everything, and he concluded with, "This time, she accepted it."

"You're sure?"

He nodded. "Yes. Oh, you were right, she had feelings for me. More than I ever realized. But once I told her what my feelings for her are now . . ."

"Ah. She's coping with the rejection by deciding she despises you." When he gave her a quizzical look, Sara said,

"She's clever, Ryan, but not complicated."

"*I* always thought she was complicated."

"You were an infatuated boy when you got to know her. Some of those impressions stuck. Besides, you don't know as much about women as you think you do."

"Yeah, yeah, okay."

She smiled, then squeezed his hand. "How do you feel now?"

"About Catherine? Relieved."

"And in general?"

"Oh, pretty unmanly."

"Unmanly?"

"Well, I let a clumsy idiot like Derrick beat me up and scare me into witless, gibbering terror—"

"You didn't *let* him—"

"I treated my girlfriend badly when she tried to help—"

"Ryan."

"—and then I cried like a baby in front of her."

"Oh, please. If you can't cry in front of me, then what kind of relationship do we have?"

"Overall, to get my self-respect back," he said, "I think I'm going to have to do something really macho, like break my fist trying to punch it through a brick wall."

"Oh, good grief."

He grinned at her. "But, apart from that, I feel pretty good."

"And your body?"

"A little sore, but I've had sex and sleep, so I'll live. And speaking of sex . . ." He toyed with her buttons. "Why are you still wearing all these clothes?"

"Actually . . . I can't do this right now."

"No?"

She shook her head. "I have to go back to my apartment.

I'm expecting a call soon from my new . . ." Her eyes widened. "I didn't tell you!"

"Tell me what?"

"The other day, I got a call from that agent who's been reading the first six chapters of my new book."

"The chapters you won't let *me* read," he grumbled.

"She loves the chapters and loves the outline I wrote!"

"Of course she does."

"She was so full of enthusiasm for my work and for my career, and she had such good ideas for marketing the book that, well . . ." Sara smiled. "I hired her."

"This is the one you described as your dream agent, right?"

"Yes."

"Honey, that's great!" He sat up and kissed her.

"It feels pretty great," she admitted. "It's really given a boost to my confidence. And to my creative energy."

"Good. The sooner you finish writing this book, the sooner you'll finally let me read it."

"I don't like to let people see work in progress. Not even you."

"I know, I know. We've been over this." He put his arm around her. "So I've got a real job, and you've got a new agent. We should go out tonight and celebrate."

"Oh, yes, let's do that!"

"And you can wear that slinky black dress for me."

"I told you it pinches."

"Don't worry, you won't be in it for long." He paused. "Um, I meant to ask. I know you weren't really going to turn tricks—"

"I would've done anything, Ryan, to make you—"

"I wouldn't have let you, and you knew it. You counted on it."

"Well, yes, I did."

"But are you really in financial trouble?"

"Oh! No. I'm right on budget."

"You're such a lousy liar, I can't believe I fell for that one."

"Well, you were a wreck. And I threw myself into the part."

"Did I mention how much I love you?"

"You did." She kissed him.

Ryan murmured, "You're sure you don't have time for this right now?"

He kissed her deeply and slid his hand under her shirt. Sara made a throaty sound that he found very promising . . . but then she wriggled away from him. He sighed in disappointment and sank backwards upon the bed, doing his best to look deprived and in need of more tender loving care.

"Later," she promised, smiling at him. "I don't want to miss this call. We didn't talk for long the other day. I was so worried about you that I couldn't concentrate, so I made up an excuse to get off the phone and—"

"I'm sorry."

"Shh." She brushed her fingertips across his stomach. "So we're going to talk more today. About the book, and her strategies, and my career."

He nodded. "Go home, take your call. I'll keep."

"Come with me?"

He rolled to his side and propped his head on his hand. "No, as long as you're busy, I'm going to take my car back to the dealer this morning and see about trading it in for an economy car."

"Oh, good idea."

"Then I want to stop by Safe House and explain to

Isabel why I'm missing my first two days of work—"

"When she sees your face, she'll understand."

"That's what I figured. I'll need to reschedule with her so I can start my training."

"After that, maybe you should come home and get some more rest."

He shook his head. "I want to find Adam after that."

"Oh! Of course."

"Three days without seeing me," Ryan said gloomily. "He might think I've abandoned him. Or he might have disappeared by now."

The phone rang, startling them. Sara started to reached for it, then laughed at herself. "That can't be my call, we're in your house." She kissed him after he sat up. "I'm going home."

He nodded, smiling as he watched her slide off the bed and head for the door. He reached for the receiver. "Hello?"

There was no reply.

"Hello?"

Still no reply. But he heard some faint breathing.

He glanced up and saw Sara looking curiously at him from the doorway.

"Hello?" He heard a slight sound, maybe a grunt. Gut instinct made him suspect who was calling. "Adam?"

Sara gasped and came back into the room.

"Adam, is that you?"

"Um . . ."

"It's me," Ryan said. "I'm here. I'm glad you're calling." No reply. "Adam?"

"Yeah. It's me."

Thank God. He looked at Sara and nodded. She sat back down next to him on the bed.

"Adam, I tried to find you the other night. But I got hurt and couldn't move for a while. That's why I haven't been around." He waited, then said, "Are you all right?"

"Um, no . . ." There was a watery sniff.

"Are you hurt?" Ryan asked.

"Uh . . . Maybe. A little."

"Okay, Sara and I are going to come get you." He waited. "Adam? Is that okay, if we come get you?"

"Yeah . . . yeah, that's okay."

"Where are you?"

"I'm not exactly sure."

Ryan's heart was pounding. "Can you give me an idea?" When there was no reply, Ryan said, "What part of town? Can you see any street signs?"

"I'll get a map," Sara said.

Ryan kept Adam talking, and when Sara returned with a detailed map of the Bay area, they started narrowing it down until they knew, within a few blocks, where Adam was.

"We're coming to get you *right now,*" Ryan said. "Stay where you are, and we'll be there soon. Okay?"

"Okay."

"I'm glad you called me. Don't scare me by not being there when I get there, all right?"

"I'll be here," the boy said brokenly.

After he hung up, Ryan said to Sara, "Something's happened to him. He won't say what."

"He's well enough to call you and speak coherently," she said. "And we're going straight to him. Right now."

"Okay. Right." He was trying to keep his head, despite the frantic pounding of his heart. "Oh, wait. Don't you have a call coming?"

"Don't be silly, I'll talk to her later or tomorrow."

"Sara."

"What?" She saw the look on his face, and she took his hand.

"Something happened to him. I was supposed to be looking out for him, supposed to—"

"Ryan, when he was in trouble," she said, "he called you."

He stared at her, aching for that scared, lost kid.

"He's finally asked for help." She kissed him tenderly. "And you're here to give it to him now."

EPILOGUE

Sara was sitting at her computer when Ryan came bursting through the door of the apartment—which was even more crowded than it used to be, now that she had been sharing it for the past six months with him, Macy, Alley, Mrs. Thatcher, and the fish.

"So? What happened?" he asked. "I tried to call you three times today, but the line was always busy."

"I've been on the phone all day," she said. "Or else online. We need a cable modem."

"Well?" he prodded.

She suddenly laughed and clapped her hands. "It's over! I have a two-book deal for three hundred thousand dollars!"

"Hey!" He hauled her out of her chair to kiss her, then picked her up and spun her around, both of them laughing with delight. His startled cat jumped off Sara's desk and ran out of the room. Macy lifted his head and gave a half-hearted bark, then decided it was too much trouble to get involved in the excitement and went back to sleep. "Wow! I'm so proud of you, sweetheart!"

"By now, I'm just glad it's over. I've been a nervous wreck!"

Since her restless anxiety had kept him awake several nights in a row, he was well aware of her nerves. He also knew that Sara would probably be too excited to sleep well tonight, either. In a day or so, however, she'd crash and conk out for ten hours.

Ryan led her over to his leather chair, which added to

the clutter of their cramped living quarters, sat down, and pulled her onto his lap. "Well, come on. Tell me everything."

Practically vibrating with excitement, she started talking about the details of the new publishing deal which, as anticipated, her agent had concluded today. Ryan occasionally interrupted her with a question, but otherwise he just sat listening to her, getting a kick out of seeing her this happy.

Sara had finished the book last month and given it to her new agent, who'd sent it to four hand-picked publishers and given them a limited period of time in which to bid on it. One of them had rejected the book, sending Sara into a depression that Ryan couldn't alleviate. A few days later, however, the remaining three publishers had made offers—all of them for much more money than Sara had been making for her mystery series. After the initial thrill, though, Sara had started agonizing again: Which publishing house would be the best one for her career, and which of the three offers was, overall, the best deal? Ryan was learning that deals like this were complicated, and the sum of money being offered wasn't the only factor to consider. Sara had spent much of the past three days on the phone with her agent discussing the details, or else keeping the telephone line open to receive yet another such call after her agent consulted the bidding publishers with questions which she and Sara had about their proposed deals.

Now, happy for her and proud of her, Ryan couldn't resist stopping the flow of her funny monologue with a long, slow, sultry kiss.

"Oh, that's nice," she said breathlessly.

When she tried to kiss him again, he said, "No, that's all you get until you finish telling me what happened."

"Hmph. Where was I? Oh, I know!"

He was so pleased that Sara's talent was finally being rewarded. So glad that her risks and her hard work were paying off. And no one knew better than Ryan how hard she'd been working. She'd scarcely touched him during the final few weeks she had spent wrestling with the book; hunched over the keyboard all day every day during that time, she would tumble into bed at night and sleep like the dead, oblivious to her pining lover lying beside her. By day, on those rare occasions when Ryan could even get her away from her desk, she was distracted and cranky.

It had been a huge relief to him, in more ways than one, when she'd poked him awake late one night, announced the book was done, and spent the next two hours giving him some of the most mind-blowing sex of their relationship. Then she'd fallen asleep for ten hours and finally woken up the next day in a good mood and showing a normal interest in real life again.

"Then *that* editor said he couldn't go any higher than one hundred thousand per book, so my agent told him he was out of the running," Sara was saying now, practically bouncing with excitement. "She said he actually seemed *upset,* Ryan."

"Of course he was upset. It's an incredible book." He nudged her. "Now that you've finally let me read it."

"Hey, I gave you a printout the day after it was done. You were the very first person who got to read it. Even my agent waited longer for it than you did." She nudged him back. "When you sleep with the writer, you get perks."

"I earn them."

She grinned. "Yes, you do."

Sara finished telling him about how the deal had been concluded with the winning bidder. "When it was all over, the editor called me so we could get to know each other.

Talk about my future there, about their plans for this book, about the revisions she wants on it."

"What revisions?" he demanded. "There's nothing wrong with it."

"Oh, there are a few things. Little things. There's a scene she thinks I should add, and a place where she thinks I should change the order of a couple of scenes." Sara added, "I like her. She was full of enthusiasm and compliments, and her only criticisms were specific and constructive. That's what I consider a good editor." She poked him. "That's what I consider a good husband, too, so you should take notes."

"We're not even married yet, and I'm getting notes already?"

"Oh! That was the other person I was on the phone with all day. My father's rabbi."

"What did he say?"

"Well, he was still fretting about you not taking any kind of instruction before the marriage. I told him no *again*. I explained *again* that you're working full time, attending class twice a week, and driving out to Bernice Village once a week. I said I'd actually like to *see* you once in a while, since I'm marrying you because I kind of like your company."

"Flatterer."

"Anyhow, he kept kvetching and—"

"What?"

"Fretting, complaining."

"Oh." He grinned. "Another word for my expanding Yiddish vocabulary."

"But I told him that all that matters to me is that I marry you. Whether or not a rabbi performs the service matters only to my father, whom I am willing to disappoint if my father's wishes become an inconvenience to my groom."

"Honey, if it's causing this much trouble, I should just agree to whatever the rabbi wants—"

"*No*. Because it doesn't matter to *me*. And you shouldn't have to do this for my father—who only goes to temple twice a year, for goodness sake!" She waved her hand. "Anyhow, it doesn't matter, because the rabbi gave in."

"He's going to marry us?" When she nodded, he squeezed her waist. "Great! When are we doing this?"

"The final Sunday of next month."

"So it'll be what we've talked about?" he asked. "A short, simple service, followed by a great big party?"

She sighed. "Well, the service is going to be longer and more elaborate than I would like. That's the concession we're making to my father."

He shrugged. "I don't mind."

She said, "You know, I'm still willing to see a priest if you want to be married in the Church, too."

He shook his head. "All that matters to me is marrying you, Sara. I haven't been to Mass or confession in over a dozen years, and I'm not really interested in going."

She touched his cheek. "All right."

"Adam's going to be nervous about the service," he said, "especially when I tell him that part of it will be in Hebrew." The boy was excited about being Ryan's best man at the wedding, but also anxious about doing everything right. "Maybe you could come out to Bernice Village with me a couple of weeks before the wedding and walk him through it, so he'll know what's going to happen? I think that would help."

"Of course."

During his final night living on the streets, Adam had been beaten and threatened with death by gang members who thought doing things like that was lots of fun. After getting his call for help, the two of them had found him injured, frightened, and ready to rely on Ryan. He had stayed with Ryan for a week, during which time Ryan had found the courage to explain truthfully, albeit vaguely, *why* Adam couldn't live with him legally. That kind of honesty had strengthened the boy's trust, and Adam had finally agreed to talk with Isabel at Safe House and to let Ryan take him to Bernice Village for a visit. Although nervous about it, Adam had agreed to try living at Bernice Village, and he had moved in there shortly before Ryan had moved into Sara's apartment. Since then, Adam had been able to establish contact with his imprisoned father—who, Ryan was pleased to learn, actually did care what happened to the boy. Adam was adjusting to life at Bernice Village and gradually becoming a more stable kid. Ryan drove out there once a week, without fail, to spend time with him.

"Hey, you know what all this money I'll be getting means for us?" Sara said.

"We can go on a honeymoon, after all?" They'd been planning to skip it, given her uncertain career situation and his modest income.

"Oh! Yes! I hadn't even thought of that! A *honeymoon*." She shifted her position so she could put her arms around his neck. "That'll be wonderful. But, actually, I was thinking that this money means we can *move*. Buy a place."

"Ah." He looked around the crowded apartment. They'd been incredibly happy living together here, but it was much too small for them. Sara needed a room for her office, and it would be nice to get the rest of their stuff out of storage. "Yeah, I guess we're ready."

"I'm *more* than ready. I want to start looking right after the wedding."

"Right after the honeymoon, you mean."

She smiled. "Of course."

"I have some news of my own," he said. "I'm getting a raise."

"Really? That's wonderful! Because you've worked so hard?"

Sara wasn't the only one whose work sometimes came between them for a little while. But they were learning together how to stay close while making space for each other.

"Well, Isabel says she's very pleased with the work I've been doing." He smiled wryly. "But I think it didn't hurt that I brought in such a big chunk of change this week."

Her eyes widened. "Your plan *worked?*"

He shrugged. "I guess I haven't lost my touch."

"Hey, you told *me* there'd be no touching involved."

He goosed her. "I'm speaking figuratively."

After working for Safe House for a while and realizing how much more funding they needed, it had occurred to Ryan that he had a number of former acquaintances (a euphemism which made Sara roll her eyes) who were filthy rich and perhaps in need of tax write-offs. Maybe the dissolution of Catherine's escort agency had even freed up some of their cash. That fellow Trevor had created such a big, juicy scandal that, even without the indictment several months ago, it would have been impossible for Catherine to keep operating. A business like hers relied on discretion. Sara hoped that Catherine would lose everything and serve hard time; Ryan thought it more likely that she'd wind up selling her memoirs for a lot of money and landing on her feet. Since his real name wasn't anywhere in Catherine's records, no one had bothered him when building a case against her. And Catherine herself had turned her back on him forever the last time he'd seen her, which was all that mattered to him.

Anyhow, with Catherine no longer in a position to charge outrageous fees for illicit services, Ryan thought some of her former clients should have enough spare change to make generous donations to a good cause. After discussing it with Sara, who found his plan so audacious she couldn't stop laughing, he'd made a list of his former "regulars" and paid them visits to discuss Safe House. Several of them seemed to suspect this was an elaborate form of blackmail, and one of them had even thrown Ryan out of her house. However, Alice Van Offelen, whom he'd always thought seemed like a nice lady, had been so moved by Ryan's pitch and so interested in the work at Safe House, she had made a huge financial commitment to the place this week. Moreover, Isabel had told Ryan today that Alice was interested in getting involved in additional fundraising efforts for Safe House.

If Isabel suspected how Ryan knew someone like Alice, she didn't say anything about it. Neither did Ryan, since he had no intention of embarrassing Alice—who would nonetheless, he suspected, feel self-conscious whenever they met.

"Well," his fiancée now said to him, her arms around his neck, "if turning on the charm with an old client raised a lot of money for Safe House, then I guess it was worth it. As long as she understands that you're retired from a certain line of work."

"She does," he assured her. "But, since my raise will be coming out of her donation, she's still the source of some of my income. Kind of ironic."

"Are we inviting her to the wedding?" Sara asked with a too-innocent expression.

"I don't think so," he said dryly.

"What about the Fergusons?"

He shook his head. "No. I mean, you were right, and I'm glad I called them." The Oklahoma couple who had employed his mother, and who had unsuccessfully tried to help him as an abused kid, had been touchingly thrilled to hear from him when, at Sara's urging, he'd contacted them a few months ago to tell them he was alive and well. They knew he had disappeared years ago and had always worried about his fate. "They seemed really pleased when I told them I was getting married, working, and starting college, but it's not as if we're going to become close now."

She nodded. "It's also not as if we need to add to the guest list." Between Sara's relatives, her friends, and the co-workers Ryan was inviting, it was going to be a huge party.

He tightened his arms around her. "So, since we're not poor anymore . . . Hey, I just realized, I'm marrying very well, aren't I?"

"You earn it," she said dryly.

"I certainly do. Anyhow, since I'm getting a raise and you've just made a big new book deal, let's go celebrate."

"Ooh, yes! Let's go somewhere expensive and eats lots of decadent food. And then we'll come home and . . ." She nuzzled him. "Well, I know I've neglected you this week."

"Gosh, I never noticed."

"Oh, please, Ryan. When you feel sexually deprived, you're about as subtle as Macy when he wants a biscuit."

"Yeah, well, I figured out a long time ago that subtlety doesn't work with anyone in your family. Least of all you, when you're obsessing about your work or your career." When she started unbuttoning his shirt, he said, "Hey, what are you doing? I thought you were going to buy me an expensive dinner first."

"I just changed my mind about the order of events."

"Oh." He watched her unbutton his pants. "You mean I have to *work* for my supper."

"Very funny, Ryan." But she was smiling.

"Come here."

He pulled her mouth to his. And then they were all done talking for a while.

ABOUT THE AUTHOR

Laura Leone is the award-winning author of over a dozen romance novels. Under her real name, Laura Resnick, she is also the award-winning author of several fantasy novels and numerous short stories. You can find her on the Web at www.sff.net/people/laresnick.

COMING IN HARDCOVER, JUNE 2004

COMING IN TRADE PAPERBACK, SPRING 2005

AN EXCERPT FROM LAURA LEONE'S CLASSIC
FEVER DREAMS

COMPLETELY UPDATED AND REVISED

CHAPTER ONE

The heat in Montedora City was sticky and oppressive, even after sundown. The dimly lighted bar wasn't air-conditioned, and the ancient electric fans overhead, which groaned with each sluggish rotation, only managed to push the hot, damp air around the room, as if trying to ensure that everyone enjoyed an equal level of discomfort. Even the omnipresent flies seemed heat-stunned; they had taken to buzzing in a strange calypso rhythm, flying straight into the walls, and then falling to the floor, apparently unconscious.

Madeleine Barrington sipped glumly on her tepid rum and coke; the Andrews Sisters would never have sung so cheerily about the drink if they could have tasted this one. Madeleine wished desperately for a glass of mineral water with a slice of lemon, a cool, fragrant bath, and the comfort of a firm mattress and clean sheets. But all of that, she acknowledged with resignation, was several thousand miles away in her Manhattan apartment. And she was stuck in Montedora for another night.

A poor South American country, Montedora boasted only one real city, Montedora City, its chaotic capital. Not exactly a tourist mecca, the entire city had only two big hotels. The Hotel Tigre, which hadn't been decorated in nearly twenty years, was the safer of the two; it really wasn't all that bad if you didn't mind threadbare towels, peeling paint, squeaking ceiling fans, and sullen service.

Madeleine minded.

She took another sip of her drink and closed her eyes,

sternly fighting the wave of depression which threatened to engulf her. What a rotten day it had been. After spending ten hours in miserable discomfort at the airport, she had been informed that her flight, scheduled to take off this morning, had finally been cancelled. The news had been disappointing enough, after a whole day of unexplained delays, but then, when she tried to reclaim her luggage, she was informed that it had been lost. Perhaps loaded onto another flight by mistake, perhaps stolen. In any case, gone.

So here she was, stuck for another night in Montedora City, and she couldn't even change into a fresh set of clothes. She couldn't even buy some, since—due to the curfew—all the shops had already closed by the time she caught a taxi back into the city. Well, she supposed she could wash out her things in the bathroom sink in her room.

She sighed and decided that she had better finish her drink in the Bar Tigre and go across the courtyard to the reception desk, where she could get a room for the night. Perhaps the taxi-sized cockroach which had shared her room last night would still be there. It could keep her company. She grimaced and finished her drink. Then, although she was usually abstemious, she ordered another. She'd need a little fortification if she was going to face one of those sullen desk clerks again. Not to mention the slightly brown water in the bathroom.

"Make it a double, please," she said to the bartender.

"Ah, you like?" The chubby man smiled.

"Actually, I'm trying to get the mosquitoes drunk," she said.

He didn't get it.

It had not been a good week, and Madeleine regretted that another trip to Montedora would probably be necessary before her goal was accomplished. Her grandfather had bought a huge plantation in this country over fifty years ago and misnamed it El Paradiso. It hadn't been a bad investment at the time; the year-round growing climate and rich soil produced tomatoes, sugarcane and other crops for Barrington Food Products.

However, social, economic, and political conditions had changed considerably over the years. Montedora had become unstable, for one thing; President Juan de la Veracruz was the country's fourth ruler in a row to seize power through violence. Moreover, the plantation was only producing half of what it used to, due to bad local management. Madeleine had been urging her father, Thackeray Makepeace Barrington, to sell the plantation for several years. Not only did she worry about losing the property to nationalization, but she also believed that Barrington Enterprises should support the U.S. agricultural economy rather than operating a feudal estate in a foreign country.

Her father had finally listened to her. Having gotten him to agree, she had come here to Montedora to inspect the property and examine the local management before putting El Paradiso on the international market.

It had been a grueling, lonesome, and depressing week, and she wished that her flight home hadn't been cancelled. She also wished she could feel more optimistic about her chances of getting out of here tomorrow. The airport seemed more like a county fair on its last legs than an international flight center.

"Another, señorita?" the bartender asked, noticing she had finished her second drink.

She shouldn't. She hadn't eaten all day, and she was feeling a little light-headed now. And Madeleine never had three drinks in a row . . . But what else was she going to do with her evening? Go check into a shabby room and stare at its four walls? Reread the two books she had brought from home and already finished? Review the paperwork which made her despair of ever being able to sell El Paradiso?

"Yes, I'll have another," she said.

She felt her elegant dress of thin silk clinging to her back, and her brow was damp with moisture. She pulled out a monogrammed handkerchief and pressed it delicately to her overheated face. She was sweating. Amazing. She never sweated. It was one of the many things her sisters disliked about her.

Oh, she knew they loved her, but there were a lot of things about her they didn't like. In fact, she supposed the same thing could be said about almost everyone who knew her. The uneasy, slightly snide jokes about her magna cum laude degree from Princeton, her mastery of every area of the enormous family business, her fastidious personal appearance, and her general competence were legion. The more she proved herself, the less affection she seemed to inspire.

Sitting here alone in a strange, seedy bar at the ends of the earth, she had to admit that, despite a large family, a prominent social position, and a vast personal acquaintance, there was no one she could call long-distance right now simply to say she was feeling lonely and demoralized. She wasn't that close to anyone.

She was thirty-one years old, healthy, wealthy, and socially and professionally successful. And, as she downed another swallow of flat coke and cheap rum, she felt . . . empty.

What had gotten into her? It must be the heat. She should stop being so maudlin. Thank goodness there was no one around to see her in this condition—sweaty, cranky, and wallowing in self-pity. She never permitted people to see her this way. She never permitted herself to feel this way. Fortunately, the bartender didn't seem to care, and the three other patrons of Bar Tigre were all involved in a poker game in the corner.

Still, she was a disciplined woman who never gave in to despondency. There was a dirty, cracked mirror lining the wall behind the bar. She looked up at it, staring forcefully into her own eyes, and ordered herself to feel capable and confident, as usual.

That was when she saw him staring at her.

Feeling moody after his final day at the Presidential Palace, Ransom walked through the dark, muggy, dirty streets of Montedora City. He had dismissed his chauffeur-driven car twenty minutes ago, wanting to clear his head with an evening stroll. Besides, despite the danger which lurked in the city's streets after dark, Ransom figured Miguel's driving was more likely to kill him than any mugger.

What a hell of a job this had been. Ransom liked working for Marino Security International, and he had willingly accepted this assignment to recommend and implement new security measures for President Juan de la Veracruz. He'd done his duty here, but he wouldn't be sorry to say good-bye to this miserable, oppressed country and its squabbling, egocentric rulers.

The assignment was finally over. Today he had finished reviewing the new security measures, and his written report would be done soon. Veracruz had invited him to spend the night at the palace, but he had declined, preferring the quiet privacy of his shabby hotel room to the ostentatious glitter of the palace, where everyone seemed to scheme and plot even in their sleep.

Ah, well. Tomorrow morning, the President's private car would pick Ransom up and take him to a military airfield, where the President's private plane would fly him back to the States.

He could hardly wait. He wanted some time off. He wanted some decent company, after putting up with Veracruz and his cronies. He wanted to get a little pleasure out of life after being stuck in Montedora for nearly a month. He wanted to undress and relax, after wearing a tie at yet another formal dinner tonight; ever since leaving the Secret Service, he seldom wore a tie for anything but weddings and funerals. He wanted someone to soothe his guilty conscience about having worked so hard to help preserve the power, position, and lifestyle of a greedy dictator. Despite the moral ambivalence he felt about it, Ransom had done a good job here, and because of that, he wanted a reward.

He pushed open the door of the Bar Tigre and saw the answer to all of his wants and needs sitting right there at the bar.

She was so beautiful she was almost intimidating. But he'd never been easily intimidated, so he stalked forward, eyes fixed on her.

Her flaxen blonde hair was starting to wilt in the heat, its fine tendrils clinging to her neck and shoulders as she pressed a lace-edged handkerchief to her cheeks and forehead. Her wide eyes were a rich, deep blue, fringed by long, curling lashes. Her skin was as fair as a pearl, as smooth and perfect as alabaster, as firm and enticing as ripe young fruit. She wore an expensive-looking dress of thin, dark purple silk with a high neck and a belted waist. It left her shoulders bare, and the hem stopped just above her knees, revealing long, shapely legs. Her simple bracelet and matching earrings were gold, and her shoes had probably cost $200.

He wondered what a woman like her was doing in a place like this. Her fine, aristocratic bone structure and perfect posture confirmed his impression that she was a class act. What was she doing sitting alone in Bar Tigre? She obviously wasn't a prostitute. No woman from the embassy staff would venture out alone after curfew, Peace Corps workers didn't dress like that, and not many foreigners did business in Montedora City anymore. Most of them had pulled out after the last coup.

If she was a traveler, she sure didn't seem to be enjoying herself. He had seldom seen such a bleak expression. What was she thinking about?

Whatever it was, it made her look into the mirror with a flash of cold fire. God, she was gorgeous! Whoever she was, whatever she was doing here, he was half-willing to believe she had been sent by the angels, expressly for him, to be his comfort and his reward. Except, of course, that Ransom's just deserts were more likely to come from someplace other than heaven.

Their eyes met in the mirror. He smiled slowly. No, this woman hadn't been sent by angels. There was too much challenge in her gaze. She had been sent by someone who understood Ransom very well indeed. He never liked anything to be too easy.

Hot as hell, he loosened his tie, undid a couple of his buttons, and joined her at the bar.

Madeleine glanced askance at the man who had looked her up and down so boldly, then sat beside her at the bar without even asking.

"Hi, there," he said easily.

"Good evening." She held his gaze for a moment, letting

him know that she wasn't shy or flustered, but that she wasn't interested in talking to him. Then she accepted another rum and coke from the bartender.

"It's on me," the man said when the bartender asked her for payment.

She said, "No, thank you. I—"

"Then do you want to buy me one?" he asked.

She frowned. "But—"

"Thanks! Señor, the lady's buying my drink. Make it a beer."

She looked at the stranger with rising irritation. "Excuse me, but I'm—"

"You're American, aren't you?"

"Yes. But—"

"So am I."

"Yes, I can tell. However—"

"You staying at the Hotel Tigre?"

She glared at him. "Your technique is very clumsy."

"I know. I usually have to rely on charm and sex appeal."

To her surprise, she laughed. It must be the rum.

He grinned. An undeniably sexy grin. "That's better."

"Better than what?" Why was she talking to this man?

"Better than the expression you had on your face when I walked through that door. You looked like you were thinking of jumping off a bridge."

"No, I wasn't."

"You looked like you were moping about being all alone in this rotten city on such a miserable night."

"Well . . ." She paid for his beer, suddenly glad for the company. Talking to anyone, even this impertinent stranger, seemed better than being alone with her morbid thoughts.

He raised his glass. "Here's to golden days and purple nights, both of which have been in short supply lately."

"As you say." She clinked her glass against his, wondering what his version of a purple night would be. Probably a waterbed motel and the sort of woman whom Mother would describe as "obvious."

"Had any purple nights lately?" he asked, his green eyes sparkling at her.

"I don't believe so."

"Nice accent. You sound like a debutante."

"Please, don't say that." Visions filled her head of the silly, overdressed girls she had never been able to understand or emulate.

"Ah, a working woman, huh?"

"Yes."

"What do you do?"

"I don't want to talk about it."

He shrugged. "Okay. No shop talk. It's been that kind of a day for me, too."

"No shop talk," she agreed, surprised at herself. She was never this blunt. Perhaps it was the heat. Or perhaps it was the man himself. It was funny how easily she had accepted his presence at her side, strange how comfortable she felt with him. She'd heard about such things, about people who told their most intimate secrets to a stranger, comforted by the anonymity, freed by the lack of a shared past and all the baggage it carried. That probably explained it.

God, it was hot! She had never known such debilitating heat. It played tricks on her mind and heightened her senses. She was aware of the stranger's body heat, his musky scent, the subtle sound of his breathing.

He was a good-looking man, though not at all the sort of man she would ever date. About six feet tall, he was slim without being skinny, muscular and athletic-looking without being bulky. His thick hair was light brown, streaked with shades of gold. One rebellious lock hung over his forehead, and he occasionally brushed it out of his eyes as he enjoyed his beer at her side.

His brows and lashes were dark, framing bright green eyes which sparkled with interest and energy. His long, lean face revealed two heart-stopping dimples when he smiled, and his mouth was full and wide. A slightly crooked nose and a faint scar at his temple gave him a certain roughness and added to his rakish air.

His clothes were ordinary. Indeed, in a less generous mood, Madeleine would have called them cheap—khaki pants, an old leather belt, scuffed shoes, a factory-made shirt, and a tie that some woman had given him. He couldn't possibly have chosen that wine-colored background and paisley design for himself.

"A woman gave you that tie," she said without thinking.

His brows moved in surprise. "That's right. How did you know?"

"I'll bet it's your only tie, except for the black one you wear at weddings and funerals."

He smiled, studying her with interest. "Have you been peeking in my closet?"

"Men are so predictable."

"Really? Then tell me what my briefs look like."

"Oh, I'm not an expert on underwear."

"Just ties."

"It doesn't look like you. And it doesn't match your shirt. You wouldn't wear it if you owned a few more." She realized what she had just said. "Sorry. That was rude." She frowned. "I'm never rude."

"Never say never."

"No, I'm never rude." She blinked at him, feeling lightheaded. "But I just was, wasn't I?"

"It's the heat," he assured her blandly.

She pushed her drink away. "I think I've had too much to drink."

He removed his tie and put it in his pocket. "I hate this thing, to tell the truth."

"Who was she?" None of her business. She shouldn't have asked, but she wanted to know.

"The woman who gave it to me?" He shrugged. "Just someone."

"She wanted you more than you wanted her," Madeleine surmised. Funny how freeing it was to say the things she always knew but usually didn't mention.

He peered into her glass. "Are you reading tea leaves or something?"

She shrugged. "It wasn't hard to guess."

He was the sort of man women wanted. Not her, of course. Madeleine had refined tastes, and this stranger was anything but refined. His shoulder muscles bulged against the cotton of his shirt. His pants were as tight as plastic wrap around his narrow hips and hard thighs. He had stalked toward that bar stool like a predatory cat. And his gaze, as he continued looking at her, was frankly sexual, yet full of enough humor and curiosity to make a woman feel singled out, special, and admired.

"Women love that sort of thing," she murmured. She took another sip of her rum, then remembered she had decided not to drink any more.

"What sort of thing?" he asked, propping his cheek on his fist.

He had nice hands. Long, strong, and neat. They were lightly tanned, like his face and arms. She noticed another scar on the heel of his hand.

"You're either a soldier of fortune or very clumsy," she said.

"Hmmm?"

She pointed to his scar. He clearly didn't understand what she meant. Emboldened by his comfortable response to whatever inappropriate thing she said, she reached over and traced the scar on his hand.

"Oh, that." His voice was husky.

"And this one." She reached up to his temple. He went very still, looking into her face as she traced the fine, white line that disappeared into his hair. "And your nose . . ." She ran her finger down its bridge. "It goes a little sideways." Her own voice sounded raspy to her. She wanted to run her fingertip across his full lower lip, too. But there was no scar there, so she pulled her hand away.

He moved a little closer. "Yeah. Broke my nose a couple of times."

"How?"

"Fighting."

"You must have quite a temper."

His smile made her catch her breath. "Nah. I'm a pussycat."

"You're flirting with me," she said in surprise.

"It's either you or those three guys in the corner, and I don't think they'd like my tie." His teasing gaze was perceptive. "You don't like flirting?"

"I'm . . . unaccustomed to it, shall we say."

"We can say whatever you like. But you must live in a guarded tower if you're not used to men flirting with you."

"A guarded tower?" She grew pensive and took another sip of her drink. "A guarded tower," she repeated.

"Are you married?" he asked quietly.

She blinked. "No." No guard needed. She was the tower.

"Oh. Okay."

"Why? Would you get up and leave if I said yes?"

"No. There's no harm in talking. But I wouldn't . . ."

"Wouldn't what?" What else did this flirtatious, impertinent stranger intend?

He shrugged and looked around the room. "If you'd said yes, I wouldn't ask you to dance."

"We can't dance. There's no dance floor."

He grinned again. "No dance floor? Damn. We sure don't want to break the rules in a fine, upscale establishment like the Bar Tigre, do we?" He slid off his stool and took her hand without asking. "Come on. There's an empty space, there's music, and there's a handsome guy like me. What more do you need?"

There was indeed music, though she hadn't noticed it until a moment ago. Blaring out from the dusty speaker of an ancient radio, which the bartender obligingly turned up, the rumba had a scratchy, tinny sound.

"How's your rumba?" the man asked, taking her in his arms.

"It needs work."

"Now's your chance."

He made her laugh, because he couldn't rumba any better than she could, but he sure knew how to enjoy trying. Anyhow, a man that graceful, that comfortable with his body, could fake it pretty well. She was giggling when the dance ended. Absurd.

"I never giggle," she said fastidiously, her hands still imprisoned by his.

"You should. It makes you look pretty."

He sounded so sincere that she flushed. She had been

complimented often by the most sophisticated of men, but it must be fifteen years since the last time she had felt shy and tongue-tied in the face of a man's honeyed words. "Oh."

The music changed. The new song was a slow, sensual Latin melody with a languid, suggestive beat. Madeleine nervously tried to pull away. The stranger held fast to her hands. She looked up, and their gazes locked. He tilted his head a little, and the suggestion of a smile played around his lips, making the corners of his eyes crinkle. He looked four, maybe five years older than she. His eyes narrowed and beckoned to her from behind their fringe of dark lashes, his expression a combination of laughter, challenge, and sexual foreplay.

"One more dance," he murmured.

"Um . . ."

"I dare you."

"Dare me?" She stepped into his arms.

He nodded. "I knew you wouldn't resist a challenge. Comfortable?"

She drew in a steadying breath but didn't respond. He'd pulled her much closer for this dance than he had for their rumba. She braced a hand against his hard shoulder, trying to keep her distance.

"Don't you sweat?" he asked.

"I am sweating."

The hand at her waist moved up and down her back in a slow, exploratory caress. She shivered and moved forward a little, seeking to escape its pressure. The movement brought her breasts into contact with his chest. He pressed her closer and drew his palm slowly across her shoulders, then back down to her waist.

"Barely sweating," he concluded. "And it's hot enough to suffocate tonight."

Her back burned where he'd touched her. Her waist vibrated under the light pressure of his hand. To her embarrassment, her nipples were growing hard where they pressed against his chest. She wondered if he could feel them.

Their eyes met. His had lost their teasing look and were growing heavy-lidded and sleepy. It made him look softer. It made her want to touch his cheek, stroke his hair, nuzzle him. She stiffened and tried to pull away.

He resisted. Not enough to force her to stay in his arms, just enough to give her time to realize that she didn't really want to pull away after all. He shifted the hand that held hers and laced his fingers with hers. She complied and let him draw her even closer, so that their hips pressed together as he slid one leg between her thighs.

He lowered his head. She felt his cheek against hers, hard and slightly rough with his five o'clock shadow. She felt him nuzzle her hair, inhaling its fragrance, and she quivered against him, closing her eyes.

"Relax," he murmured, sensing her tension. "Don't you ever let your spine sag?"

"Never."

"Never say never," he whispered. His hand slid up her back to gently knead the tight muscles between her shoulder blades.

She sighed and slid her arm around his neck, running her fingers through the soft hair at his nape. He was a feast of different textures: warm, smooth skin; slightly abrasive stubble; hard, bulging muscle beneath damp cotton; silky soft hair; soothing, stimulating hands.

She felt dizzy. Her head was spinning. Was she under the influence of the rum or the man? Both, she supposed.

His strong, clever fingers unlocked all the secrets she

carried between her shoulders. All the anger she never showed, all the fears she kept hidden, all the weariness she never gave in to; he freed it all and let it flow between them. She sighed and pillowed her head on his shoulder, wondering at his skill, his understanding. It was as if this perfect stranger knew things about her that no one in her life had even guessed.

Wanting to hold him with both arms, wanting both his hands to be free to touch her, she pulled her other hand out of his grasp and slid it around his shoulder. He responded by embracing her and letting his hands roam freely over her shoulders, back, and waist.

The intensity of his touch increased, his warm hands releasing other, more deeply buried instincts. She clung to him, feeling the depth of her loneliness, wondering how she could bear it if he stopped touching her. Her belly throbbed with desire, with a pulsing, insistent need to be even closer to him.

The song ended. The chirpy voice of the disc jockey intruded on this drowsy, magical feeling. Madeleine raised her head. The man in her arms stilled, then caressed her cheek lightly before tilting her chin so that their eyes met.

"Ask me up to your room," he whispered, his eyes glowing with lush, emerald highlights, his voice heavy with promise.

"I can't."

His expression didn't change. "I won't hurt you."

"I . . . believe you." Crazily enough, she did.

"I've got condoms." When she lowered her gaze in embarrassment, he pointed out, "Well, it makes a difference. I thought that might be why you—"

"No. I mean, I haven't got a room."

He gave a short puff of laughter. "Then come up to my room."

"Uh, I . . ." She bit her lip, confused and astonished. She was actually considering it! She, Madeleine Barrington, was considering accompanying this total stranger to his hotel room and going to bed with him.

She had only gone to bed with three men in her whole life, and she knew everything about them, their families, and even their trust funds before taking that step. She never slept with a man unless she was dating him seriously and exclusively.

"What are you thinking?" he asked.

"I'm . . ."

Her behavior tonight would shock everyone she'd ever known. She was always the model of propriety, good sense, and self-control.

"It's okay to be nervous," he said. "We're strangers, after all." He pressed his forehead against hers and closed his eyes. "But I don't feel like a stranger with you. And I want you as much as I want to go on breathing."

She trembled in response to the hot longing in his voice. He smelled sharp and tangy, and his breath was a little faster than before. Of its own volition, her hand moved to cup his cheek. He turned his head and pressed a kiss into her palm. His lips were hot and soft.

She started breathing like a swimmer, struggling for fast pants of heavy, humid air. The music started again. She ignored it, focusing on the man who held her in his arms.

Who would ever know? She was all alone here in the middle of nowhere. She could be someone else for a night in Montedora City, someone wild and irresponsible, someone free and driven only by desire.

There was no one here to see her do something sordid, unconventional, and wholly out of character. She was so tired of being perfect, so tired of being Madeleine

Barrington. And tonight, she was so lonely. She couldn't bear the thought of letting this man go.

No one would ever have to know. It would be her secret. Their secret. She made a silent pact with this nameless stranger. For this one night, they would be partners in her detour from the straight and narrow. And then tomorrow, it would be over. She'd get on a plane for New York and forget about him. He'd forget about her, too; he didn't even know who she was.

She could do whatever she wanted tonight, and then put it behind her.

"Where's your room?" she whispered.